THE
BUSHMAN

By Tricia Statter

Copyright ©Tricia Statter 2016

FOR KEITH

LOVE ALWAYS, ALWAYS LOVE

PROLOGUE

1897

Ningan could feel the music take over his body as he moved to the beat. The deep-throated growl of the didgeridoo was like an animal in their midst and the tapping of sticks made a pulse pound in his head. He was enjoying himself and couldn't stop smiling and yelping with delight. He loved to dance, he loved to feel the rhythm of the music and join in with the singing. He raised his voice, chanting and grunting at the appropriate times.

Glancing down at his painted body he felt proud. He had daubed the design in ash and the blobs of white flashed like fish scales as he moved. He smiled as he looked across to where his father was doing an old man's dance with his uncle. They both swayed and stamped their feet in one spot. He frowned as he watched them and tried to remember when his father had become old.

The music grew louder and faster and Ningan threw himself about letting the sound tremble through his body. Suddenly it stopped and he joined the others in a final shriek, the spirits had been thanked for the food they had caught. As the dancers passed him they patted him on his back and ruffled his hair. He shrugged off these affectionate touches. Just because he was the youngest they treated him like a tame wallaby.

After the harshness of the music the sounds of nature at night were comforting. The chirruping locusts, far off call of a dingo and the shuffling in the undergrowth of small animals. The night was warm and humid. The trunks of the ghost gums stood out against the blackness of the bush, they looked like motionless dancers. Once the dancing was over and the dust had settled it was time for the important thing, food.

His stomach rumbled as the smell of sizzling meat wafted through the trees. He was sure he must be the hungriest. When the food was cooked he had to stand back and let the older members of the group eat first. He watched as his father ripped chunks from a cooked bush turkey. The blackened flesh tore easily from the carcass. He was handed a piece of meat which he wolfed down, fat oozing down his chin and onto his bare chest. Sparks flew as he poked a yam from the ashes with a stick. He tossed the hot vegetable from hand to hand, blowing on it, hastily trying to cool it before eating. Every mouthful was ecstasy and he couldn't help groaning with pleasure after each bite.

'You've earned your food today, my son,' his father said.

Ningan grinned, his mouth too full to answer.

'First kill?' his uncle Managi asked.

His father answered for him. 'First kill and a good sized wallaby it was too.'

'Been a good hunt, plenty to thank the spirits for,' Managi said, indicating the pile of carcasses that were covered in flies.

Ningan had enjoyed hunting kangaroo and wallaby and was beginning to master his boomerang. This hunt was the first time he had actually hit a wallaby. It had only been stunned and he had to spear the animal to kill it. He had faltered as it lay on the ground and looked up at him with soft brown eyes. With closed eyes he had plunged his spear into its belly. His father had been watching and nodded his approval. The first time was the worst.

After eating so much Ningan's stomach felt as though it would burst. He sat down and leaned against a tree on the edge of the camp. He didn't want to be too near his father and the elders of the tribe and still felt a bit clumsy with the others. They were older than him and laughed at what he had to say. As he made a bed of moss and leaves his body felt heavy with tiredness, his eyes began to droop and the day's events ran through his mind.

A loud noise made him jump and his eyes sprang open. At first he thought it was the crack of dry wood on the fire but then it came again, louder. He ducked and covered his head with his arms. Someone was attacking them. Men began scrambling to their feet shouting, 'the shooting sticks.'

The whitefellas came on horses, trampling through their camp, firing their shooting sticks at anything that moved. They hooted and yelled and it sounded like the devil himself. They hid under their hats, their faces in shadow, men of death.

Ningan's father was running towards him yelling, 'run, run, get out of here,' but he was stopped as though he had run into a tree. He hit the ground face first and lay still.

Ningan wanted to run to him but was rooted to the spot, too scared to move. All he could do was hide, gibbering and shaking, glued to the solidness of a tree trunk. The noises that came to him were like none he had heard before, screams, groans, the thud of bullets in human flesh, neighing horses and woops of joy from the killer men. The sound of his people in their death throes grew less and the gun fire stopped before he dare look what had happened.

Slowly he peeped out from behind the tree, expecting to be shot at any moment. He gasped as he saw the remains of their camp. His father lay still where he had landed earlier but now a black pool surrounded his head. His uncle was nearby, a pulpy mess stuck to his chest. He was also motionless. The other members of their hunting party lay sprawled on the ground. His people could have been sleeping except for the grotesque way they had fallen.

Bile rose in his throat at the smell of blood and the sight before him but anger made him swallow as he watched a whitefella go to each body, lay his shooting stick on every still head and fire. Ningan's legs began to shake and felt as though they wouldn't hold him any longer. Was he the only one alive or had some escaped to the bush? What could he do, if he moved he would be killed?

The hairs on the back of his neck tingled. He was aware someone was behind him. Was it friend or enemy? Before he could turn a hand clamped over his mouth and pulled his head back. He was yanked from the safety of the tree and thrown to the ground. The power in the arms that held him prevented him from lashing out. He was puny against such strength. He was dragged backwards, one arm round his chest the other over his mouth. His feet were being scraped over stones and through bushes. He kept his body stiff, waiting for the pain of a bullet to ram into him. He couldn't see his attacker, he didn't know where he was being taken, but was certain he was going to die. He felt a wetness run down his leg and at first thought it was blood, but realized it was pee.

Eventually he was dropped on the ground, his head banged against a rock, his teeth clattered together. He was free and his instinct was to escape, to crawl into the bush and get as far away as possible.

As he looked around the whitefella spoke. 'No you don't.'

The weight of him as he sat on Ningan made him want to heave. He thrashed his arms about as he tried to catch his breath but they were caught and held. The noise of the camp sounded a long way off and he held his breath as he waited to die.

The man spoke but Ningan didn't know all the words he said. His only experience of whitefellas was when they came to tell them about their God. He looked up into the face above him. The man's hat had slipped off and he could see his face. It was as pale as a ghost gum and the eyes that looked at him were the colour of the morning sky. The skin looked soft and not lined from the sun and wind, it was a young face. It was not taut with hatred and sneering with vengeance. There was a frown on the forehead but then a small smile crept to his lips.

'That's better young fella.'

The thing that fascinated Ningan most was the man's hair. It was nearly white against the blackness of the night, with not a curl or kink in its smoothness.

'Understand?'

The man nodded his head and Ningan did the same.

The whitefella slowly moved off Ningan's stomach and waited for his reaction. For a moment he lay still unsure what to do. Was it a trick, when he tried to escape he would be shot in the back?

Nodding the whitefella beckoned Ningan to get up. He wobbled to his feet like a new-born colt and looked at the man who had saved his life. It was the first really white man he had seen with the strange hair and sky coloured eyes. Was he a spirit man? He must be. He had been sent from the spirit world to protect him.

Ningan backed away from him and nodded. He would do anything the spirit man told him.

The whitefella held out his hand and smiled. Ningan looked at it unsure what to do. He looked friendly enough now but so did a snake before it attacked. Picking up his hand the stranger shook it.

'Go,' the spirit man said and pointed to the bush.

Ningan turned his back on him and began to run expecting a bullet to tear through his skin. He didn't know where he was going, his long legs crashed through the bush, and were lashed by branches and scratched by thorns. He was too scared to feel anything and couldn't rid himself of the image of his father's slaughter. He was so frightened tears ran down his cheeks his face screwed into a grimace.

His feet thumped on the ground as he ran and sweat trickled into his eyes, mixing with his tears that blurred his vision. He ran as fast as he could for a long as he could and then stopped to listen. Was anyone following him? The only sound he could hear was the thumping of his heart and the rasping of his breath as he gulped air. He began to trot to conserve his energy. He had to get back to his homeland and let them know what had happened.

Had any of the others escaped? He hadn't waited to see. Should he have gone back to make sure his father was really dead?

Where had the white spirit man come from? Why had he been saved?

PART ONE

1910

CHAPTER 1

Maggie

'Billy? Is papa going to die?'

'No.'

'Are the twins going to die?'

'No, no one's going to die.'

'What's it called, what they've got?'

'Geez, you ask a lot of questions. Diphtheria Doctor Burns says.'

'What's diphtheria?'

'It's a disease.'

Maggie wasn't sure what a disease was but it sounded nasty and it made the twins look terrible. Mama said it was very catching, so they had to stay out of the house. When the twins coughed it was really raspy, like a new saw on dry wood and she'd seen mama boiling smelly rags they had to spit in. Every time they tried to swallow they cried and there was nothing she could do to help them. No, it was not something she wanted to catch, she hated being sick. That was why she hadn't complained too much when mama said she and Billy had to sleep on the veranda, even though the thought of snakes crawling into her bed kept her awake most nights. She hated snakes, even more than she hated being sick.

'C'mon sis.' Billy prodded her in the arm. 'We'd better get the firewood and head back.'

Maggie brushed the dust from her skirt and wriggled her toes into the shoes she had kicked off. She could feel the grit between her toes as she followed Billy towards the river where there were more trees for firewood. Because he was three years older than her he always led the way, to protect her, Maggie liked to think.

"Follow the Leader" was one of her favourite games, she would copy everything Billy did. He would do silly things to make her laugh, jumping over logs, running round tree trunks and screaming at the sky. They would fill their lungs with air, open their mouths and let out as much noise as they could. Maggie opened her mouth and then shut it quickly when she remembered what happened last time. Billy had swallowed a fly. The memory of the surprised look on his face brought a titter to her lips.

'What are you laughing at?'

'Nothing.'

The river, when they got there, had no water. There was a dead sheep half sunk in the mud with blowflies covering its matted wool. The sight of it made Maggie shudder. It was as though when the river dried up everything else did too. Leaves on the trees were all shrivelled and there wasn't a blade of grass in sight. All the starving sheep had eaten it and left only dusty soil that clogged in her throat and nose.

She looked across at Billy who was frowning. His thumbs were hooked in his braces and he stood just like papa.

'Let's just get some wood and go home,' he said.

Maggie nodded and held out her arms for him to pile on as many branches as she could hold. The bark felt scratchy through her sleeves as she hugged the load to her and started for home. A big bitey ant scurried across the branch right under her nose and she almost dropped the lot but she knew Billy would shout if she did. She hummed as she dawdled along but when her arms began to ache, her tune came out more like a moan.

'Gawd sis, you sound like a constipated bee.'

By the time the house came into view the sun had begun to set. The sky was streaked with orange as though God had painted it himself, Maggie thought. She loved coming home. The homestead nestled in a small basin of land that made it seem protected from the outside world. A few gum trees huddled round the house, guarding the metal roof from the heat of the sun and the wooden walls from strong winds. The dogs ran out to meet them.

'Hi yuh, Jessy.'

After they stowed the wood Billy ruffled the older kelpie's fur. She whined and leaned against him, while the younger dog nearly tripped Maggie over trying to nip the hem of her skirt. She sank to her knees and put her arms around his neck, letting her face be licked.

'I don't need a wash now, do I Bob?' She wiped her face. 'Come on, time for dinner.'

'Ah, here you are.' Mama always said that when they came home. She stood in front of the fireplace wiping her hands on a cloth. Walking into the bungalow was like hitting a wall of heat, yet the warmth was comforting to Maggie.

Billy hung his cap on the chair back and sat down at the table.

'How are the twins?'

'Fair to middlin'.

Maggie wasn't sure what "fair to middlin" meant.

'Now, you two can have your food on the veranda, it's a bit cooler out there'.

Maggie perched on the top step with Jess beside her. Billy brought her a metal plate with her portion of damper. Her mouth watered at the smell of it and Jess's saliva dripped on the floor. The dripping spread on the bread-like food slid through her fingers as she ate, and she let Jess lick them clean.

'That was good,' she said.

Billy gobbled his down. He wandered back into the house and Maggie knew he was after seconds. Normally he would come back with an empty plate but today he had another large slice.

'How come you got some more?'

'Mama says papa and the twins aren't eating and she's not hungry, so I could have theirs.' The end of his sentence was muffled by food being crammed into his mouth.

Hoping for another helping, Maggie rushed inside with her empty plate. Before she could ask for more one of the twins began coughing in the next room. Mama looked worried and sighed before disappearing to see to the twins. Maggie stood there wondering what to do. She didn't really feel hungry anymore, just sort of sad. She wanted to help but didn't know how. Perhaps papa would like a cup of tea.

She hadn't been into their bedroom for almost a week to talk to him and she missed him. Mama said he wasn't well and needed his rest, but Maggie knew the real reason they weren't allowed in. Her father didn't like anyone to see him when he was ill. It was like when he was off droving and they didn't see him for weeks, but he usually bought them back boiled lollies, fresh honeycomb or apples.

Maggie loved to follow her father round when he was home. She would watch him do his chores. He made everything look easy, but when she tried she wasn't strong enough and he would laugh at her. Whatever he was doing he would stop to roll a smoke and Maggie always watched with great interest. His rough hands would gently work the fine cigarette paper, making a thin trough in which he laid the tobacco. His tongue darted out to lick the edges, he'd roll it up and then pull all the dangly bits from each end. Once he let her have a go but hers turned out too fat and the edges wouldn't stick because she had made them all sloppy. After the smoke was made he used one hand as a windbreak, while he lit up with the other. The first puff always made him sigh. It then became a part of him, stuck to his bottom lip.

The room was in semi darkness. Maggie edged her way across to the bed, the bare floorboards creaking under her weight. At first she thought he was asleep. His face looked a strange, pale colour. He was usually brown from working outdoors. His mouth drooped and he looked as though he would never laugh again. His breath was raspy in his throat. Maggie felt scared when she looked at him. The large man that was her father had disappeared and this thin sickly looking one lay in his place

'Papa?' she whispered.

His eyes opened. Maggie smiled, feeling a bit shy, and was about to speak but before she could he shouted, 'get out of here.' The effort to talk brought on a bout of coughing and Maggie rushed from the room.

Her father never shouted at them, but that wasn't her papa in there. She stood by the fire and felt like crying. Clearing her throat, she tucked her long blonde hair behind her ears as she had seen her mother do and went outside to Billy.

Flopping down beside him she sat quietly for a moment before asking, 'Are you sure papa won't die?'

Billy shrugged.

She wanted to be told that everything would be all right but Billy wouldn't lie to her. Just this once she wouldn't mind if he did. She nuzzled into Jess's neck for comfort and stroked her. The old dog moved her head against her hand. The action soothed her and she whispered to the dog, 'You're a good old girl aren't you?'

As she stroked Jessie, her mother came out onto the veranda. Maggie didn't want to look at her sad face but instead stared out at the blackness that surrounded their house. The darkness didn't usually bother her. She was used to it, but tonight it made her shiver and it wasn't even cold.

She jumped when mama laid a hand on her head. 'Time for bed now sleepy head,' she said.

Maggie didn't question mama or try to make excuses to stay up like she did sometimes. With a last ruffle of the dog's fur she said, 'night, night Jessie.'

She kissed mama goodnight and went to her bed which was on the veranda at present, so she didn't catch germs from the twins. It felt like an island to her where everything was normal, where she couldn't get in trouble or see sick people. Burying herself under the blankets she forgot her nightly inspection for snakes. She had also forgotten to say her prayers. She didn't think God would mind if she said them under the blankets instead of kneeling.

'Now I lay me down to sleep, I pray the Lord my soul to keep, if I should die before I wake, I pray the Lord my soul to take.' She wondered if God would mind if she asked for something else and added, 'and please, please, please God look after the twins and papa and make them get better soon.'

The following morning Maggie woke to sounds she didn't recognise. The first was a tapping on the corrugated iron roof, like a small animal was dancing up there. She couldn't work out why something should be on their roof. She sniffed, there was definitely something different in the air. Her eyelids flew open and throwing off the blanket, she padded across the veranda to look. Drops of water plopped onto the dry soil.

'It's raining,' she whispered to herself. 'It's really raining,' she repeated, half afraid if she said it out loud it might only be a dream that would stop at the sound of her voice. As she watched the water immediately disappeared into the thirsty dirt. More and more fell until the ground was dark with moisture. Perhaps enough water would fall to fill the river again and then they could go swimming. She began to feel excited which made a huge grin light up her face.

She was about to run into the house, but the other sound that had woken her came from inside. At first she wondered if Jess was ill but then realized it was a person. Mama was making the noise. Standing in the doorway in her vest and knickers she could see mama in the gloom of the kitchen. She was sitting at the table, her head in her hands. Her body shook and a sort of hiccupping groan came from her. Maggie watched for a moment unsure what to do. Her mother never cried and the sight brought a huge lump to Maggie's throat.

'Mama?' she whispered. 'What's the matter?'

Her mother didn't answer. Where was Billy when she needed him and what was wrong with mama? Had she hurt herself or was she sick, so sick it made her cry? Sitting down next to her, Maggie clutched her arm. She could feel her mother's body shaking. Tears pricked her eyes and it was an effort not to cry. Mama's sobs began to die down and she turned so Maggie could see her streaming face.

'Oh Maggie,' she said. 'Come here.'

The feel of her mother's arm around her shoulders made her feel better. They sat for a little while until mama was calmer and Maggie had given her a big hug.

From where she sat, Maggie could see into the twin's room. There were two small figures lying on the old wooden bed. The blanket was covering their faces. On impulse she took her mother's arm from around her.

Tutting, she said, 'I'll just go and see to the twins, they've got the blanket round their heads.'

'No Maggie.'

At her mother's words Maggie turned half way to the bedroom and looked at her. The sadness on her face made her carry on, she couldn't leave the twins, she had to go to them, even if she got into trouble.

She stood over them for a moment and gently removed the cover from their faces. She didn't want them to suffocate. Dulcie and Ben lay together, their young faces smooth in sleep. There was no crying with pain now and Maggie wondered if they were better. Perhaps they would wake up after a sleep and she could tell them about the rain. A blowfly droned round the room as she stroked Dulcie's hair. Her dark brown curls were not as springy as they usually were. They felt dry and dirty. She stroked her arm but it was cold to her touch.

'Dear me,' Maggie whispered. 'You need warming up.' Tucking the blankets round Dulcie's body she talked to her as she worked. 'You'll never guess what, it's raining outside, so you'd better get well soon so we can go and play in the river.'
Talk of the river made Maggie remember the sheep that was stuck in the mud. The stillness of the twins reminded her of that poor thing. That awful feeling she had when she saw it came back to her now as she looked at Dulcie and Ben. She shook her head, that's silly she thought. What happened to that sheep couldn't happen to the twins. They weren't starving or thirsty, they were just a bit sick.

She shook Ben's shoulder trying to wake him up. 'Ben?' she whispered. 'Wake up.'

Mama's voice came to her from the other room. 'Come away now.'

'They aren't coughing anymore, so they must be getting better?'

'No. They are at peace now.'

Maggie didn't know what her mother meant. If they were at peace surely that meant they were better, but it was strange that they wouldn't wake up.

Billy came into the room. 'Come on, sis,' he spoke quietly. He began to cover the twin's faces again. 'We'll have to go for the vicar.'

'No, no, don't cover them up. They'll be frightened in the dark.'

He dropped the blanket and Maggie tucked it neatly round their faces again.

'Now you two,' she could hardly speak, her voice came out all trembly. 'You stay here and be good for mama, while we're away.'

Mama stood in the kitchen, staring into the fire. She seemed to be ignoring everything that was going on around her.

'Mama? Do you want me to do anything?'

Her mother shook her head and continued staring.

'Come on, let's get going,' Billy said.

Maggie followed Billy out the door and looked at the torrential rain that was now falling. She should have been happy, she would have run round in it, screaming and shouting and feeling the coolness of it on her skin.

While Billy went for the horse she got dressed and joined him in the shed. Within minutes of riding out into the rain they were drenched. Maggie held Billy round the waist and leaned her head against his back. She could smell him, it made her feel better being so close to him, but still her tears fell. They mingled with the rain and washed down her cheeks. She could taste the saltiness and let them fall.

Her body shook with crying and Billy asked if she was all right. She nodded but didn't seem to be able to stop. She felt so sad, sadder than she had ever felt before. She knew the twins were dead like that sheep. How would things ever be the same without Dulcie and Ben?

Constance

The house would have been very quiet but for the rain drumming on the corrugated iron roof. Constance sat motionless a while longer, wondering what to do. There was nothing more she could do for the twins, her babies, her beautiful babies, gone. At four they were such characters, Dulcie always the leader and Ben trailing after her. But he had a little temper at times and when Dulcie pushed him too hard he lashed out. No more would their little arms go round her neck and their sweet smell of innocence fill her senses.

Maggie adored her little brother and sister and Constance wondered what effect their deaths would have on her. Billy probably wouldn't show his feelings very much, he took his role as the eldest very seriously and she knew he would try to hide his emotions.

And Jack, he would be devastated, if she told him. Slipping into his bedroom she stood beside the bed and took his hand. It felt cold. His breathing was laboured and he was sleeping. She really didn't like the look of him. She knew he wouldn't be long in this world, so, maybe he didn't really need to know about the twins. Trying to make him as comfortable as possible she plumped up his pillow a little and straightened the blanket.

She touched his face and said, 'God bless you, Jack.'

Leaving the room her next task was uppermost in her mind. She had to see to the twins before Maggie and Billy got back. The thought of laying out their bodies sent a shiver through her, but she was the only one who could do it.

As evening fell Constance lit the lantern and decided it had been the worst day of her life. Jack had died late in the afternoon. She felt as though it wasn't happening to her, how could three of her family die, on the same day, just like that?

The children had come back with the news that the vicar was up country seeing to other deaths from diphtheria. He wouldn't be coming so it was down to them to say a few words over the graves. Well, she knew her babies and Jack better than any vicar and if they had to do without the blessing of the church they would. God hadn't done a great deal to help them lately.

She had told Maggie and Billy about their father but they had just stared at her. There was only so much grief a body could take, then numbness descended and you began to work like a clockwork toy. Bending to the task in front of her Constance thought she would never get used to this, preparing a loved one for burial.

It was the first time in thirteen years of marriage that she had seen Jack completely naked. By the light of the candle she gazed at his body, it was as though she was looking at a stranger.

She dipped the cloth into a bowl of water, squeezed it out automatically, as though she was going to clean down some shelves. With the greatest of care she smoothed it over her husband's suntanned face. Deep wrinkles were etched round his eyes from years squinting against the glare of the sun, constant exposure to the elements had made his skin leathery. His moustache looked untidy and stubble clung to his chin and caught at the cloth as Constance worked. She dampened his once soft lips but his infectious smile had gone. Billy had inherited his deep brown eyes that were now closed. Her fingers combed through his dark hair, curls springing back when she crushed them. Grey hair at his temples made him appear more mature, even though his face was boyish. As she wiped the cloth over his body she noticed the dramatic contrast in skin colour as the tan gave way to the whiteness of his torso. He never went without his shirt. She had always liked his broad shoulders. Muscle clung to his chest and upper arms even though his physique was wiry. He looked quite good for a man of thirty five.

Picking up his hand she felt the broad solidness of it. They were man's hands, not white and limp but stubby and strong, they were forceful and took control, a reflection of Jack's character.

At first she avoided looking at his manhood, but with no witness to her inquisitive gaze she studied the thing with interest. Not Jack's best asset, she decided, shaking her head as she tentatively washed around it.

When she had finished washing him she delved in the old tin trunk for his suit.

It was the same suit he had been married in. The image of him standing at the end of the aisle in that little church on their wedding day was one she would never forget. His hair had been plastered to his head with oil and one curl sprung up and flopped disobediently over his forehead. He looked so handsome and she had thought she was lucky to be marrying him.

Heaving and pulling Jack's body, Constance tried to cram his stiffening limbs into trousers, shirt and jacket. She couldn't believe how heavy he was. Perspiration trickled down her back and made her blouse stick to her. When his body was completely covered she collapsed into the chair beside him. She stared at the floor lost in grief. Unchecked, tears filled her eyes and overflowed down her cheeks. Her nose began to run and she subconsciously wiped it on her skirt as sobs heaved at her body.

Finally exhaustion swamped her and she dozed off.

The brightness of daylight woke Constance and at first she was disorientated, until she saw Jack. Leaning over she gently kissed his forehead. She noticed the scent of him had gone. That masculine mustiness that was always present on his hair and body had disappeared with his soul. Tenderly she stroked his cold arm and left the room.

She felt the need for fresh air and went outside to inhale the smells of the new day. It was still raining and the moisture-filled air felt invigorating. The fetid odour of the bedroom had made her head throb. She needed to rally herself and start the day, her first day as a widow. Her eyes felt heavy and gritty, she had hardly slept for weeks, her nights interrupted tending her sick husband and the twins. Now it was all over. She felt empty, their passing leaving a void that would never be filled.

Sitting on the veranda, she kicked off her shoes and stretched out her legs. Pulling up her skirt she let the rain fall onto her legs. It felt good, water on her skin was something she had missed. To soak in a bath full of warm soapy water would be heaven. The drought had lasted so long it was ages since she'd had a good soak. Unhooking the tin bath from the wall, she laid it out in the rain and wondered if a bath would wash away her sorrow and make her feel new again.

The squeaking of a floorboard made her look round. Maggie stood there in her underwear and bare feet.

'Mama, what are you doing?' Maggie's voice had the slow monotones of someone who is not quite awake.

'Filling the bath.'

Maggie frowned, looking dishevelled. Constance suddenly realised how much she'd neglected her lately.

'Come here.' She held out her arms to Maggie and the child stumbled to her. They clung to each other for a few minutes swaying, as though they had been reunited after a long absence. Their grip on each other relaxed and they sat in silence, watching the rain splash into the tin bath.

Maggie couldn't stay quiet for long. 'Mama, will the twins be put in a box in the ground?' The abruptness of the question made it obvious it was something that worried her.

'Yes, that's what happens when people die. The box is called a coffin.'

'Is there going to be enough room in the box for Dulcie and Ben?'

Constance realised it was important for Maggie that the twins stay together.

'Oh yes, plenty of room.' Her voice trembled as she fought to control her emotions. 'They'll be as snug as a bug in a rug.' Hastily she added, 'but they won't be there long.'

'Won't they?' Maggie looked at her with hope in her eyes.

'Oh no.' Constance tried to sound convincing. 'They'll be going to heaven for God to take care of them.'

Maggie's face lit up. 'Will they?' She thought for a moment and added, 'will papa be with them?'

'Of course.' It wasn't really a lie since none of them knew what happened when someone died.

'What's heaven like, mama?'

'Oo, now then.' Constance was trying to think of something that would make it sound realistic and not like a fairy tale. 'It's like another life, the next life. You see, no one really dies, they just go on to the next life.'

A small smile turned up Maggie's lips. She waited expectantly for her mother to continue.

'If you are good on this earth then you go on to a better life, one where there are only nice things and nice people.'

'And what do they do there?'

'Much the same as they do here, but it's better, there's no droughts or floods or anything nasty, just goodness and happiness. Now,' Constance changed the subject, 'let's find your brother.'

'I know where he is, he's up on the hill.'

From the veranda Constance looked towards the hill and saw Billy alone in the rain. For a moment she wondered what he was doing, but his actions told her. He was digging the graves. She was torn between helping him and comforting Maggie. Was this how it would be from now on, she would have to be mother and father?

CHAPTER 2

Billy

When the first rays of the new day crept over the horizon, Billy set off to dig the graves. He noticed the watery dawn and the newly washed countryside looked fresh and smelled earthy. The dawn chorus seemed noisier than usual and the kookaburra led the eruption of birdsong. Billy hadn't actually thought where he would put the graves. Not too far from the house but not close enough for the ghosts to pop in for a midnight visit. A lone tree on the hill was outlined starkly, but beautifully, against the grey morning sky. Under its branches, overlooking the homestead would be the perfect spot, he decided.

He had spent most of the night making a coffin by the light of the kerosene lamp. He had cobbled together slats of wood and used a hessian corn sack for the lining. It looked messy but it was the best he could do. He wasn't even sure if it was the right size, but he couldn't face going into the house and measuring the twins. At least he only had to make one for the twins. The thought of them being parted even in death was unthinkable. He didn't have enough wood for papa's coffin.

For a moment he stood staring into space, his thumbs hooked into his braces. Sadness enveloped him like smoke from a bushfire and even the effect on his eyes was the same. Tears trickled down his cheeks, he dashed them away with his sleeve and began digging.

When he thrust the shovel into the ground, it sank into the thin layer of mud and crashed into what seemed like rock. He hadn't realised how hard the ground was, with no rain for months the soil was baked solid like an overcooked damper. How was he going to dig two holes deep enough? He wished he had his father to help, but he didn't and never would again. He had to work it out himself and stood for a moment scratching his head. There was nothing for it but brute strength.

The wooden handle of the shovel was slippery from the rain and Billy found it hard to grip. He made an oblong shape on the ground, miles too big. He worried about it not being big enough and the coffin getting stuck, half in and half out. The thin layer of topsoil was easily removed but then he began to hack at the earth, trying to break it up. It crumbled under his onslaught and he shovelled the lumps to one side. Before long he was breathing heavily and grunting as he worked. His heart was pounding so loudly in his ears he felt he would burst. He leaned on his shovel and rested watching the rain fill the hole.

A solitary worm poked its head out of the earth, it was the first worm he had seen in a long time. The rain drew it out, like pus from an infected sore. He thought of it slithering over the twins and shuddered. If it were dead it wouldn't be able to. He jabbed at it with his shovel.

The digging seemed to be taking forever as the rain mixed with his sweat and soaked through his clothing, which stuck to him like another skin. With the dark clouds covering the sun it was hard to tell what time it was. He pushed his exhausted body on, but his lack of energy affected his accuracy with the spade. He picked the spade up with two hands and plunged it into the ground. Jumping on the blade shoulders with his full weight, he forced the steel into the earth but one foot slipped. He sliced his flesh on the metal, opening a gash round his anklebone. Blood poured out and mingled with the mud on his shoe.

'Bloody hell!'

He sat down and covered the cut with his hand. The blood flowed through his fingers and he couldn't stop it. Maybe he would bleed to death, what would they do then? If he had diphtheria bleeding must be a good thing. It would mean the germs would flow out and not make him ill. He took his hand away and let the cut bleed.

His eyes felt sore and his bottom lip trembled from the damp that seemed to have soaked through to his innards. Shaking his wet head like a dog, he got to his feet. There wasn't much he could do about his foot, except carry on, even though it throbbed painfully.

His mind wandered to less depressing things as he worked. He had always dreamed of being a sea captain. It was probably the silliest thing anyone who lived in the outback could want. It all began years ago when his mother showed him a book with a drawing of a pitching ship on a high sea. He was fascinated and ever since he had tried to find out as much as possible on the subject. Mama had come all the way from England on a ship, so knew what it felt like to be surrounded by water. His father had never been on the ocean.

Billy planned to run away to sea and stow away on a ship. One that was big and new, not a dirty tramp steamer, but maybe a sloop or one of those new passenger liners his father told him about. Of course he would miss Maggie and the twins, but when he came home he would be rich from all the gold sovereigns he captured from pirates. Did they still have pirates? There must be some somewhere. He would come home and relate his adventures to Maggie and the twins. But it wouldn't be the same now. There were no twins, just Maggie. He didn't think she would be as excited as Ben would have been. He could see Ben now, his eyes wide with wonder as he told him of his daring sea journeys. Dulcie would lean against him, fiddling with her curls like she always did when she was quiet. The prospect of life without them made him stop digging. He looked at the sky and rain sprinkled on his face.

'You bastard,' he yelled. 'What did they ever do to you?' He felt so angry with God, why couldn't he leave things as they were?

He kept digging, trying not to think of the damn sad things that made him into a blubbering idiot. How would he know when the grave was deep enough? Exhaustion dragged at his limbs and his stomach rumbled with hunger and his arms ached. He couldn't do anymore. He climbed out of the hole. He'd go home, get some food and have a rest.

The sickly smell in the house was more overpowering than the previous night and his appetite disappeared. His mother placed a bowl of watery porridge in front of him with a mug of black tea.

'You alright, lad?'

What a question, Billy thought. How could he possibly be all right after just digging a grave?

He grunted, 'Yeah,' and ladled the food into his mouth.

Maggie watched him eat and asked, 'what have you been digging?'

'A hole.'

'But what for?'

'The twins and papa,' he mumbled.

'Oh, is that where their graves are going to be?'

Billy nodded.

There was silence for a moment and Maggie said, 'but it's good that they'll all be in heaven together.'

Billy looked at her.

'When the twins start their lovely new life in heaven papa will be there to look after them,' she said.

Billy was amazed, Maggie had it all sorted out in her head. At nine years old she had the problem solved. He wished it was that easy and felt like saying, 'but what about us, who's going to look after us?'

'Maggie, lass can you go and let Blue Boy out into the field?' Mama asked.

Once Maggie had gone, his mother said, 'thanks for getting on with the graves. How far have you got?'

Billy felt uncomfortable with her. She looked so sad and her eyes were red rimmed.

'I've dug one grave so far and I've made a coffin for the twins, but there isn't enough wood to make one for papa. Sorry.' He felt as though it was his fault that papa didn't have a coffin.

She rested her hand on his shoulder and said, 'you're a good lad.' Her voice was tired and slurry.

Billy wrinkled his nose at the smell that filled the house. The humidity and dampness was having an effect.

His mother noticed.

'We'll move the twins into the shed,' she said, 'and get the other grave dug. We'll bury them tomorrow, alright son?'

Billy nodded. They weren't talking about papa and the twins any more, they were just smelly bodies now. The thought of digging another grave filled him with dread.

'Better let me have a look at that foot before we do another thing.'

Billy took his shoe off and propped his muddy foot on the table. The gash was covered in congealed blood and dried mud and looked quite swollen. With a cloth dipped in water she began gently cleaning the wound. As the skin was washed a purple bruise appeared around the gash.

'That's nasty,' she commented. Reaching up to the shelf, she grabbed the black ointment that fixed everything. Billy wished it would fix the sadness he felt. He could feel his eyes drooping and his body begin to relax as his mother tended to his foot. Steam was rising from his wet clothes as they began to dry in the humid indoor atmosphere.

She rummaged round for a piece of rag, which she wound round his foot. 'There, how's that?'

He jumped when she spoke. 'Good,' he mumbled.

Before he got too comfortable, he decided to get on with some more digging. Dragging himself from the chair he walked towards the door.

His mother spoke to him. 'I'll come and give you a hand in a minute.'

He sat on the veranda step, pulling on his shoe. His motivation had evaporated like water in a drought. It was all down to him now. He would be the breadwinner, the hunter, and the only male heir. The thought was frightening. How could he do it all?

'That's the end of sea captaining,' he muttered to himself, 'but knowing my luck I probably would've been sea sick anyway.'

Maggie

They had cleaned the house to get rid of the killer germs. The twins' bed had been chopped up for firewood, the blankets burned. All the furniture had been scrubbed and the cups and plates boiled. The diphtheria was driven away but it felt to Maggie as though they had washed away any traces of papa and the twins. She was glad mama didn't cry as much, but she did sit staring a lot and Billy wasn't very happy doing woman's work.

Since she couldn't catch the disease anymore she didn't have to sleep on the veranda. The room she had shared with the twins was now hers. It was such a shame it was full of ghosts. Sometimes she could hear them giggling and whispering to each other. Once she saw Dulcie standing in the corner looking very worried. Maggie asked her what was the matter, but of course as soon as she spoke the twin disappeared. Perhaps she wasn't happy in heaven.

Maggie got up from the bed and walked over to the window. The new curtains her mother had made from an old skirt, made the room look bright and cheerful. During the day she could forget about the ghosts.

On the shelf were her treasures. A colourful rock, a wooden horse her father carved when she was younger, which wouldn't stand up, a piece of a clay dish they'd dug up the previous summer and a rag doll her mother made when she was a baby. There was also a brightly coloured spinning top her grandfather in England had sent. It didn't work any more as it was full of dirt and kept falling on its side but Maggie liked its bright colours.

Her clothes were hung on nails on the wall, except for her best dress. That was kept in a box under the bed. It was a lovely dress but it was too small now. When she put it on for the funeral the skirt was nearly up to her knees, the sleeves were tight under her arms and she could hardly do up the buttons that ran down the back.

Having her own room wasn't that good. She felt lonely without the twins to look after and cuddle up to. She didn't think Billy would let her cuddle up to him, but he was all she had now, and mama of course. Billy kept his bed on the veranda. He said he could guard them better outside. Maggie wondered what he needed to guard them from.

The rain had lasted a week and it was such a sad time Maggie wanted to forget it. The sun shone again and life was beginning to get back to normal, well, as much as it ever could with no papa or the twins.

Maggie still felt that heavy sensation in her stomach, like when mama overcooked a damper and it sat like a rock in your belly all day. Billy said it was sadness and would go away in time. She wondered how they would live without papa to bring home the money for food. When she was in her room she did a lot of thinking and tried to work out why things happened the way they did.

A knock on her door stopped her thoughts. Billy popped his head in and asked, 'Coming down to the river, sis?'

'Yeah.' She jumped up off the bed glad to have something else to do.

Mama's voice came to them from the next room. 'But only if you have done all your chores.'

'Yes mama,' they chorused.

Billy's head disappeared again and Maggie heard him talking to mama.

'I thought there might be some fish in the river, now it's back to its proper level.'

'Just be careful, lad,' Mama said.

Maggie wondered what they had to be careful of but shrugged and ran from the room shouting, 'I'm ready'.

'Right, let's get the nets.'

Billy mumbled something about how the nets could be full of holes it was so long since they'd been used.

It felt good to be free, to escape from the house, its memories and mama's sad face. The countryside seemed alive. The trees were full of the sound of bird song and the cark of crows echoed round the hills. Lizards darted out of their path and ants crawled busily across the dirt. They walked down the track that led away from the homestead. They were on a mission.

'Watch out fish, we're coming for you,' Maggie shouted.

The gnarled old ghost gums that grew along their route where like old friends. They had been there before Maggie or even Billy was born and each had its own shape. Today all the shrivelled up leaves had fallen off and a hint of new buds were starting to show. Their bark was rain washed and looked white against the brown earth.

When they reached the river it was flowing fast, rushing past the trees along its bank. It gushed over rocks and dragged things down river. Branches, sheep bodies, pieces of wood all washed past.

'Geez,' Billy commented, 'I didn't think it would be so full.'

A shiver ran down Maggie's spine as she watched, the force of it fascinating her.

"Hmm, this could be a bit tricky.' Billy was doing that thinking out loud thing. 'I think we'd better go down stream and see if we can find a spot that's a bit calmer.'

He set off along the side of the river with Maggie running to keep up. The distance between them widened as Billy marched off ahead.

'Where's he going?' Maggie began talking to herself. 'If he's not going to wait for me, I'll just have to catch my own fish.'

She would love to catch the first fish. She stopped and approached the bank and stared at the water, unable to drag her eyes away. It was alive, moving like hundreds of giant eels, thrashing about and gobbling things up as it went.

Maggie didn't notice her feet begin to sink into the earth until the bank started to give way. She shrieked as she struggled to regain her balance, her feet back pedalling up the crumbling sides. The net was ripped from her hand by the gushing water, the force made her tip further forward and splash into the river. Her scream ended as she swallowed water. She coughed and spluttered. The sudden coldness made her gasp and tense all her muscles. The current swiftly carried her out into the middle.

Maggie thrashed her arms trying to keep afloat. She had never learnt to swim, it hadn't seemed important in a land where there wasn't much water. Her wet clothes weighed her down, her legs felt heavy and clumsy as she tried to kick her way back to the bank. She pushed her chin into the air and clamped her mouth shut, so she wouldn't swallow any more water. When she sailed past Billy she tried to shout and wave her hand. She wasn't sure he'd seen her, he was fiddling with his net and not looking in her direction. Her body tumbled about like a rag doll. There was a whack on her knee and her shins scraped over stones. Her fingers clawed the water, trying to find something to hang onto. More water rushed into her mouth as her head went under again, it seemed a long time before she could get to the surface. Her chest was burning, each time she tried to gulp for air she got a mouthful of water. She couldn't breathe, she was going to die.

She could let the river have her, she could close her eyes and let it eat her. She could go with papa and the twins to heaven, in the place of goodness her mother told her about. It would be great to see them again, that little grin Ben had when he wanted something and to feel Dulcie's arms round her neck. But she could see her mother's sad face and the words she spoke before they left. And Billy, what would he do without her? Her arms began to move again and she managed to gulp another mouthful of air.

The bank was getting nearer and she was suddenly jolted to a stop. Her arm had hooked round a tree root that stuck out of the water and felt as though it would be ripped from its socket. The river dragged at her, hungry for her to be part of its meal. Maggie grabbed the root, desperate to get a firm hold but her arm was trapped, wedged between root and rock. Pain shot down it as the river pulled at her. Her arm was twisted behind her back and she struggled to pull her weight off her shoulder. She kicked with her legs and found she could touch the bottom, but only on tiptoes. Floating her knees up she tried to roll on her side so her trapped arm was in a better position. She wrapped her legs round the root but it began to give under her weight, so she had to drop back into the water. Her teeth began to chatter, her body shivered like a nervous dog and her fingers and toes felt numb. Perhaps she would die here after all. She looked up into the branches of the river gum that had caught her.

'Please dear old gum tree help me.'

She closed her eyes and began to sink to the bottom, all her strength gone.

Something gripped her round her waist. In panic she tried to scream and bashed at it, thinking it was an eel or something horrible. Her eyes flew open and all she could see was a black body leaning over her.

A gentle voice said, 'he alright girlie, I got yuh.'

His hands eased her trapped arm from its twisted position. Maggie flinched and couldn't stop herself from yelling, 'ouch,' as the pain bought tears to her eyes.

The aborigine lifted her out of the water and laid her gently on the bank. She didn't feel frightened of him as his black face smiled down at her. Maggie tried to smile back but her teeth were chattering too much. Every time she moved pain shot down her arm and she gasped.

'Keep still girlie.'

Billy rushed over and grabbed her. He hugged her saying, 'thank God', over and over. She knew he would be lost without her.

Maggie felt herself being lifted off the ground and carried. She opened her eyes and looked at the face of the black man. She had never seen black skin so close before. It was perfectly smooth and his curly hair stuck up everywhere, he even had little black ears. It was as though he had been dipped in chocolate, his blackness was solid with no white bits anywhere. His arms felt warm and she could feel his muscles moving under his skin as he walked. With her head resting against his chest she could smell him. It reminded her of when she hugged Jessie or Bob, a sort of animal smell.

She could hear Billy's voice. He sounded a bit shaky. 'Will she be alright?' The aborigine nodded and smiled.

'Mother is going to kill us,' Billy said.

Maggie's shoulder was throbbing. Once she realised she wasn't going to die the pain got worse. Each step the black man took jolted it more. She could feel sweat on her face but she didn't groan or yell. She just wriggled.

The aborigine stopped and asked 'What's a madda, girlie?'

'My shoulder, it's hurting.'

'Mmm, him river spirit want you. You not want him so he hurt you,' the aborigine commented.

He laid her down on the ground under a tree where the grass was soft and cool.

'You wait, I fix,' Very gently he held her arm and shoulder. His touch was cool. 'Close em eyes.'

Maggie did as she was told and suddenly she felt her shoulder yanked and pain explode down her arm. She yelled out all the swear words she knew.

Billy rushed to her side. 'What do you think you're doing?' He tried to push the black man aside.

'Girlie be alright now.'

'You said that before, but she wasn't, was she?' Billy sounded as though he was going to cry, but he would never do that.

'Give me him shirt.' The black man nodded at Billy, the demand stunned him to silence. 'Hold him bad arm up,' the aborigine explained.

Maggie sat up, her shoulder was still sore but not that pounding that went right through her. The black man wrapped Billy's shirt round her body and her injured arm and it immediately felt easier.

Maggie would probably have been all right on her own two feet but the aborigine still carried her, so she let him. She felt a lot better, she had relaxed into his strong arms and was nodding off to sleep.

Maggie woke when she heard the dogs barking and sighed with relief to be home. The black man stood her on her feet and held her gently until she stopped swaying. Billy rushed over and put his arm around her waist. She was too heavy for him to carry, but she managed to walk to the house. She turned round to thank the black man but he was gone.

CHAPTER 3

Constance

'What the hell were you doing?' Constance was very angry. 'Why didn't you stop her, fancy letting her go so near the edge… absolutely stupid… she could have died.'

Billy stood motionless and didn't say a word. She thought he would try to defend himself, but he didn't.

'It wasn't his fault, mama,' Maggie interrupted.

'And you should have known better. Haven't you got a brain in your head? Isn't it enough that we had to bury your brother and sister, did you want to join them, you silly girl?'

She turned back to Billy.

'You're supposed to be the man of the house, protecting your sister. What would have happened if that abo hadn't come along? She'd be dead that's what and you'd be digging another grave.'

The words spewed from Constance' mouth and she didn't seem to have any control over what she said. It was as though the stress and sadness of the past few weeks had been curled up inside her like a hibernating snake and now spat venom at those closest to her. She wanted to hug Maggie, to protect her but how could she when the child thought so little of her own safety.

Billy's expression was belligerent.

'And you can take that look off your face.'

'Mama, stop pickin' on Billy.'

'It's alright, Maggie. I don't need you to stick up for me.' He finally spoke.

'Well, what have you got to say for yourself?'

'Nothing.' His tone was aggressive.

A reflex action made Constance raise her hand to slap him, but his voice stopped her in mid air.

'Go on, slap me.' He was practically sneering at her. 'Yes it's my fault. Everything's my fault, father's death and the twins too. You can blame it all on me since you seem to need someone to blame. But what about blaming yourself.' His words were gushing forth now. 'Did you ever think anything was your fault? We have to get out of the house to escape from you. The way you just sit on father's chair most of the time, staring at nothing as though it's only you that's suffering, well it's not, we're all upset. When was the last time you smiled or said anything nice to either of us? You make me sick.'

Billy stormed from the house. There was an awkward silence after he had gone. Constance looked across at Maggie who was studying her feet. Billy had never spoken to her like that before. She felt hurt and embarrassed in front of her daughter.

'Do you feel the same way as Billy?' she asked Maggie. 'Don't be frightened to tell me the truth. Do you think papa and the twin's death was my fault?'

'No mama.' Maggie spoke firmly as though there was no doubt in her mind.

'Are you sure?'

Maggie nodded.

'Do you think I have been a bit too mopey?'

'Just a bit but I haven't heard you crying for ages.'

Guilt made Constance turn away from Maggie. Perhaps some of the things Billy said were right, she had been full of her own grief.

'Come here Maggie and let me look at that shoulder,' she said changing the subject.

As she gently administered care on her daughter her thoughts turned to her biggest worry. How was she going to put food on the table with no money? There was practically nothing to eat, only a few handfuls of oats and a bit of flour in the bottom of the bin. They hadn't eaten fresh meat for weeks, long before Jack got sick. The money situation was tight even then. The situation was dire.

Maggie interrupted her thoughts. 'Mama, I was thinking, you shouldn't feel bad about having a fight with Billy, he didn't really mean what he said.'

'I know.' She tried to sound unconcerned but wondered if her relationship with her son would ever be the same. 'Right now, young lady,' she went on. 'That abo did a good job on your arm but you need to rest it a bit or it may pop out again.'

'I don't want that to happen.' Panic crept into Maggie's voice. She still looked a bit pale and her eyes were drooping.

'I suggest you have a little lie on your bed until supper time.'

'Yes mama,' Maggie said as she shambled out of the room.

Constance wished she could reason with Billy as easily as she could Maggie. She realized he was still upset and frustrated at the death of his father and she would have to make allowances for his behaviour. It did explain why he had been so short with her lately. She didn't know whether to tell Billy about their situation or would it make matters worse.

She flopped dejectedly into Jack's chair. He hadn't been earning the money he did in the good times, with the drought there was fewer cattle for the drovers to take to the railheads, which meant not as many men were needed. Consequently their stocks of all the staple necessities were very low. The few milking cows had been slaughtered months ago when their milk dried up. The hens had been taken by some starving creature and had left only their feet. Not that they'd had any eggs for weeks, anyway. Blue Boy looked all skin and bones, there was no hay or grass, and Constance had to give him a spoonful of molasses everyday to keep him going. The dogs managed to scavenge food, they ate frogs and small lizards and Jess licked the ants off trees.

They were stuck out here in the back of beyond, ten miles from the town of Bangala and one hundred miles from the nearest large town. Her next door neighbour Fred, lived five miles away, and he was always drunk.

Years ago Jack had a dream of building this little homestead into a large sheep station. He went so far as to buy a herd of sheep. It was an exciting time in their marriage, she was pregnant with Billy and they were going to be rich. The prices, when he bought in 1897, were rock bottom and Jack couldn't believe their luck. As beginners in the business, neither of them had realized why they were so cheap. The drought, that was in its second year, looked set to break and had it done so their dreams may have come true. But nature has a way of being contrary and it was another six years before rain came. It was the worst drought anyone could remember, it lasted eight years and all forms of livestock production and agriculture were drastically affected. The price of sheep plummeted and the drought reduced the country's livestock population by half. Jack's little herd soon perished. That was one of many times they had to pick themselves up and start again. In those days she used to get terribly homesick for a bit of green English countryside.

Constance kicked off her shoes and pulled her feet up onto the chair. She hugged her knees, wrapping her skirt about her legs for comfort. The look of absolute devastation on Jack's face when he found the last of his sheep dead, was something she would never forget. They were left with nothing only a large hole in their finances. The wool prices never really recovered and it didn't seem viable to buy anymore. Jack had gone back to droving to put food on the table. That was twelve years ago. She eventually got used to the harshness of the outback but life was hard, especially when Jack was away. Somehow they had managed to get by over the years.

'It's not fair, why aren't I mistress of one of those big sheep stations, with people working for us, and the table groaning with food? Why aren't my children away at school, safe in the city where they never have drought or famine?'

She knew she was being melodramatic and childish. Perhaps Billy was right. I am sitting around feeling sorry for myself, she thought. Gingerly she got up and straightened the chair. Things were going to have to change around here. We need food and it's up to me to get it anyway I can even if it means lying and stealing.

Reaching for her purse on the mantle shelf, she peered inside. She tipped the contents on the table. A few pennies were all she had. Optimistically she picked the old tea caddy from the cup shelf and shook it. No sound of rattling coins could be heard, but to make sure, she opened it. It was empty apart from the musty smell of tea.

She would have to sell something to raise some money. Constance knew there was nothing of any real value in the house. The few pieces of furniture were looking well worn and shabby. Her good, black dress smelt of moth balls and looked faded. Maybe there was something in the shed they didn't need. Without realizing she began to fiddle with her wedding ring, twisting it round on her finger. The firmness of the ring between her fingers made her stop. She held up her left hand. She stared at the gold band as if seeing it for the first time. It would fetch quite a bit of money, it was gold and the years of dipping her hands into all kinds of things hadn't done any damage. It looked relatively new.

But she couldn't sell her wedding ring, could she? Was she being disloyal to Jack? Her thoughts drifted back to when she received it. Sydney 1893 on a hot February day. She remembered Jack standing at the end of the aisle looking very uncomfortable in his borrowed suit but smiling all over his face. She had been upset that none of her family was there but none of Jack's were either, just Bluey, his best man and Mrs. Maguire from the boarding house. Constance could still recall how strange it was having a ring permanently stuck on her finger but it didn't take long to get use to it. Now it was part of her and hadn't been off her finger since her wedding day but it was no good being sentimental and starving.

She tried to pull it off but it got stuck at her knuckle and wouldn't budge. Maybe fate was intervening and she wasn't meant to sell it. She went to the water jug and dipped it in before vigorously applying soap to the surrounding skin. Thrusting her misgivings to the back of her mind she pulled and wriggled the ring until it slid off. The white mark and indentation in her skin was a reminder of where it had been. It was the last remnant of her marriage.

She would have to go to Bangalla and see if old Mr. Sullivan would give her anything for the ring. She knew she would get one of his disdainful looks at selling the wedding ring her man had bought her, but she couldn't worry too much about that, so long as he gave her the money.

The following morning Constance dressed as usual. She put on her apron and tied it at the back. Her optimism had been dented during the night. She had lain awake with doubts like huge obstacles in her way. A bit like this skirt, she thought. It felt cumbersome and hot, the gathers round her waist making it stand out to twice its girth and the hem that dragged along the floor was a hindrance. The leg of mutton sleeves felt bulky, accentuated her shoulders and looked ridiculous. Of course they weren't the fashion now, this dress was over ten years old. The material had faded but hadn't got any thinner, still as hot as ever. Men didn't have to wear such clumsy clothing and who needed to look feminine out here?

Men's clothes, that's what she needed, something that would allow her some freedom. The idea was foreign to her but she had heard of women wearing trousers. There must be something she could wear in the tin trunk, since she never threw anything away. It was jammed full of old clothes. Some had painful memories. Baby clothes and her wedding dress wrapped in calico, a simple style that she had never worn again.

She laid everything carefully on the bed, but couldn't help burying her face in the folds of a soft baby rug. The fresh baby smell had gone years ago. Near the bottom she found an old pair of Jack's trousers that had split under the crotch. She remembered how she had laughed at Jack when he described how they'd ripped. She could see where she had repeatedly sewn them up. Holding them against her waist she decided they were just the job with a few alterations. Once everything was packed away again, all the memories secured firmly in the trunk, she set to with a needle and thread. She stitched the baggy waist, shortened the legs and repaired the crotch.

It was a strange feeling wearing trousers, having her legs wrapped in scratchy material. She bent over and stuck out her bottom. There was a bit of tightness, her rear end was definitely bigger than Jack's. She hoped her new bit of stitching would hold. She dug out one of her old blouses and pulled on her shabby boots. Her outfit was complete.

It would probably cause all sorts of gossip, and when she sold her wedding ring the rumours would be rife. Pinning her hair up, she clamped her battered hat on her head and looked in the mirror. Was it her imagination or did she look different, more self assured. If that's what a pair of trousers could do for her, she would wear them more often. As she looked at herself in the mirror both children wandered into the room.

Maggie spoke first. 'Why are you dressed like that, mama?' The frown on her face was comical.

Billy scowled and shook his head. 'Yeah, why have you got papa's pants on?'

Constance decided she wasn't going to explain herself. 'Because I have and I will probably dress like this a lot in the future, so you'd both better get used to it.'

'That's stupid,' Billy stated and walked out.

Driving the cart had been difficult, with deep ruts in the dirt road worn by countless wagons. Mud from the recent rain made Constance worry that the cart would get bogged. Homesteads speckled the landscape, some near the road and others set back away from the dust of passing wagons.

As she approached the town Blue Boy slowed down. The main street of Bangalla consisted of shops, hotel, church, and town hall huddled together in a jumble of seediness, neatness and well-worn prosperity. A veranda protruded from each shop front to protect the merchandise from fading. Corrugated iron roofs abounded, painted in dark colours or left to rust. There was a blacksmith's forge attached to the ironmongers, the bakery that stood beside the hotel and the clothing store with its sensible styles for both men and women. She would have loved to be able to buy herself and the children something. There was also a bank that only opened two days a week, when the wealthy sheep station owners came to draw out money for wages. A Cobb and Co coach stood outside the post office, the driver nowhere to be seen.

The horse came to a stop outside Mr. Sullivan's store as if he knew where to go. A mid day sleepiness hung over the town and the main street was almost deserted. Constance climbed down from the cart and stretched her aching joints. The whole idea of wearing men's clothing suddenly seemed silly and she felt very conspicuous. As she entered the shop she pulled down the brim of her hat.

There were no customers in Mr. Sullivan's store, which was just as well. It was a fascinating shop, jammed full of food and household goods. Merchandise hung from the ceiling and shelves, the floor was crowded with stock. Metal cans hung precariously at head height and galvanized buckets threatened the shins. Copper jelly moulds in different sizes and shapes were stacked on a crate of horse liniment. Sacks of flour, wheat and oats stood drunkenly with their contents spilling on the floor. In one corner was a small counter with an ineffectual metal grille. Constance moved towards this section of the shop. A voice made her jump.

'Gudday.' Mr. Sullivan stood behind the counter with a cigarette hanging from the corner of his mouth. He was short and fat with a full greying beard. His hair was a mass of unruly grey curls and his eyes a faded blue.

'Hello.'

'Geez, you're a woman, are yuh?'

Constance smiled and nodded.

'What's with the get up?' Before she could answer he said, 'I know, you're one of them suffragettes, aren't yuh?' Recognition suddenly dawned. 'Hang on, aren't you Jack Lang's wife?'

'That's right'. Constance wasn't sure whether she was confirming being a suffragette or Jack's wife.

'Oh, we was sorry to hear about old Jack. We heard he'd met his maker.' He bowed his head for a moment as though saying a prayer and then briskly enquired, 'Now what can I do for yuh?'

Constance cleared her throat. 'Well,' she said, taking her wedding ring out of her pocket and laying it on the counter. She could feel her cheeks burning. 'I was wondering how much you would give me for this?'

'Ah, wedding ring eh?'

Mr. Sullivan studied her a moment and his accusing look made her add, 'it was my mother's.' She hid her left hand as she spoke.

'Of course it was.' He nodded. Delicately holding it in his rough hands, he put a jeweller's loupe to his eye and made appreciative noises. 'Forty shillin's, how about that missus?'

To Constance it sounded a fortune but she knew he would only offer her his lowest price first.

'I'll have you know, Mr. Sullivan, that's an heirloom, it's been in my family for generations.'

A smile spread over his face at her reply. 'Really?'

'Most definitely.'

They both knew it was a pack of lies.

'Well, since you are such an honest woman and a suffragette with it I'll give you fifty shillings, but that's my last offer.'

Constance could tell by the tone of his voice that bargaining was over.

'That will do nicely, thank you Mr. Sullivan.'

She was excited as she left the shop. There was enough money to buy what they needed and perhaps a few luxuries. But by the time she had walked around the other shops and seen the prices her happiness had dissolved. What Mr. Sullivan had given her was only equal to a few weeks' wages and there would be no more. Her purchases barely covered the bottom of the cart.

Her spirits recovered when she got nearer to home. The children ran out to meet her. Constance felt as though she had been away for a week instead of only a day. Even Billy had a slight smile on his face when they began to unload the supplies. Over a reviving mug of black tea and a slice of proper bread, one of her little extravagances, she described what she had seen and the reaction to her outfit.

Even though they had enough basic supplies to stop them starving they still needed fresh meat. Constance had seen quite a lot of game on her way to town and didn't think it would be that difficult to shoot something. Jack had given her shooting lessons some years ago when he first started going away.

The next day she decided to go hunting. Clutching the gun she clumsily hoisted herself into the saddle and headed off. She had no real idea where to go but would just ride until she found something.

The untidy bushland gave way to a more open and deserted area. The red earth was bare except for mulga bushes, spinafex and an occasional tree. The heavy rain had left large muddy areas, which were gradually drying out. She spotted paw prints in the mud and dismounted to investigate.

'Boar,' she muttered. The hairs on the back of her neck tingled. 'Come on Blue Boy, I don't think we'd better hang about here.'

As she began to remount, she heard rustling in the bushes. She froze hoping it would go away but Blue Boy was spooked. He neighed and shook his head pulling the reins from her hand. He rushed to the edge of the clearing. The movement made the boar attack. It burst through the bushes. The horse reared up on its hind legs and the gun and Constance clattered to the ground. The boar charged the horse. Blue Boy's eyes were wide with fright and he took off into the bush.

Constance didn't have much time to think as the boar turned in her direction. Desperate to get up the nearest tree, she launched herself at the trunk, clawing at anything she could get hold of. The boar was swiftly upon her. Her legs scraped on the rough bark as she tried to get out of reach of its tusks and teeth. She kicked at its snout, gibbering and crying with fright, her arms clamped round the tree. She couldn't hold on, her hands began to slide down. Regaining her grip she forced herself upwards, her muscles burning with exertion and her body trembling. A protruding knot of wood saved her life as she grabbed it and hauled herself onto a branch. She was safe, for now. Constance shuddered as she looked down at the destructive animal, its beady eyes staring up at her. Over the years she had seen the damage wild boars could inflict on livestock and people.

She balanced on the thin branch as the wind ripple through the foliage. The dull leathery leaves rustled and she clung tighter. After a while her arms and legs began to stiffen up with the effort of clinging on. The boar moved away, but she stayed where she was, just in case it was still lurking about.

The gun would be the first thing she would grab, once she worked out how to get down. She began to pull herself along the branch. Movement made her wobble like a drunken monkey. When she got to the middle she laid along it wrapping her arms round the limb. She knew she only needed to shift her weight slightly and she would fall. If she could let her legs drop and keep hanging on with her arms she might have more control. Before she could master this manoeuvre she felt herself going. She couldn't stop herself and fell to the ground with an almighty thud.

She gasped as the air was knocked from her lungs on landing. One arm was pinned beneath her. For a moment she lay still wondering what she had damaged. Her whole body seemed to hurt. She staggered to her feet, moving her limbs, waiting for an excruciating pain to tell of a broken bone but none came. She breathed a sigh of relief, she was tougher than she thought. She rushed to the gun and slung it over her shoulder. Hopefully she looked about for Blue Boy but he was long gone, probably galloped all the way home.

She couldn't believe how stupid she had been, thinking she could just ride off into the bush and come back with a plump, neatly slaughtered piece of game. It was going to be a long walk home.

At first she was worried the boar might still be in the area and cursed herself for not shooting it. What a meal he would have made. She began walking, not even sure if she was going in the right direction. Recalling how the sun was in her eyes when she rode out, she tried to guess how long she had been up the tree. The sun was still high in the sky so it was probably afternoon. The hostile terrain stretched away in every direction looking identical no matter which way she turned. What if she got lost, she could easily perish out here, it happened all the time and what would happen to the children? She didn't even have any water.

It seemed as though she had been walking for hours, her aching body needed to rest. A fallen Mallee tree, its roots exposed to the air like lifeless tentacles, looked the perfect place. She eased her bruised body down onto the tree trunk. The hot breeze flapped the baggy sleeves of the shirt she wore. Perspiration trickled down between her breasts and she undid a few buttons. She took off her hat, letting her hair loose. Sitting completely still, with the gun on her lap, her head back and her eyes closed, she began to relax. She was so tired she could have slept but instinctively opened her eyes, feeling another presence.

The snake that was crawling between her boots was flicking its tongue, sensing the air. Constance jumped to her feet and the snake's reaction was swift. It lunged for her foot. She grabbed her gun, fumbled with the trigger and managed to fire at point blank range. The sound of the gunshot was deafening and erupted through the trees. Birds clattered into the air, screeching and squawking. Constance fired again even though the snake was already lifeless and bloody. Her heart pounded, the adrenalin pumped through her body and she visualised the snake venom flowing through her veins.

She looked down at where she had been bitten. The deadly venom trickled down the dusty leather of her boot. Her hands began to tremble as she breathed a shaky sigh of relief. She looked down at the mutilated corpse. It couldn't do her any harm now. She had heard that snake meat was a delicacy and the black bushmen ate it.

Sheepishly she grabbed the tail, half afraid it might attack her again and began dragging it. As the sun began to sink she had an eerie feeling that she was being watched. Perhaps it was Jack, she thought. Familiar terrain began to surround her and her fears evaporated. She practically ran the last part of her journey, back to her children and the safety of home.

'Where have you been?' Billy demanded. 'Blue Boy has been back for ages.'

He was speaking to her as though she was the child.

'Hunting,' she replied, holding up the dusty, headless snake.

'Yum,' Billy said sarcastically while Maggie screwed up her nose.

'It will be fine when I boil it up,' Constance tried to sound convincing.

As the morning sun spilled over the horizon Constance sat on the veranda step, within easy reach of the outside privy. The feed of snake the night before hadn't been a great success. She felt sore and bruised from the previous day's exploits. A movement, near the edge of the tree line, made Constance alert. It was probably a feeding roo. An uneasy feeling settled on her as she stared into the darkness that lingered under the trees. It wasn't an animal, but a person.

The man moved away from the camouflage of bushes and walked towards the house. What did he want? Thoughts raced through her mind. Who would be loitering around her property at this time of day? Should she run indoors for the gun? It would look threatening. She could yell at him but her five feet five inch stature would hardly cause him to run. A red wash of sunrise lit up the sky behind him. By squinting into the glare and shading her eyes, Constance could see the distinctive silhouette. It was an aborigine.

Exaggerated tales of black men massacring defenceless women and children clawed at her logic. She wanted to run but couldn't leave Billy and Maggie. As Constance watched, he stealthily approached. His eyes darted from house to bush, his bare feet hardly making footprints in the dusty soil. He was dragging something that left a snaking trail behind him through the dirt. His fluid movements made the task look easy, but the bushman trod with a wary step. Constance breathed out the trapped air that had lodged in her pounding chest. As he drew nearer he walked slower and finally stopped in front of her.

Rays of the rising sun bounced off his mass of unruly curls. It spread warmly over his bare torso accentuating the muscles in his arms and chest. His broad shoulders looked as smooth as finely sanded wood, his skin the colour of polished boot leather. The lower half of his body was clad in a pair of moleskin trousers, turned up at the cuff until they were half way up his calves.

'What do you want?'

'Tucka, missus.' He held up the carcass of a dead goanna by its tail and dropped it at her feet. Flies buzzed round it as it lay in the dirt.

A huge grin, full of perfect white teeth, split the black man's face in glaring contrast to his dark skin. 'Him taste bedder 'an that snake,' he stated.

At first Constance wasn't sure what he was talking about until the memory of her catch yesterday came back to her.

Acknowledgement must have showed on her face, because the black man smiled and nodded his head. Hesitantly Constance smiled back and said, 'Thanks.'

She watched him unsure what to do next. Before she could think of anything else to say, he moved back from his bounty and still smiling said, 'See yuh,' and loped off into the bush.

The whole incident was like a dream except for the dead lizard on the ground.

CHAPTER 4

Billy

Billy was still sulking. He sat on the veranda lethargically pulling on his boots, thoughts festering in his mind. Two things had upset him. Firstly, being blamed for Maggie falling in the river, and secondly his mother going bush. What made her think she could go hunting when she didn't have a clue what she was doing? Didn't she realize he knew more about it than she did? Didn't she trust him to provide for them? Fair enough, his attempt at fishing hadn't been too successful, but it was all right for him to make that coffin and dig them graves, wasn't it? I would've liked to see her do it, he thought. She was too busy sitting indoors crying. The memory of her tending his cut foot came back to him, the expression on her face as though she really did care. Maybe she did, a little.

'Females,' papa used to say. 'You can never please 'em'.

There was no use driving himself mad trying to figure them out. Thoughts of proper food made his mood brighten, he was starving. The supplies his mother had brought back from town meant a decent bit of tucker.

Billy sidled into the kitchen, but instead of finding food on the table there was a grotesque animal lying there and Maggie was playing with it.

'Look at this, Billy, isn't it horrible?'

She was barbarically examining the goanna's floppy body, lifting a clawed foot, letting it drop and manually swishing the long tail. She stroked the hard skin, opened and closed the animal's mouth and growled, 'hello everybody, I'm the ugliest animal in the whole world and I'm not happy 'cause I'm dead.'

Billy tried to stifle a laugh but it blurted out in an uncontrollable gush of grunting which turned into a full-blown laugh. It felt great. It had been ages since he'd had a good laugh and once he started he couldn't stop. His face creased up, his eyes filled with tears and his stomach hurt. It was as though all the pent up emotion he had been feeling these past few weeks bubbled out. As he laughed the tears fell and his face changed. His lips began to turn down and the laughter was replaced with crying. His mother and Maggie watched him but he couldn't stop. He just stood there in a confusion of emotion, making a fool of himself.

His mother came over to him and put her arms around him.

'Shh, my lad, it's alright now.'

She stroked his brow as she used to when he was little and Billy held on to her. It was good to have physical contact with someone, to be held and comforted. He felt bad about all the horrible things he had been thinking about her. He wanted to tell her he was sorry but the words wouldn't come.

'What's the matter?' Maggie was looked very concerned. 'It's not that scary, these claws won't really get you.'

Billy pulled himself from his mother's arms and strode out of the house. He looked like a right ninny, crying in front of everyone, he didn't know what was wrong with him. He hadn't meant to cry, after him thinking himself so grown up, the man of the house and all that rubbish. His father once told him that men only cry inside and not out. Well, he hadn't got the hang of that yet. Maybe you had to reach a certain age. Was twelve the right age? Obviously not. A deep shuddering sigh exhaled from him. He felt stupid as he wiped his face with his sleeve. He supposed his mother and Maggie were family so it wasn't really that bad.

Once he composed himself he went to the shed and got his father's hunting knife. Someone was going to have to skin that thing and he must be able to do a better job than his mother did on the snake. He rubbed a piece of sandstone up and down the lethal looking blade to sharpen it. He tested it by running his thumb tentatively along the razor sharp edge and grinned. He was ready for action.

Returning indoors brandishing the knife he ordered his mother and Maggie to 'stand back.' He examined the carcass. 'I wonder how it died?' he said. There was no evidence of how it had been killed, no blood or gashes and its neck wasn't broken.

His mother explained how they had come by the dead goanna, she told them about the aborigine that had left it on the step.

Billy was intrigued. 'It could have been the same abo who saved Maggie.'

'Perhaps, since we haven't seen any around here for ages and then all of a sudden two decide to help us.'

'Right, well, I'd better get on with it.' Billy tried to sound as though he was in control of the situation. 'This could get messy, so don't get too close.'

He laid the animal on its back and slit it from neck to hind legs. He wasn't sure how to skin a goanna but he'd seen his father do a rabbit like this once. Hacking at the carcass his hands soon became covered in blood and as it dried it turned sticky. His fingers slithered round the internal organs and the smell of warm flesh mixed with the overpowering odour of rancid stomach contents made Billy want to heave. The skin was not pliable and soft like a rabbit's, but more like leather and he chopped it off in chunks. He sliced muscle from bone, dropping the meat into a pan ready for cooking.

As he worked large blowflies were drawn to the smell of fresh meat and tried to settle on the exposed pieces. They buzzed round Billy's head and he swiped at them, leaving a trail of blood on his face and shirt. It was a very strenuous task and he could feel the sweat on his back and under his arms. At last he ended up with two pots full, one with meat and the other with bones.

'That'll make a beaut dinner,' he said, laying the knife on the table.

'Well done, lad.' His mother was smiling her approval.

Billy went out to the water tank and washed his hands thoroughly, shuddering as he did so. He'd never cut up an animal before, usually his father did that sort of thing. He would have to get used to all these horrible jobs.

He began to wonder about the bushman who had left it. Could it be the same one who saved Maggie, sort of like a guardian angel watching over them, only with a black skin instead of wings? The thought made him smile. He wondered if he would come back again and had a feeling he would. Billy decided he'd be ready for him when he did.

The following morning Billy was the one awake at dawn and sure enough a figure walked stealthily across the yard. Apprehension made Billy scowl as the black man came to stand in front of him. Their eyes met and Billy nodded a greeting. They stood for a few moments studying each other, the black man and the white boy. Well not really a boy anymore, Billy thought as he straightened his back and squared his shoulders. The aborigine thrust a bowl towards Billy whose reaction was to step back.

'More tucker?' the aborigine offered.

Billy peered at the contents in the bowl. Fat, white grubs wriggled in the bottom and he unconsciously screwed up his face with distaste.

'Him good witchetty grub,' the aborigine stated, looking slightly hurt at Billy's reaction.

'Thanks.' Billy tried to smile but didn't have a clue what to do with them.

As if reading his mind the aborigine suggested, 'Cook him in ashes of fire.' Billy understood and nodded his head.

'What's your name? I'm Billy.'

'Billy?'

'Yeah that's right.'

The aborigine smiled. 'Me Ningan.' He poked himself in the chest as he said it as though that was how he had been taught to introduce himself.

'Go steady mate, you'll do yourself an injury pokin' yourself like that.'

The aborigine's face fell and he looked puzzled.

'So, Ningan, now what?'

'See yuh tomorra, Billy.'

'Yeah, if you like'.

Neither Billy nor Ningan were very big on conversation, but they didn't need to be. Billy felt as if he had found someone on his wavelength, blunt and to the point, no beating about the bush. He looked at the witchetty grubs.

'I guess they won't kill us,' he mumbled.

The next day Ningan was back. But this time he didn't have an offering, much to Billy's relief. The witchetty grubs hadn't been very appetizing, the womenfolk wouldn't touch them but he thought he had better not waste food, even abo food. He cooked them as instructed, their bodies swelled and the skin stiffened. They were a bit smelly when they were cooking but he held his nose and had a nibble. They were quite nutty in taste and if he forgot they were grubs, they would have been passable.

'Gudday, Billy,' Ningan greeted him.

'Gudday mate.' Billy stood on the top step of the veranda so he was as tall as the aborigine.

'Wanna come huntin'?' Ningan asked as though it was an everyday event.

'Yeah, sure thing,' Billy couldn't help grinning and eagerly replied, 'Just a sec I'll get me knife.' Billy disappeared into the house and came out with his father's lethal weapon.

Ningan shook his head and said, 'don't need that.'

'Why not?'

Ningan put his hand behind him and retrieved a boomerang that was stuck down the waistband of his trousers. He held it up and raised his eyebrows. No explanation was needed.

'Oh, yeah, I've always wanted to know how to throw them things.'

They headed off across the yard, Billy fairly swaggered with the importance of their mission and Ningan had an amused look on his face. Their footsteps were halted for a moment when a voice called, 'where're you going?' Maggie was running after them. 'Can I come?'

Billy's answer brooked no argument. 'No, sis, we're off to do men's work.'

They walked in silence. Billy really didn't know what to say to Ningan. What do you say to an aborigine? Been to any corroborees lately or how's yuh didgerdoo? He smiled to himself.

At first he could keep in step with Ningan but soon the aborigine was striding off and he had to run to keep up with him. He didn't want to say anything, he just jogged and skipped at his side hoping they would soon get wherever they were going or have a rest.

All of a sudden Ningan stopped and examined the ground. He broke a stick off a nearby tree and began scraping the soil.

'Ah… there he is.' Ningan pointed to a small hole.

'Oh yeah,' Billy replied not having a clue what he was looking at.

Next the black man pushed the stick down the hole and waggled it about. Very gently he pulled it back out and the end was teaming with ants. Billy stepped back, he didn't want them buggers to get on him.

Ningan was smiling and offering Billy the insect infested end of the stick.

'Him good.'

Billy looked in horror as Ningan gently picked one off the stick and ate it. The ants looked very unappetizing with peculiar large bulbous bodies. The bushman helped himself to another and ate it with relish. He nodded to Billy to do the same.

With faltering hand Billy tried to disentangle one of the insects from his mates but as he grabbed round the fat bit it squashed and a sticky nectar covered his fingers.

'Errr…' Another had managed to get on his finger when he touched the stick and was crawling up the back of his hand. 'Get off yuh….'

'Ged him,' Ningan's shouted.

Billy's reaction was to smack the thing and kill it before it got any further, but with a control he didn't know he possessed, he quickly picked it up and popped it into his mouth. He could feel its legs tickling his tongue and when he closed his mouth fully it squashed and a wonderfully sweet sensation erupted on his tongue.

He widened his eyes in disbelief. 'You're right, it does taste good.'

Ningan offered him the teaming end of the stick again.

'No thanks, mate. I'm a bit full at present.' Billy couldn't quite believe they were sitting in the dirt, eating ants, but anything this abo can do, I can do, he thought. He just wished they would get on with the boomerang business.

The aborigine wiped his mouth with the back of his hand and stood up. He stopped and looked at the ground again. Oh no, not more ants, thought Billy.

'Wanna bush turkey for yuh dinna?' He pointed to some footprints on the ground. 'Him looks like a fat one.'

Billy studied the footprints and wondered how Ningan knew it was fat. The aborigine began walking very quietly, his bare feet making hardly any sound. Sitting down again, Billy pulled his boots off and followed Ningan, but Billy's feet weren't hardened like the black man's and he felt every stone and twig under his weight. Gritting his teeth he trod gently, placing each foot gingerly in front of the other. He finally reached Ningan who was standing behind a tree looking intently at something Billy couldn't see.

'See that bush?' Ningan pointed ahead of them.

Billy nodded not sure which bush he was talking about, since there were loads.

'Turkey thinks he can hide there.' Ningan chuckled to himself. Very slowly he raised his arm holding the boomerang and flung it into the bushes. It flew decisively through the air and thumped into something in the undergrowth. A short squawk was heard then nothing. Billy rushed to the place the boomerang had disappeared and came out dragging a fat, dead, bush turkey.

'Can you show me how to do that?'

Ningan shook his head. 'Nah, yuh godda be an abo to do that.'

Billy's face fell. 'Can you show me how to make one of them things, then?'

The black man nodded. Billy decided if he had his own boomerang he could teach himself to throw it, it couldn't be that difficult.

Ningan looked at the sun. 'We'd bedda ged yuh home.'

Billy wasn't as enthusiastic on the way home. He felt a bit annoyed that Ningan wouldn't show him how to throw a boomerang and now he was trying to get rid of him. But at least they had some proper meat for tea, not lizard or creepy crawlies. As he neared the house he suddenly realized Ningan was no longer in front of him. He stopped and looked around him. 'Sneaky abo,' he muttered smiling to himself. 'See yuh tommorra,' he yelled at the trees.

'See yuh Billy,' the reply came back.

Billy giggled and threw the bush turkey over his shoulder and went home like the conquering hero.

They saw each other most days after that. In the weeks that followed the larder was stuffed with salted meats and all sorts of other aboriginal delicacies. From wild peaches that Billy's mother had bottled to vegetables such as yams and spinach. The friendship between Billy and the black man grew. He was like one of the family although his mother didn't really know him only over the goanna episode. Maggie thought he was the dog's bollocks after he saved her life and was always trying to follow them. He did feel a bit mean not doing anything with her lately, but it was important stuff he was doing with Ningan, not some silly games. Perhaps he should include her sometimes.

Maggie

When Billy started going off with Blackie every day Maggie felt very jealous. She had given the black man that name after he had rescued her, when she didn't know what he was called. She remembered how warm his skin was when he carried her, how protected she had felt and really, he should have been her friend, not Billy's. Her injured shoulder had been painful for a few days and her mother had rubbed liniment on it and now it was completely better.

In those few days when she had to rest, Billy came into the bedroom and sat and chatted to her. She had felt very important, but once she was better he was gone again for hours, off with that abo. She was so used to doing things with Billy, but now, all of a sudden she was left at home with mama.

She tried to follow them once but couldn't keep up. Eventually, after a few weeks they did let her go along with them.

They made a bit of a fuss of her, which she enjoyed, Billy showed her things he'd learned and Blackie, or Ningan as she had to get used to calling him, asked if she would like him to make her a digging stick. She said she would love one but wasn't sure what it was for.

Maggie stood with Billy and watched as Ningan scoured the trees for a suitable stick. It had to be sturdy but light, not too long but not too short, he told them in his funny talk. When he found the right sort he sharpened one end and held it over a fire. This was to harden the wood. Next he smoothed the bark so it wasn't rough and gave it to her. She felt quite shy taking it from him, a gift he had made her.

'Erm, it's very nice,' she said holding it at arms length and studying it.

'You don't know what it's for or how to use it, do you, sis?' Billy smirked at her.

'Course I do.' She tried to sound convincing but didn't have a clue. 'Stick it in the ground and dig.'

'But what are you digging for?' Billy was being a bit too smart for her liking.

'In case we need a hole.' She was getting quite cross watching them smiling and sniggering at her.

'I show missy,' Ningan announced. 'Come, we'll find him good root.'

They both followed the black man and Maggie watched very closely which plant he dug up for the roots. She stared as he scratched around in the dirt, not bothering about the soil that got on his hands or the dust that coated his bare feet. When he got the root out of the ground he wiped it on his trousers and gave it to her.

'Missy need a dilly bag,' Ningan stated.

'Yeah you do,' Billy echoed his sentiments.

'What's a dilly bag?' Maggie was getting fed up being made to look stupid.

'What women carry things in,' her brother informed her.

'Oh, like a shopping bag?' Maggie wanted to show she wasn't as stupid as they thought. Billy nodded and Ningan copied him.

Sometimes, she did catch up with them when they eventually stopped to rest under a tree. While they sat, Ningan would tell them stories about alchera or the dreamtime. At first Maggie thought they were fairy stories, like mama told them when they were little. But he spoke so seriously, maybe it really had happened. His stories fascinated Maggie and she could imagine the pictures he described of spirits travelling across an empty place. As they journeyed they created land and sky. Wherever they rested they left living creatures that took over the safe keeping of that creation. Maggie's favourite creature was the rainbow serpent that shaped the valleys by dragging its tail across the land. When the spirits were finished creating things they went to live in caves, water holes or other secret places. She wasn't really sure what a spirit looked like, perhaps it was a bit like the wind, invisible yet able to move things. Her imagination became a bit too over active and every time the wind rustled the leaves in the trees she thought it was spirits escaped from their cave or resting place. She wasn't frightened of them, Ningan said they were friendly unless you did something to annoy them. Maggie wondered what you would have to do to annoy a spirit, but she tried not to think about that too much.

When Maggie and Billy were at home they talked about Ningan all the time and sometimes she wondered if her mother got fed up with it. Perhaps it was time for mama to meet him properly not over a dead goanna. She wanted to share him with her, she felt sure mama would like him too. She couldn't understand why he kept making excuses not to come. Perhaps he was shy. Finally Billy managed to talk him into it and they all trooped back to the homestead like visiting royalty.

As they got nearer home Billy showed Ningan their favourite gum tree for climbing and their hiding place which was a circle of coolabahs trees surrounded with bush and a big open space in the middle. It was where they went when they wanted to be on their own, it was their secret place.

They stood on the ridge that overlooked the house and gazed down at the shabbily repaired tin roof and broken fences that surrounded the property. Long grass sprouted round the old shed and the water tank was battered and rusty. Maggie decided it looked a sight even though it was home. Who was going to repair it all now?

Her mother was pegging washing on the line. Even the washing looked drab and lifeless, in colours that blended with the dusty surroundings, browns and fawn, black and grey. It would be lovely to have something red, Maggie thought, or even bright yellow like the wattle flowers. As they approached, their mother looked up from her chores and waved to them. They all waved back including Ningan and they ran down the incline towards her with Ningan hanging back a bit.

'Hello mother,' Billy greeted her. 'We've brought a visitor. This is Ningan.'

Maggie noticed how Billy had stopped saying "mama" and now sounded very posh calling her "mother".

Ningan held out his hand to shake their mother's, as he had practiced with Billy. It was not something the black man did, it was not one of their customs.

'Nice to meet yuh.'

Billy had taught him what to say. Ningan's rough, black hand gently clasped her pure white skin. She nodded and smiled, looking slightly uncomfortable with the black man.

'I'd like to thank you for saving my daughter's life.' Now Ningan looked embarrassed. 'It was very brave of you,' she added.

Maggie didn't know why she had to bring up that subject.

'Aw, come on, mother,' Billy interrupted. 'You're embarrassing the poor bloke.'

'Sorry.' She looked away and a little grin turned up her lips. 'Would you like to come in?' she asked, but Ningan shook his head.

'Bad luck, missus,' he replied. 'Spirits not like me goin' in white man's house.'

'Sorry.'

It was as though her mother didn't know what to say to the blackman, Maggie thought. They were strangers, from different worlds.

'I've heard a lot about you from the children.'

Ningan smiled one of those smiles that Maggie loved, where his white teeth lit up his black face and sent crinkles round his eyes.

'Erm, I'm Constance.'

Maggie was surprised by her mother's words. Why didn't she call herself Mrs Lang? "Constance" seemed a bit too friendly.

Ningan frowned for a moment, then his face lit up. 'Goodday Connie,' he said. Maggie laughed, she realized he couldn't say Constance and even her mother looked amused. She seemed to like Ningan and now he had a nickname for her they would all be friends together.

'Godda go now,' Ningan said as he turned and walked away.

Later that night Maggie thought back over the day's events. The visit by Ningan had been a bit strange. She was surprised by her mother's reaction to him. She thought she would be stern and stand offish but she wasn't. In fact after he had gone mama seemed to be in a good mood. Why did Ningan have such an effect on her family, Maggie wondered? They all seemed to like him, which was good but she would like to be able to spend more time with him, on her own, without Billy being all smart and thinking himself so clever. She thought back to the day Ningan rescued her from the river. It was good being the centre of attention and having the black man make such a fuss over her and what about Billy? He was crying when he thought she was going to die. Now none of them cared what happened to her. No one seemed to notice that she had to do some of his chores when he wasn't there, it was 'Maggie, nip out and get some more firewood' or 'Feed the dogs and horse, Maggie'. They were jobs that were always Billy's.

She looked up at the wooden rafters of the ceiling in her bedroom and fantasized about being Ningan's wife. He would carry her back to his shelter or gunyah as Ningan called it, and they would snuggle up safe together all cosy and warm. She would have children, she wasn't sure how that happened, but she would have a black one and a white one, of course the white would be the girl and the black would be the boy. With these thoughts drifting round in her mind she finally fell asleep.

Next morning all thoughts of the previous night had disappeared from Maggie's head. She was too excited. They were going on a fishing trip and Billy had said she could go too. Billy and Ningan had spent the evening making nets of grass and bark woven together and talked about how they would catch the biggest fish. Maggie had the important job of carrying the dilly bag to bring home "them big buggers" as Billy said.

When they got to the river she was given strict instruction not to go near the edge, which was silly since the river wasn't fast flowing now and she could have waded out to her knees without any danger. Maggie sat on the riverbank clutching the dilly bag and watched as the boys waded out and placed the net across a shallow part of the river. Ningan and Billy stood motionless on either side of the net with their spears at the ready. Maggie smiled at the picture,

Billy would never catch a fish with his spear, she decided. It took years of practice.

She edged back under a tree and watched the proceedings. Her eyes began to close from the glare and the warmth of the day made her drowsy. She tucked the dilly bag behind her head as a pillow and dozed off.

She was woken abruptly by the sound of raised voices. Maggie scrambled to her feet still half asleep. Billy was jumping up and down with his back to her yelling. Panic attacked her thoughts. What's wrong with him? Was he hurt? Thoughts flashed through her mind as she flew to the water's edge.

'Please God don't let anything poisonous have attacked him.' She prayed.

'Billy, Billy, what's the matter?' she yelled as she ran. 'Are you alright?'

As she came level with him along the bank he turned. The grin that lit up his face was not what she expected.

'I've caught a fish.' He held it aloft for her to see.

Maggie sighed with relief. 'Oh, is that all?'

'What's the madda, sis? You look like you've seen a ghost.'

'No, just a big galloot who nearly scared me to death.' She was cross and threw the dilly bag down on the ground. 'You can carry your own fish home,' she said as she stormed off.

Dawdling home, she felt like kicking something or someone but since she was in bare feet she couldn't. Instead she took her frustration out on the sky. She stopped and looking up opened her mouth and screamed. She didn't even care about flies, she let all the pent up emotions out, shrieking until she felt hoarse but calmer. Stupid boys and men, she thought. They were just so selfish, they only cared about boys' stuff and getting dirty. It was like they had this secret club or something, where no women were allowed. They winked and nodded at each other and Maggie had no idea why.

Billy and papa always had secrets. Maggie used to ask what they were talking about and her father would say, 'Nothing you need to know about.' Now she was getting older is was becoming more annoying especially since Ningan was involved, it seemed to go across races, this man thing.

As she approached the house she saw her mother sitting on the veranda step.

It was a comforting sight.

As she sat beside her, she asked, 'Everything all right?'

Maggie gave a half hearted nod.

They sat in silence for a few minutes before Maggie said, 'Mama, why do men have to be such pains?'

Her mother gave a snort of laughter before answering. 'It's because they think they're better than us.'

Maggie looked at her with a frown on her face. 'Why?' she asked.

'Ah, because we were the reason they were thrown out of the Garden of Eden.'

'What?' Maggie was beginning to regret starting this conversation with her mother.

'Don't you remember your Bible, Maggie?'

'Which bit?'

'The beginning, you know, when Adam and Eve were in the Garden of Eden and Eve took a bite of the apple?'

'But that was thousands of years ago, they can't still hold a grudge about that.'

'Men have always felt superior to women and probably always will.' A smile played on her mother's lips. 'They haven't realized yet that without us women they would be lost. Men are not very good at surviving on their own.'

'Aren't they?' Maggie was surprised.

'No, you can always tell a man who doesn't have a woman, they look untidy and messy and there's usually a spark missing.'

Maggie thought for a minute about Ningan. He didn't have a woman and he was definitely dirty and untidy. 'What's a spark, mother?'

'Well it's hard to say, it's a sort of glint in their eye, a self assurance, they relax in the knowledge that someone is looking after them.'

'Mmm.' Maggie was mulling over her mother's words and it all made perfect sense.

'But us women have our own secret,' her mother went on.

'Do we?'

'Yes, we can manage quite well without men.' Maggie noticed her mother's voice had become more serious.

'Yeah.'

She leaned her head on her mother's shoulder and they sat quietly together, both deep in their own thoughts. At that moment Maggie felt closer to her than she had ever done before. She felt more grown up, mama had shared a secret with her that only another woman could understand.

After a few minutes mama sighed and said, 'well, I suppose we'd better do what God put us on the earth for.'

Maggie looked at her. 'What's that?'

'To serve men.' They both laughed at their female secret. They got up together and went into the house to begin preparing the evening meal.

CHAPTER 5

Constance

Constance sat in front of the fire. It was the only light in the room and she gazed at the images that flashed in the flames. The children were asleep and the house was still. The evening held a slight chill even though the days were getting warmer as summer approached. She slouched in the wooden chair, the only one they had with arms, the one that Jack had always used, and stretched out her bare feet to the hearth. Pulling her long skirt up to her knees she let the warmth toast her legs. As she relaxed her mind began to wander.

She remembered back to the first time she had set eyes on Ningan. The fluid way he moved across the yard dragging that goanna. The memory made her smile, she hadn't been able to take her eyes off him, at first it was fear but then a sort of fascination. Constance had seen aborigines before, but there was something about this one that compelled her to watch his every movement. She wasn't sure why. Was it his bare chest and torso rippling with wiry muscles, she wondered? Maybe it was because she could brazenly stare at him without having to worry about her husband or the tittle tattle of townspeople.

With men she was a bit of a novice. The only serious relationship she'd ever had was with Jack, and living out here she had rarely thought about other men. When she went to town she never openly looked at the opposite sex, she was a married woman and that was that. Some of the young shearers and horsemen would occasionally doff their hats and say 'Gudday', but it was just being friendly, nothing more. The thought suddenly struck her that she was now an unattached, single female. Did that mean she was fair game? She was a new recruit to the eligibility stakes. It was a strange feeling since she'd been married since she was nineteen.

Before she left England, her father had betrothed her to a plump middle aged man, three times her age. She had fled the country before his fat white fingers had touched her. Her whirlwind courtship with Jack had been exciting but there was no flirting or sentimentality, it was a serious business for Jack to find himself a wife. He had been a good man who had looked after her and the children in his own way. He provided for them as best he could, and had never raised a hand to her, but in her heart she knew there had always been something missing from their relationship.

Constance leaned back in the chair and stretched her arms above her head. She was being fanciful and it wouldn't do her any good. She decided to get ready for bed in front of the fire, instead of wasting kerosene on the lamp in her room. Standing in the glow of the fire she stepped out of her skirt and petticoat and laid them on the chair. The air against the skin of her legs felt wonderful, freedom from her layers of clothing. She unbuttoned her blouse and laid it with the rest of her clothes. As she stood in her drawers and bodice she could feel the warmth of the fire on the front of her body through the thin material. Her back was cold so she turned and toasted herself like a large joint of meat on a spit, it was the first time she had done such a thing. She sighed with pleasure.

When Jack was alive she had always changed in the privacy of the bedroom where there was no fire. She usually whipped off her outer garments, threw her nightgown on and jumped into bed before he saw her or she got cold. Even in the hot weather she hadn't dallied in her underclothes. But now she could do as she liked. Slowly she untied her bodice, shrugged it off and let it slip to the floor. She looked down at her bare breasts, pale against the brown of her arms. They were not her best asset she decided, they had lost their pertness from feeding babies.

'I'll have to get myself a decent pair of stays to make them look better,' she said to herself as she roughly pushed them upwards to give herself some cleavage. Constance tried to span her waist with her hands and grunted. 'Nowhere near a hand span anymore.' But at least with all her physical labour her body was firm. She had one more slow turn in front of the fire without her clothing then slipped her night wear on and flopped back into the chair.

The flames of the fire had died to glowing embers, she would soon get cold, but she didn't want to go to bed yet. Her mind was flitting over memories and images like a bee hopping from flower to flower and she knew she would never sleep.

Thoughts of Ningan continued as she recalled the second time she had seen him. It was the day the children brought him home. She knew Billy spent a lot of time with him, learning aboriginal skills, he was a kind of replacement for Jack. When Ningan walked towards her again, this time with the children, she experienced that quivering sensation in the pit of her stomach. Was it nervousness or excitement? She had continued pegging out the washing, trying to pretend she hadn't noticed him.

When Billy introduced them she could no longer ignore this man, after all he had saved her daughter's life. She had officially thanked him and embarrassed everyone in the process. The children had been watching avidly for her response and she had tried to act normally. When his black hand momentarily encompassed hers she felt the warmth and dryness of his skin. It seemed intimate to her, she had always felt that hands were a very important part of the human anatomy. A person's hands did all manner of personal things, as well as the harsh manual tasks that kept a person alive. Everything a person did relied upon the hands, raising food and drink to the lips, showing love in a hug or touch, toiling on the land or killing game for the table. When the hands moved the body moved and when the hands were still and relaxed so was the rest of the body. As she remembered that handshake an uncontrollable shiver ran down her spine. What was wrong with her? She was acting like an adolescent.

She cringed at her ignorance when she had asked him into the house. That was really stupid, she should have known that was against his customs. Constance didn't know why she introduced herself by her first name, she just felt comfortable and at ease with the familiarity of the situation. The title Mrs. Lang seemed too formal and stuffy, not that Ningan would call her that anyway. Aborigines always called each other by their status in the family so she would be Billy's mother. When he called her Connie in that almost comical way, it had surprised and secretly thrilled her. She had watched him walk away with that spring in his step, his stance erect and his limbs flowing and hoped she would see him again.

Constance shivered with cold. She rose from the chair, yawned, and wandered over to the window. A waning moon sat above the trees and the sky was a black ceiling with twinkling stars scattered through the heavens. Outside it was still and peaceful. She had not felt so positive in a long time.

Billy

Over the next few months Billy's confidence grew as he mastered new skills. Even though he didn't talk much to the aborigine, Ningan's English improved. His relaxed attitude rubbed off on Billy, the idea that everything was in the hands of the spirits and therefore not worth worrying about, sounded good to him.

Eventually, with much persuading the black man finally showed him how to make the secret boomerang. This strange weapon was much more complicated to make than it looked. Finding the materials to use in the first place was difficult, it had to be made from a curved piece of wood, which was cut and filed against a stone until it was perfectly smooth and balanced. Billy spent hours working on his until Ningan deemed it was acceptable. But when he threw it for the first time, it sailed into the distance and crashed to the ground with no sign of it coming back to him. It was all in the wrist action Billy supposed and tried all different techniques to master the art. Ningan didn't help, he was a bit vague about the way it was done and Billy felt sure he didn't want a white boy learning their sacred skills.

As they became closer Ningan told Billy about gubura which was the name for a youth after he had been initiated, the turning of a boy into a man. Secretly Billy wished that whites had such a thing then he would know where he was. At the moment he felt torn between being a boy and being a man. Sometimes he wanted to sulk and be childish. At other times his gawky limbs felt strong and tall, and he was ready to take on the world, just like a man.

Ningan told him how, at a certain age, a boy was taken away from the women and taught sacred rituals. They got him ready to take on new powers, all to do with the spirits and stuff. Billy supposed it was a bit like that in the white man's world. The men go off to the pub and get initiated into the world of drinking alcohol and telling tall stories. Women were not allowed near the place.

Billy became very interested in the subject. 'You know this initiation thing?' Ningan nodded. 'Does it hurt?' Billy tried to sound unconcerned.

'A bit.'

'Oh,' Billy frowned and asked, 'What happens?'

'I already told yuh'

'Could you give me an initiation ceremony?' Billy thought for a moment. 'But without the dancing.'

'Godda have the dancin' or it's not proper.'

'Geez,' Billy would feel a prize idiot dancing about.

'And yuh godda have the paint.' Ningan added.

'What paint?'

'Yuh godda paint your skin, to let them spirits know you're glad to be changin' into a man.'

'Oh, right.'

'And you need a new name.'

'What? Why do I need another name?'

'It's yuh grown up name, so whadda yuh want to be named after?'

'Erm....' Billy was feeling a bit out of his depth, painting his face was one thing, but having a new name was something else.

'Animal, tree, somethin' the spirits 'll like,' Ningan tried to explain. 'But once you've got his name, you can never kill him again. So don't pick him good eatin' ones.' Ningan chuckled at his own joke.

'Well, I don't like eating snake.'

'OK then, wanna be a "yabaa" or a "nhiibi"?'

Billy was stifling a laugh as Ningan told him his choice of names.

'What's a bird called since I don't eat many of them either?'

'Thigaraa.' Ningan answered with a serious expression on his face.

'I think I'd rather be a yabba.' Billy couldn't help smiling every time he heard the word.

Ningan turned his back on him and started to walk away mumbling as he went, 'If yuh not goin' to do it proper him spirits be angry.'

'No, no, I will.' Billy ran after him.

Constance

As the months passed there seemed to be a bond between Billy and Ningan and Constance was pleased to see the change in her son. His whole demeanor was different, he didn't seem as angry towards her and he was full of confidence and he was learning to hunt. He could move about without a sound, which was disconcerting when he sneaked into the house and she didn't know he was behind her.

On a warm day, when Constance was chopping kindling for the fire she could sense some one behind her. She spun round and came face to face with Ningan.

'Oh, hello,' she said as she put the axe down and tried to compose herself. She wondered how long he had been standing there.

Hi yuh, Connie.' He smiled broadly as he addressed her.

'Is Billy not with you?'

'Nah, missus, I got him doin' some boomerang practice.' Ningan grinned.

Constance shook her head. 'You are a tease with that boomerang, Ningan.'

The bushman looked puzzled. 'Tease? What's that?'

'Never mind.' She looked at his smiling face and noticed his perfect white teeth and a sparkle in the dark brown depth of his eyes. She cleared her throat and looked down at the wood she was cutting up. She could feel her cheeks flushing with embarrassment and she said without looking up, 'is there anything I can help you with Ningan?'

'I've come about initiation.'

Constance was confused. It was a subject she knew nothing about. 'I don't think I can help you with that.'

'Billy's initiation to be man,' Ningan went on.

She looked up at his face, trying to gauge if he was joking, but his smile had disappeared.

'But Billy's too young to become a man, he's still a boy, he's only thirteen next month.' Constance said the words quietly, half to herself.

'Billy, he wants to be a man.' There seemed no argument as far as Ningan was concerned.

'Oh, does he?' Constance frowned and thought for a moment. He had been taking his duties seriously lately and he did seem to have matured, but he was a long way from being a man. She was curious though. 'What does it entail?' She asked trying not to sound too ignorant.

'No tails, he do things like he's man.' Ningan was looking serious.

'What sort of things?' Constance asked, trying not to smile. Was Billy ready for all this? Wasn't it all a bit too uncivilized, a black man thing, not something whites did. So far Ningan's influence on Billy had been positive so what harm was there?

'Secret things, not for womens' eyes or ears.' He gestured towards his eyes and ears just in case she didn't know what he meant.

'Will he be in any danger?'

Ningan shook his head as though he was dealing with a child. 'Him big, him no boy now.'

'I suppose you're right.' Constance stood contemplating when Billy had stopped being a boy. It was probably when Jack died.

'Well, so long as I can trust you to look after him.'

The grin returned to Ningan's face. 'No worries Connie,' he said, 'I watch him like lizard watches fly.' He chuckled and Constance laughed with him. 'I bedda go.' A cheeky smile crossed the blackman's face, 'See yuh later.'

'Bye, Ningan.'

After Constance told Billy about this conversation with Ningan, he did nothing but talk about the impending initiation ceremony, which would happen round his birthday. Tipping from excitement to apprehension, like the makeshift see-saw the children used to play on, Billy prepared for the event. Constance realized the build up was all part of it, instilling new ideas and learning new skills.

But while Billy was becoming more grown up, Maggie seemed to be spending more and more time on her own. Constance tried to get her involved in chores around the house, but the child's heart wasn't in it. She missed her brother and the things they used to do together. She knew they would always remain close after all they had been through together, but just at present Billy thought himself a man and Maggie a little girl. She talked about Ningan a lot and Constance had a sneaking suspicion that she was very fond of the black man, as they all were. It was funny really, how they all liked him. It was as though he had been sent to them for a reason. She smiled at her own silliness. Constance quietly followed her religious beliefs, not sure whether it was fate or God that ruled their lives.

Billy

In the dead of night, Billy sat in the bush, with just a small fire for light and warmth, completely on his own. He had no idea it would be so cold and sat as near to the fire as possible. He was shivering but wasn't sure whether it was from cold or fear. The night seemed to go on forever and the strange noises had Billy's head spinning from one direction to the other, trying to see if anything was about to attack him. He had the distinct feeling that someone was watching him. Stories Ningan told him about the dreamtime and the black demons that lurked behind trees, waiting to take over your body, fought with logic in Billy's mind. He sat with his legs crossed and his hands wedged under his arms for warmth and so nothing would crawl on him. His eyes felt gritty and he wanted to close them, but was too scared. He tried not to think too much about snakes, there could be one slithering right in front of him and he wouldn't know. At other times he thought how childish he was being, he had grown up in the bush. He knew about the animals and creatures but in the dark everything was frightening. This was part of the initiation ceremony. He had to stay in the bush for three days and find his own food and water.

As the sun rose and its rays clawed their light over the horizon Billy breathed a sigh of relief and stretched his stiff joints. The thoughts of another night in the dark made him wish he hadn't decided to do this stupid thing, but he couldn't chicken out now. He was feeling ravenously hungry and using his digging stick he poked a few honey ants out of a hole for starters. Next he broke some branches off an acacia tree to find a few witchetty grubs and cooked them on the fire. With the spear he tried to kill a wallaby but missed it. The bush turkeys seemed to be hiding today and he couldn't eat snake. He tried not to think of food, but images of his mother's stew kept creeping into his mind. Billy tried to concentrate on the task set for him, he had to get to the Bora Rocks and back, a distance of ten miles. It was another part of the test. He set off with a bounce in his step hummed a tune as he walked and convinced himself he could do this. He would be victorious and never again would his mother doubt him.

When he finally succeeded in his mission, three days later, he was filthy, but he glowed with pride. He had done it. He had survived. He was a man. He was Yabaa.

That evening Billy didn't mind being decorated. A pattern of white dots ran down his body and arms and Billy felt proud to be painted like an abo. They danced round the camp fire with Ningan singing weird songs. Billy joined in and their out of tune voices mixed with the natural sounds of the bush at night. It was a shame his mother and sister couldn't see him now, he wanted to share his experience with his family, but that was not the aboriginal way.

The following morning, after their celebratory dance, Billy went back to the homestead, a man. He was still only thirteen but felt as though he had changed. He felt proud of himself for staying out in the bush for three nights on his own and overcoming his fear. When he walked back into the house, with the whites of his eyes the only clean part of him, the body paint smudged on his face and hands, he was smiling from ear to ear. His mother rushed over and hugged him. He suddenly realized he was taller than her. Had he been that big before he went into the bush or had he grown in the past few days?

Maggie hung onto him round his waist and looked up into his face. 'I missed you, Billy'

He ruffled her hair. 'Come on, sis, and I'll tell yuh all about it.'

'I think you'd better get a wash first, lad' His mother was ever practical, but he didn't mind anymore. He felt like saying, 'I'm not "lad" anymore, it's Yabba now', but didn't. He hadn't decided whether to tell them his aboriginal name yet, or keep it a secret a bit longer.

Constance

The initiation ceremony seemed to be a turning point in their lives. They saw more of Ningan after that. He called at the homestead quite often and sat on the step and told them stories. Constance appreciated having another adult to talk to, even though their backgrounds and customs were so completely different. Ningan, being a man of a few words, was a great listener.

As spring turned to summer she spent many evenings sat with the black man talking of life and the universe. His tales of how the world began fascinated her. He seemed to make them all more aware of nature's beauty with his stories from the dreamtime and Constance sat smiling, watching the rapped expressions on Maggie's face as he related the story of "Why the Crow is Black?" or "How the Sun was Made?"

Every time Constance saw the black man she felt that flutter in her stomach, a physical reaction that never changed. She was becoming very fond of him, which made her feel guilty. It was only eight months since Jack had died although what she felt for Ningan was nothing like the lasting bond she had with her husband. With Ningan she felt gratitude, he made her laugh and he made her feel good about herself.

Constance often wondered why Ningan didn't have a woman and some piccaninnies, he would be the perfect father and husband. It was his gentleness that fascinated her, his hands with their long fingers and almond shape nails that could do such intricate tasks and yet kill in a moment. Sometimes he seemed so wild and untamed, with his hair all frizzy and his musty smell. The brightly coloured headband he wore was like his talisman, a bit of his own identity that made him stand out from the rest. His strength was formidable, encased in the wiry frame and slender build. It was hard for Constance to gauge how old he was, but she guessed by the lack of lines round his eyes that he was probably still in his twenties.

For the first time in many years Constance became more aware of her body. Years of living in the outback with drying winds and hot sun had drained her skin of moisture and after studying herself in the looking glass she decided her complexion looked like a peach that had begun to shrivel. There were creases round her eyes from squinting into the sun and lines had begun to form round her mouth. She started putting turkey fat on her face at night to try to reverse some of the damage, but she feared it was a useless task. Her hands also needed attention with their broken nails and rough skin. She cut her nails so they were neat and rubbed her hands in grease to make them smooth.

Her blonde hair was her best asset, which she thoroughly brushed every night before she went to bed. No matter how much dust or sweat clung to her hair, once washed it always shone sleekly with golden tints. It hadn't been cut for years and when loosened from its pins fell in waves across her back. Jack had loved her hair. Sometimes he would brush it and lay it gently over her shoulders. They were very personal moments, times when he was tender towards her.

Sometimes when she was rubbing grease into her face and hands she thought how shallow she was being. Who was she trying to impress, what did it matter how she looked? It was not important, the graves on the hill were what mattered, the people that had been part of her life, now gone. She had to keep their memory sacred. Constance visited the graves regularly and put fresh flowers or leaves in a jar at the foot of the green mounds of earth. There were no headstones for them just the grass that had spread from the surrounding ground. She regularly brushed away the fallen leaves from the gum tree that guarded them. She would sit and talk to the twins and tell them some of the stories Ningan related. Other times she would tell Jack what Billy and Maggie were up to.

In these quiet moments as she stood by the graves and spoke to her deceased children, Constance felt the loss keenly. She missed their little bodies snuggling into hers and their need of her. She missed teaching them new things and she desperately missed their childish giggles. Ben had been hopeless at tying shoelaces and Dulcie always took an age to do up a button. She knew they would never be replaced in her heart but as the months passed she began to want another baby. Her motives were purely selfish, she wanted something to hold and protect, she wanted to feel the soft skin of a baby and the peace that came when a child was feeding at the breast. She wanted to kiss the downy head and smell the cleanness of a baby's skin. Constance knew at thirty three she was getting too old to have a child but the yearning struck her at times like a craving, tormenting her and leaving her feeling sad at the loss of her other babies. But it was all hypothetical. She needed a man to fall pregnant and that was one thing she didn't have.

CHAPTER 6

Constance

As spring turned to summer the weather became uncharacteristically hot. Usually it didn't get so unbearable until well into the New Year. Everything was tinder dry, even after the rain earlier in the year. The bush was baked brown and warm winds whipped across the open spaces. Constance had an uneasy feeling about the weather, it didn't feel right somehow, but she wasn't sure why. The animals became scarce, not that they were starving and falling down dead, they just weren't there. It was as though they had moved out of harms way, to a different area, to avoid, what? She tried to convince herself that she was being melodramatic. There was nothing wrong it was just a bit of hot weather.

Ningan wore a grave expression and when he announced that the spirits were angry she knew her feelings had been right.

'Can you feel it too?' she asked him.

'Hmm, him big evil spirit,' the bushman announced, throwing his arms out to indicate its size.

Constance felt the hairs on the back of her neck tingle. It was ridiculous, they were worrying about an invisible thing. There was nothing tangible just a feeling. She tried to make light of it.

'It's just the heat making us nervous.'

But Ningan shook his head. He didn't elaborate any further but Constance could tell he was worried. He wasn't his usual carefree self.

A few days later the skies darkened in the middle of the day. It looked as though the heavens would open and all their water problems would be solved. Instead great claps of thunder reverberated around their little valley and lightning pierced the sky. Maggie clung to Constance trying to hide her face.

'It's alright,' she tried to calm her. 'It's only a storm.'

Billy stood on the veranda watching the lightning flash until Constance told him to get in the house so he wouldn't be struck. Ningan was nowhere to be seen and she hoped he had found a safe place to weather the storm. No rain fell, just the thunder and lightning. As it came over their house the claps of thunder rattled the china and the little house seem to quake from the onslaught.

An almighty bang, followed by the crack and screech of tearing timber, sent them all rushing to the window. A tree had come down, struck by lightning and as they watched small tongues of fire licked at its base. Within minutes the fire had engulfed the surrounding dead leaves and with a wind behind it, was spreading in their direction.

'Oh my God,' Constance groaned. The thing that instilled fear in her more than anything was bush fires. The thought of her house being burnt down made her panic.

'Billy help me,' she yelled as she rushed from the house. 'Get any sacks we have in the shed and bring the shovel.'

Her voice was carried on the wind and drowned out by more thunder. She ran towards the fire and tried to kick dirt on the small flames. In desperation she picked up hands full of soil and threw them on the flames. The tree trunk caught and she knew when the fire reached the branches they were in real danger.

Billy was at her side in moments. She grabbed the shovel from him and threw soil over the burning tree, managing to extinguish some of the flames. With the sacks Billy beat the spreading flames trying to prevent more trees catching alight, but it was useless. Bits of the burning branches blew off in the wind, landed among the tinder dry undergrowth and started more fires.

Both of them coughed incessantly, tears streamed from their eyes. They stumbled around fighting in vain against a formidable enemy. The flames were getting bigger and building into an impenetrable wall, the heat was overpowering, causing sweat to trickle down Constance' hot skin. She was oblivious of the bottom of her skirt brushing the ground and the insidious flames reaching for it, smoldering on the heavy hem before catching the finer material and bursting into flames.

'Mother, watch out.' Billy rushed at her and wrapped his sack round her legs to smother the flames. Fortunately her petticoat had protected her skin from being burnt. Without even thinking she dropped the skirt round her ankles and stepped out of its hazardous folds, fighting the fire in her petticoat.

She became aware that Ningan was beside her, she didn't know where he had come from, but she was very grateful he was there. With his strength and stamina he was much more effective at beating the flames. He worked rhythmically and methodically instead of just whacking at the licking tongues of fire. But no matter how hard they worked the fire out ran them. A flaming tree had fallen and was touching the shed. Once that went it would almost certainly spread to the house. They continued to thrash at the flames but the heat was making their hands blister and the smoke made their lungs feel as though they would explode.

Constance ran to the house to find Maggie and the dogs huddled in a corner. She led them to safety up the hill, her breathing coming in short painful bursts, she was exhausted, it was futile, nature was going to destroy her home, her belongings and her life.

'Leave it,' she yelled at Billy and Ningan. 'It's no use.'

As Constance watched, the timbers on the back of the shed caught and Billy tried to beat them with his sack which also began to burn. He stood back coughing, his body trembled with fatigue and his eyes were nearly closed with the effects of smoke.

'Ningan, look out,' he screamed and ran towards the black man, who managed to jump out of the way of a burning branch that fell next to him.

'For God sake leave it.' Constance was nearly in tears, her voice shook as she yelled at them. There was nothing they could do but stand back and watch the fire consume everything in its path.

From the safety of the hill that overlooked their home, they saw the flames jumped from the shed across to the roof of their house. Constance put her arms around Maggie and closed her eyes. She didn't want to see the destruction of her home. In those few moments when her eyes were closed she felt something plop on her head. Her eyes flew open and she looked up. Another plop of water landed on her face and another.

'It's raining, it's raining,' she screamed in her excitement.

'But is it going to be enough to save the house?' Billy was still breathing heavily.

Big fat drops of rain landed all around them and quickly wet the dry soil. Within minutes it was raining torrentially. As the water landed on the flames they hissed and spat as though trying to fight off a predator. Small pockets continued to burn for a while longer until all was still except for the calm drumming of the rain.

'Thank God.' Constance was overwhelmed with relief. She lowered her head and covered her face with her hands.

In her moment of uncontrollable emotion she felt a presence in front of her.
She could smell Ningan, he placed a hand on her shoulder and whispered in her ear, 'We beat him big spirit.'

She looked into his kind face, the pressure on her shoulder gone, but the memory of that contact lingered.

'We did, didn't we?' A smile was spreading across her face. It was so good to be alive.

'Come on you two,' Maggie called as she and Billy ran towards the house to see what the damage was.

Constance and Ningan followed. Constance had an urge to hold Ningan's hand and run down the hill like sweethearts, to throw back her head and laugh until tears streamed down her cheeks. But she restrained herself and walked sedately, never looking at Ningan for fear that her real feelings would show on her face.

The house was still intact. One corner had taken the brunt of the fire with some of the wall timbers burnt through and the roof blackened and buckled. Everything inside was covered with a black film, the smell of burned timber and eucalyptus leaves was overpowering. The shed was a burnt shell that looked as if it would fall down in the next strong wind. Fortunately Blue Boy was out in a field, well away from the fire, so they had come off quite lightly. The same could not be said for Constance's emotions that had taken a helter skelter ride through fear, fortitude, and forbidden feelings.

Maggie

It was two months since the fire. All the repairs were completed. Ningan showed them how to use bark when they ran out of wood, so at least it was wind and water tight. Maggie thought the house looked a bit patched and battered but at least they still had a roof over their heads, as mama kept saying. They had pulled the remains of the shed down and a blackened patch of soil was all that was left.

By December things were getting back to normal and Maggie began to think about Christmas. It would be strange without papa and the twins. Could they really have Christmas without them? It was as though mama was thinking on the same wave length.

'I think it would be very nice if we made a bit of an effort at Christmas this year,' she said.

Billy frowned. 'Why?'

'Do we need a reason?' Mama replied. 'Is the birth of Christ not enough of a reason?'

Billy shrugged again. 'It will be our first Christmas without them,' he muttered. 'So really we shouldn't do anything.'

'Well, I just thought it would cheer us up to have a proper Christmas, for Ningan…' Mama spoke quietly as though she was having second thoughts about her idea.

'I think that's a good idea,' Maggie said, trying to sound grown up.

Mama looked at Billy, as though she wanted his approval, since he was the man of the house.

'I guess we could do something,' he said.

'That's settled then, we'll have a real English Christmas.'

'Without the snow,' Billy added.

It was the main topic of conversation for Maggie for the next few weeks. She became very excited as the day drew nearer. Mama told them what needed doing and she put her in charge of the Christmas tree, which meant she had to make all the decorations to go on it. They didn't have any from previous Christmases and there wasn't much to make them with. Maggie scoured the bushland for things to use. She found brightly coloured stones and tied wool around them to attach them to the tree. With bush flowers she made dangly ornaments to drape over the boughs. Ningan showed her how to make paint, which she daubed on bark shapes of stars and bells. Nearer the time she was going to help mama bake biscuits with holes that she could thread onto the tree. She dipped gum leaves in whitewash and sprinkled on yellow pollen while they were still wet and made gum nuts into little stick men.

Billy was given the job of finding and chopping down a suitable tree on Christmas Eve. Of course Maggie had to go too, just to make sure he picked the right one. It wouldn't be like the ones she had seen on pictures that people in England had, because nothing like that grew near where they lived, but it would be their very own Australian tree.

It was difficult to find a tree that was small enough to fit in their house but Maggie thought of an idea. 'We could have the tree outside.'

'Don't be silly, all the decoration would blow off in the wind.'

If it was windy, it might not be.'

'And what if it rains?'

'As if it would at this time of year.' Maggie could feel herself getting annoyed, Billy was doing his sensible thing again, he did that a lot lately.

'Don't worry Sis,' he said, patting her on the head. 'We'll find one.'

They seemed to have walked miles, Maggie's legs were aching and she really felt like moaning, but didn't. This was her challenge, to make sure they had a really good Christmas tree even with the hindrance of an older brother.

As they walked along the riverbank, Maggie sloshing bare footed through the mud at the edges, she looked up and there it was.

A sapling stood on the side of the river dwarfed by the other river gums.

Maggie's eyes lit up. 'That's it,' she shouted and rushed towards it. Billy sauntered after her with the axe slung over his shoulder.

'Hmm, not a bad choice,' he commented. 'The leaves will shrivel pretty quick though.'

'Trust you to be a spoil sport.' Maggie wasn't going to let him say anything awful about her tree. 'It won't matter once it's all decorated.'

They carried it home between them, Maggie carried the top half and Billy took the heavy end. It was placed in a metal bucket in the corner of the main room of the house, right next to the fireplace. Maggie decorated most of it, although Billy had to reach some of the high branches. When it was finished they stood back and admired it. The ornaments dangling from the branches shone in the firelight and it looked magical. The twins would have loved it, Maggie thought.

'It looks wonderful.' Her mother put her arm round her shoulder and stood next to her. Her voice sounded a bit quivery as though she was going to cry.

'You alright, mama?'

'Yes, I just wish your father and the twins were here to see it.'

'They can see it from heaven.'

'Course they can.'

Christmas Day arrived with a ground mist that soon disappeared to reveal clear, blue skies. In the cool of the early morning mama cooked a bush turkey Ningan had brought for Christmas dinner. Maggie had never seen such a plump bird. Its feathers were removed and it was stuffed with a wild sage stuffing. When it was cooking the smell made her mouth water. While the bird was baking she helped do the vegetables. Yams and roots washed, peeled and chopped. She beat the batter for Yorkshire puddings, which mama said were supposed to be eaten with beef. They even had pudding, not something Billy and Maggie were used to. They had watched a few days before when mother had mixed up flour, lard, sugar and egg. She had added wild berries and the smell when it was cooking had made Maggie's tummy rumble.

Billy and Ningan took the table and chairs outside and placed them in the shade of one of the trees that had escaped the fire. Ningan would be able to sit with them if it was not in the house. A white damask cloth and some pretty plates had appeared from inside the tin trunk. Mama set the table with sprigs of shiny berries in the middle. It all looked wonderful.

Once the preparation was out of the way it was time for presents. A brown paper parcel had appeared under the tree with Maggie's name on it. It was so long since she'd had a present she jigged with excitement. She asked who it was from and mama said 'Father Christmas'. Maggie knew there was no such person, but she wished she did still believe in him. Perhaps she could believe for today.

With her present on her lap, Maggie felt and shook it, delaying the moment when she ripped off the paper. It was soft and squashy. She hoped it wasn't one of Billy's shirts made into a nightgown like she had once before. Slowly she pulled off the string from round her parcel. She was holding her breath but when her fingers touched new material she let out a sigh of relief and happiness. It was a new cotton dress in a pretty shade of pink with lace round the neck and cuffs and a gathered frill round the hem. It was the most beautiful thing Maggie had ever seen.

'Oh mama,' she sighed with pleasure. 'Look what I've got.'

'Do you like it?'

'I love it.' She hugged her mother. 'Can I put it on to eat Christmas dinner?'

'I think so.'

Maggie buried her face in the crisp material.

'But don't run off to get changed just yet, let's finish the presents first.'

'She can run off if she likes,' Billy said, 'but she won't get my present if she does.'

'Did you get me a present?' She felt awful, she had no idea he was going to do that. 'Oh Billy, I didn't get you one.'

Billy tousled her hair. 'It doesn't matter, here you go.' He gently placed a small parcel in her lap. 'Be careful, it'll break.'

With care Maggie gently unwrapped the odd shaped parcel. She couldn't stop smiling. The brown paper slipped from the item once the string was cut to reveal a large emu egg painted in bright vibrant colours.

'Oh…. it's beautiful.'

'I thought it would look good in your bedroom.' Billy said. 'See, I made you a little stand for it.' From out of his pocket he produced a small, carved wooden stand.

Maggie held it up and admired it. 'Aren't you clever?'

'Ningan showed me how to blow the egg and paint it.'

Billy got some new trousers from Father Christmas. After the presents the meal was served. They all sat down and attacked the food. Maggie wanted to eat her meal with her fingers like Ningan but her mother wouldn't let her. The sight of Ningan using a knife and fork was funny as he chased food around his plate trying to get it on the fork. He did manage the spoon for his pudding and seemed to enjoy the different flavours. Maggie felt as though she would explode if she ate another bite and they all sat groaning with pleasure when the meal was finished.

Afterwards Ningan told them stories of his life as a boy playing tricks on the old women of the tribe. The stories made Maggie laugh, she couldn't imagine him being a naughty little boy.

While Billy and mama cleared up after the meal, Maggie decided to tell Ningan about the baby Jesus. Maggie thought it would be good to tell him a story for a change.

He sat very quiet and listened, and when she had finished he asked, 'Where this Jesus piccaninni now?'

'In heaven, with his father, who's God.' Maggie answered. 'We killed him you know.'

Ningan looked startled. 'Did we?'

'Oh yeah,' she said. 'We sinned and then they hung him on a cross.'

'No, missy telling untruth.'

'No, I'm not.'

Ningan looked annoyed and asked, 'Where this heaven place?'

Maggie thought for a moment and said. 'It's in the sky somewhere.'

'Ah, he must be mighty spirit.' Ningan nodded and smiled.

'Umm, I guess he is. Well, it's God who does all the punishing.'

'What is punish?'

'If you don't say your prayers something bad will happen.' Maggie grew serious. 'Sometimes bad things happen even when you do say your prayers.'

'What are you two looking so serious about?' Billy asked as he and mama returned to the table.

'Baby Jesus,' Maggie answered. 'Ningan didn't know why we had Christmas.'

'Oh.' Billy raised his eyebrows and looked at his mother with a slight smile on his lips.

The heat of the day and over eating made them all feel tired. Maggie did a giant yawn and mama said, 'I think you better go and have a rest.'

She went to her room where she stepped out of her new dress and hung it carefully on a hanger her mother had given her. She lay on her bed in her drawers and vest and thought about the presents she received. She smiled at the fun they had had until her eyes began to droop and she dozed in the heat of the afternoon.

Constance

Finally all the work was finished. The meal has been eaten and Constance was enveloped with a sense of wellbeing and contentment. She couldn't remember the last time she felt like this. It had been a grand day after a year of heartache and pain. The spirit of Christmas had descended on them and all was right with the world. Her body had relaxed into a pleasurable stupor of over eating and warmth. The children had taken themselves off for an afternoon nap and she and Ningan remained at the table.

She looked across at the bushman and smiled. The quietness between them was comfortable. She placed her hand across the table and brushed bits off the cloth. It was an unconscious action that needed no response. After a few moments she stopped fiddling with the cloth and let her hand go still. It was as though it was reaching out for him and she had no inclination to retrieve it. She should have pulled it back and hidden it under the table out of harm's way but she didn't.

Ningan placed his hand in front of hers. She longed to feel his touch, she raised her eyes to look at his face. Their eyes met and she could see a softness of spirit, a yearning to be accepted and she smiled assent.

His hand moved and covered hers. His touch was as gentle as a spider's tread, sending shivers down her spine. She placed the other hand across the table. Their fingers entwined and joined them together. They were reluctant to break the hold.

Constance felt as though she was inside someone else's body, inevitably moving towards something risky, dangerous and completely out of character, but she couldn't help herself. She rose to her feet still holding Ningan's hands and led him away from the table. They never spoke as she showed him the way to the grove of coolabah trees. She walked almost in a trance of need, of longing and desire. She never looked back at the house or the Christmas debris left under the trees. If she had she might have seen sense, stopped and taken stock of her feelings and the moment would have been lost.

In the glade of trees and bush the air was cool, a breeze wafted around them cooling Constance' hot skin. No birds twittered in the heat of the afternoon, all was still and quiet apart from the comfortable humming of insects.

She felt serene and calm as she stood facing this blackman. Slowly she let his hands go and stepped back from him. Kicking off her shoes she felt the roughness of the grass beneath her feet. All her senses were alive, heightened by the enormity of what she was doing. She undid her skirt, pushed it over her hips and let it fall to the ground. She unbuttoned her blouse and paused a moment before pulling her arms through the tight sleeves.

Constance smiled at the puzzled look on Ningan's face when she stood in her underwear. Aborigine women didn't wear all this paraphernalia in the heat. She took off the rest of her garments and stood in front of him. The warm breeze on her skin made her body tingle. She reached up, arching her back as she undid the pins from her blonde hair and let it fall loose round her shoulders. She wanted him and knew he wanted her.

His skin felt warm to her touch as she ran her hands down the smooth contours of his chest. She pressed her body into his and her nipples tightened of their own accord. Resting her head against his shoulder she could smell his strong scent, it reminded her of the wildness of him.

She began to undo his trousers but he gently pushed her hands away and did it himself. Within minutes he was also naked and their flesh touched, black against white. Holding hands they sank to their knees and lay on the grass. The earthy smell filled her nostrils and the harshness of the ground increased the sensitivity of her skin. As Ningan lowered himself onto her she felt a warmth between her legs. A rhythmical motion began, so gentle at first she wanted it to go on forever. Luscious waves of euphoria spread through her body until she could stand it no longer. As Ningan increased his rhythm she cried out as the pain of ecstasy enveloped her.

CHAPTER 7

Billy

The heat of the afternoon made Billy feel sweaty. It was too hot to lie for long on his bed. He roused himself and wandered outside. It seemed unnaturally quiet, there was no one around. Probably all gone for a snooze, he thought. Even the dogs were asleep under the house. They had enjoyed all the turkey scraps and probably felt like the rest of them, too fat to move.

He wondered where Ningan was, he would probably be laying down somewhere cool and not move for the rest of the day. Billy smiled as he thought of his friend and some of his strange habits. Maybe he should move the table back indoors but he couldn't be bothered. He sat at the table remembering what a beaut day it had been with all that lovely tucker. They had laughed and joked like old times. It was funny that, he thought they would never enjoy themselves again after papa and the twins died and here they were, having a proper Christmas with a blackman and laughing their heads off. Should he be feeling guilty? Maggie's face was a picture when she opened her present. It was the first time she'd had any grown up stuff, usually she got one toy if that, but there had been years when they couldn't afford food let alone presents.

The heat made him feel lazy, he needed to cool off. He thought of the place where he and Maggie used to hide when they wanted to get away from mother. It was always shady and cool, he'd find a tree with a patch of soft grass and have forty winks.

The grove of coolabah trees was like an old friend but as he approached he realised something wasn't quite right. With his aboriginal training he noticed the odd snapped twig, crushed leaves and footprints in the sandy soil. Some one had recently come this way, two pairs of human footprints lead into the grove. Who could possibly be so near to their homestead? Who would know about this place?

Quietly he crouched down and hid behind the screen of bushes. Moving forward he froze when a twig snapped under his foot. He peeped over the scrub. There were branches in the way but he could see two people lying on the ground. Billy backed out of his position and crept further along, where he could get a better view. Sweat beaded on his brow as he stealthily moved through the bush. This time he had a perfect view of the clearing.

There were two bodies writhing on the ground. A black one and a white one, joined, legs and arms entwined, bodies jerking like mating dogs. The worse part was they were completely naked. He was unable to drag his eyes from the scene in front of him even though he knew it was wrong.

The sudden realisation of who it was mating like a pair of over sexed animals, out in the open, for all to see, made Billy feel sick. His stomach churned and he heaved. Bile rose in his throat and threatened to choke him. He didn't want to be involved in their dirty secret. It just wasn't right, or decent. He wanted to rush from this place and pretend he hadn't seen them. He walked backwards as quietly as he could. When he was far enough away, so they couldn't hear his footsteps, he ran. Back to the homestead, back to normality, back to the moment before he'd walked towards the clearing and saw his mother and Ningan.

The image of them locked in each other's arms was disgusting. Why were they doing that? Can they do that if they're not married? Is it breaking the law, what would happen if anyone found out his mother was mating with a blackman? People didn't carry on like that they did it in the privacy of their bedroom.

By the time he got home Billy was breathless. Everything was the same as he had left it a short while ago. It was as if nothing had happened, but it had. He checked on Maggie, she was fast asleep in her room. He didn't want her seeing them like that.

Billy couldn't let them know what he'd seen. He went back to his bed and buried his face in the pillow and tried to blot out the image of them.

'This is a nightmare,' he said to himself. 'I've fallen asleep and I'll wake up in a minute and everything will be normal again.' He knew he was kidding himself, it had happened and he had witnessed it.

Closing his eyes tightly he tried to sleep but the feeling of disgust and embarrassment flooded over him. Why hadn't he stayed here and not ventured into the bush? He would never have known about them, and now nothing would ever be the same again, even though he desperately wanted it to be.

He remembered a conversation he'd had with his father a few months before he died. His father had explained the differences between men and women. His explanation of human sex had been likened to animals. The only difference, his father told him, was that humans face each other when they did it. He wasn't embarrassed when his father talked about it, in fact Billy thought it quite funny. After that conversation he had known what the strange noises were that sometimes came from his parents' bedroom. It was all a bit sick, thought Billy, adults going at it like rabbits whenever they got a chance.

After a while he heard movement in the house, but pretended to be asleep. He felt a presence near him then Maggie's loud whispering.

'He's still asleep, mama. Should I wake him?'

'No, leave him,' his mother whispered back.

She sounded the same, how could she be normal after what she'd done. He felt as though he would never be able to face her again and as for Ningan, supposedly his friend, the person he had trusted. The black mongrel just wanted to sneak off with his mother, like a snake in the grass.

Billy stayed on his bed until the sky began to glow red with the onset of evening. He knew he would eventually have to face them and pretend nothing was wrong. His mother was in the kitchen alone. She was bending over the stove lifting a heavy kettle onto the hob. Her back was to Billy. In that moment Billy hated her. She had spoiled everything, she always did.

She turned when she heard him and said, 'ah, there you are. Fancy a cuppa?'

For a moment Billy stared at her, she looked the same, there were no brown hand prints on her skin, not that he could see much of her now she was all covered up again.

He turned away from her as his face reddened. 'No,' he grunted, 'I don't want anything from you.' He moved to leave the house but stopped. 'Where's Ningan?'

'I don't know, lad.'

He found him by the river sitting under a tree.

'Hi yuh, Billy.' He had a big smile on his face.

He wasn't even embarrassed, thought Billy, but then perhaps black men don't regard sex as a private act. Billy couldn't look at him, he felt as though there was an invisible barrier between them. Ningan was an uneducated man, he would have been no match for his mother with her English education. He scowled as he sat on the ground and picked savagely at bits of grass.

'What's a madda, Billy?'

'Nothin'.'

'You look like a horse before it bites its owner.'

Billy could feel his mouth drooping as though he was going to cry. He could hardly get any words out his voice was trembling. He shook his head.

Ningan was quietly studying him and said, 'Things bad eh?'

'Yes', Billy said before stumbling to his feet and rushing away.

In the weeks that followed, Billy's moods swung from deep unhappiness to a white anger that made him want to hit someone. So far he had taken it out on the surrounding trees and hacked at them with the axe. They had more firewood than they knew what to do with. He spent long hours roaming through the bush, honing his hunting skills and getting away from the house and his mother.

He felt sorry for being awful to Maggie, but there was nothing he could do. When they were on their own he tried to be nice to her but she kept asking him what was wrong and why was he always in a bad mood. He couldn't tell her.

He spent very little time with Ningan these days. It was over, the blinkered view he had of the black man being the greatest thing since the wheel, had changed. He had grown up and realized that he couldn't stay round here anymore. He had to move on, get away from the vision of the two naked people in the clearing that haunted him day and night. Perhaps if he didn't see them he could forget it.

Billy planned his departure for weeks. He would have to wait until the hot spell was over. February could be a stinker of a month with not much water and everything brown and dried up. It would be much harder to survive in conditions like that. He would bide his time until March or April.

Rain clouds rolled over the horizon the first week in April. It rained off and on for a week or two and the draining humidity gave way to the beginning of a pleasant autumn. Billy decided it was time. He rolled up a pair of trousers and a shirt in a blanket. He filled a hessian sack with a water bag, his knife, boomerang, a length of rope, a piece of flint and his digging stick. He was ready for the road. With his father's old hat pulled down over his eyes he left the homestead at dawn.

From the top of the hill Billy looked back at the house that had been home to him all his life. It looked a bit dilapidated after the fire but he loved it. The dawn was strengthening and a mist lay trapped in the valley round the house. Kneeling in front of the graves he said goodbye to his father and the twins.

As he stood he remembered the morning he waited at dawn to see Ningan, and was treated with a handful of witchetty grubs. That was the beginning, the start of a friendship that should have gone on forever. But forever was a long time, nothing lasted that long. He turned from the house, the lump in his throat took a few attempts to swallow but he gritted his teeth and blinked rapidly to stop the tears from falling. He headed south towards the Bora Rocks and beyond.

Once he was away from familiar surroundings Billy thought about his plan. He decided his best bet was to find a sheep station to get some work. They were always looking for men although it wasn't shearing season for a few months. With his father being a drover he would have to be careful. Jack Lang would be known around these parts. Billy would have to go further a field where no one would know who he was. He would lie about his age, with his height he looked at least fourteen. He tried not to think about what he was doing or why, he just kept putting one foot in front of the other and eventually he would end up somewhere.

By the end of the first day the landscape was beginning to look different. Billy made a fire in the shelter of a kurrajong tree. He had killed a lizard earlier as it lay sunning itself on a rock and now he stuck a stick through its body and rested it over the fire to cook. He found water at a spring and took a long swig from his water bag. Leaning against the tree he pulled his boots off. His feet hurt, they felt as though the soles were rubbed off but were just red. He buried them in the sandy soil to cool off. After his meal he felt much better, he packed what was left of the carcass in his sack and curled up in his blanket.

What a good thing he had been initiated and knew how to survive in the bush. He wasn't doing too badly. He smiled to himself, who needed people. They only upset you and got your mind in a spin so you couldn't think straight. He was so tired his eyes drooped and within minutes he was asleep.

When he awoke he felt stiff, he'd forgotten how hard the ground was. He finished off the cold lizard for breakfast and had a long swig of water. His boots were full of ants and he cursed as he banged them against the tree to get rid of them. He felt a lot better, looking forward to the future and the challenge of what lay ahead.

The routine of Billy's travels continued for three days and nights. On the fourth day Billy decided the next place he saw that looked half decent he would stop and see if he could get work. His feet were covered in blisters and his socks were hard with dried blood. He was limping badly when he approached a long drive with a sign over the top.

'Taroola Station', he read out loud. 'This'll do for a bit.'

The clatter of horses' hooves and the grinding of cartwheels made Billy look round as he walked down the track to the homestead. He moved over to the side to let it pass but the cart pulled up beside him. A burly looking man with a beard greeted him.

'How yuh goin' mate?' his voice boomed.

'Fine thanks.' Billy tried to tidy himself up he dragged his fingers through his hair.

'Where you off to then?'

Billy was thinking on his feet and said, 'Down to Taroola Station, I … eh… got a job there.'

'Ah, right.' The man didn't question his lie. 'Hop in then and I'll give you a lift.' As Billy climbed into the wagon the man added, 'that's the ticket. My name's Robert Dinkerman but they call me Dink'

Billy smiled at the name and said, 'pleased to meet you Dink. I'm Billy……eh,' he looked down at the floor of the wagon and ended with '…..Carter.'

Dink looked across at him, and Billy wondered if he could tell he was lying but he only added, 'right.'

They drove the rest of the way in silence until buildings came into view. 'I'll drop you here by the bunkhouse. Dinner's at five on the dot and Mrs. Pringle doesn't like anyone to let their food go cold.'

'Thanks, Dink,' Billy got gingerly to the ground and limped over to the large shed where the men slept.

'You need some metho on them blisters,' Dink shouted after him. 'I'll bring you some later.'

Billy nodded and waved. As he entered the shed the heat hit him like a wall. The corrugated iron roof seemed to draw the sun, but come sundown, it would soon go cold. He glanced around at the beds. Only about half of them looked occupied with shirts and trousers hanging from the walls. A pot bellied stove stood in the middle of the room and Billy decided he would try to get as close to that as possible. He threw his stuff on a bunk and sat down heavily, just to take the weight off his feet. He yawned and put his head against the wall.

The sound of raucous voices woke him from a deep sleep. A group of men had come in and it seemed as though they were all talking at once. When they saw Billy they stopped and the silence was unnerving. Billy sat up and waited.

'Who's this then?' One of the men asked. He approached Billy and said, 'how yuh goin' mate, my name's Mick.' He held out his hand.

'Pleased to meet yuh.' Billy shook the outstretched hand. 'I'm Billy.'

'Ah, Billy eh?' The other men all watched the exchange until Mick said in a louder voice, 'meet Billy, boys', at which point they all ambled over and shook his hand with words of greeting.

Dink followed the men into the bunkhouse with a bottle of methylated spirits in his hand. 'Here you go, son, whack this on your blisters.'

After the men had gone back to their bunks Dink sat on the bed opposite Billy scratching his head and asked, 'so, what you doin' here?'

'Working'.

'Ah huh.' Dink nodded his head. 'How old are you?'

'Old enough.'

'You look a bit young to work here.'

Billy could feel his face redden but he was not going to back down or look away. He looked Dink straight in the eye and said, 'I'm fifteen and I need a job.' Then rather boldly he added, 'and since I know a bit about sheep I thought I could help you out here.'

'Why didn't you say so?' Dink smiled and nodded. 'Now Billy, have you been up to see Mr. Pickett?'

'No, why?'

'He's the boss round here, he's the one that pays us.' Dink smiled. 'No need to look so worried, you can meet him at tucker time.'

Billy sighed with relief. So far so good, but what if this Mr. Pickett threw him off the station, he was an imposter after all?

Dink good-humouredly cuffed Billy round the head. 'Come on squirt, I'll give you the low down on what goes on round here.'

He told Billy what he would be doing, times of meals and the wage he could expect. Billy wondered if he should have known all this if he had worked on a sheep station before.

The other men started drifting out of the shed and Dink got up to leave. 'Come on, it's grub time.'

Dink was still giving advice as they walked across to the veranda that ran the length of the huge house. 'If anyone asks what job you'll be doing just say helping with the lambing.'

Billy nodded.

Mr Pickett welcomed him with a slap on the back after Dink's convincing introduction. The men shuffled along a bench to let him sit down at the long table, too intent on their food to have much conversation. Billy breathed a sigh of relief, he was in.

The next day his working life began. He was given a horse called Gert, a bedroll and a billy can. After that he followed what everyone else did. Dink and some of the other men rode out from the station into the barren sheep farming country with Billy tagging along behind. Their task was to fix all the fences before lambing season began. To do that they had to ride long distances and sometimes they were away for days. Billy was told the sheep station was thirty thousand acres in size so that was a lot of fences. Sometimes they had to replace the posts and other times it was just the wire where kangaroos had smashed through. Billy never got used to finding animals caught in the wire, usually dead or badly maimed after thrashing around for days.

At first he was very nervous about everything. He longed to be at home with Maggie curled up in his familiar bed instead of sleeping on the ground. They rode hundreds of miles to check on all the sheep and it was exhausting. His horse was skittish, while they were both getting used to each other. Dust and dirt penetrated every stitch of his clothing and seemed to have lodged permanently in the back of his throat. His body ached from hard riding during the day and hard ground at night. It took a while for him to become accustomed to the life on horseback. But he was one of the blokes now, no one asked questions or pried into his past. They were all escaping from something otherwise why would they be in this God forsaken place?

The days rolled into weeks and the weeks into months and the next thing Billy knew the ewes had begun lambing. It was up to Dink and the boys to ride out and check on the mothers and babies and help with any complications. They brought any undernourished lambs into the poddy field where Billy learned how to look after them. Since every ewe and lamb was worth money they all had to be cared for or it was money down the drain.

At night he usually fell straight to sleep from exhaustion, but sometimes he thought about Maggie. He missed her so much. Occasionally his thoughts strayed to mother and Ningan. When that happened he gritted his teeth and closed his eyes tight against the image of them that wouldn't leave him.

Dink seemed to have taken him under his wing. Billy liked him. He was a cross between a father figure and an older brother. He looked out for Billy and checked up on him all the time. His bear like physique was capable of incredible strength. He could easily lift a fully-grown ewe. He would sling it round his neck if he was going any distance and hold the poor struggling creature by its feet. When it came to delivering the lambs, Dink had an uncharacteristic gentleness with the newborns. Many a time Billy had to help him pull a slithery lamb from its mother's belly after it had become stuck. Billy liked those moments.

Once the lambing was over they had a short respite from the long hours in the saddle. There were chores to be done back at the station. The pens had to be repaired ready to hold all the sheep that would be bought in for shearing. The shearing sheds had to be scrubbed and all the equipment oiled.

Billy's boss was a fair man who didn't tolerate laziness or fighting. Both were punishable with the sack. The men worked very hard and tolerated each other. Now and again one of the men would go off on his own and not mix with the rest. When this happened everyone knew that he was ready to blow for whatever reason. He was left alone, no questions asked, no good humoured banter until he was ready to come back into the fold. Some of the men had a great sense of humour and managed to get everyone laughing. One such hand was Curly, every time he opened his mouth something funny came out. He had the straightest hair Billy had ever seen and at first he couldn't work out why they called him Curly. As time went on he began to understand the sheep hands' sense of humour.

After a hard day working, the boys liked to play cards or games with dice. At other times they would just lay on their bunks putting the world to rights or talking about women. None of the men were married, it was not a life the wives liked. Billy listened to their crude conversations and tales of conquests with women. Most of the time it was amusing and Billy had finally stopped blushing at all their rude remarks and constant swearing.

Winter slid into spring and the outback burst into blossom. The wildlife seemed to make more noise as if celebrating the coming of warmer weather and as summer hovered in the wings the shearers arrived. Suddenly the bunkhouse was full. Dink warned Billy to keep an eye on his things since some of these seasonal wanderers were not that honest. Taroola Station was a hive of activity.

The shearing shed was like a production line with sheep trailing in one way all woolly, madly baaing and then skipping out the other side, shorn to within an inch of their lives. Billy was fascinated watching the shearers at work. Lying the sheep on their side and starting at the back end their electric shears glided up the body of the animal, then it was flipped over and the other side done.

Billy's job was to pick up the fleeces that were thrown into the middle of the floor and put them on the large slatted tables for the classers to sort. The heat in the shearing shed was intolerable and all the men were wet through with sweat, Billy included. Mid morning the shearing machines were turned off and the men went outside for a smoko. Mugs of tea were given out and they rested, usually with a cigarette in their hand. Billy had begun smoking, it made him look older and he did enjoy it once he got the hang of it and stopped coughing.

With the shearers came gossip from other areas. They were worse than women when it came to nattering about other people's business. Some of the stories they told shocked Billy, station hands having it off with the boss's wife or the boss's daughter going through the men in the shearing shed like a dose of salts.

One shearer in particular knew everything about everyone. His name was Norm Bartlett. Billy wondered if half the stuff he said was made up just to get everyone's attention.

One particularly hard and hot day, they were all sitting under the trees having a smoko, when Norm came out with another of his gems.

'Eh, have yuhs heard about that woman over Bangalla?'
Billy froze.
'Nah,' came the mumbled replies from the boys.
'Well it appears there's this woman who lives out in the sticks on her own.' Norm stopped to light his cigarette. He took a long drag at it before continuing. 'Seems her husband died of the diphtheria. I think some of her kiddies did too. Now, whether that's what's turned her brain I dunno.'
'Come on Norm, get to the point.' Curly interrupted.

Norm continued, 'This woman's only having it off with an abo.'

'Get away.'

Billy was getting hotter. It couldn't be, nobody would know about his mother and Ningan. It must be another lady from back home. Was it another lady with Ningan, was he two timing his mother? Billy's mind was in a whirl.

'That's not the worst of it mate.' Norm went on.

'Go on.' The men were all leaning forward, eager for more information.

'She's only having this abo's baby.' Norm shook his head. 'Can you imagine that. Her husband must be turning in his grave, poor bloke.'

'Bit of a tart, I'd say.' Dink put his tuppence worth in.

Billy could feel the flush traveling up his neck, across his cheeks.

'Well, anyway, the town's people are not very happy with her, especially since she's about to drop the bastard baby any day,' Norm went on.

'They want to lynch that bloody black man, don't they?' Dink was getting himself worked up.

'Seems they're trying, but can't find him.' Norm embellished his story. 'As for her, well the locals want her out. Sad thing is she's got a girl of about ten. Bet she's having a hard time of it.'

Billy got up to move away from this story he didn't want to hear. It couldn't possibly be his family Norm was talking about.

'What did yuh say her name was, Norm.' Dink was looking thoroughly disgusted.

'Ah, geez, what was it, now?' Norm scratched his head. 'It's got an "L" in it.'

As Billy walked away with his head bent he muttered to himself so no one could hear, 'Lang.'

None of the men noticed Billy leave the group. It was mid afternoon before they missed him from the shearing shed. Dink went to the bunkhouse in search of him. His stuff was gone, not a trace of Billy Carter was left. Dink stood, scratched his head and then shrugged his shoulders. Billy was now just another person that passed through his life. He thought there had been a bond between them but evidently not.

Constance

The effort of carrying the unborn baby made Constance exhausted. Her bulging stomach was a constant reminder of what had happened between her and Ningan all those months ago. She was still quite confused as to how she felt about the impending birth. Sometimes she shuddered at the thought of what she had done, and other times she was glad she had conceived while she still could. She looked forward to holding the little helpless bundle but the bigotry she experienced every time she went to town upset her.

Billy's departure had been a shock to Constance. At first she thought he was off with Ningan, but as the day turned to evening and there was still no sign of him Constance began to worry. Ningan tried to reassure her that he would be able to look after himself but she was still terribly worried. Constance had no idea why he went away and at first kept expecting him to walk in as though nothing had happened. The nightmare of not knowing where he was or if he was safe haunted her for months.

At first she made excuses why she had no period, it seemed too remote a possibility that she could be pregnant. The guilt she felt was unbearable, she had soiled Jack's memory. For a while she pretended it hadn't happened, she carried on as normal, doing the heavy jobs as before. When the morning sickness began she was convinced it was something she ate.

She closed her mind so completely to her condition that she carried on going to town even when she was showing, in the belief that no one would notice. Of course they did. People who passed her in the street looked without shame at her stomach as though that was the most important part of her. They would look at her larger figure and then look her in the face and tutt or shake their heads as though she was an errant child who had done something wrong.

Constance could have handled that but when the attitude towards her and Maggie became malicious, she realized what an isolated position she was in. She didn't know which was worse when they completely ignored her and looked down at the ground or when they made some nasty comment as they passed.

Of course Maggie noticed the change in people and asked, 'why doesn't anyone like us anymore?'

'I don't know.' Constance tried to think of an explanation for Maggie but none came.

'They don't say hello any more.' Maggie frowned and added, 'and when we walk into a shop everyone stops talking.'

'Do they, I hadn't noticed.'

On one trip to Bangalla Constance was very annoyed when she went into a shop and left Maggie outside only to return and overhear children calling abuse at her. Maggie was trying very hard not to cry as the children scurried off giggling. That episode had made their trips to town a lot less frequent and they tried to manage with their supplies as long as possible even coping without some things just to avoid the upset. Consequently Constance didn't have much in the way of baby supplies but with summer approaching the child wouldn't need many clothes.

Constance wondered if they knew it was a black man who was the baby's father and if that was the reason for her and Maggie treatment. She felt sure they did. The old bush telegraph, Jack used to say, was more reliable than the national newspapers.

The maliciousness of the townspeople made them stay fairly close to the homestead and Ningan subsidized their diet with whatever he could find to eat. Constance convinced herself that they didn't need anyone else and could manage on their own. She didn't dwell too much on the actual confinement.

Ningan's excitement at the forthcoming birth of his first child amused her. He was so thrilled he would frequently pat her stomach and say, 'him good piccaninny,' and when he actually felt it move the look of delight and happiness on his face brought tears to Constance' eyes. She couldn't remember Jack being so thrilled when she was pregnant with Billy.

The relationship between her and Ningan grew, she was his woman and she felt protected when he was there. They were careful not to show any affection in front of Maggie.

She also seemed excited at the prospect of another baby in the house. It was going to be difficult to explain the colour of the child when it was born. Maggie was only ten but still knew that white women had white babies. Fortunately she wasn't all that wise as to the mechanics of how babies were conceived. One of the good things about the pregnancy was that it had brought them closer. With the imminent arrival of the baby Maggie had more of an interest in feminine things. Many evenings she would brush her mother's hair in a very gentle, soothing fashion and Constance would talk about her childhood in England.

They were content and felt cocooned by distance from the wagging tongues of the townspeople. A feeling of well being enveloped her and the homestead, even though supplies were short. She had lulled herself into a sense of security and didn't consider the consequences of her pregnancy.

A favourite time for Constance was early morning when it was still cool. She would sit on the veranda step and listen to the dawn chorus. As the sun rose it would warm her outstretched legs and bare feet as she relaxed.

One morning the sound of galloping horses interrupted her peace. At first she thought it was a herd of wild horses passing their way, but then she heard voices. She wasn't unduly worried, it was probably bushmen trying to find a short cut to Bangalla. She got to her feet and stood on the veranda with a welcoming smile. The horses and their riders rode into the clearing in front of the house.

'There she is, the slag,' menacing voices sneered. 'Look at her, barefooted just like an abo's whore.' They rode right up to the veranda rail and spat at her. 'What would your old man think of yuh, with a belly full of black man? Where is the black bastard, anyway? We've come to get him missus, so don't try to hide him.'

Constance stood rooted to the spot, too shocked to move, her smile gone. She knew what could happen when a group of het up men confronted a helpless woman. She wasn't going to be that helpless woman, she wanted to lash out and yell abuse back at them. Who did they think they were, riding onto her property and threatening her? After all she had been through she was not prepared to take this from a bunch of jumped up blokes who thought they could scare her. She began to move forward but felt Maggie's presence beside her and a tugging on her arm.

'Mama, come inside.' The pleading in her voice stopped Constance. If she antagonized them she may put Maggie in danger. At least they weren't drunk so she may be able to reason with them. But she didn't want to, she wasn't going to make feeble excuses to this bunch of rabble. The pressure on her arm from Maggie was insistent and she began slowly to walk backwards towards the door of the house.

'And the poor kiddie, having a mother like you,' another sneering rider shouted. 'You should be banned from having anymore.'

Maggie was whimpering and pulling her.

'Hiding in there'll not do you any good.' The ringleader was someone she recognized from town, but wasn't sure of his name. In fact they were all fairly young, angry men, full of hatred that had to be focused on some one.

Once in the house Maggie clung to her mother. 'What do they want mama?' She was shivering with fear.

'Oh, they're just being silly.'

The men were still outside yelping with glee. She could hear their footsteps on the wooden planking of the veranda and expected them to burst through the door any minute. Maggie was petrified, hiding her face and gripping her mother tightly. The more frightened Maggie became the more the anger grew in Constance. Gently she shrugged Maggie off and strode to the door picking up the rifle on the way. She stepped outside and aimed the gun at the ringleader's horse.

'Get off my property, you rabble before I shoot your horse.'

'Now look what you've done,' a sarcastic voice nodded at the leader. 'You've upset the whore.' Gales of laughter followed.

The gun in Constance' hands was shaking but she aimed it at the trees and pulled the trigger. The blast sent all the bird life flapping into the air and spooked the horses. 'Did you hear what I said? The next shot will be through your horse's chest.'

The laughter suddenly subsided and the men looked at each other but Constance went on. 'Aren't you all very gallant, coming here and picking on a woman on her own with her child. You're all the scum of the earth. Haven't you got any jobs to go to or wives and children to feed?' She was so furious she couldn't stop her outburst.

One of the men who had stayed at the back of the pack spoke, 'Come on boys, I think we've done enough here.' One last glob of spit was aimed at Constance as they rode away from the house. Within moments the morning was quiet and peaceful again. The whole experience had shaken Constance and her hands still trembled. She put the gun back in its place behind the door and went to Maggie.

'It's alright now, Maggie, they've gone.'

'They were horrible men.' Maggie looked worried. 'Will they come back again mama?'

'I don't think so. They were just being nasty, they wouldn't have hurt us.'

'Mama, what's a whore?'

Constance could feel her face redden and had to think before she could answer. 'It's a certain type of woman.'

After that experience Constance was more on edge. When she told Ningan of the unwanted visitors, he didn't say a word, but she could tell he was very angry. The peaceful haven that she had made had been violated, the world outside had crossed the barrier of distance and invaded her home. She didn't sleep easy in her bed at night and worried they might find Ningan. What would they do to him? Wasn't there a law against such things?

A few weeks after their disturbing visit, Constance was feeling particularly tired and uncomfortable. It was a week before her thirty fourth birthday and she was feeling every bit of her age. She sat on the veranda in a chair with a pillow to her back and her feet propped up on a box. The unborn child was moving but not as vigorously. It had filled its cramped space and was sluggish in its tight enclosure. Constance knew the child would be born any day. Maggie would be the only one to help her when the time came.

As Maggie stood over her, brushing her hair, Constance decided to broach the subject.

'Maggie?' she began, 'You do realize that when the baby is coming you'll have to help me.'

The brushing strokes slowed. 'Will I?'

'Yes.'

'Well don't worry, mama,' Maggie continued, 'I'll be able to take it for walks and feed it.'

'Well, that will be good, but even before that, I'll need your help.' Constance cleared her throat. 'I'll need your help when it's coming out.'

The brushing had completely stopped.

'But I don't know anything about having babies.' Maggie said pathetically.

'I'll tell you what to do, but you mustn't be scared. Having babies is a very natural thing and may look horrible but millions of women have them everyday.'

'Why would I be scared mama?'

Constance didn't know how much to tell her, but decided the gory details may upset her.

'You won't be because you're a very brave girl.'

'Am I?'

'Of course you are. I will have some things ready that I have to use. I want you to keep them very clean and give them to me when I need them.'

'Well I can do that. What things?'

'Well, when the baby is born it will be still attached to me by the tube that has been feeding it all these months. It's called the umbilical cord and needs to be cut.'

Silence greeted Constance biology lesson but she went on. 'But first we have to tie some string around it to make it safe before I can cut it. You will be in charge of the string and scissors.'

The brush began to stroke Constance hair again. 'That doesn't sound very scary.'

'Everything will be alright, just as long as you do as I say.'

Maggie came round to the front of her mother and knelt down at her feet. 'Don't worry, mama, I'll look after you.' She laid her head in her mother's lap.

Two days later the contractions began. Constance lit the fire in the grate to boil water ready for sterilizing the scissors and string. She got her bed ready and laid clean sheets over sacking. She closed the window so no flies got in and placed a bowl with cool water and a face cloth beside the bed. She also put a chair at the head of the bed for Maggie to sit on.

As if he sensed the imminent arrival of his off spring Ningan arrived. A beaming smile lit up his face when he saw the pain Constance was in.

'Him baby come soon.'

Constance nodded as she grimaced, which made him smile even more. She wished he would stay to help but knew that wasn't the aboriginal way.

'This women's work, I come back when him here.'

'Where has Ningan gone? Isn't he staying to help with the baby?' Maggie asked.

'No, but don't worry, we'll be alright.'

A particularly severe contraction made Constance groan involuntarily. Sweat was standing out on her forehead and she felt wobbly.

'From now on I'll be in a lot of pain and I may even make a noise but it's alright,' she explained.

Maggie was looking very concerned but Constance hugged her and whispered, 'We'll have this baby together, you and me and it will be our little treasure.'

Constance waddled into the bedroom feeling as though her stomach was about to explode. She lay on the bed on her side and tried to get as comfortable as possible. A pain cut into her stomach and she gritted her teeth. As a contraction began she mentally counted. When she got to ten it was at its worse and by twenty it had subsided. With them coming every five minutes she knew it shouldn't take long before the baby was born.

Between contractions she talked to Maggie who sat stiffly in the chair at the head of the bed. Constance was relieved when she began to relax and took on the role of carer. She was a sensible girl and seemed to know what Constance needed, cooling her face with a damp cloth and giving her sips of water. The roles had reversed, Maggie stroked her mother's arm and talked in soothing tones. She chattered on about what they would call the baby and who it would look like. She hoped it looked like Dulcie, a replacement little sister.

Hours passed and Constance got off the bed and walked about the room. As each contraction came she squatted down hoping gravity would help. The pain was intolerable, she felt exhausted and short tempered. Maggie had gone outside, the atmosphere in the room was stifling. Constance prayed for relief.

She was feeling uneasy about this birth, it wasn't like the others something was stopping the baby from coming.

A wave of nausea came over her and she heaved. As she did the pushing contractions began and Constance let her body do its work. She panted and groaned as the pain became excruciating, then momentary relief. A flood of warmth flopped between her legs but even in her half conscious state she realized it wasn't the baby. A wash of red spread over the bed as Constance yelled for Maggie. The after birth had come first and Constance knew her baby was in trouble. Should she lay back and let nature kill off the unwanted child in her belly. Her problems would be solved, she would have no more shame and guilt, but she couldn't. This child had been a child of love even though she had not wanted to admit it to herself. She loved Ningan, and she wanted to have his baby.

Constance felt lightheaded and a white light spread in front of her eyes. She was fainting with the loss of blood. She sensed the door opening and knew Maggie would be beside her any moment. She hoped she wasn't going to die in front of her child.

A deep voice addressed her, 'Mother, mother... God...What's happened here?' Was she hallucinating, it sounded like Billy, but it couldn't be? He had left, gone, not seen or heard of for months.

'Mother, mother, can you hear me, it's Billy.'

'Billy?' She felt too weak to speak.

'Yes, I'm here.' His voice was deeper, he sounded like Jack, he was going to take control and everything would be alright.

'Now listen,' he said. 'I know you're feeling weak and ill but I still need you to help deliver this baby.' His voice sounded less serious. 'Hell, it can't be that different from delivering a lamb and I'm a dab hand at that now.'

Constance tried to smile but another contraction was building. She didn't feel as though her body could cope with any more pain.

'Now mother, with this contraction I want you to push as hard as you can and I will pull this little mite out.'

The thoughts of her son seeing her private parts flashed through her mind but she just wanted rid of the pain and didn't care how it was achieved. She groaned ascent. As the pain increased she pushed with all her strength but nothing seemed to be happening.

'Push, mother, push.'

Constance took a deep tired breath and bore down as hard as she could. There was a pulling between her legs as her baby entered the world. The relief was overwhelming, tears pricked at her eyes. Was it still alive or dead? She raised her head to see it. The little mite was lifeless in Billy's arms. He laid it on the bed and rubbed it with the towel, gently stroking warmth into its tiny body. His calloused hands expertly helped the baby's circulation. Finally it began to move as though to shrug off its tormentor. It screwed up its face and mewed like a little animal.

'Come on little girl, get them lunges full of air.'

As if answering the baby opened its mouth, took a breath and began a healthy wailing. A smile lit up Billy's face. 'There she blows.'

The baby's cries bought Maggie into the room. 'Ahh..,' she cooed.

Billy wrapped the baby in the towel and laid it on his mother's chest. 'There you go, mother, she's all yours now.'

Billy had cleaned up the bed and wrapped up the sacking ready to dispose of. He helped Constance to sit up and brought her in a cup of tea. While he was doing all this she didn't ask him why he had left home or where he had been.

Maggie put her arms around Billy's waist and said, 'I'm so glad you're back.'

He ruffled her hair. 'Come on squirt, let's get some food, I'm starving.'

Constance laid back and studied the little bundle in her arms. It was perfectly formed with a shock of black hair and tiny hands and feet. She had forgotten how small newborn babies were and how wonderful it felt to hold one. Another little girl and she had no name for her. Should she call her an English name like Mary or go for something more natural. At present her skin was pale and looked as though she had a light suntan. A name would come but she was too tired to think, she settled herself in the bed, sleep was what she needed.

The movement in her arms woke Constance. It was dark and the house was quiet. She had no idea what time it was or how long she had slept but she felt refreshed. The baby began a complaining cry and Constance placed her at her breast.

The memories of the previous day replayed in her mind. Billy was home, she felt so happy having him back. She felt sure the reason he ran away was her relationship with Ningan. She didn't know how he had known but he was back so he must have forgiven her.

No matter what happened between her and Billy she would still be shunned by the locals. It wasn't a healthy environment to bring up a baby or for Maggie. There was only one answer. They had to move. She would approach the bank and see if they would buy the land back. It must be worth something. They would sell what they could and get enough money together for the fares to Sydney. Constance was sure she and Billy would be able to get jobs there. She would wean the baby and Maggie could look after it for a few hours a day. She wondered if Mrs. Maguire still had her boarding house, perhaps they could stay there when they first arrived.

As her thoughts rambled on over their future the sky began to lighten. She pushed the shutter open to let in the new day.

'Look my little one, this is the first day of your new life.' Constance gazed down on her child and as she did so a ray of sunshine shone on her face. The little face screwed up from the light and Constance knew what she would call her. Her name would be Dawn.

PART TWO

1913

CHAPTER 8

Emily

Sunlight burst into the room as Emily opened the heavy brocade curtains. The person in the huge double bed groaned and a female voice muttered, 'Close those curtains.'

'I can't Mrs Rhodes.' Emily moved towards the bed with the tea tray. 'Have you forgotten it's the picnic today?'

Another groan came from under the bedclothes.

'Come along now, marm. The children have been up for hours waiting to go.'

'Yes, yes, Emily.' A head appeared covered with an abundance of tangled black hair. 'Put the tea tray down and come back in half an hour to help me with my toilette.'

'Yes, Marm.'

Emily closed the door quietly on her mistress's bedroom. She walked with a spring in her step. The family was going out for the day which meant, hopefully, she could have a bit of free time. Maybe she would be able to nip down to the stables to see Dan. He hadn't been working at the house long but he seemed very friendly and he was so handsome. Then she remembered that Dan would be driving the family on their outing. That meant she would be bored around here, dusting and polishing and doing all the dreary things a housemaid did.

She made her way to the kitchen, she'd been told to help Mrs Lovelock with the packing of the picnic lunch, which was not really her job, but she enjoyed being in the kitchen, it was like the hub of the house.

The noise as Emily opened the kitchen door was a complete contrast to the quietness of the rest of the house. Two children sat at the huge scrubbed table talking animatedly, their voices raised with excitement. Master Thomas sat with Mistress Anna on his lap. He was the older brother and was always very protective of his four year old sister.

'Emmy, Emmy,' Mistress Anna squealed as Emily entered the room.

'For goodness sake Emily can you help me with these two.' Mrs Lovelock heaved a big sigh and added, 'I don't know what's happened to the governess.'

'She's being sick,' Anna stated.

Emily and the cook exchanged glances over the children's heads.

'Oh dear, she must have eaten something that didn't agree with her.' Emily tried to tone down the glee that sprung to Anna's eyes at the prospect of the governess being sick.

'She says she has a weak stomach,' Thomas enlightened them as he dipped his finger in the thick icing of a sponge cake Mrs Lovelock had put on the table. The smack of a wooden spoon coming down on the table right next to his fingers made them all jump.

'Come along you two,' Emily held out her hand to Anna who jumped off Thomas's lap. 'We'd better get you ready.'

Thomas at seven was too old to hold hands and shuffled along behind Emily as she made her way up the back stairs to the nursery.

Half an hour later she reappeared in the main entrance with the two children dressed ready for a picnic. She had knocked on the mistress' door while she was upstairs and been told her help wasn't required. Anna looked adorable in a white smocked dress with loads of gathered material and frills. Her feet were clad in white stockings and black patent leather shoes. Perhaps the choice of white was not practical for a picnic but it went so well with her dark hair. It was the same colour as her mother's and just as wayward. Emily had tied it all together with a matching silk ribbon but it would probably fall out before the day was done.

Thomas was in a sailor suit, also white but with navy trim. It even had a lanyard draped round the shoulder just like the officers wore and with his blonde hair he looked a picture. Anna and Thomas were as different as chalk and cheese in appearance one taking after her mother and the other after his father. Emily was pleased she had managed to get the children ready in time. They had been instructed by Mr Rhodes to have everything and everyone ready by ten o'clock exactly.

As the hall clock chimed ten, the master appeared and Emily breathed a sigh of relief.

'We aren't quite ready…..' he spoke hesitantly as though he was afraid of upsetting someone. That was the thing about Mr Rhodes, he was such a lovely man. Sometimes Emily felt sorry for him, having such a bossy wife. And he was so handsome with his blonde hair and blue eyes.

Mr. Rhodes absolutely adored his children. Emily thought he would probably have liked more, but his wife was a bit obsessed with how she looked and Emily guessed she wouldn't want to lose her figure again. They didn't even share the same bedroom.

Even though Mrs Rhodes was so nasty, Emily felt sure Mr Rhodes still loved her. He still bought her presents from time to time and always tried to do things to please her. He never raised his voice to her or spoke to her unkindly, which is more than could be said about her behaviour. Some of the screaming sessions she had were really uncalled for.

Emily could tell that Mr Rhodes was feeling awkward and tried to ease his discomfort by saying, 'don't worry Mr Rhodes, we can find loads to do 'til it's time to go.'

'I knew I could count on you, Emily.' He patted her gently on the shoulder.

She beamed and ushered the children away, back into the kitchen. Mrs Lovelock sat in a wooden chair, her legs spread out in front of her as she wafted herself with her apron.

'Put the kettle on, girl,' she addressed Emily.

Emily raised her eyebrows but did as she was told.

'She running late again, is she?' Mrs Lovelock asked as she raised her eyes to the ceiling.

Emily made a face at her and looked expressively at the children as if to say not in front of them.

'Do you think you two can eat a biscuit without making a mess of your clothes?'

Both children answered noisily in unison. 'Yeah.'

'It's yes, and before you do anything you have to have an apron on.' Emily briskly tied a tea towel round Anna and draped one of Mrs Lovelock's aprons over Thomas. The children sat quietly eating some of cook's homemade shortbread biscuits, which seemed safe enough. A small glass of milk was given to each of them with Emily holding Anna's so she didn't spill it.

'When are we going?' Thomas was getting impatient. 'Why is it taking mama so long to get ready?'

'Well, it gives us time to have a story.' Emily could see how bored they were.

'Yeah,' Anna yelled but Thomas' face fell.

'It'll be a baby book won't it?' he stated.

'I'm not a baby.' Anna lashed out with her foot.

'Now, now.' Emily got between them. 'Anna, go upstairs and get your favourite book.'

An hour later when the story was finished and Mrs Lovelock had got the children drawing at the table, Mr Rhodes popped into the kitchen.

'Are you ready?' He was smiling but Emily could tell it was a false smile.

The children rushed to him and he enfolded them in his arms.

'Oh, Emily?'

'Yes Mr Rhodes.'

'Would you mind coming on the picnic with us, the governess is not feeling very well and I need someone to help me with these two.' He ruffled Thomas' hair as he spoke.

'I'd love to, but I'm not really dressed for it.' Emily was gauging how swiftly she could get changed into her outdoor clothes.

'Don't worry it will take us a while to get everything loaded into the carriage. I'm sure you won't take long to get changed.'

'No Mr. Rhodes, thank you Mr Rhodes.' Emily rushed for the stairs.

At long last they were on their way. Emily sat up front with Dan. The beaming smile he gave her when she climbed up next to him made her feel shy. The family sat in the back of the open carriage nestled in amongst pillows and rugs. The French perfume Mrs Rhodes wore wafted over them and Emily thought it smelt wonderful, even though Dan looked at her and screwed up his nose. She raised her eyebrows at him to indicate what a heathen he was.

As they rode around the circular driveway Emily looked across and admired the house. She was very lucky to live in such a place. The sandstone walls looked white in the spring sunshine and the contrasting tile work took the starkness off the design. An upstairs veranda ran across the front of the building and around both sides. The railings were decorated in cast iron lace work and on the ground floor decorative black iron pillars held up the balconies. Tall chimneys sat on the roof along with an elaborate belfry that made it look very grand. Two palm trees stood either side of the entrance, giving it an exotic look as though it should have been in the tropics instead of a suburb of Sydney.

The street was wide with houses scattered along its length, and unpaved until they reached the junction of the main road. A tram trundled past them, the service had only become electrified this year and Emily longed to ride on it. It was so quiet after the noise and danger of the steam powered ones that used to run.

Emily could still recall the tram tragedy that happened when she was only thirteen. She lived not far away in Stanley Street when the explosion happened. Eight people had been killed when two trams passed each other and one exploded. The silence after the disaster was something Emily would never forget. She was one of the first on the scene and saw the blood everywhere. A shudder still ran through her at the memory. A huge headlights from one tram was hurled into the air and landed on the lunch shed of the school. The whole area had been in mourning for weeks.

Emily shook her head to dispel the memories, fancy thinking about things like that on such a perfect day. As they travelled she could hear some of the conversation coming from the carriage behind her, even over the noise of the cartwheels clattering on the road.

Mrs Rhodes' raised voice let them all know she was not pleased. 'There's no need to keep going on about it, John.'

'Lower your voice dear.'

'Why should I?' she argued. 'I think the world should know what a tight fisted husband I have.'

'Now, you know that's not true.' Mr Rhodes tried to placate her.

'Well you're making such a carry on about spending a little bit of money on a few dresses.'

'It wasn't a little bit of money, and I don't see the point of spending hundreds of pounds on dresses that you will never wear.'

'Who said I won't wear them?'

'You don't wear the ones you've got.' Mr Rhodes was getting annoyed.

'We can afford to spend, and don't forget whose inheritance it was......'

'Mama, mama, look at that.' Master Thomas was trying to divert his mother's attention.

His ploy worked. 'Yes my darling, it's a dog.'

'I know it's a dog but isn't it cute.'

'Not that I would have noticed, my darling boy, but if you think it is then it is.'

'It's dirty.' Anna said.

'So would you be if you lived on the streets.' Thomas sulked.

Dan and Emily looked at each other and raised their eyebrows.

It wasn't a very long drive to their destination, just as well because the children started to fidget and Anna began asking if they were nearly there. Carriages snaked slowly through the gates of Coronation Park, it seemed everyone had the same idea on this perfect Sunday morning. The children were gigging with excitement as the carriage passed the swings and merry-go-rounds, and Emily loved the floral displays and the exotic looking trees and shrubs.

Dan drove the carriage towards the river as Mr Rhodes had instructed. The sun glistened on the water as the carriage came to a halt and the children spilled out. Emily held their hands firmly as Mr and Mrs Rhodes elegantly disembarked.

'Come along children, we'll have a little walk while Daniel sets up a spot for us,' Mr Rhodes said.

'Yeah,' the children shouted.

The family promenaded along the walkways and Emily noticed all eyes were on them. Mrs Rhodes looked sensational in a pale peach gown with a satin sash around her waist that emphasized her hour glass figure. Emily felt quite envious of her. She, in contrast wore only a serge brown skirt and white blouse that denoted her position in the ladder of success. Her straw hat was positively shabby compared to Mrs. Rhodes creation adorned in fluffy white ostrich feathers. She carried an Empire scarf of embroidered muslin that she had draped over her hat while travelling so it didn't blow off. She looked so elegant.

They wondered down to the river and watched the ferry boat from Parramatta disgorging its day trippers. Emily held the children's hands tightly as they walked near the water, afraid that they might go too close. It wouldn't do to have them wet or dirty before they ate their lunch.

A cluster of rowing boats nudged each other on a small jetty and Thomas pointed at them. 'Look father, can we have a ride on one of them?'

'I don't think so.'

'But why? It'd be so much fun.'

'I think you and your sister are a little too young for boat rides.'

'Oh for heaven's sake John, it's only a rowing boat.'

It seemed to Emily that Mrs Rhodes tried to upset her husband at every turn.

'Yes a rowing boat that can easily capsize,' he pointed out.

Anna joined the persuading team. 'Please papa please, please, please.'

'That's enough, we'll see after lunch.' He had given in, Emily knew.

By the time they returned to their carriage Dan had unpacked everything and laid it out.

Under a willow tree a collapsible table and four chairs were placed in the shade. It was set with a white cloth and napkins. The silverware shone in the sunlight that filtered through the leaves and the wine glasses sparkled. A bottle of white wine stood in an ice filled bucket. The hamper of food sat on the middle of the table and the savoury smell that came from it made Emily's mouth water. She knew she wouldn't be getting any of it.

The children rushed across to the chairs and sat down. Thomas exclaimed, 'I'm starving.'

'I hardly think so, darling,' his mother corrected him.

'Me too,' added Anna.

'There are children in this world, who are really starving, who eat bread and water.' Once again she had made everyone feel bad, thought Emily. Thomas was now frowning.

'Would you do the honours, Emily?' Mrs Rhodes nodded at the picnic hamper.

Emily reached over and unpacked sliced roast beef, a large meat pie, a crusty loaf, a big piece of poached salmon and pickled onions. The children watched her every movement.

Mrs Rhodes put some meat, fish and bread on the children's plates. Dan poured out the wine and Mr Rhodes took a sip to taste it. He nodded and Dan continued pouring. Emily hovered near the table ready to help the children. Thomas ate his food hungrily and Emily shook her head at him when he began stuffing too much in his mouth. Anna ate small amounts of everything and Mr Rhodes seemed to enjoy the wine more than the food.

Mrs Rhodes picked at her lunch before pushing back her chair and rising. That was the signal that everyone should be finished. Mr Rhodes hastily finished his glass of wine, he still had food on his plate but left it.

'Now, shall we see about that boat ride?' Mrs Rhodes announced.

The children dropped their forks and jumped to their feet. The meal was over.

'I wish you would reconsider, my dear.' Mr Rhodes looked worried.

His words went unheeded as the children grabbed their mother's hand and began skipping in the direction of the rowing boats.

Once the family moved out of ear shot Emily could say her piece. 'Everyone has to do what she wants all the time, it really annoys me.'

'She wants a good hiding, that one,' Dan put in his opinion. 'But he's too weak to do it.'

'No,' Emily took Mr. Rhodes' side. 'It's not that he's weak, he's just too kind for his own good.'

'Well being too kind is a weakness.'

'How can you say such a thing?' Emily felt annoyed. 'We should all be kind to each other.'

Once the hamper was repacked and the table brushed clean of every tiny crumb of left over food, Emily and Dan could relax for a while. They walked along the paths that meandered through the gardens. They knew the family would be a good hour in the boat, which gave them some time to themselves. As they strolled Emily glanced at Dan. His handsome face was quite brown from all the outdoor work he did and a half smile played on his lips. His felt hat sat at a jaunty angle, dipped over one eye and his dark brown, curly hair escaped from beneath the brim. He hooked his thumbs in the pockets of his waistcoat and his jacket swung open as he walked. He was so good-looking and seemed so full of confidence it made Emily feel a bit out of her depth.

The brass band on the bandstand played rousing music and families gathered to watch. Further on the peace and quiet of the walled garden was like a sanctuary as they sat on a bench. Soft humming of a bee in the flower heads nearby added to the harmony of the spot.

'Ah,' Emily sighed. 'What a perfect spot on a perfect day.'

'Yeah,' Dan agreed, 'it's a pretty nice place. We'll have to come down one afternoon if we ever get the same day off.'

Emily thought for a moment before shyly saying, 'that would be lovely.'

He moved nearer to her and Emily could feel her face growing hot. He put his arm along the back of the seat behind her, it rested against her in an almost protective manner. He was so close she could smell him, the outdoors, horses, leather and soap, not unpleasant, the scent of a man. Emily wondered what she would do if he leaned over and kissed her. The thought made her blush more. She didn't have much experience with men. She turned away from him, her body felt tense, her mind in turmoil. She felt him move away, the moment lost, disappointment engulfed her.

'Perhaps we should be getting back,' Dan said.

Emily nodded and rose to her feet. As they walked back the way they had come the cloak of professionalism covered them and they reverted back into their roles of maid and coach man. As they approached the river people ran past them, one or two at first, then more. There was an atmosphere of alarm in the air.

'What's going on?' Dan was frowning.

'I don't know, where's everyone going?'

'Come on.' Dan began to walk faster.

They could see in the distance a crowd of people gathered on the shore. Emily had a feeling of dread in the pit of her stomach. What were they all looking at? They reached the edge of the crowd. People were hushed, women stood with handkerchiefs clutched to their faces. An undercurrent of despair came out in low groans and gasps.

Dan pushed through the crowd, Emily followed. They could hear splashing and people yelling. There seemed to be lots of activity beyond the bank of onlookers. Finally they got to the front. Men were diving into the river with their clothes on, but no one was laughing. It wasn't a game. An empty rowing boat floated in the middle of the water, not attached to anything, as if it had escaped from its moorings.

'Oh my God,' Emily gasped and began running.

Mr Rhodes sat on the sandy bank with a rug wrapped round his shoulders.

'Emily,' he shouted her name when he saw her. 'They're still in there.' He pointed to the water.

At first Emily didn't know what he meant. Who was in there? Where were Mrs Rhodes and the children? But Dan had realized straight away and hurriedly sat down, pulling off his shoes and shrugging out of his jacket. He ran for the water and dived in, one more pair of hands to feel the river's depth for the children and Mrs Rhodes.

Emily held Mr Rhodes tightly and tried to reassure him. 'Don't worry, they'll be alright. They are probably sitting on a rock further upstream absolutely fine.' She hoped with all her heart that was true.

More shouting came from the river, and the crowd surged forward.

'Get hold of him, quick.'

Mr Rhodes got to his feet and ran to the waters edge as Thomas was being carried out. He was completely still and his lips were blue.

'Put him down here, I'm a doctor.' A man from the crowd took control of the situation. He pumped Thomas' chest a few times and then laid him on his side. A stream of water gushed from his mouth and the process was repeated.

The crowd was silent and all that could be heard was Mr Rhodes pleading. 'Come on son breathe.' The anguish in his voice was heart wrenching.

After more water trickled from Thomas's mouth, his body jerked, his chest rose and uncontrollable coughing wracked him. The crowd cheered. Mr Rhodes hugged him and thanked God.

'We need to get him to the hospital.'

The doctor still looked concerned. Thomas hadn't regained consciousness. He was breathing on his own but there was still cause for concern.

'Has anyone got a car?' the doctor shouted.

A man stepped from the crowd. 'Yes, I have.'

'I need to get this boy to the hospital as soon as possible.'

'Right you are.' the man practically saluted.

Emily was kneeling beside Mr Rhodes watching the proceedings. This couldn't be happening, not to her family.

Dan had gone back to the waters edge. Other men stood next to him and they were all shivering in their wet clothes, even though the day was warm. They seemed unsure what to do next.

The ringing bell of a police car could be heard in the distance as Dan said, 'Keep looking.'

CHAPTER 9

Dan

Dan shivered as the sun slowly sank behind the trees. It would have been a beautiful sunset but he was too shaken to appreciate the sky streaked with shades of pink and red. A cacophony of twittering could be heard from the bird life as they vied for roosting spots for the night. The onlookers and people who had been enjoying their afternoon until the accident, drifted away. The other men who had helped to look for the bodies had all gone home.

Leaning against a tree Dan rolled a smoke and inhaled deeply. His deep breaths helped the shuddering that ran through his body. He needed a stiff drink and judging by the look of Mr Rhodes he did too. Turning his back on the river he walked across to his boss. The police had been, taken a statement and they would resume the search for the two bodies in the morning. Mr Rhodes was in shock and had sat looking at the river for what seemed like hours. He probably expected his wife and child to emerge from the water like two water babies, completely unscathed and the nightmare would be over.

'Right, Mr Rhodes,' Dan decided to take matters in hand. 'It's time to go home.'

'No.' John Rhodes refused. 'I have to be here when they come back.'

'Now look, mate,' Dan tried to reason without being too harsh. 'They may not come back.'

'They will.'

'What about the boy, it's ages since Emily went to the hospital with him and we don't know how he's doing?' Dan got hold of his boss's arm and gently coaxed him to his feet as he talked. 'Don't you think we should go over there and see him?'

'But what will I tell him?' The anguish on Mr Rhodes face upset Dan. Even though he didn't like the man he still felt sorry for him.

'Best not tell him anything just yet.'

They walked in silence to the carriage. Dan helped Mr Rhodes into the back seat as though he was an old man and tucked the rug round him before climbing onto the driver's seat and setting off at a slow pace.

At the main entrance to the hospital a reporter from the local paper thrust himself in front of them. Dan urged the horse on and shouted abuse at him.

They found the children's ward without too much trouble. Emily was sitting in the waiting room.

She rushed towards them. 'At last you're here, did they find them?'

Dan shook his head. 'How's the little fella?' he asked.

'He's still sleeping, but they think he'll be alright.'

'Thank God,' Mr Rhodes said.

'Do you want me to ask the nurse if you can see him,' Emily suggested.

Mr Rhodes nodded.

Emily left and after a few moments a starched white nurse returned with her. She introduced herself.

'My name is Sister Pritchard and you are Thomas' father, is that right?' Once again Mr Rhodes nodded. 'Come with me,' the nurse held the door open for him and they disappeared.

'What happened after I left?' Emily hastily asked Dan.

He gave a quick run down of the police questioning and how the search had stopped for the night. He didn't mention the conversation he had had with police about where the bodies would probably turn up downstream. They sat and spoke in hushed tones. Emily told Dan how Thomas didn't seem to be rallying.

'He just lays there.'

Dan could see she had been crying and the slightest thing would set her off again.

When Mr Rhodes returned his expression was grave as Emily asked, 'how is he?'

'Well, he seems to have blotted out the incident.'

'What do you mean?'

'He woke up when I spoke to him, but he didn't know who I was.' There was a long silence. Neither Dan nor Emily knew what to say. 'Anyway,' Mr Rhodes continued, 'they say there is no use us waiting around any longer. He will sleep now.'

Dan saw the tear that trickled down Emily's cheek and decided he needed to get her away from these morbid hospital surroundings.

'Right, let's get you both home.'

The house was hushed when they got there. The news had preceded them and everyone avoided eye contact, as though it was irreverent to be normal. Mr. Rhodes shut himself in his study and nobody saw him again until the following morning. The place seemed empty without the sound of children's laughter and the governess sat in the kitchen with a screwed up hankie in her hand sniffling and sighing. Mrs Lovelock busied herself cleaning things that didn't need cleaning.

Dan took in the scene, the feeling of depression hung in every nook and cranny and there was only one way to get rid of it.

'Come on Mrs Lovelock,' he ordered. 'Crack open some of that home made beer you've got in the cellar.'

'Oo Dan,' she tutted. 'Do you think it's appropriate in the circumstances?'

'I think it's very appropriate.' He winked at her and nodded at Emily. 'It'll numb the pain a bit.'

The rest of the evening was spent with Dan and Emily relating the events of the afternoon. There was conjecture as to what would happen next and how Mr Rhodes would cope. Dan noticed how every time their boss's name was mentioned Emily jumped to his defence. If the man had any gumption he would have saved his family, Dan thought. Mrs Lovelock tutted more and the governess shook her head continuously. After a few hours they just slumped in their chairs as the effects of Mrs Lovelock's potent brew took effect.

The next morning the newspaper was plastered with the story of the boating accident and all sorts of speculation into what had happened. Since Mr Rhodes hadn't told his part of the story to the newspaper, the article was made up of observations from onlookers. For a few days reporters stood at the end of the drive snapping photographs of anyone who came and went from Brunswick House. They were like blowflies on raw meat. Dan came across a persistent one that had sneaked in the back way and was peering through a downstairs window. It had given him the greatest of pleasure kicking the bludger in the backside and dragging him by the scruff of the neck to the gate, but the chap was persistent.

'Get in touch if you hear anything juicy, I'll make it worth your while,' he said, popping his card into Dan's pocket as he left.

After a week in hospital, Thomas was brought home and everyone fussed over him. His memory still hadn't returned and the worried look on his face made them treat him very gently. He would flinch when anyone touched him and he hardly spoke. His young body was finding relief in sleep as he dozed most of the day. The doctor came regularly but there was nothing he could do. It would take time.

But for Dan it was back to normal, working in the stables and coach house doing his usual chores. He felt sorry for the lad but it wouldn't do for them all to sit around moping. He took himself down to the pub on a Friday night as was his custom and still had his Saturday bet on the horses. He felt as though the events of the big house were of no concern to him. He would do whatever was asked of him and no more.

Emily seemed so involved with the family and their tragedy she had no interest in him. He thought he was making a bit of headway with her at the park but that was another time, before all this happened. Now she only had eyes for "poor Mr Rhodes" and the boy.

During the first week after the accident no one saw much of Mr Rhodes. He shut himself away and only saw officials from the police, the vicar and one or two relatives. The bodies still hadn't been found and rumours were rife. Dan heard them all when he went to the pub. Some said he tipped her out since they didn't see eye to eye and she was worth a bit. Other said it was all a scam and that she had swum off to be with her lover. One offering was that a shark had eaten them but they argued that bits of them would have washed up if that had happened. Dan never got involved in these conversations. He kept his own council but noticed the changed attitude towards the Rhodes family. They were no longer the perfect, well-to-do family, they had fallen from grace and the name Rhodes was greeted with a wry smile these days.

A few weeks after the accident, Dan came across Mr Rhodes in the stable. At first he was wary as he approached the stall where the big grey mare was tethered. Someone was talking and Dan armed himself with a pitchfork thinking it was one of those annoying reporters. Silently he approached but as he got closer he realized it was a solitary voice, talking softly. The mare was making blowing noises and a slight whinny as though she was responding to someone. It couldn't be a stranger. Dan stealthily crept into the adjoining stall and slid down on his haunches and listened.

'You're a nice old girl, but I'm afraid I forgot your sugar lumps.' It was Rhodes. 'Sorry I haven't had you out for a bit, but things have just got to me and I haven't had the energy.' There was a silence filled by Nelly's nostril blowing. 'I just don't know what to do….'

Dan could hear the other man's voice tremble with emotion. He shook his head and thought how pathetic he sounded.

'I'm not sure whether to have a funeral or not. How long should I wait for their bodies to appear? And what if they don't?' A long groaning sigh could be heard. 'What a mess, this should never have happened. I didn't want to go in that boat but you know what Beattie was like when she got an idea in her head, we all had to do what she said. I should have been firmer with her.'

There was a pause and Nelly answered him with another snuffle.

'Why didn't I ever learn to swim?' he went on. 'I could have saved them if I had. I should have drowned too. Why did God spare me? What right does he have to pick and choose who lives and who dies? It just happened so suddenly. We must have hit a rock or something. Oh God I miss Anna so much, my darling little girl, and Beattie.'

His voice changed and Dan detected a hint of bitterness. 'She could be so unreasonable.'

Dan raised his eyebrows. Perhaps he wasn't as kind and well meaning as everyone thought.

'And so wrapped up in herself.' There was a pause. 'She never really loved me. The children she lavished with affection when it suited her but at other times she could be just plain nasty with them.'

Dan listened to more recrimination.

'God, what am I saying, how could I speak ill of the dead? I married her for better or worse and because my parents wanted me to. Even when she had her little fling with Matthew Pennington I forgave her. God, I'd give anything to turn back the clock.'

Dan wasn't sure whether he meant turn the clock back before the accident or before he married Mrs Rhodes. It was all a bit of an eye opener for Dan who decided he'd heard enough and discretely crept out of the stable.

As Dan slunk away from the barn he thought about his boss and what a hypocrite he was, talking about his dead wife as though he was doing her a favour not kicking her out. He no more loved her than fly in the air. It was all an act, their loving, perfect family. Well, now it was over. He deserved to feel guilty. Dan began to wonder if there was any truth in some of the rumours he'd heard. Was his wife really worth a bit? And if she had an affair did Rhodes secretly want revenge. Of course he hadn't meant to kill his little girl as well. It beggared belief what the rich thought they could get away with. Dan shook his head, and wondered how Emily could think the sun shone out of the man's back side. Perhaps he should enlighten her. Next time he got a chance he'd pay her a little visit.

'Hello Dan?' Emily's voice sounded curt. 'I'm a bit busy at present.'

'Sorry for interrupting your work.' Dan tried to keep the sarcasm out of his voice and failed. He had seen Emily pegging washing on the line and strolled over. She looked at him all prim and tight-lipped.

'It's all so hectic at the moment.' Her voice softened.

'You're doing too much for Mr Rhodes.'

'I have to do all I can to help the poor man.' She sighed as though she had the weight of the world on her shoulders.

'But what about you?' Dan gritted his teeth as he tried to sound sympathetic. 'There's no point running yourself into the ground.'

'I suppose.' She looked as though she was battling to keep control.

He felt like smacking a bit of sense into her but instead said, 'why don't we go out somewhere, to cheer ourselves up?'

He watched her cheeks go red and her eyes widen with surprise before she answered.

'Are you asking me out on a date, Daniel Turner?'

'Why not?' He moved closer to her. 'Any reason why I shouldn't ask out an attractive lady like yourself?'

'Um... I have never ......'

'Never what?' Dan was smiling. He guessed Emily had never been out with a man before.

'Nothing,' she said. 'Where would we be going?'

'Wherever you like.' He looked thoughtful then added, 'but it would have to be evening as we are both so busy during the day.'

Emily nodded.

'We could just go for a walk.' Dan tried to make it sound as tame as possible. 'We could go to town, look at the shops and grab a drink somewhere.'

A smile spread over Emily's face and Dan realised what a beauty she was. 'Since we were getting on so well in the park the other week I thought....' As soon as the words were out of his mouth Dan realized his gaff. Memories of that terrible day would not get Emily on his side. 'Sorry, I shouldn't have mentioned that.' He tried to look contrite and changed the subject. 'Shall we say Friday night?'

'That would be lovely'. She was falling under his spell. 'But what should I wear?'

'You will look good in anything.' He flattered her.

'Oh you....'

He leaned across and gently placed a kiss on her cheek. 'I mean it,' he reassured her. Before she could be shocked or blush again he walked away saying, 'see you here Friday seven thirty.'

Friday night came and Dan stood waiting outside for Emily. She was already late and he could feel himself getting more and more annoyed. He heard her footfall before he saw her. It was the first time he had seen her without her uniform and she was quite a looker. Her floral dress had a nipped in waist which accentuated her superb body, her ample breasts strained against the cotton bodice. Her mass of red curly hair hung down her back but was tamed by a ribbon at the nape of her neck. She looked almost angelic. The knowledge that Mr Rhodes never saw her dressed up like this gave him a sense of satisfaction.

She looked coyly at him and said, 'I'm ready'.

So am I, thought Dan.

'Where are we off to?' she asked.

'Well I thought we could get a tram down to town, call in at the dance hall and see what's going on there. After that it'll be a cuppa and a bun in Mrs Fitzroy's café and home again. How does that sound?'

'A dance?' Emily's voice in the darkness sounded worried.

'Don't worry,' Dan soothed. 'I'll take care of you.'

He held her hand and guided her through the badly lit streets to the tram stop.
They sat in silence as they travelled. Dan thought he would have to treat this one a bit gently to start or she would bolt like a startled filly.

Once they got to town he attempted to take her hand again but she pulled away. 'We don't want people to think we are courting.'

He tried not to let his irritation show as they walked along the row of shops.

Emily loved looking at the shoes and a window full of hats had her gasping with pleasure. 'Oh, look at that dear little hat, Dan.'

'I'll say it's dear, cop a load of the price tag.'

He hurried her along and up the hill where the shops sold less attractive things like medicines for horses and corsets that looked like they'd been made at the ironmongers. Eventually they reached the church hall. Young couples were wondering in, hand in hand, the men delving in their pockets for the entrance fee of sixpence each. Once inside a stringed quartet was playing a lively tune to get everyone in the mood. Groups stood round the dance floor tapping their feet but everyone seemed too embarrassed to launch into a dance on their own.

After about half an hour, as if a secret signal had been relayed between groups, couples ventured onto the floor on mass. Within minutes it was crowded with people jostling against each other.

Dan finally had Emily in his hold. He had been longing to feel her body against his since he'd first laid eyes on her earlier that evening. They waltzed around bumping into people and the more crowded it became the closer Dan held her. He could smell the soapy cleanliness of her and feel the warmth of her skin through her dress as he pressed his hand to her back. The hand that held his was smooth but there were rough patches on her thumb and index finger that hinted at her occupation as housemaid. He murmured in her ear, asking if she was enjoying herself and breathed against her skin. At one point they were bumped and their bodies brushed against each other. The feel of her breasts against his chest was exciting, the soft mounds squashing against him. The gap between their bodies was maintained which was just as well as Dan could feel a sensation in the front of his pants that could prove embarrassing.

The heat that emanated from the dancing bodies was overpowering even with all the windows of the hall thrown open and the doors kept wide. Dan began to feel sweat dripping down his back and decided it was time to get Emily out of this oven.

'What's say we go outside for a breather?'

Emily nodded.

Much to Dan's annoyance, there were more people outside who had the same idea. He led Emily to the fringes of the group and gently eased her away into the darkness where the lights of the hall hadn't penetrated. He threw his jacket down on the cool grass and sat down next to it. Patting the jacket he said, 'come on Em, have a pew.' She sat down leaving a decent gap between them but didn't look very relaxed. Dan, being a dab hand at getting women in the mood, moved further away from her so she wouldn't feel threatened.

He leaned back on his hands and sighed. 'Look at that sky.'

'It's beautiful,' she said. 'I wish I knew all the constellations but to me it's just a mass of stars. I can't make head nor tail of it.'

Neither could Dan really but he did know one and it was always a good ploy to get closer to a woman.

'Well the easiest one to see is the saucepan. See those three stars in a row there.' He pointed vaguely at a spot in the sky.

'No, where?'

He edged closer to her.

'There.' he pointed again.

When no answer came, he knew she hadn't spotted it, which was what he intended.

'Look,' he leaned even nearer until their heads nearly touched and pointed directly at the stars in question. 'See those three in a row and the others going off like a handle.'

'Oh yes.'

'Well that's it, the saucepan.'

Emily seemed pleased and gave a little giggle. As she turned to face Dan he kissed her on the lips, long and lingering. Her hands pushed against his chest but his senses were so aroused he ignored her protests. He put his hand behind her head and pulled her to him when she tried to pull away. She thumped him hard in his chest and the shock made him lose his grip.

'Dan, what do you think you're doing?' She had begun to get to her feet.

He pulled her back down to the ground with a thud. 'You know you're enjoying it.'

She twisted from his grip and stood up. 'Take me home, now.' The light of laughter had gone from her eyes. She looked at him with distaste as though he was an insect.

'You don't mean that.' He tried to make light of her overreaction. 'Come on let's go back into the dance.'

'Just take me home, Dan.'

'Don't be silly,' he tried to calm things down. 'We're here to enjoy ourselves so come on.'

'I've not come out to be embarrassed.'

'Embarrassed?' Dan could feel himself getting angry. 'I bet if it was poor Mr Rhodes you wouldn't be embarrassed.'

'What are you insinuating Daniel Turner?'

'Well he's a rich single man now he's got his wife's money and you have the hots for him.'

'How dare you.' Emily's anger exploded in an onslaught of scathing words. 'He's a better man than you'll ever be and he doesn't need his wife's money.'

'Has he put your wages up or does he just pay you on the side to stick up for him? He must be giving you something to be such a loyal servant because that's all you are, a servant.'

The slap that hit his cheek made him stop his tirade and stare in amazement at Emily. She looked at him for a moment, as though she too was surprised at her assault, before turning her back on him and striding off.

He couldn't help calling after her. 'Ah, so you do have some backbone.' He let her walk away. She could find her own way home. With unsteady hands Dan lit a smoke and inhaled deeply. The words she had spoken buzzed round in his head. He was infuriated that she actually did prefer Rhodes to him but at least he had found out that Mrs Rhodes did have money and it had been in Rhodes interest to get rid of her.

Dan smiled as he walked back into the dance hall. With a bit of luck he may find himself another willing woman to spend his evening with. If not it didn't matter because after tomorrow he would have a bit of money himself. The Sydney papers would love to have this story of a rich businessman murdering his wife and child. Rhodes had motive and opportunity, even if it wasn't proven, the people of Sydney would judge for themselves. John Rhodes your days are numbered, he thought.

CHAPTER 10

John

The weather was humid and sticky as John sat beside his son's bed. The boy slept. He longed to stroke the child's face to sooth him and try to rid him of the frown that seemed permanently planted on his young forehead, but he was afraid his actions would wake him. If that happened he knew Thomas would curl up in a ball and cover his head with the blankets. John ran his fingers through his own blonde hair instead, an unconscious gesture that meant his hands were doing something instead of lying helplessly in his lap. He didn't seem to be able to sit still lately, always fidgeting, his hands always moving. A great depression surrounded him, isolating him from happiness and peace of mind. It felt as though his life had taken on the realms of the worst nightmare imaginable. He had lost his wife, daughter and mentally his son. Thomas was still there in the flesh but wanted nothing to do with him.

It had been weeks since the accident and Thomas had not responded to him at all. The only person who could get near him was Emily and even she had to coax him to do everything. The doctor's prognosis was not very optimistic. Evidently, sometimes after such a shock a patient's memory never returned. They blotted out that part of their lives and everything that went before.

John studied the contours of his son's face, the soft downy skin with freckles sprinkled across his nose. Angelic curls hung over his brow, which was smooth in sleep with no hint of the worry lines. What must it be like to lose your memory and not know anyone around you? He tried to imagine the fear and confusion that his son must feel and longed to hug him and tell him that everything would be all right. Thomas wasn't even aware that his mother and sister were dead, maybe that was a good thing.

A flash of lightning shone through the curtains and a few moments later a crack of thunder shattered the silence. John was startled out of his reverie at the same moment as Thomas was wakened by the storm. The room was dark even though dawn had passed an hour ago and the sun should have been filtering through the crack in the curtains. Thomas made a mewing noise like a lost puppy and without even thinking John went to him and held him tightly in his arms. The child didn't fight but clung tightly as the next crash of thunder trembled through the house.

John could feel how thin his son was through his nightshirt and wanted to protect him against all the terrible things in the world, but it was too late. He had already witnessed the worst, the death of a parent and sibling. Even though his mind had blacked out the incident, it was still in there, buried. Momentarily John hugged him until he was pushed away.

'Emily, I want Emily.' The boy's voice sounded as though he was about to cry.

'Alright son, I'll get her.'

Before he could get up the door burst open and the maid rushed into the room. It was as though she had been waiting outside and came when she heard her name but why would she be doing that? Practically pushing past him she went straight to Thomas.

She held him in her arms and shushed him, rocking him back and forth.

'The storm frightened him,' John said feeling helpless. Low rumblings could still be heard and rain drummed on the window.

'I realise that Mr Rhodes.' Emily looked at him and held the boy tighter as though to protect him.

'You'll smother him, Emily if you're not careful.' John said it almost as a joke but Emily scowled.

'I'm not likely to kill a child.' She said it quietly and at first John wasn't sure he heard her. Emily seemed in a foul mood. There was definitely something bothering her. The usual caring, smiling disposition that made her such a nice person had deserted her.

'Are you alright, Emily?'

'Fine, thank you,' she practically spat out the reply. 'Mrs Lovelock said to tell you your breakfast is ready.'

'Thank you, Emily.' He watched her momentarily as she turned her back on him, dismissing him and directed her attention to the boy.

On his way to the dining room he thought about Emily. It was so out of character for her to behave like that she was usually so obliging and friendly. He wondered what had upset her. She was the only person who seemed able to get through to Thomas. It would be disastrous if she were to leave.

John went to the huge dining room and sat at the table on his own. He should really take his meals on a tray, he thought. Mrs Lovelock kept preparing tempting meals for him but most of it was sent back to the kitchen, he had no appetite.

The newspaper was next to his place setting and he unfolded it to read the headlines before he ate his first mouthful. It was just as well he hadn't taken that first bite or he would have choked. Staring back at him was a head and shoulders photograph of himself taken a few years ago.

'Where the hell did they get that from?' His voice was loud in the empty room. The greyness of the print made him look drab and lifeless with a fixed smile plastered to his lips. The headlines jumped out at him and he could feel himself tense with anger. His eyes scanned the print, it seemed he was to blame for the death of his wife and child. It was not an accident, according to the author of this drivel. The article went on about "inside knowledge from a reliable source".

As his anger rose he banged his hand down on the table. 'I'll sue them for this, this is outrageous.' He stood up and began pacing the room. 'Who is responsible for this, who decided to feather their nest at the expense of my reputation?' As he ranted and raved, a knock sounded at the door.

'Come in,' he practically shouted at the unsuspecting caller. The door opened gingerly and Daniel walked in.

'Mornin', sir.' Daniel stood some way from John. 'Just wondering what time you want me to take you to town this morning, but maybe this isn't a good time.'

'Oh, Daniel, have you seen this morning's paper?'

'No sir, can't say as I have.'

'Well look at that.' John thumped the paper again, smacking the photograph square on the nose. 'It's disgusting, how can they spread such lies about perfectly innocent people?'

Daniel moved forward and glanced at the newspaper but the big black words made no sense to him. He squinted at the print and John realized he couldn't read.

Without being patronizing John explained the outline of the story interspersed with swearing and exasperated shaking of his head. 'It says here that some insider gave them all this information but if it's someone who works for me, they won't be for much longer.'

'It's disgusting sir, people spreading rumours like that.' There was silence for a few moments before Daniel went on. 'Do you want me to keep me ear to the ground and see if I can find out who's been saying these things, sir?'

John dragged his eyes from the newspaper and looked at the coachman. He didn't like to spy on his staff but if this sort of thing was going to happen maybe it would be a good idea to have his own person on the inside.

'Yes, perhaps we should try to find out who told them this load of nonsense.'

'Right, sir.' Daniel replaced his hat and began to back out of the room. As he got to the door he asked, 'will you be going to store today, sir?'

'Of course, usual time.'

John could still feel the anger seething through him. His muscles felt tense and his head was throbbing, he tried to calm himself. His uneaten breakfast lay in front of him, the egg congealing in the fat, the steak now like leather and the tomatoes shriveled to inedible mulch.

Pushing the food away he rose and left the room. The solace of his study was more comforting. Its smell of leather and polish reminded him of the army and a time in his life when he had no worries or problems. But those times would never return. He went to the drinks tray and poured himself a stiff brandy. It was a bit early in the morning for a drink but he needed something to get through the day.

Sitting in a comfortable chair he nursed his drink and wondered if he had done the right thing letting Daniel into his confidence. There was something about the coachman that made John feel as though he could trust him. It might have been the fact that he was there to help on the day of the accident or that he seemed a quiet discreet man. Not that John really knew him, he'd only worked here a few months. He'd always been in the background and apart from arranging times of trips and the occasional comment about the weather when they were driving along, he'd never had much to do with him.

There were more important things to think about than the character of his coachman. He needed to go to work and sort out a few things. Since the accident he hadn't set foot in the place but Simms his manager seemed to have everything in hand.

How could he face his staff with this plastered all over the papers? He didn't have anything to hide, it was a boating accident. He knew that and felt sure most people wouldn't believe all this rubbish in the paper but if Emily's reaction was anything to go by things could get very nasty. John gulped down the brandy and was about to pour another but thought better of it. Speaking to his employees smelling of alcohol would not help his cause.

During the long trip to the city John was immersed in paperwork. He read through minutes of meetings that had transpired in his absence and lists of new employees and people who had left. He had a quick look at the overall accounts and was surprised to see the shop was still expanding even without him. Their turnover was better than ever. Some of the new ranges were exciting and the advertisements eye catching.

Once the coach reached the city, the streets were clogged with every imaginable piece of transport. Greetby and Co was an imposing department store, right next to the sandstone edifice that was the General Post Office.

It wasn't really John's business it belonged to his wife's family. It had been in their family since the 1850's, starting as a smaller establishment that boasted new and exciting importations. It had all been Alfred Greetby's brainchild, a great uncle of Beatty's. The only problem was that there was no male descendant to take over the reins. Great Uncle had always had a soft spot for Beatty and when she got married to John he asked if the new bridegroom would like to come into the family business.

In those days, John was still in the army and looking for a way out, without losing face with his father, so he accepted the offer. He had worked closely with Alfred and learned the business quickly becoming head of imports in his late twenties. It had meant traveling to exotic places and leaving Beatty at home.

Twelve months ago Uncle Alfred had died and in his will left the running of Greetby & Co solely to John. It was a big responsibility for someone who was only thirty five but John knew he could do the job. Well, he could before the accident. He wasn't so sure now.

John always felt a sense of satisfaction when he entered the building. It was the epitome of affluence, with merchandise arranged in tasteful displays. He fingered the cloth of a man's suit as he passed and straightened a scarf on a dummy's shoulders. The sing song voices of the female shop assistants wishing him good morning as he passed usually had him tipping the brim of his hat.

But today there were no welcoming voices. In his office his secretary was waiting for him. Miss Burrows had only been working for him for six months but her efficiency was a credit to her. He had never had any reason to reprimand her and she always looked immaculately dressed. Granted she was an older woman but John loved the way she almost mothered him without realizing she was doing it.

'Good morning, sir.' A ghost of a smile crossed her lips. John immediately felt the awkwardness between them.

'Morning Miss Burrows.' She looked at her feet as he spoke to her and a flush ran up her face. 'Is everything alright?'

'Yes, sir, I'll just get your coffee.'

John sat at his desk and swiveled his chair so he looked out of the huge corner window down George Street. People bustled back and forth along the pavement and John was jealous of them, jealous of their ordinary lives. He craved an existence where he was a nobody. He longed to escape prying eyes, to run away from his life, somewhere where malicious tongues didn't wag about him.

A knock on the door made him turn back into the room. 'Come in'.

Samuel Simms walked over and shook hands with his employer. 'Nice to have you back sir.'

John sighed with relief that his manager hadn't judged him like everyone else. The coffee arrived and the two men settled down to discuss business. Thankfully no mention was made of the newspaper article.

After two hours Samuel glanced at his watch and cursed. 'Oh God, I'll have to get going I've got some girls to interview.'

'Can't someone else do it?'

'Normally it would be Mrs Hawkins but she's off sick and there's no one else,' Samuel rose from the chair, 'unless you want to do it?'

'It could be amusing. What's the job?'

'Gloves.'

At least the applicants would be complete strangers, John thought, and if they look down their noses at me they won't get the job. It felt like a bit of revenge for all he had endured.

'Right, Samuel, I'll do your interviews if you get the monthly returns out for me.'

'You're on.' A smile lit up Samuel's face as he added, 'can you remember how to pick a good worker?'

John gave a wry smile at the impudence of his second in command. 'Tell Miss Burrows to bring them up here, will you Samuel.'

'Right sir.'

John couldn't remember the last time he interviewed anyone for a job. What did one look for in a new employee? Looks, brains, good time keeping or maybe all three. How hard could it be to choose someone to sell gloves?

Within ten minutes there was a knock on the door and Miss Burrows put her head round.

'Show the first one in, please.' As an after thought he asked, 'how many are there?'

'Only ten Mr Rhodes.'

John groaned inwardly. He could really do without this, what was he thinking, getting involved in job applications when he had so much work to do.

The first lady was neat, young and prim but not very approachable. Once John got the hang of putting himself in his customer's shoes he realized what he wanted in his sales staff. Unfortunately the ladies that passed before him all made him feel awkward and uncomfortable. He supposed they all had their merits but overall they were a bit serious and seemed to be lacking in something. John wasn't sure what. Once again paranoid feelings assailed him. Maybe it was because they were talking to a murderer. By the tenth candidate he was feeling bored by the whole thing and had no idea who he was going to choose. He could put their names in a hat and just pick one.

When the last interviewee walked into the office John studied her. She was completely the opposite of the women he had already seen. She was bright and smiling. Her hair was tied up but wisps had escaped and fell gently over her face. A few wrinkles appeared around her eyes when she smiled but her skin was brushed with a light brown glow from the sun. She made John feel relaxed right from the start and he knew his customers would feel the same way.

'Good morning, Mr Rhodes.' Her voice was steady with no hint of nerves and she looked him directly in the eye.

'Good morning,' he answered. He got his notepad and pen ready and asked, 'And you are?'

'Constance Lang.' She held out her gloved hand to shake his.

John gently shook it, feeling more relaxed in this woman's company than he expected.

'How do you do Constance?'

Her smile lit up her face. They chatted about the job for a short while until John realized he was talking for talking sake, just to keep her in the room a little longer.

Finally he said, 'Well Constance, when do you want to start?'

The look of delight on her face made John smile.

'Tomorrow if you like?'

'Shall we say Monday, eight o'clock sharp?'

'Yes, Mr Rhodes, I'll be here.'

John was smiling when he said, 'I hope you enjoy working for Greetby and Co.'

As she gathered up her skirt and handbag she said, 'I'm sure I will.' She stood and turned to walk away but as an after thought faced him again and said, 'I'm so sorry to hear about your wife and daughter.' A genuine look of concern crossed her face. She slowly walked towards the door.

'Thank you,' John spoke to her retreating back.

John didn't stay at work much after one o'clock. He felt fidgety and couldn't concentrate and the only member of staff that spoke to him without looking embarrassed was Samuel.

The trip home was depressing. For the first time he noticed mothers and their children, the protective holding of a young hand, the pride of pushing a pram and the happiness that being part of a family brings. He no longer belonged to a family group, no longer the breadwinner to his wife and children. There was only Thomas now. His jaw began to ache from gritting his teeth as he tried to keep his emotions under control. He felt if he let his jaw slacken a great sob of self pity would blurt out.

Finally he got to the sanctuary of his own home. His head was throbbing and his hands were shaking. John went immediately to his study before he even took his coat off. He needed to be on his own. He threw his jacket and silk scarf over a chair and without stopping went to the drinks cabinet. Filling his glass with neat whisky he slumped down in his chair.

His mind darted from one depressing topic to another and dwelled on the utter uselessness of his life. Refilling his glass again and bringing the whisky bottle with him he flopped back in his chair and let the alcohol overwhelm his senses. His eyes began to droop and his mouth became slack as the bottle emptied. It slipped from his hand and spilled onto the carpet but he didn't care. It was only a carpet and besides he didn't have the energy to mop it up. He smiled to himself, it would make his office smell nice. It would be his alcoholic den, no women would come in, they would turn their noses up and walk out. Beattie would be furious that he was such a soak. He chuckled to himself, it was about time he did what he wanted. All those years he had pandered to her moods and tantrums, trying to keep everything sweet, well not any more. If he wanted whisky on his study floor he would have it.

The effort of keeping his eyes open became too much. The room spun when he closed them but it might be nice to spin, like he was on a merry-go-round, a ride at the fair, swirling round, having fun, closing his eyes and feeling the wind in his hair, like he did as a child. His body relaxed and his breathing became heavy as sleep overwhelmed him.

His mind opened on a beautiful scene. Willow trees were dipping their leaves into the river. The sun filtered through the branches and glistened on the water. He leaned back in the boat, stretched his legs out and let his hand dip in the water. Thomas sat on the seat opposite him, smiling and chattering about something but John wasn't listening. Anna sat on the same seat as her brother with her back to John. She was talking to Beatty. John smiled at the picture of him and Beattie lazing back, relaxing and the two children in the centre of the boat chattering away at odds with each other. They were in the middle of the river, probably a bit to far from the shore but it was as though they were in their own little world. No one came near them and he let the boat drift dreamily along. John's lids felt heavy with the heat and laziness of the day. The first slight knock on the hull of the boat made him open his eyes and look around to make sure they hadn't hit anything. He looked across at the shore, which was now further away. They'd better get back, if they went too far out they would be in the way of the ferry boat and then they would really be in trouble.

As John reached for the oars the boat was bashed with such force it tilted to one side. Anna slid off the seat and splashed into the water with Thomas right behind her. As if in slow motion, John stood up and tried to rush to the middle of the boat. Beattie was screaming and shouting as she also scrambled to save her children. The boat was destabilized further and John couldn't stop himself from falling in as well. He grabbed for the side of the boat and pulled it so hard Beattie overbalanced and went in. It was like a comedy act with bodies falling in the water and everyone would bob to the surface in a moment and laugh at their dunking.

But no heads came up. John clung to the boat too scared to move since he couldn't swim and knew he would go straight to the bottom if he let go. Where were they? He put his face into the water and tried to see them but it was a pink mire of churning, churning what? A black shape was thrashing about, his mind couldn't lock onto what it was. He had to help them. If he died in the process so be it. He pushed himself away from the boat and floundered about not getting any nearer to them. He couldn't see clearly, he pulled with his hands through the water in front of his face trying to clear his vision but he was sinking. The weight of his wet shoes and trousers was dragging him down and his family was going further and further away from him. He tried to scream at them but his mouth filled with water and gushed down into his lungs. His body reacted of its own accord, he went limp and a white curtain closed over his eyes and then blackness.

'No, no, no, help me, help me,' He woke himself screaming. His eyes flew open and his heart was pounding. His hands were trembling and he was covered in a film of sweat. It was the same nightmare. It had haunted him since the accident but this was the first time he realized what he was seeing under the water. His mind didn't want to accept what had happened to his Anna and Beattie. He put his head in his hands and wept. Great sobs wracked his body and his tears dripped between his fingers. It was too horrible to contemplate.

Emily

Emily could hear the yelling when she got to the bottom of the stairs. It was coming from the study. She hovered at the door momentarily wondering whether to go in or run for Mrs Lovelock. It wasn't really her place to barge into the master's study, she might get into all sorts of trouble. But the words "help me, help me," had galvanized her into action. She rushed into the room and closed the door immediately behind her when she saw Mr Rhodes.

For a moment she was dumb struck by the sight of him. He had his head in his hands and was crying, well not really crying, sobbing as though he would never stop. He hadn't noticed her standing at the door and she felt as though she was intruding on his private moment. She stood motionless for a few moments waiting for him to compose himself but he didn't seem able to. It was as though a tap had been turned on and a gush of emotions poured out of him. She moved towards him and at first he still didn't know she was there.

When she was practically next to him he looked up. 'Oh Emily, this can't be happening,' his voice trembled with emotion.

She knelt down beside him and put her arm round his shoulder. She really should apologise for the way she had spoken to him earlier, practically accusing him of killing his own child. When she saw him in this depressed state she was shocked at the change in him. From a mild mannered, kind man to a wreck of human suffering, all within a few short weeks. He turned his head to speak and she was not ready for the alcoholic fumes that assailed her nostrils. She screwed her nose up and pulled away from him.

'It was a shark,' he blurted out.

Emily didn't know what he was talking about but leaned over and picked up the empty whisky bottle from the floor.

'I think you've had a bit too much to drink, Mr Rhodes.' There was disappointment in her voice.

'Forget about that, it was in my dream again.' He looked pleadingly at her. 'It was a shark that got Anna and Beattie.'

Emily retreated to the door. He was drunk and confused and she couldn't believe a word he said. For a brief moment she felt sorry for him but this story of a shark seemed very convenient after the article in the newspaper.

'I'll go and get you a nice cup of tea, Mr Rhodes, it may help you …erm…feel better.' She couldn't say sober up.

'I don't want any tea I just want my wife and daughter back.'

He was almost ranting like a spoiled child and Emily was at a loss what to do. She thought of telling Mrs Lovelock about this convenient revelation but thought better of it. There was enough plastered all over the newspaper about him without her adding to it. Besides she didn't really know what to believe.

As Emily waited for the kettle to boil she wondered what she should do? She couldn't very well ignore the state he was in but it wasn't really her place to interfere. She couldn't remember Mr Rhodes ever getting drunk before. It wasn't in his nature, well the nature she knew anyway. Perhaps there was a side to him that she didn't know. Had she been taken in by the impression of the perfect husband and father when there was a violent and uncontrollable side to him that she hadn't seen? Could what the papers say be true? Her mind went back to the day of the picnic. No, it was Mr Rhodes who didn't want to go in the boat, but his good nature gave into his wife's wishes. She remembered how happy he had been before they went and how excited the children were, but everything had changed and the niceties of the day were obliterated by tragedy.

'Penny for 'em.'

Mrs Lovelock interrupted her train of thought as she emerged from the pantry. Emily smiled half-heartedly at her. She made the tea in silence and took it back to Mr Rhodes. As she got to the end of the corridor she stopped. Some strange men were entering the study. Who had let them in, Emily wondered? One of them was wearing a policeman's uniform and the other wore a suit and looked very official. Their expressions were stern, not at all friendly. She approached the closed door with trepidation. She knocked and went in pretending she didn't know there were guests.

'Oh, sorry sir,' she apologized when she entered. She put the tea tray down on the desk. The two gentlemen sat looking intently at Mr Rhodes. He looked dreadful, his hair was untidy, his eyes were red rimmed and his suit was crumpled with his necktie shoved at an odd angle round his neck.

Emily decided he needed some time to get himself together and asked, 'would you like me to get the gentlemen a cup of tea, sir?' If they were drinking tea, Emily thought, they wouldn't be asking questions.

'Yes, please Emily.'

She rushed back to the kitchen where Mrs Lovelock helped her arrange an afternoon tea tray with cups, teapot, milk jug, sugar bowl, hot water, a plate of scones and chunks of fruit cake.

'This should keep them busy,' Emily muttered to herself as she lugged the tray back to the study.

Mr Rhodes had gained some of his composure by the time she returned and she hoped the food and drink would help him sober up. Closing the door, she stood listening, trying to make out some of the conversation. She heard Mr Rhodes raise his voice and say, 'so what exactly are you accusing me of?'

'We're not accusing you of anything, Mr Rhodes. We just need to clarify a few things.' The voices reverted back to low murmurings and Emily couldn't make out what was being said.

There was nothing she could do for him, he had to sort it out himself. Feeling upset she sought solace in the nursery. Thomas was in the room on his own which made Emily feel guilty. She had been running around taking care of Mr Rhodes when the real victim was here. He was quite happy to be on his own and played with the toys as though they were all new to him. But recently some of his games turned quite destructive and he would try to break whatever he was playing with. It was as though he was taking out his pent up anger on his toys.

She sat quietly next to him. He was drawing a picture, leaning on the big wooden table. Emily looked at his work ready to praise him but the page was filled with black crayon scrawl that didn't resemble anything.

'What's that, Tom?'

'It's blackness.' He put the crayon down and leaned his head on Emily's shoulder. She stroked his face for a few moments feeling terribly sorry for him. She knew what it was like to lose a parent.

When Emily was ten her father committed suicide. Being the eldest of six children she was the one who had to help her mother pick up the pieces of her life. Before that they had lived in various parts of New South Wales, her father always moving on to find work. They only stayed in one place a year or two and then off they would go again. It meant Emily was always making new friends. Fortunately she wasn't shy and was clever enough to be able to learn, even with all the upheaval. She could still remember being hungry at times and living in houses that were practically shacks but there was lots of love in her family. Her mother and father adored each other, that was why it was such a shock when her father did what he did. He left a note apologizing and saying they would be better off without him, he had dragged them down to an existence of animals and he was sorry. Emily never forgave him for leaving them.

Almost immediately they had moved back to Sydney to her Gran's house. The plan was that Gran would look after the children while Emily's mother worked but in reality Gran wasn't well enough. So when Emily was ten she was looking after her brothers, sisters and her Gran. They had a roof over their heads and food on the table.

In fact Gran's house wasn't far from where she now worked and she slipped home to see the kids every chance she got. The baby, Mary, was now nine and very grown up for her age. Gran didn't go out much and loved to hear all the gossip from the "big house" as she called it. She'll be agog with the latest news Emily thought and smiled to herself.

At that tragic time in her life Emily had been too busy looking after her family to mourn her father. It was completely different for Thomas, there's just him, on his own. Well, he has his father, but he doesn't seem to be much use.

She patted his arm as a gesture of reassurance and said, 'I nearly forgot.' Thomas looked at her. 'I've got a new story to read to you.' It was one she had found downstairs in the library and hoped Thomas would like it. She would have to read it to him, it might take his mind off things. 'It's called "Black Beauty" by Anna Sewell.'

'It's not a girl's story is it?'

'No, it's about a horse.' He looked more interested and Emily fetched the book. She made herself comfortable in the rocking chair and Thomas curled up on the shabby chaise lounge. He pulled the patchwork rug around himself and snuggled down. They looked the epitome of nursery harmony, Emily thought, but looks could be deceptive.

Emily read to him for half an hour in which time he remained completely engrossed in the story. When he began to get fidgety she decided they'd had enough.

'Is it time for milk and biscuits now Tom?' He nodded half-heartedly. 'Do you want to come to the kitchen with me while I get them?'

He shook his head. 'I'll stay here and play with my soldiers.' The lead soldiers were Thomas' favourite toys.

Emily nodded and left the room. On her way downstairs, she thought about Tom. She'd begun to call him by the shortened version of his name, it sounded less formal. Once the governess left Emily had become quite close to him. The woman seemed to lose interest when there was just Tom. It was a relief when she went.

Emily decided she needed to do something to make life more appealing for Tom. There didn't seem to be anyone else who was interested in his future. She needed to get his brain focused on something new and exciting.

By the time Emily got back to the nursery she had a plan of action whizzing through her head. Tom couldn't be left to stagnate like a mosquito infested swamp, he needed stimulation to get his brain thinking and perhaps his memory would come back. It would be back to lessons. The only problem was that Emily hadn't had much schooling and didn't consider herself to be clever. But she could read, write and add and subtract basic numbers. So it would be a learning process for her too.

That evening, once she got Thomas tucked in bed she wandered down to the library and began looking for books that could help in her quest for knowledge. She found a shelf full of encyclopedias. Each book seemed to be split up into sections through the alphabet. The best idea was to start at the beginning, she thought and reaching up pulled down the book marked "A – C" and was amazed at the weight and size of it.

Emily took it to the table and began to glance through it. The information and pictures crammed in the book were enthralling, she had never seen anything like it. She nodded to herself and clutching the heavy volume took it upstairs to her room.

The subjects that unfolded in front of her were of things she could never have dreamed of. There were animals that looked very peculiar and took some pronouncing like the "Armadillo". She was fascinated by historical events that happened on the other side of the world, battles and wars in places like Agincourt and the Armada. She knew Tom would love anything to do with soldiers and fighting. It was much more interesting than the things she learnt at school, that Burke and Wills stuff, and Captain Cook and the Endeavour was all a bit boring. English history happened so long ago, before Australian was even discovered.

There was so much information. She had to be blinkered and read what she thought would interest Tom. Her eyes darted from page to page then she would stop at something that was quite unbelievable and revel in the facts.

The following morning Emily woke, sitting up in her bed with the book still opened on her lap. She had no idea what time she fell asleep but was eager to start her new teaching regime. Once out of bed she splashed cold water over her face and eyes from the jug on the chest of drawers. The cool water woke her up and the lanolin soap felt smooth between her hands. Quickly Emily put on her drawers and camisole followed by her heavy, black dress. She brushed her frizzy mass of hair and gathered it up with combs and pins. Looking at herself in the mirror she decided she already looked more intelligent with all this new knowledge floating around in her head.

First she must convince Mr Rhodes that what she had planned would be the right thing for Tom. She could have just gone ahead with her idea but she needed access to the library and probably a new writing slate, chalk, paper and pencils. Any encouragement his father could give might help Thomas remember his past.

It was still quite early when Emily went down the main staircase. The grandfather clock was just chiming six, there was plenty of time to have breakfast and do a few chores before she spoke to Mr Rhodes. As Emily was on her way to the kitchen she noticed a suitcase next to the front door. Who was going away? Was it some of the governess' things that she had to collect. The suitcase with its shiny brass clasps and rich brown pungent leather looked too expensive. A traveling cloak hung on a hook above it and could only belong to Mr Rhodes. Emily frowned as she wondered where he could be going. As she stood contemplating the suitcase Mr Rhodes came out of the study. He faltered momentarily when he saw her.

'Ah, Emily.' He busied himself doing up his jacket and placing his trilby hat on his head, all the time averting eye contact with her.

Emily was too curious to keep silent, 'Is everything alright, Mr Rhodes?'

She suddenly remembered the men that were questioning him yesterday and gasped. She had been so consumed with plans for Thomas she had not even thought about the outcome of that meeting. Perhaps Mr Rhodes had to report to the police station or go to gaol even. Was that how things were done? She had no idea.

'Everything is fine Emily.' He reached past her to get his cloak and she got the distinct whiff of alcohol. He still wouldn't look at her.

Emily was worried about where he was going but needed to address the issue of Thomas' education before he left. She didn't know how long he would be away.

'Mr Rhodes, there was something I wanted to discuss with you.'

'Well, as you can see I'm going away.' His voice sounded disinterested.

Emily didn't feel it was her place to ask where he was going but instead said, 'It's about Thomas, sir.'

His eyes suddenly met hers. For a moment his guarded expression slipped away and revealed the fear and torment in his eyes. His expression softened further and his whole face seemed to droop. Wrinkles had appeared round his eyes that Emily couldn't remember being there before. His cheeks were sunken and he appeared gaunt and pale. His hair needed cutting and looked lifeless and dull. Emily had an overpowering urge to put her arms round him, to hug him to her, like she did Thomas and tell him that everything would be all right. But he was the master and she was the maid.

'Take care of him,' he mumbled as he bent down and picked up his suitcase, his body moving stiffly as though he was forcing himself to do it.

'When will you be back?' Emily gently touched his arm and he hesitated.

He looked at her and slowly shook his head. A nerve twitched on the side of his face as he gritted his teeth together striving to control his emotions. A moment later he was gone, the front door closed behind him and clicked with finality into place.

Emily stood, unsure what to do. Mr Rhodes couldn't just leave like that. He was in charge, he was the master, what would they do without him? How would the house run if he didn't pay the bills and the wages?

Stirring herself Emily went into the study to look for something that would give her a clue as to Mr Rhodes' intentions. In the middle of the green leather inlay on the big desk was a white envelope. It was addressed to Thomas in Mr Rhodes' large scrawling hand. Emily picked up the envelope and put it in the pocket of her skirt. She had a feeling it was a letter that would not help Tom's recovery or stop tongues from wagging. It was better in her safe keeping until she decided what to do.

CHAPTER 11

Dan

The house was in an uproar once it became common knowledge that Mr Rhodes had left without telling anyone where he was going or for how long. Emily had seen him leaving but said she assumed he was just going away for a day or two. A few days later Samuel Simms came to the house to gain information as to his boss's whereabouts, at the same time trying to keep it quiet before the authorities or the press got wind of his disappearance.

Dan watched all the comings and goings with a certain amount of curiosity and also relief that the man who was a threat to his relationship with Emily had left. He had achieved his goal without too much effort and without anyone realising it was he who went to the papers. As far as everyone was concerned he was still the loyal servant.

In his present mood of optimism, Dan enquired if Mr Simms would like him to scout around and find out where Mr Rhodes had disappeared to. Of course he made it sound as if he genuinely cared what happened to his boss.

'There couldn't be too many well dressed gents about early in a morning,' he remarked to Mr Simms, smiling at his own powers of deduction.

Mr Simms nodded his agreement. 'Only make enquiries discreetly,' he said. There's been enough gossip about him lately without adding to it.' His abrupt manner made Dan feel annoyed.

'Um,' Dan cleared his throat, 'not the easiest thing in the world to do. Folks round here can be real sticky beaks.'

'For goodness sake Turner use your loaf.'

Dan was rapidly going off Mr Simms, who seemed to think he could speak to him like he was dirt on his shoe.

To top it off he handed him a pound note saying, 'that should cover your expenses.' It was practically a brush off. He wasn't happy about the situation but decided to play at the pretence of finding Mr Rhodes.

The obvious place to start was the local railway station. The stationmaster was a busy body and a chatterbox. When asked, he did remember Mr Rhodes because it was so early and he was done up like a dog's dinner in all his fancy clothes. There weren't many posh folk travelling at that time of the morning, mostly workmen and shop girls. He also recognised his photo from the newspaper. He remembered that Mr Rhodes bought a single ticket to the city and asked about travelling on to Parkes. He said he had some business there and was staying for a few days, hence the suitcase. The stationmaster's opinion was that it was all a bit suspect, him going off like that after he drowned his wife.

Dan sensed the railway worker was ready for a good chin wag but he managed to dodge his verbal diarrhoea and get away on the next train bound for the city.

The train ride was pleasant enough, Dan had only been on a train once or twice before and found the experience quite entertaining. He could look at the slim ankles of the young women and even winked at one. To his delight she blushed and looked the other way. Of course she couldn't help peeping at him, trying not to let him see her ogling his good looks. His curly hair was probably a mess but he knew women liked the rugged look. They loved a bit of rough.

His father used to always say that and regularly gave his mother a back hander. Men weren't supposed to be mamby pamby like Rhodes, they had to stand up for themselves and let women know who was boss and usually they came back for more.

Dan thought back to his childhood of beatings, hiding under the house with the spiders and roaming wild, away from his drunken father. His sister got pregnant and no one knew who the father was, but Dan had his suspicions. Poor Gert had never really recovered when she had to give it up for adoption. She got pneumonia and died soon after. He shook his head as he gazed out the window. Well, his tough childhood hadn't done him any harm, but he did need to find himself a woman and settle down and have a few kids. But things seemed to happen, he always got the blame and then he had to move on.

The view from the window brought him back to the present. The houses shouldered nearer and nearer to each other the closer they got to the big smoke. It was as though the builders hadn't realised there was plenty of land. They'd squashed everything together, then finally got to grips with the enormity of Australia and relaxed into the placing of houses on bigger plots. It was all very interesting looking down into people's back yards, some neat and tidy and others full of rubbish and junk, which showed the types of people who lived inside, Dan thought.

He was beginning to feel like a bit of an authority on human nature. Recently Mr Rhodes had confided in him and then there were the blokes at the pub, banging on about the rich and famous and all their foibles and of course Emily, the delightful, delectable Emily. He would still like to get into her good books and her knickers. A smirk crossed his face at the thought. Good job people can't read my mind, he thought as he looked around at his fellow travellers. That interested female was still glancing at him every now and then. Women, they made Dan laugh. One minute they were all coy and the next they were leading a poor bloke on.

The train finally jerked to a stop and let out a long hiss of steam that jolted him from his reverie. He looked around, people began to rise from their seats, as they pulled into Central Station. Passengers poured from the train and streamed down the platform to the exit gates. Dan followed the tide of people and ducked through the gate as the ticket collector momentarily turned away.

Dan was not convinced that Mr Rhodes had gone to Parkes. He had an idea that the information he had given the stationmaster at Burwood was a bum steer to get people off his scent. What earthly reason would anyone have for going to that place out the back of beyond, Dan wondered? He sauntered across to a ticket window, the one that had the smallest queue and began chatting with those around him.

'A mate of mine's gone off up country and I think he may have gotten on the wrong train.' He spoke to no one in particular.

'How's that then?' The man in front asked.

'He's new to this country and gets a bit confused'

'Eye tie, is he? Geez, you look a bit like one yourself.'

'No mate, I'm not from Italy, true blue Aussie, that's me.'

'Yeah? So what about this mate of yours?'

'Well he got here early this morning and got on the first train he saw.'

'That'll be the one to the back o'Bourke. Bit of a silly bugger, wasn't he?'

'Yeah, well as I say, he's new to the area.' Dan scratched his head. 'Back o'Bourke you say, are you pullin' my leg mate?'

A smirk appeared on the strangers face. 'Maybe, maybe not.'

Dan stood in the queue, feeling peeved with the smart arse in front of him. When he got to the counter he leaned against the metal grille. 'What time was the first train out of here this morning?' he asked.

'Ah, that'll be the eight o'clock to Bourke stopping at Newcastle, Tamworth and a few other places.' The man seemed to know his trains.

'Can you remember a posh looking bloke buying a ticket on that train?' Dan felt more annoyed that the fella in the queue had been right. This was like finding a flea on a dog.

The ticket seller leaned forward as though he didn't want everyone else to hear. 'As a matter of fact I do.' He cleared his throat and looked around for effect before continuing. 'It was a bit strange really. He didn't seem to know where he was going, he couldn't decide, can you imagine that, bit odd if you ask me. Anyway, said he'd go to the end of the line.'

'So that'd be Bourke then would it?'

'You got it, mate.'

Dan walked away undecided what to do next. There was no way he was going to Bourke, his pound for expenses would never get him there and who would want to go there anyway. It was a joke, "the back o'Bourke" meant anywhere in the interior that was so far out no one knew where it was. Nobody actually went there. He'd have a stroll and decide what to say to Mr bloody Simms.

Since he was in the city, Dan decided to have a look around.

He strolled down the long ramp from the station and looked over a park on one side and a road with horse and carts rushing along on the other. One or two of the new motor carriages were puttering along and Dan leaned on the rail and watched. He shook his head at the silliness of the human race. Fancy anyone thinking that those things would ever replace the horse and cart.

Building workers were scurrying up and down the ramp with materials for the new clock tower that was being built at the station. Looked like a mammoth undertaking to Dan, great slabs of stone were piled in readiness for use and he had heard that the clock face was going to be huge. So far it was pretty impressive and it was only half built.

Dan was drawn into the hustle and bustle of the metropolis. Street after street of shops and businesses had Dan's eyes darting from window to window. Men with bowler hats walked briskly along the pavement, satchels clung under their arms, their expressions grave, the success or demise of some business their sole thought. Burly men rolled barrels down ramps into the cellars of public houses. Dray horses munched on bags of chaff hanging round their necks while they stood with their cart waiting for their next delivery.

The sights and sounds were fascinating to Dan. He walked and walked and after a while realised he was near to the store that Mr Rhodes owned. Of course he'd been there before as a coach driver but had never had a chance to walk around this hallowed place, but now he had an excuse, he was looking for Mr Rhodes. He strolled about as though he was going to buy something.

He swore under his breath at the prices and muttered to himself, 'Now I know how he got rich.'

A voice in his ear startled him. 'Can I help you sir?'

Dan turned abruptly and came face to face a very attractive woman. And woman she really was, a bit older, not the young giggly floosies that Dan usually went for, the easy catches that were flattered with any old flannel he told them. This was a mature, smartly dressed lady with her blonde hair sleekly pinned up to show her long elegant neck. Her flawless skin looked tanned and healthy and even the lines in the corners of her eyes didn't detract from her good looks.

'Ah, um…,' Dan could feel the flush coming to his cheeks, he hadn't been tongue tied in years. What could he say, he was just having a nose? He quickly looked around to see what department he was in. There were gloves everywhere and his quick brain seized on a fictitious reason for him being there. 'Yes,' he lied. 'I'm looking for a pair of gloves for my sister. It's her birthday next week and I thought I would surprise her.'

She smiled at him, and he revelled in the role of doting brother. 'What sort would you pick?' he asked trying to sound helpless.

'Well, sir, that depends on her taste and what she will be wanting them for.'

'Oh.' Dan's confidence ebbed.

She went on, 'But I imagine a brother like you would want her to have a piece of frippery, something pretty and yet serviceable.'

Dan looked at her and nodded his head. He noticed a faint accent in the way she spoke.

'Where're you from?' He was curious to know more about her.

'Oh,' her face brightened. 'I didn't realise I still had my Lancashire lilt'.

'Not much of one, but it's still there.'

'It's years since I left England.'

She laid out lacy gloves and changed the subject. 'Do you know what size she takes?'

Looking down at the gloves Dan noticed her hands. The nails were short and the knuckles red, she had working hands. Even more interesting, Dan thought. She saw him looking and put her hands behind her back. 'Size, sir?' she prompted.

'Erm,' he looked at the gloves while he thought. 'Well, it's her sixteenth birthday and she comes up to here on me.' He put his hand to his shoulder.

'What style would you like, sir?'

'You choose.' He treated her to one of his winning smiles and said, 'I'm sure you'd have a better idea of what a young girl would want than I have.' He tried to sound like an innocent, unsure of the wiles of women.

She separated a pair of gloves from the others and laid them on some tissue paper. Suddenly Dan realized what the next step was. She was about to wrap them and he had no money to pay for them. 'I'm certain she will love this pair, sir,' she said as she began to tuck the tissue paper around them.

'Actually, I'm not sure gloves are what she really wants.' He sounded pathetic he knew, but he couldn't let her know he had no money. 'I'd better check and let you know.'

'Of course sir.' Her professional mask never altered.

He edged away from her, reluctant to end this brief encounter. 'I'll find out.' He winked as he walked off. 'Be seeing you.'

She immediately began attending to the gloves that lay on the counter and he watched her from a distance. An older woman briskly approached her and Dan could tell by her stance that she was not being friendly. Curiosity made Dan sidle nearer. He hid behind a dummy and listened to the conversation.

'You should have made that sale, Mrs Lang.'

'Yes, Mrs Knowles.'

'I know it's your first day, but I think you were a bit too over familiar. I hope you were just trying to impress me and that you won't be so friendly to our male customers in future.'

The bitch, Dan thought. Guilt made Dan feel unsettled, it was her first day and he had blown it for her. He brightened at the thought that at least he knew her name, Mrs Lang, a married lady eh? A woman of experience that would make a nice change, Dan thought. As he made his way out of the shop he decided he would come back and buy some gloves, perhaps he could give them to Emily, win her over.

By the time Dan got back to the house most of the day was gone and he had made up a good story as to his boss's whereabouts. It was obvious to him that Mr Rhodes had gone out the back of whoop whoop to do away with himself which suited Dan just fine, but he didn't want anyone chasing after him. It would be better if they didn't find him, people disappeared in the outback everyday and most of the time no one even knew about it. A pile of bones found under a tree didn't even raise an eyebrow, it was just some silly bastard thinking they could outwit the outback.

Dan's good mood soon changed when he walked into the kitchen. Mr Simms, Mrs Lovelock and Emily were sitting at the table laughing about some private joke. They all went quiet when he entered and stared at him as though he had two heads or something.

'Ah.' Mr Simms looked up at Dan and became serious.

Emily looked guiltily away, the smirk still on her face. Were they laughing at me, Dan wondered?

'Come into the study, Turner where we can discuss business.'

Dan didn't like this jumped up fella from the city. Who did he think he was, walking in here and taking over? At least Rhodes, for all his faults, didn't talk down to him. Well there was no way he was going to co-operate with this galah.

'So?' Mr Simms began once they were closeted in the privacy of the study. 'Where's he gone then? I imagine you managed to find out something.'

Dan was getting more and more irritated. 'Yes, sir.'

He began spouting the story he had come up with and hoped this twaddle would be believed.

'Seems he's gone down the South Coast. Evidently he told the ticket seller at Central he had relatives down there. Yeah, he was going to "visit his sister" was what he told this bloke.' Dan took a breath and added, 'said he'd be staying a few weeks.'

'Very good memory this station worker has, wouldn't you say?'

'He remembered Mr Rhodes because it was so early in the morning and he recognised him from his picture in the paper.

'I see.' Mr Simms sniffed and preened his moustache. 'That'll be all Turner and don't go blabbing about this to the rest of the staff.'

Dan returned to the kitchen but Emily was no longer there. He could feel his anger simmering under the surface, he felt like lashing out. Shoving his balled fists deep into his pockets he asked Mrs Lovelock, 'Where's Emily gone?'

'She's working, as you should be.'

Dan fought down the urge to walk over to the cook and thump her in the face. He'd always liked Mrs Lovelock but everyone was speaking to him as though he was a bit of mould found between their toes. It was that Samuel Simms stirring things up.

'Tell her when you see her that I've some important news of Mr Rhodes she should know about.' That should get Emily rushing to him, he thought. Before Mrs Lovelock could say anything he walked out, adding as he went, 'I'll be at the stables if she wants me.'

Dan felt listless and not at all in the mood for work. He half-heartedly brushed the horses, thinking of the woman in the department store, Mrs Lang. He fantasised about her and what sort of life she led. Dan imagined she was a widower she wouldn't be working unless her husband had died. She would definitely have kids, but how old? Not babies, that's for sure, she was past that stage. He visualised her neat little house with neat little children, she wouldn't be silly enough to have a shed full. He would go and visit, dressed in his Sunday best and she would make him a beaut meal, a proper baked dinner with all the trimmings and after the food the kids would go off and play and they would spend Sunday afternoon in bed. He imagined the curtains in her bedroom wafting in the warm afternoon breeze and Mrs Lang lying naked on the bed. Dan wondered what her first name was and ran through a few in his mind. Hetty, nah, Elizabeth, too posh, Mary, too religious, whatever it was he was sure it would suit her just fine.

A voice at the stable door made him jump.

'Daniel, are you in there?' It was Emily. 'Mrs Lovelock said you had something to tell me about Mr Rhodes.'

He could tell by her voice she was back to being her prim self and it annoyed him. She was not like that with Mr Bloody Simms an hour ago.

'There you are,' she said as she moved across to where Dan was brushing the horse. 'So, what was this important piece of news you have about Mr Rhodes?'

Her hands were on her hips and her head was tilted to one side and he could have slapped her. Of course there was nothing to tell Emily, it was just a way of luring her away from them at the big house and getting her full attention. He had hardly seen her since the night she walked off and left him at the dance. He still had to pay her back for that.

Dan moved away from the horse to the bales of hay that were stacked against the wall. He sat on one and leaned forward his elbows resting on his knees. Patting the bale next to him he said, 'come on, sit you down.' He noticed her hesitate and added, 'I thought you might like to know where Mr Rhodes was going when you saw him.'

Emily sat down. It was as though any mention of Mr Rhodes made her feel secure.

Dan turned and looked at her. He felt like the spider about to eat the unsuspecting fly that had wondered into its web.

'What?' Emily acknowledged his look.

'I was just thinking how attractive you look.'

Emily went to get up but Dan grabbed her arm and pulled her back down. 'Don't rush off we haven't finished our talk yet.'

'If you've got something to say, say it and stop all this cat and mouse nonsense.'

The laughter bubbled from Dan's lips, he felt excited. 'Emily, Emily, why are you in such a rush.'

'Some of us have things to do.' Dan could hear the slight tremor in her voice, which aroused him even more. 'And if I don't get back soon Mrs Lovelock will send out a search party.'

Dan knew that was a hollow threat. He moved closer to Emily. She stayed completely still. Gently he fingered a curl of her hair. 'You have lovely hair, Emily, it makes you look wild.'

He bent over to smell it and she elbowed him in the ribs.

'Get off me you pig.'

Dan grabbed her hands and clamped them together in his strong grip. She struggled trying to wriggle from his grasp. With his other hand he pulled her head back with a handful of hair. He stood over her, as she tried to yell he placed his mouth over hers. The scream was muffled and her lips relaxed. Ah, he thought, she was beginning to enjoy his rough treatment. That was all she needed, a firm hand. Her body went limp and her breasts were protruding as he pulled at her hair to make her back arch more. Any minute now and she would be squirming in his arms asking for more. His tongue began to investigate the interior of her mouth. He was enjoying himself until an excruciating pain ripped through his mouth as Emily's teeth clamped onto his tongue. Her action was so sudden he released his hold on her and leapt away. With blood trickling down his chin he yelled muffled profanities into his blood soaked hand. He spat on the ground and cursed even louder.

Emily had moved quickly while he was preoccupied with his bleeding tongue and was on her way to the door when Dan whirled round. He lunged at her, he was wild with anger and felt like killing her. He grabbed for her skirt and managed to get a small piece. Emily shrieked, real terror in her eyes as she yanked her skirt from his grasp and continued to run.

Dan lost his balance and fell to the floor. 'I'll get you,' he shouted after her. 'Don't you worry about that, luv, I'll get you.' Emily kept running he wasn't sure she'd heard him but he vowed to himself. 'I'll get that little cow if it's the last thing I do.'

CHAPTER 12

John

The countryside rushed past the train window but John Rhodes hadn't noticed any of the sights or sounds. He was cocooned in his own world, noises came to him as though he had wool in his ears, a sort of muffled blur. He closed his eyes pretending to be asleep. He didn't want anyone to speak to him. Fortunately there was only a stockman sharing the compartment and they were not known for their conversation.

The same thoughts were going round and round in John's head. Guilt overshadowed everything. He winced at his own stupidity and cowardice on the day of the picnic. He felt as though he was in a nightmare that wouldn't end. That feeling of overwhelming relief when you wake up after a bad dream was something he yearned for. Instead it was like being stuck in a mire, being dragged down further and further each day. He longed for the blackness of oblivion so he could at last feel free of the quicksand of depression. John had finally admitted to himself that he wanted to die. He had no idea what happened after death but he didn't care. It couldn't be as bad as the hell he was living. He could pump himself full of laudanum and exist in a semi conscious stupor but what would Thomas think of him?

Thomas his boy, how could he ever face him and admit to killing his mother and sister? It would be better if he was out of the boy's life, he would be orphaned but he would be a rich orphan.

After hours and hours of stop start train travel and a night that seemed to go on for ever, John finally arrived in Bourke. The station was deserted, the few passengers that remained on the train descended onto the platform and scuttled away like cockroaches when a light was lit. John stood in the blistering sun. Within minutes his bare arms, where he had rolled up his sleeves were burning. He stepped into the shade of the platform awning for relief but the intense heat made sweat break out on his body as soon as he moved.

Slinging his jacket over his shoulder, clamping his hat on his head and picking up his case, he struck out towards the township. It was devoid of habitation, not a soul could be seen. All the houses had their windows flung open and curtains billowed in the hot breeze. Front doors were left wide and he could see right through some houses to the back door. A dog slept on a veranda and raised its head to watch him pass only to flop back down again when he posed no threat.

By the time John reached the row of shops he was breathing heavily and his throat felt parched. His hair was wet with sweat and his shirt was sticking to him. Outside one shop a solitary horse was fastened to a post, a bucket of water in front of it. Reaching the shade of the shop awnings was a relief. He glanced into each shop as he passed but most of them looked as though they were closed. At the top end of the street was the Port of Bourke hotel, its open door beckoned him inside.

Momentarily John wondered why it was "Port of Bourke". Was it someone's idea of a joke to name such a land locked location a port? He walked to the bar and a man appeared from a back room.

'Gooday, yuh look like you could do with a drink.' He was tall and burly with a ruddy face and bulbous nose, his mouth creased into a smile sending wrinkles criss-crossing over his face.

John nodded and said, 'that would be much appreciated.' Putting his suitcase and jacket on the floor at his feet, John grasped the proffered glass of beer and gulped it down in one go.

'That'll be another, then eh?'

Again John nodded and a second beer was put in front of him. This time he drank it more slowly.

The hotelier held out a meaty hand saying, 'Bill Barstow's the name, or as the locals call me "Bastard Barstow".' The shocked look on John's face made the stranger add, 'it's a term of endearment round here. If they call yuh bastard you're well in.' There was a pause in the conversation before Bill went on, 'come from the city by the look o' yuh.'

'Yes, just arrived on the train.' John was trying to think of a feasible reason for him being in such a God forsaken place but nothing came to mind.

'Oh, here on business are yuh?'

'You could say that.' John smiled and nodded.

'I expect you'll be looking for a place to stay?'

John looked round at the bar area and decided it was fairly clean and tidy and this chap was definitely friendly enough.

'You won't find anywhere as clean as this and the food's pretty good too. It's three shillings a night and an extra shilling for clean sheets. It's the water, see. Can't use too much of it. It's not like the city up 'ere, water's a bit scarce.'

'Right, I'll have a room then.'

'How many nights will that be for?' Bill looked enquiringly at him.

'I'm not sure at this stage, depends on my business arrangements.'

Bill Barstow nodded his head and John thought it was going to be difficult to get one over on this fellow.

In his room John sat on the bed and let his body flop. For a few minutes downstairs, he had stood erect, pretending he was a normal person with a valid reason for being here. He had been an upstanding pillar of the community, a businessman not a murderer. John wondered what his reception with Bill Barstow would have been had he known the recent events in his life.

The room was hot and stuffy. He crossed to the window and threw it open wider. He leaned out and looked down into the back yard of the hotel. The grass was brown from the searing heat and lack of water and a pile of wooden kegs were stacked against the fence. A mangy looking dog lay in the dirt under the shade of a spindly looking gum tree. A caste iron water tank dominated the yard, at some stage it had been painted green but the paint was peeling off in large scabs revealing the rusting metal beneath. Lying back on the bed John gave into the exhaustion that overwhelmed him.

It was dark when he woke. He could hear the noise of men in the bar downstairs, a happy chunnering of deep voices interspersed with throaty laughter. John wondered what the time was and peered at his fob watch in the gloom. It was a quarter to seven he couldn't believe he had slept so long. It was the most sleep he'd had in weeks.

He felt hungry for the first time in ages and hoped dinner was still being served. He poured water from the jug into the bowl and splashed his face. It was cool and refreshing. He dipped his hair in and let the water run down his collar. Scraping a comb through it made him look neater.

As he descended the stairs of the hotel he could smell the delicious aroma of roasting meat.

'Hello, you must be our new lodger.' A buxom woman stepped out of the kitchen holding out her hand as she spoke. 'Sorry luv, I don't recall your name.'

'It's John, John Riley.'

He didn't know why he gave a fictitious name. It had slipped out before he realized, probably the overwhelming urge to be treated like everyone else, to be normal and not the subject of gossip. It wouldn't do any harm, he wasn't going to be here long enough for it to matter.

'Well, John, you just sit yourself down in the dining room and I'll bring your supper.'

'Thanks very much.' John smiled at the woman.

The baked dinner was delicious, the potatoes done to perfection, the pumpkin singed at the edges just how John liked it and the cabbage cooked to a tasty mush. Thick slices of lamb lay on his plate and everything was swimming in a rich gravy. A rice pudding followed and when John had finished he felt as though he could hardly move.

After the meal he strolled into the bar and had a glass of rum since they didn't have any whisky. Everyone was friendly and the alcohol made him feel relaxed. People were curious about him and he managed to make up quite a believable story as to why he was here and where he came from. It had been a long time since John had enjoyed himself as much, the last bit of pleasure for a man about to die. He felt as though the alcohol had washed all his troubles away. His sadness and depression was covered with drunkenness. People patted him on the back and shook his hand as though he was the new boy at school that everyone wanted to meet. He was the centre of attention once again but this time it felt good. The other men looked at him with smiles on their faces not anger in their eyes.

John didn't remember going to bed but the harsh rays of the morning sun made his head ache even through his closed eyelids. He had the mother of all hangovers. He stumbled from the bed, washed his face and rinsed the taste of mouse droppings from his mouth. The remnants of his life came back into perspective with a rush once the numbing effect of the alcohol had worn off.

Today was the day he needed to plan what he was going to do. On the train he had preconceived ideas of walking into the unknown. He realised the locals wouldn't let him walk off and perish. If he didn't return within a certain time they would probably send out a search party. So he would have to plan his departure without causing suspicion.

John dressed in his coolest pair of grey trousers and a white shirt, without its collar. Instead he tied a large handkerchief round his neck and rolled up his sleeves. With his hat plopped on his head the transformation was remarkable. The façade of a wealthy businessman had disappeared to be replaced with the casual attire of the country folk.

His breakfast was waiting for him and the smell of food made his stomach heave but he didn't want to hurt the cook's feelings. He took small mouthfuls of the steak and eggs. Somehow he managed to eat it and surprisingly felt a lot better afterwards.

Passing through the bar on his way out, Bill called, 'Here yah mate, a hair of the dog.' A glass filled with some vile looking concoction stood on the bar.

'No thank you,' John answered politely.

'Yuh look as sick as a dog to me and this little potion will definitely work.'

John approached the bar, and looked suspiciously at the drink.

'What's in it?' he asked.

'Now that'd be tellin'. It's a special recipe that works every time.'

John grabbed the drink and swallowed it in one gulp, as it reached his throat he gagged but clamped his mouth shut and let the slimy consistency slither down his throat. It was worse than eating oysters.

'Good boy.' Bill clapped him on the shoulder.

John shook his head and let out a long breath. 'What was in that?'

'Well if yuh really want to know it was rum, raw egg and a dash of milk.'

John gave one last shudder before grinning. 'Can I complain to the management if it doesn't work?'

'Seems it's already worked, you're smiling aren't yuh.'

Once outside the hotel John looked about him. There were more people around today, but no one seemed to be rushing. Women with baskets over their arms stood talking, their long skirts swishing in the dust as they articulated enthusiastically with their hands. Young children were pulled along by the hand or pushed about in perambulators. The sight of aboriginal children sitting in the dust was a novelty to John. These children leaned against the wall of the Post Office in the shade as if they belonged there. They were playing in the dirt, giggling and enjoying themselves. There weren't many men about, probably all working.

He wasn't sure which direction to go. He needed to find out where everything was. As he walked, a selection of carts passed him loaded with sacks of wheat, boxes of oranges, timber, corrugated iron and other things. John wondered where they were going.

He could smell the water before he could see it, an expanse of river wide enough for cargo boats to moor along a huge wharf. This obviously was the Port of Bourke and John was amazed at the activity there. Like ants on a sugar bowl men and wagons streamed over the wharf loading and unloading their goods. This was the Darling River the men in the bar had told him about the previous night.

John tried to remember from his school geography where the Darling flowed. It may be a way of getting out of town. He needed to know where the boats stopped along the river.

A voice nearby said, 'Here mate, give us a hand.'

John looked around. 'Are you talking to me?'

'Sure thing.' He nodded as he struggled with large sacks. 'I've got to get this load to Louth before the shearers run off the job in protest.'

John looked puzzled and the man sighed and explained, 'If they don't get their tea with plenty of sugar at smoko they'll walk off the job.'

The large sacks contained tea and sugar and the man was struggling to load his cumbersome supplies into a flat-bottomed boat.

'What do you want me to do?'

'I just want a lift with these sacks. By the way the name's Frank Crawford.' The stranger held out his hand.

'John Rhodes.' John immediately realised he should have said "Riley" if his secret was to be safe. It was too late now.

They shook hands and began the work. By the time everything was stowed on board John was a lather of sweat and perspiration trickled down his face.

'Look like you could do with a drink.' Frank walked to one side of the boat and pulled a piece of string that was dangling in the water. At the end of the string was a bottle of beer. 'Only way to keep it cool,' he commented before opening it and taking a swig. He handed it to John who let the cool liquid trickle down his throat. 'Thanks mate that was real good of yuh helping like that.'

While John had been labouring away a plan had begun to form in his mind. 'Well,' he said in a slow drawl, 'I do require payment for my services.' The shocked look on the face of Frank Crawford was a picture.

'Well.... I haven't got anything....no money...' The words spluttered from Frank's mouth as he tried to gain his composure.

'Don't worry, mate.' John had realised that if you called people "mate" they were more amenable. 'I just want a lift.'

Frank sighed with relief. 'Yuh could give a bloke a heart attack carrying on like that. If it's a lift you want that's not a problem. Back to town is it?'

'No, in the boat, down river or where ever it is you're going.'

A puzzled look furrowed Frank's brow. 'Ah... going down river to look for work are yuh?'

'You could say that. What time are you leaving?'

'In about an hour, just got to nip into town and buy some boiled lollies for the abo kids and have a drink for the road or river in my case and we'll be off.'

Exactly an hour later the top-heavy boat was manoeuvred away from the wharf and out into the watery hands of the great Darling River. It bobbed along like a cork while Frank got the little steam motor working and they puttered away from Bourke until the town was lost from sight round a curve in the river.

John's suitcase was beside him, which he had managed to get from the hotel room without any questions being asked. He left the money on the bed for his room and a bit extra, he felt like being generous when it came to Bill and his wife. They were good people.

He was embarking on the next step of his journey, away from civilisation and into the unknown where he would be in the hands of God. But since God had recently seen fit to kick him in the teeth, John knew He wouldn't help with his survival. John Rhodes would be just another statistic gobbled up by the indiscriminate hunger of the unforgiving outback.

It was late afternoon when they approached a battered wooden jetty. A group of black men wore the clothes of the whites. They hung around the jetty as the boat approach. As the wooden hull bumped against the wharf John watched as the men moved forward to help their boss unload the cargo. A wagon stood ready and the driver sat up from his slouched position in readiness to hold the horses while the loading was done.

As soon as the boat was tied up Frank Crawford began ordering the aborigines about, geeing them up, making their black limbs move quicker. The muscles on their sinewy arms stood out as they lifted the sacks of tea and sugar and plonked them unceremoniously into the cart.

The black driver watched the proceedings over his shoulder, gently calming the horses as the wagon was rocked by the weight of the sacks landing heavily in the back.

John felt as though he was in the way. He was a stranger, someone to stare at.

'Come on Ningan, get on with the job and stop staring.' Frank spoke good-humouredly to the black driver who immediately averted his gaze. 'Anyone would think you'd never seen some one from the city before. Maybe you ain't.'

Ningan

Ningan looked down at the shaft of the cart and held the reins slackly in his fingers, his mind not registering anything but the white stranger. He seemed so familiar to the black man, his light coloured hair flopped just the same but his face was more worn by time. He couldn't resist turning round again but this time he meet his gaze, the stranger looked away. Could it be him? He couldn't be sure, they all looked alike except for the hair. The whiter whitefellas, Ningan called them. He hadn't seen many over the years.

That white hair reminded him of Connie. He still thought about her a lot. He knew he would never be able to get her out of his head. Her image was burned on the inside of his skull and their time together would stay with him forever. He had forgiven her for taking his child to the big smoke. His child would have a whitefella's life and become like one of them, but still he yearned to see her. Sometimes the pain was like when he had no food for a week, a hunger that was a gnawing ache that nothing could shift. The thought that his seed had grown into a piccanini who was now a stranger to him, felt all wrong. But his life was no match for what a whitefella could give his daughter.

Once again Ningan glanced at the newcomer. There was something about this whitefella that Ningan found different to the others. This one was surrounded by sadness and defeat. It reminded him of a beaten dog, the way he walked and didn't look anyone in the eye.

'Ningan, this is Mr Rhodes.' Frank Crawford introduced him.

'Gudday.' Ningan held out his hand to shake Mr Rhodes' hand, it was a whitefella's custom that Ningan knew was expected of him. Some aborigines wouldn't touch strangers, you never knew what spirits may be lurking below the skin.

The cool fingers of the white man clasped Ningan's and almost made him shudder.

'How do you do?'

The city voice sounded strange to him and he nodded and smiled his greeting.

'Mr Rhodes is going to be doing a bit of book work for me.' Frank informed no one in particular. 'Not that you'd know much about that.'

'Yes boss... ah...no boss.' Ningan wasn't sure how he was supposed to answer he was too preoccupied trying to have a good look at the stranger.

The boss climbed up next to Ningan and the other man squeezed on the end of the seat. The labourers jumped into the back of the cart with the supplies and Ningan coaxed the horses to start. It took him all his concentration to steer the horses round the potholes that littered the track into town. They passed through Louth without Ningan noticing the post office, pub and general store. It was so small if you blinked you'd miss it.

On the open road a miasma of dust followed them, it settled on their hats and clothing and felt gritty on Ningan's lips. The heat would bake them alive, he thought. He squinted into the sun and once they were away from the town, let the horses drift along at their own speed. He kept glancing at the stranger at the other end of the seat. All he could see of him, round the boss, were his hands in his lap and his trousers that looked much better than the rough ones worn by the workers around here. The hands, Ningan noticed, were fairly clean not ingrained with dirt, the nails not chipped and broken. His were women's hands not the hands of a worker. The stranger's fingers twitched like a mating cricket. He was uneasy in his mind.

The boss yattered on but Ningan didn't pay much attention. He knew not to speak until he was asked a question.

By the time they got to the sheep station it was dark and the boss showed John Rhodes to the white men's sleep house. Ningan went with the black workers into the bush to a makeshift camp they had set up. There were no squeaky beds for them only the ground. Ningan didn't mind that, he would rather sleep outside so he could watch the stars and listen to the wind spirit singing in the trees.

Thoughts chased round in Ningan's head as he lay on his back looking at the star speckled sky. The new whitefella had got him thinking. It was the white hair and the resemblance to that man all those years ago. Could it be the same man who rescued him when his father was killed by the whites? How long ago was that? He was on the edge of manhood then and now he was….. ? Ningan thought of events in his life and tried to work out how old he was. His body had stopped growing long ago but the signs of age had not yet begun.

If it was the spirit man who rescued him what should he do? Had he come back to take him now, or to help him again? Was something going to happen to him that he would need the spirit man? Ningan decided that if he watched the white spirit man he would find out why he was here.

For weeks Ningan watched and waited for the spirit man that went by the name of John Rhodes, to do something. During the day he worked in the house and at night he went to his bunk and stayed there. He didn't join in with the other whitefellas although they all seemed to like him and did much patting on his back. Sometimes he sat on the veranda with the boss and had a beer. Ningan could tell that missus boss liked John Rhodes by the way she looked at him. Her eyes sparkled, her face softened like when lubras looked at piccaninis and her lips smiled. Ningan wondered if the boss knew his missus liked Mr Rhodes. It was as obvious as smoke meant bush fires. Ningan knew trouble was brewing, the boss got drunk more, the sun made Mr Rhodes browner and missus boss undid her top button.

One night shouting rattled around the house. It was the boss yelling at missus boss, the beer had pickled his brain again and he had gone off into one of his rages. She screamed and things smashed and no one went to her aid. In the morning everyone acted like nothing had happened, even missus boss.

The next day the boss came into the yard yelling. 'Ningan get your black arse over here.'

Ningan rushed towards the house, the boss looked as angry as a grass snake when you tread on its tail. He thought he would have to go for the doctor like he did once before after they'd had a row and the boss had broken missus boss's arm.

He stood on the veranda, his hands on his hips and looked down at Ningan.

'The new man's gone walkabout.'

It was almost like he blamed the aborigine.

'Walkabout boss?' Ningan was confused.

'Yeah, and him being a city slicker I don't want his death on my conscience.'

'Right boss, you want me find him?'

'Since you're the best tracker we've got it shouldn't take you too long.'

Ningan beamed, he couldn't help being pleased when the boss said he was good at something. 'Don't worry, boss, I ged him back quick.'

'Well see that you do, there's plenty of work around here waiting for yuh.'

Ningan was glad to be getting away from the mundane jobs round the station. The blacks were given all the bad jobs like finding lost sheep or killing old ones with fly blown rumps that wriggled with maggots.

Finding the white spirit man would be easy but he could take his time and see where he was going. Maybe, Ningan thought, he would learn something about a spirit man's life if he followed him.

Before the sun was high in the sky Ningan had found John Rhodes. He didn't walk up to him, he just watched him from a distance. His boss didn't need to know he found him so soon.

The flat, bare terrain made it quite difficult for Ningan to follow the whitefella without being spotted although this fella didn't seem to be noticing anything. He had struck out away from the road across the nothingness. As the morning turned into afternoon Ningan kept following him. When night fell and the cool blackness descended over the land the whitefella lay down on the ground and slept. In the morning he stood and continued to walk. He ate nothing, did nothing, just walked.

Ningan scratched his head. Usually, in the mornings, the whitefellas have to scrape the whiskers off their faces, or make a fire to cook some food but John Rhodes did none of these things. He was being forced on by something but Ningan wasn't sure what. He didn't seem to feel pain or hunger. He was like an animal going off to die.

The landscape was lush with long grass that licked at Ningan's legs. It felt cool on his tramping bare feet during the day but at night, when the spirits sprinkled the water, it was cold and wet. Even in the springtime the temperature dropped during the night and so far inland it had been known to freeze over the waterholes.

Ningan longed to light a fire at night and warm his bare toes by the embers, but the whitefella would see it. He hadn't lit one either and Ningan wondered if it was because he didn't know how or got his flint wet or whatever white men used to light fires.

For three days Ningan followed John Rhodes. Dark clouds began banking on the horizon. The whitefella wasn't looking for shelter he just shambled along as though nothing could touch him. The breeze grew stronger and whipped into a wind that rushed across the plains. Ningan watched as his hat blew off and was left to bounce and roll across the ground.

'What's wrong that fella?' Ningan grumbled to himself. 'Him need that hat to stop his brains geddin' boiled.' It was like the man was in a trance. Had a medicine man pointed a bone at him, Ningan wondered?

Thunder began to rumble and lightening forked. Ningan laid flat on the ground and waited for the storm to pass but Mr Rhodes was standing in the open, as though he wanted to be struck. Rain began to pelt down and he finally reacted. He ran towards a tree.

'Him real stupid fella,' Ningan muttered as the lightening drove at the ground. The noise of the thunder was deafening and Ningan lay watching. The lightning strike made the ground shake and the crack of breaking wood was hard to hear over the sound of the storm. A puff of smoke rose from the tree but the rain put it out.

Jumping to his feet Ningan ran towards the tree where the whitefella had thrown himself on the ground. The tree trunk was creaking like an old man's stiff limbs. It was about to fall and Ningan rushed over to the body on the ground. He got hold of the whitefella under his armpits and dragged him. The force of his movements rallied the stunned man.

'What're you doing?'

'Him tree gunna fall, look out.'

As he shouted the tree swayed and began to slowly bend in their direction. Ningan clawed at the whitefella's clothes, pulling him, desperate to get him out of the path of the falling tree. More sounds of breaking wood and Mr Rhodes suddenly realised what was happening.

'Damn.' He cursed as he began to propel himself with Ningan still scrambling beside him. As the tree thudded to the ground they also fell, together, in a lovers clinch, breathing heavily as lovers do, covering their faces with their arms as bits of flying branches crashed around them. For a moment all was still.

Ningan was the first to whip away from the whitefella as though he had been stuck with a heated spear. The body odour of John Rhodes was strong in his nostrils. The memory of it from all those years ago was like a rock crushing into Ningan's skull. It was him it was the man who saved his life when he was a boy.

The whitefella propped himself on his elbows as Ningan stared at him. They looked at each other, they were both wet through, their clothes streaked with mud, lying in the middle of nowhere with a storm raging overhead.

The whitefella began to chuckle to himself which turned into a laugh. Ningan looked about them wondering what he found so funny, his white spirit man, the one he had been looking for all these years without even realising it. The sheer relief of finding him, and saving him from death were unbelievable to Ningan. His laughter began to bubble in this throat and titter between his lips, and he couldn't stop grinning, life was good. They continued to sit on the ground like children playing games, laughing and giggling with the rain lashing around them.

Mr Rhodes laughed and talked at the same time. 'That beats all, I'm out here trying to kill myself and you save me.' His giggling continued. 'It would have been perfect, to be killed by lightening, a real accident not something staged. God obviously wanted me dead to strike that tree just when I was under it, but this abo decides it's not time for me to go.' He looks at Ningan and shakes his head. 'I don't believe it.'

Ningan still laughed, slightly confused at the white man's words. His white spirit man was here but what should he do with him now? A thought suddenly struck him, maybe all whitefellas smell the same. He had only ever been that close to one other whitefella and that had been a long time ago.

CHAPTER 13

Emily

Emily looked down into the garden as she ironed her new uniform. It was three months since Mr Rhodes had left and she did miss him. She smoothed her hands over the grey material as steam rose from the damp patch.

Her new governess's uniform looked very smart even though it was only a grey skirt and white blouse. Not having to wear an apron made her feel important, she had more responsibility. She'd moved up in rank, instead of gaining a stripe she had lost a pinny. She smiled at the thought.

It had been Mr Simms idea to make her a governess. It felt very official having such a title and sounded so English. All her hours of learning and book reading had paid off with an increase in pay. She was no longer a maid and Mr Simms had employed a youngster to take over her cleaning duties.

She did wonder whether Mr Rhodes would have done the same thing, or would he have always seen her as a maid. She sighed when she thought of him. No one had heard from him and Emily still worried about him.

Sometimes she fretted that she had done the wrong thing opening the letter he had left on his desk that morning. It had been addressed to Thomas, but he was too young to understand it and at the time he wasn't well. It was obvious an adult would find it and read it first. Had Mr Rhodes meant for her to find it or Mr Simms?

Emily had read the letter in the solitude of her room. It had been a letter of love from a father to his son, but the way it was worded sounded as though Mr Rhodes didn't expect to see Thomas again. At first Emily dismissed it as the ramblings of a disturbed mind, but as the months went on and no word was heard from him, she wondered if he was desperate enough to take his own life. A year ago such a thought would not have entered her head. The image of his smiling, caring face flashed in her mind. He had been such a mild and gentle man. She would keep the letter hidden under her mattress in the hope that he would soon contact them and put their minds at rest. Emily's optimism returned as she held up the ironed skirt and smiled.

A noise behind her made Emily turn as Thomas entered the room balancing a plate of biscuits in one hand and a glass of milk in the other. He kicked the door closed with his foot sending splashes of milk onto the floor.

'Sorry,' he said as he walked carefully across the room and laid his little feast on the table.

Emily bent to wipe up the spilt milk with the damp cloth she was using for pressing. 'Don't worry Tom,' she said as she ruffled his hair. 'There's no use crying over spilt milk,' she added and laughed.

'You alright Emily or are you in one of your silly moods?'

'You cheeky little brat,' she ruffled his hair again and kissed the top of his head.

The relationship they had wasn't one of teacher and student or servant and son of the house it was something all together different. A closeness, a friendship, a bond. Was it like mother and son, Emily wondered? She just knew she loved him and he could do no wrong in her eyes.

'I see Mrs Lovelock is spoiling you again, making your favourite biscuits.'

A smile played at Thomas's lips as he dipped a biscuit into the milk and took a big bite. 'She said you could have one too,' he mumbled with a full mouth.

'That's very kind of her, when you've finished that we'll read the next chapter of your book.'

'Yeah,' Thomas yelled sending biscuit crumbs spraying from his mouth.

The story before bed had become a routine, which Thomas seemed to enjoy. Before they began Emily asked him what happened in the story the day before and he could always remember. His memory was improving. With day to day things he was very good, there just seemed to be a gap when the tragedy happened. Emily couldn't blame him for blacking the event out, but she worried what would happen when he did remember that day on the river.

Every time a frown appeared on his face, she wondered what was upsetting him. She usually managed to snap him out of a sad mood. One day he asked if she was his mother. Emily stumbled over her reply. She would have loved to answer 'Yes' and seen the relief in his eyes but no matter how much she wanted to be his mother, to love and protect him forever, she had to answer 'No'. There had been silence for a moment before he asked where his mother was? Emily said she was in heaven and of course he wanted to know where that was. She described a wonderful place but then he wanted to know why his mother hadn't taken him too. She quickly changed the subject as the tears began to choke her.

After Emily had put Thomas to bed she tidied herself in front of the mirror. Mr Simms had asked her to see him in the library when Thomas was settled. He quite often chatted to the staff in the evening making sure everything at the house was running smoothly.

Emily studied her complexion in the mirror, at least during the winter months her freckles didn't stand out quite so prominently. She pinched her cheeks to make herself look healthier. She dragged the brush through her hair, her curls bounced in all directions before she pinned it up again, leaving a few tendrils dangling round her face.

Moving to the full length mirror, Emily tucked in her blouse and put on her freshly pressed skirt. She looked at herself, turning first one way and then the other. Her figure was quite trim although her bottom stuck out a little too much. Finally she liberally dabbed rose water behind her ears and round her throat.

As Emily floated gracefully down the main staircase, Dan was coming out of the library.

He looked up at her. 'Hello Emily.'

'Hello Daniel, haven't seen you for ages.' Emily tried to sound pleasant.

'Been too busy, this new boss is buggering me about something rotten.'

'Shhh, he'll hear you.' Emily looked meaningfully at the closed library door.

'Couldn't care less.' His eyes narrowed. 'You're looking a bit spruced up for this time of day. Got an audience with the pope in there 'ave yuh?'

Emily didn't answer. She didn't like his attitude. He had changed from the person she had tried to impress all those months ago. She blushed which made her look guilty, as if she had something to hide.

'Thought so, don't tell me you're all sweet on this boss as well?' he tutted derisively. 'You women, you make me sick,' he muttered as he walked away.

The cool, calm demeanour Emily had felt as she descended the stairs had been replaced with nervousness and loss of confidence. She walked into the library feeling conspicuous, all done up for a man she couldn't hope to have.

Samuel Simms sat on Mr Rhodes' plush leather chair with his long legs sprawled out in front of him and most of his body hidden by the large newspaper he was reading.

She cleared her throat as she stood inside the closed door and immediately the newspaper was collapsed in a crackling mass and disposed of on the floor.

'Hello, Emily,' he smiled at her good naturedly. 'And how are you today?'

'Fine, Mr Simms,' she answered. She didn't feel as comfortable in Mr Simms presence as she had with Mr Rhodes. He was much better looking in a less refined way, taller and more powerfully built, more your bushranger type with that Australian masculinity.

'Sit yourself down.' He pointed to a chair opposite him.

'You wanted to see me?'

'Did I?'

'Yes.'

'So I did Emily, please forgive my lapse in memory. That's right,' he went on. 'I just wanted to tell you that you'll be having a relative of Mrs Rhodes coming to stay.'

'Oh, right.' Emily raised her eyebrows in surprise.

'It's her aunt, a Mrs Hilda Tasker.'

A worried look crossed Emily's face as a vision of her aunt Myrtle came into her mind, her with all the cats.

Mr Simms went on. 'From what I've heard she is a nice little old lady and shouldn't cause you too much upset. I imagine she will sleep all day when she's not sewing or doing whatever it is that little old ladies do.'

Emily gave a little titter at that remark and Mr Simms smiled. 'You should smile more often Emily it suits you.'

Her smile became fixed falsely to her face. 'Yes Mr Simms.'

'So, I expect you to make her feel welcome and encourage Thomas to get to know her.'

'Right Mr Simms.' She turned to leave but stopped at his words. 'The new uniform looks very good on you Emily.'

She could feel her face redden but said, 'thank you.'

Dan

The meeting in the hallway, with Emily, had left Dan feeling furious. The way she stood in front of him looking like the mouse that was about to get the cheese. Well the trap was going to snap on her one of these days and the big cheese wouldn't want her anywhere near him.

He brushed the horse's flanks with strong forceful movements taking out his anger with physical action. The horse almost flinched from his rough onslaught and jerked its head round and curled its lip back in protest.

'Easy girl.' His voice was not calming, more demanding. 'Stop complaining, you need a good brushing you dirty mare.'

Dan's thoughts went back to Emily and the horse continued to suffer under his heavy handedness. He had watched the way Emily carried on with the boy. That spoiled brat who did whatever he wanted with no father to give him a good thrashing. She pampered him and was making him into a right little ruffian. He needed a good smack but Emily was too busy hugging and kissing him.

Since the river tragedy things had really changed around here, Dan thought. He didn't like to admit that the incident had more of an effect on him than he realized. Black moods descended on him and he was powerless to snap out of it. He blamed bloody Rhodes and Emily. Maybe he needed to get away from this place.

Emily

The following week Aunt Hilda arrived. The staff members were all lined up to greet her, which had never happened before. It was as though royalty were visiting. The house had been thoroughly cleaned and even Emily had been asked to take some time off her teaching duties to help. Thomas had run around completely out of control while everyone was so busy. Hopefully things could get back to normal now the old lady was here and they could stop preparing for her arrival. She had been collected from the station by Daniel and descended from the carriage leaning heavily on his arm, cursing at every movement.

'This dreadful carriage is just too high. Why haven't you got one of those new cars?'

Daniel's sour look told them this probably wasn't her first complaint. Once she was standing steady, she addressed the waiting staff.

'Now then, who's in charge?' No one stepped forward. 'Well, who is going to introduce me to everyone? Come along don't be shy.'

The women looked demurely at the floor so Dan stepped in and brashly told her their names. They all stood back while she climbed the three steps to the front door with great difficulty. It was obvious she should have a stick and at one moment Dan rushed forward as she tottered on the top step. As she entered the house she called over her shoulder, 'I'll have tea in my room and then I don't want to be disturbed.'

Emily couldn't help curtsying to the old woman's back and the young maid stifled a titter. Mrs Lovelock put her finger to her lips demanding quiet.

It was a few days before Emily saw Mrs Tasker again. She came up to the nursery enveloped in a cloud of camphor, to meet Thomas who was sitting at the table drawing. Great scrawls of red and orange crayon gouged the piece of paper as Tom let out his inhibitions on his artwork. They had been busy all morning leaning about nouns and verbs a subject that Emily had only recently begun with him. After an hour of English she had let him have his head and go wild with a piece of paper and crayons. This method seemed to work with Tom, an hour of hard work then time to unwind and do something he enjoyed. Most of the time she had no problem but occasionally he just wouldn't do the work and she didn't force him. He stared at the strange woman when she entered the room.

Mrs Tasker walked over to him. 'Haven't you got a kiss for your great aunt Hilda?' she demanded.

Thomas looked at Emily with a pained expression on his face. She nodded encouragement. The old lady was not much taller than him so he stood on his tiptoes and wrinkled up his nose as he kissed her on the cheek. She drew him to her and enclosed him in her arms.

'My poor boy,' she said. 'You are a little orphan aren't you?'

Emily was horrified at her words and couldn't hold her tongue. 'No, he is a very clever little boy and there's nothing poor about him.' Fortunately Tom didn't know what an orphan was.

Mrs Tasker went stiff mid embrace, and looked over to the table at the drawing he'd been doing.

'Well,' she said. 'If that's an example of the work you are teaching him he's never going to learn anything.'

Tom struggled from her embrace and rushed to Emily's side. 'At least Emily doesn't smell.' He stood and faced Mrs Tasker insolently.

Her sharp intake of breath and the bulging of her eyeballs made Emily cringe and she realized in less than ten minutes she had made an enemy of the aunt.

The old lady limped to the door but stopped with her hand on the handle. She turned and said, 'I will expect Thomas to have tea with me every afternoon and I will teach him some important things, like manners.' She swept from the room as best she could for someone who was having trouble on her legs.

Emily didn't know whether to laugh or cry, the way Tom had defended her was surprising, but it would have been better to have Mrs Tasker as an ally.

Things carried on more or less as before except Emily now had a free hour in the afternoon while Thomas was with his great aunt. Some of the things she told him made Emily very angry. He was at such an impressionable age her ramblings about how she was bought up as a girl with a strict Victorian outlook were not relevant to Tom. It only confused him although he probably went off into a little world of his own while she chattered on. She told him the only books that he should be reading were the Bible and a good encyclopaedia and that fiction books corrupted people's minds and he was not to read such things. She had also decided that he needed elocutions lessons as she didn't like the Australian twang in his speech. He would never grow into a fine gentleman if he couldn't speak the Queen's English, she told him. The mother country was very important to her and she informed Thomas that he should always put England before Australia. It all seemed very negative and Emily was glad Mrs Tasker only got her claws into Tom for an hour a day and not more, although even that amount of time could be enough to knock the boy's confidence.

Dan

The unreasonable anger Dan felt for Emily simmered under the surface. He would never admit it was sheer jealousy, he didn't like her preening herself for other men. He was all the man she needed.

But another woman had come into his life. She was much more mature, she didn't go round making eyes at anything that wore trousers. Mrs Lang was poised and calm and had an air of dignity that Dan loved. She didn't look down at him and those big, blue understanding eyes of hers made him feel boyish under her gaze.

With running Mr Simms back and forth to Greetby's Dan had managed to see her fairly regularly. Once he dropped his lordship off at the department store the day was his own. Of course he should have been scuttling back to Brunswick House to polish carriages and brasses but who was there to check up on him. He could spend as long as he liked in the city.

One day he had followed her when she finished for the day and bumped into her, making it look like an accident of course. He had chatted to her on the street and tried to get her to go into Braddock's Tea Shop with him but she had to get home to her kids. At first he thought she was married but by the time he had walked her a few blocks he had discovered that her husband had died. He pretended he had to catch a train but instead followed her home.

It was about twenty minutes walk from the store to the Rocks area of Sydney. He watched as she opened a front door on a small terraced house and disappeared inside. He had to be a bit careful in a place like this people would notice a stranger loitering about.

Things were really looking up for him. The dramas at Brunswick House with Mr Simms and his menagerie would soon be a thing of the past for Dan. He had landed himself a new position. He was to be a courier, with a new city based firm. He would have his own wagon, delivering supplies from wharf to door. His patch would be all around Sydney, but the best part was that one of their biggest customers was Greetby & Co. He would be delivering to them at least once a week and there was nothing stopping him from sneaking in and having a chat with Mrs Lang while he was there. He wanted to take her somewhere nice, and once he was earning more on this new job he would be able to afford it.

In the meantime he had a few weeks of work to do at Brunswick House and then he could walk away. He had two weeks to sort out that floozie Emily before he moved on to greener pastures, but it would take a lot of planning to get her alone.

The following day as Dan was leading the horse out of the barn to a nearby field, he saw Emily disappearing round the back of the house. Quickly he removed the horse's head rein and smacked its rump so it galloped across the field. He rushed back into the tack room throwing the rein inside before running across the courtyard to see where Emily was going. She was strolling down the drive towards the main gate.

Dan hid until she was out of sight round the trees that bordered the front of the house. He remembered it was her free time when the brat sat with the old lady. He wondered where she went, when she had this time to herself. He was determined to find out and followed her staying well back so she didn't see him. She was strolling, as though she was in no rush. Once past the boundary of Brunswick House the dirt road continued and Emily walked ahead along the rough road verge.

She came to a large grassy area with boulders dotted about like large marbles, scattered by a giant. It was a very picturesque spot Dan had to admit with a view across to the river. As he watched Emily went behind a rock and disappeared. He smiled and looked around. Perfect, not a soul in sight, no passing wagons no nosey neighbours, no one to see what was going on.

Dan retraced his steps, smiling as a plan evolved. If he could way lay her here, he could teach her the ways of men and disappear before she could raise the alarm. He'd be off to the other side of Sydney with no forwarding address.

In the following week Dan watched Emily's movements and trailed discreetly behind her when she went outside the gate. It seemed she didn't go to her special spot everyday but only Mondays and Wednesdays. He planned his altercation with her for the following Wednesday.

The weather held and the warmth of the sun made Dan sweat. He pulled his hat down over his eyes to shade them from the glare and to hide his face from anyone who might see him. Once again he watched as Emily disappeared behind a large boulder. His stomach was churning and his hands were shaking. He had rehearsed this moment in his mind and still wondered if he could pull it off. She was strong, healthy and could bite and kick as good as any horse he had tamed but Emily would be just another frustrated filly waiting for his firm hand to make her docile.

He walked past the boulder as though he didn't know she was there and turned when he heard her sharp intake of breath. He knew he would scare her. She wouldn't be expecting anyone to come round the rock.

He pretended to jump at her sudden appearance. 'Ooo, Emily', he said, 'yuh scared me.' He put his hand to his chest in a theatrical gesture of shock.

'Daniel, what are you doing here?'

'Well, I could ask you the same thing.'

Erm, oh, well I'm just ......' A book lay on her lap and she picked it up and said, 'reading'.

Dan looked across the scenic area. 'Yeah it's a beaut spot for it, isn't it?' He turned to look at her. 'I come here quite often, to dream and ... You don't want to hear about all that.'

Emily smiled warily. 'Great minds think alike.'

He took his hat off and wiped his sweat soaked brow with his sleeve. 'It's very warm isn't it?' He had to make her feel comfortable or she would scarper like a frightened rabbit, he tried to sound polite and caring. 'Don't you feel hot, Emily?' He couldn't resist looking at the top two buttons of her blouse which she had undone. She grabbed at the neck and pulled the opened edges together.

'I'm fine,' she said the smile disappearing from her lips.

She pulled her legs up clasping her skirt to her for decency as she began to stand. 'I'd better be going I have to get back to Thomas.'

Before she could stand fully, when she was in that awkward crouching position between sitting and standing, Dan rushed across and pushed her back down. She fell with a thump, the air knocked out of her with the surprise of the attack.

'What are you doing?'

She struggled to stand again but Dan lunged at her throwing his weight against her. They both fell to the ground, the force of the fall taken by Emily. She grunted as his weight settled over her.

For a moment she was still then she began to struggle and shout. 'Get off me, get off me.' Her hands thrashed out and pulled at his hair and scratched his face.

'You bitch.' Dan put his knees between her thighs to push her legs apart. He grabbed her hands and held them round the wrist with one hand, with the other he ripped at her clothing his energy heightened by his desire. She began to scream but he crushed her windpipe with his forearm and her screams died in her throat. Her face was going red under his pressure and she was making a gurgling sound, trying to breathe.

'Now, you bitch, I'm going to give you what you have been wanting for a long time.'

'No, no,' Emily croaked.

'So you may as well lay back and enjoy it because if you don't I'll only hurt you. And we wouldn't want that would we?'

Her body went still and Dan released the pressure on her neck. Had she fainted, or was it just an act?

He slapped her face. 'Come on wake up you bitch, I want you to feel everything I do to you.'

He undid the buttons of his trousers and his organ sprang from its restriction.

He entered her and her body jerked and bucked trying to rid herself of him. He thrust deeper and deeper inside her and she shrieked in pain. That surprised him, he was sure she'd had it off with every Tom, Dick and Harry round the place. It was even more exciting to think he was the first man to have her, the first to leave his mark on her. Well she would definitely remember him, her first sexual experience. His rhythm grew faster as he craved satisfaction, the nerves in his body tingled and his breathing became heavy. Sweat trickled down his face and he could smell himself, a manly dominant smell of sweat and semen. All his sensed became focused on one part of his body as he continued to thrust and groan. He was completely oblivious to Emily or any discomfort she may be feeling. When the pinnacle of ecstasy flooded over him he groaned louder before finally collapsing onto Emily his body feeling leaden, the endorphins in his brain making his spirits soar.

'There y'are, luv, all done.' He looked Emily in the face. The hatred he saw in her eyes shocked him.

She raised her head and spat at him. 'You scum.'

Her response was like cold water over his head. The scared little maid had turned into a demon and Dan hadn't expected that. He thought perhaps she would curl into a ball and have a little cry but her actions made him angry.

He smacked her across the face. 'You'd better watch your mouth, woman.' He pushed himself to his feet and did up his buttons.

Emily hurriedly sat up pulling her skirt round her for protection. 'You haven't heard the last of this,' she spoke with venom.

'Oh yeah and whose going to believe you, it's your word against mine.'

'Of course they will believe me, why wouldn't they?'

Dan sniggered at her remark. 'Do you think Mrs Tasker will appreciate the governess having it off with the coachman?' He looked down at the ground and added, 'and then you have to find me?'

'Oh, you're going to run off and hide? Don't worry, they will find a low life like you no matter which rock you are hiding under.'

Emily's rage was annoying. Maybe he should get rid of her and then no one would know anything.

'I'm warning you, I'm losing patience with you.'

'Oh are you?' she began to get to her feet. 'Well I can promise you one thing Daniel Turner, I will get you, one way or the other.'

He'd had enough of her threats, she was supposed to lie back and enjoy it, women liked forceful men, they liked a bit of rough and tumble and he hadn't done anything wrong. She was just a mouthy bitch and he couldn't stand her harping on any longer. She was standing in front of him, yakking on at him.

'For Christ sake shut up.' He reached out for her, grabbed the front of her blouse in both hands and backed her up against the boulder. He smashed her into it and she grunted as the air was knocked out of her lungs. Again he thrust her against the rock and he heard the crack of her skull hitting the hard surface. Her body went limp and her legs couldn't support her. He pulled her away from the rock and saw the blood on its surface where her head had hit. In horror he let her body go and it slid to the ground, her mouth gaped open and her head lolled to one side.

Dan stepped back from her prone figure. He had killed her.

'Oh my God.'

The fear that gripped his brain was unreasonable but he was convinced she was dead. For a moment he couldn't move, he should do something for her, call some one, get help, try to revive her but shock made him stick to the spot like a statue that had dropped from the skies into the wrong place. His primeval fleeing instincts took over even before he checked to see if she were still breathing. He turned his back on the situation he now found himself in and began to run, but not towards the road, away down the hill into the scrub where no one would see him. No one would know he had killed Emily Smith.

For a few hours Dan wondered round in the bush planning what he would do. He had to go back to the stables to get his things and the money he had hidden under his bed. He was due to start his new job next week and was going to leave tomorrow anyway, a fact Mr Simms knew. Fortunately he hadn't told him where he was going and there was not much chance of him seeing anyone from Brunswick House again once he left and started his new job. It just meant he was going a day early. That would look suspicious to the police so he would have to leave a note explaining his sudden disappearance. Perhaps he could say his old mother was ill. Would Mr Simms know he had no mother? Why would he? He didn't know anything about the staff at Brunswick House he just came along and pretended to care what went on there.

All was dark when Dan managed to find his way back to the house. His clothes were filthy but he didn't have time to change. There was no police wagon out front and everything looked normal. Stealthily he crept up the stairs that led to his room above the stables, half anticipating someone would be waiting there for him. The room was empty but he couldn't light the lamp and draw attention to the fact that he was back. He stumbled around in the dark gathering up his things and stuffing them into a hessian sack. He felt under the straw mattress and found his small wad of money. He ripped a piece of paper from the Equipment and Supplies ledger that rested on a box beside the bed and jotted a short note, explaining that his brother had been thrown from a horse and was in a bad way, so he had to go and see him. He didn't state where or when but added that he would call back for the wages that were owed to him in due course.

Of course he would never come back for that pittance although he could do with it at the moment. Carefully Dan crept down stairs and out into the darkness keeping to the side of the building so no one would see his silhouette. He left the note on the mounting block outside the stable with a stone on top to stop it blowing away.

Away from the house he made his way across the fields to find somewhere to shelter for the night. Walking in a huge circuitous route he ended up back on the main road a few miles from Brunswick house. He headed towards the river and Coronation Park and knew there would be a ferry along in the morning to take him to the city. It took Dan a good hour to walk there, being so late he didn't see a soul. By the time he got to the park he was tired and very hungry but managed to scale the gates and find a bench under a willow tree. The branches screened him from the curious eyes of park keepers. He made himself comfortable and tried to sleep but the slumped figure of Emily haunted him. Killing her wasn't part of his plan. Would her death play on his conscience for weeks, months or even years to come? Silly bitch. Why did she have to have the last word, why couldn't she just lay there and not be so mouthy? Dreams of being chased haunted Dan's few nodding hours before dawn.

As daylight edged across the park and the sun burnt off the early morning mist Dan's spirits improved. In a place like Sydney they would have no chance of finding him. All he had to do was get on that ferry and get lost in the hustle and bustle of city life.

But he needed to spruce himself up a bit. His first port of call when he got to the big smoke was to see Mrs Lang. Thoughts of her filled his head as he changed his shirt and trousers and rubbed the dust off his boots. He tried to shave in a nearby pond but the cut throat razor nearly lived up to its name. Blood trickled down his neck and he swore and clamped a piece of lily leaf over the slight wound. His empty stomach was rumbling wildly and he gazed hungrily at the fish swimming nonchalantly around the pond. As he heard the voices of the park keepers he hurried down to the riverbank, hid behind a tree and waited for the ferry that would take him to freedom.

It was Friday morning when he arrived at the Port of Sydney and alighted from the boat with a crush of workers that had been picked up all along the Parramatta River. At the first teashop he came to he ordered bread and butter and a mug of tea which calmed his nerves. Dan felt more human and able to face the tasks of the day. A place to live was his next concern. He was going to ask the blokes at work on Monday about that, they would be sure to know somewhere, but now he had to find a room a few days earlier so there was no one he could seek advice from.

Dan wondered if Mrs Lang would know somewhere but since she was still fairly new to the area herself she probably wouldn't. A bit of silliness slithered into his mind, what if she felt sorry for him and said he could stay with her. If he gave her a real sad sob story she might be taken in although he doubted she would have room. He could sleep on her sofa or floor for a few days and he would be so helpful and charming she wouldn't be able to resist marrying him. He laughed at his little dream. No self respecting woman would take a single man into her home to live unless they wanted to get a bad name for themselves. No, he would have to find a place for himself. As he looked at all the ships in the harbour, he had an idea. Sailors, they were always looking for somewhere to stay and would know all the good and bad boarding houses in the area.

By mid afternoon Dan had found a room in a house in Argyle Street and he was feeling very pleased. It was quite close to where Mrs Lang lived, in fact she was only in Playfair Street, which was just around the corner. He couldn't believe his luck, now he could watch her and he had good reason to be in the area. But the downside was that he had to pay a week's rent in advance and he would be a bit strapped for cash until he got his next pay packet. But life was good he had a new job and a new woman.

The fleas in Dan's bed and feelings of guilt kept him awake. Saturday morning he felt ready to see Mrs Lang. He really must find out her first name and get to know her better. He knew she would be working at Greetby's but would have to think of some excuse to see her. Well for a start he could tell her all about his new job, he had told her a few lies about his old one, which was good since he didn't want her to know what had really happened. As he walked down George Street there was a spring in his step and a smile on his face. He sighed with satisfaction as he waited to cross the road. Horses and carts clattered past but a strident voice amid the noisy onslaught brought Dan to a complete halt, frozen to the curb side, unable to move.

'Read all about it, woman's body found, come on get your newspaper here.' The newspaper vendor repeated his selling spiel and Dan's head spun round and looked at him. Her death had made the headlines already. She had been found. Dan stumbled into the road oblivious of the swearing dray driver whose horse nearly crushed him. He bumped into people who swore at him thinking he was drunk. He staggered into the nearest pub and sat down heavily at a small table. The sound of men's voices bounced off the tiled walls and echoed round the large room and Dan put his head in his hands and covered his eyes.

What was he going to do? He was a murderer, a killer and a rapist. How could he every look Mrs Lang in the face?

'You alright mate?'

Dan peeped through his hands and saw the soiled apron of the publican directly in front of him. 'You look like you could do with a stiff drink, I know the signs of shock, mate. Beer with a rum chaser should do the trick.' He sounded friendly and jolly.

Dan nodded his head but kept looking down until his drinks arrived. He drank the beer straight down and looked at the patrons of the pub who were milling about chatting and telling stories. No one looked at him they weren't the slightest bit interested in him. The vision of people pointing at him and calling him a killer faded. He took a deep breath and decided he was being dramatic. No one knew anything about him. This was a new life. The authorities would never know where to find him in this rat race. It would be practically impossible. One good thing, Emily wouldn't be able to tell them who had killed her. Dan smiled to himself although he still felt uneasy. He decided he wouldn't go to see Mrs Lang today. His nerves were a bit stretched, better to leave it a few days when he was feeling a bit better.

On Sunday Dan knew Mrs Lang would not be working and decided it would be a good day to suss out her house and see if he could find out more about her. The day was sunny and lots of people were out strolling, taking the air. Doors and windows were flung open and Dan could hear the sound of children's laughter, the boom of a male voice or the shriek of a fishwife filtering onto the street. He leaned against a gas lamp, rolling a cigarette, looking quite comfortable in his surroundings. He spent an age fiddling with the cigarette as he observed Mrs Lang's house for signs of life.

As he watched she came out of her front door with a bucket. Dan hastily tucked himself out of sight. She put the bucket down and thrust her hand into it drawing out a dripping soapy brush, which she proceeded to scrub the step with. A smile lit up Dan's face, that's what he liked to see, a woman looking after the home.

'Mama, mama, we can see you.' A piping young voice made Dan look above her head. On the balcony of her house was a child or rather two children. One was carrying a youngster. Dan stared. The bigger girl was fair like her mother, the same blonde hair but the one she carried was dark, very dark. An abo, well not a true abo, she wasn't that black but she was definitely halfy halfy.

Dan squinted up his eyes with distaste. As the child spoke Mrs Lang looked up at them and scolded the older girl. 'Maggie, don't lean over the edge carrying Dawn, you might drop her.'

What was she doing with a half caste child? She must be minding it for some one else, but why? Why would she want a black child in her house? He knew she was a lovely person and all that but sheltering one of them was going a bit too far. That child stuck out like a sore thumb, there weren't that many abos in the big smoke. He could tell the child wasn't that old only about a year he reckoned. What if it was her child? No, his woman would never have it off with a black fella.

CHAPTER 14

Ningan

For years Ningan had thought about this white man. On dark nights as he looked at the stars scattered in the sky, he had envisaged a spirit person with magic powers who saved people from death. He never thought the man who saved him all those years ago would be stupid.

'Him silly fella,' he kept muttering under his breath.

After the storm and the falling tree, when he smelt his sweat and knew this was his white whitefella, Ningan had jumped away from him and sat on the ground at some distance. He could feel the anger coming from John Rhodes like rays from the sun, even though he was laughing. Ningan wasn't going near him. He knew when white men got angry anything could happen. He decided to keep out of reach but watch him. He certainly needed watching, he wasn't safe to be let loose on the creatures of this earth. He was like a cat that had been dumped in the outback, wild and spitting at everything in sight and upsetting the native animals.

'What are you staring at?' John Rhodes spat. 'Just leave me alone,' he yelled as he got up and stalked away.

He didn't seem very happy to have his life saved, thought Ningan. And another strange thing was that this man didn't have anything with him. No bed roll that the white men used or sack of food, nothing but the clothes on his back. Next thing he began heading away from the river in the direction where there was no water for miles and miles. Ningan shook his head.

What was he doing here? The words he muttered after he saved him came back to Ningan. Something about trying to kill himself but that was really stupid. The mere skin and bones of a man couldn't decide a thing like that. It was down to the spirit of death to decide. Ningan felt very worried for this strange whitefella. If he did kill himself what would happen? The spirits might cry and their tears flood the earth or they may breathe air of badness and make people sick like they had done before when the white men first came to these parts. No, it was too risky he would have to look after this man and save him from himself if he had to. Ningan scratched his head, the ways of the whitefella were very strange indeed.

For the next few days Ningan followed him. He kept his distance, stalked him like any wild animal that was wounded and ready to thrash out if it was cornered. Perhaps when this man had a chance to lick his wounds and rest, the health of his brain would come back.

On the first day Mr Rhodes just walked and walked with hunched shoulders, his hands thrust in his coat pockets. At the end of that day he lay down using his coat for a pillow and slept. The next day he got up and walked off leaving his coat behind. He didn't eat or drink. The following day his pace was slower and he began to limp. When the sun was high in the sky the whitefella didn't look for shelter he just kept stumbling along.

Ningan had seen many corpses of white men in this place and knew it was a horrible way to die. He didn't want his Mr Rhodes to go like that, but what could he do? Some bush animals were very silly like the bilbi when it sees a grasshopper or the mallee foul when it tries to dig its nest in a rock bed, but none of these creatures were as silly as this whitefella. Is dying of stupidity the same as taking your own life, Ningan wondered?

He hoped the spirit gods could heal John Rhodes who had closed his mind to beauty and feelings of good. On the third morning he left his shoes behind at his campsite. It was as though he was torturing himself, making his body pay for the bad things he had done. All day he stumbled in the blazing sun, how he kept upright Ningan didn't know. In some ways he had to be admired, he didn't sit down and let his body rest he pushed himself on, towards certain death.

Ningan was feeling desperate he couldn't help him and knew that if he gave him food or water it would be pushed away. That night he stayed close. Although Mr Rhodes was unaware of his presence Ningan could see him through the bushes.

He heard him crying and making his peace with the people from his life.

'Please forgive me Thomas…..I am not worthy to be your father.' Ningan frowned at this plea, but the whitefella went on. 'I'm going to be with your mother and sister if they'll have me.'

Time was getting near, Ningan knew, when the spirit leaves the body and the remains would collapse like clothes without a person inside.

Shaking his head Ningan cursed 'No John Rhodes you not going die.'

The sound of his sobbing died away and finally he took a deep sigh and closed his eyes. Ningan sat still, watching his chest. It continued to move up and down, occasionally the whitefella mumbled in his sleep and threw his arms up as though fending off some unseen attacker. Was he going through the trip to the other land, Ningan wondered or fighting the fever of hunger? All night he sat watching and felt fear as the demons continued to tug at John Rhodes' body.

By morning he was still. Ningan went to him.

'John Rhodes, don't be dead.' There was a faint breath as Ningan held his hand in front of the whitefella's mouth and gently spoke to him like a sick child. 'You can't die, I won't let you.'

As gently as he could he dragged the unconscious man to the shade of a nearby tree and tried to make him comfortable. He was obviously in need of liquid and Ningan thought for a moment before he took a sip of water from his water pouch and held it in his mouth. He leaned over and placed his lips over the open mouth of the whitefella. Gently he let the water seep from his mouth to the other man's and the automatic swallowing function did its work. Ningan repeated the process until Mr Rhodes began moaning slightly. His hands moved like a creature coming out of hibernation, the fingers giving an occasional flutter as life was restored.

'Now Mr Rhodes, lay still till your dried up blood begins flow again.' The whitefella's chest was moving up and down more forcefully now and Ningan was glad. He studied the rest of his body. His face was red from sunburn and his feet were a mess of blisters, blood and peeling skin. Ningan could feel his ribs through his shirt and put his hand round the scrawny wrist.

'Mr Rhodes, you not bin eatin' much,' he tutted, as though he was reprimanding a small child. 'Don't yuh know you haffa eat. Eatin's good. Them plump witchetty grubs, ummm, cooked till skin bursts and him whitefella food, him good.' Ningan screwed his nose up at the thoughts of the white mushy stuff the whitefella called porridge. 'We gunna have do something bout this bag of bones.' He gently patted the prone man's rib cage.

Ningan delved into the kangaroo skin bag that hung round his waist and produced a hand full of furry berries that had begun to go mouldy. 'Dunno how long em berries bin in there but him still good berry.' He put the fruit into his mouth and slowly chewed it until in was a wet pulp and then spat it into his hand. Gently he forced the masticated fruit between the whitefella's lips and followed it with more water. The sick man coughed as the fruit hit his throat but did swallow it. Ningan gave him more water but this time let it dribble straight from the pouch letting some of it trickle over the dry, scabby lips.

'That bedda Mr Rhodes, but yuh godda do himself.' Ningan shook his head, it was pathetic really that this spirit man had come to such a state after only five days in the wild. It would take a healthy man a bit longer than that to be dying of thirst and hunger. This man that he had placed in the realms of a spirit was only human and in great need of soul healing. It was obvious to Ningan that this man was dying from the brain out. His mind had closed on reason and commonsense and decided not to let the rest of his body live. This was the sort of thing the very old did when they felt they were no more use to the tribe, a burden to their relatives. Ningan studied Mr Rhodes, he wasn't that old. Could it be that whitefellas felt useless younger than black men, their lives had no meaning or purpose so they decided to go bush to die? No, if that were so, the bush would be full of men walking to their death. The idea made Ningan smile.

Perhaps these whitefellas weren't as hard and unbeatable as they made out.

A moan came from the prone figure and Ningan lifted the lolling head and placed it on his lap. It was about time this poor man felt some human warmth. Leaning over, he smelt the whitefella's hair. His scent was stronger and once again the smell bought back the memories of the day his father died and the way this man had saved his life. With one arm across Mr Rhode's chest and the other cradling his head Ningan crooned a native lullaby to the man he felt such a bond with. He wanted the strength of his body to travel to his whitefella and make him well again.

The whitefella lay still, the small fluttering of his hands had stopped, his chest was still going up and down with a regular movement and Ningan knew he was asleep. Every hour or so he would trickle more water into his mouth but decided to let him sleep to gain more energy to eat.

After a short while the crooning stopped and Ningan leaned back against the tree but still had the whitefella's head on his lap. He made himself comfortable and began talking quietly. Occasionally he stroked Mr Rhodes' head and realized it was the first human contact he'd had himself since Connie.

'Ah Mr Rhodes, this funny old life, she drags us long, from one heartache to next, like going over a bumpy track. There's parts that hurt feet, there's so many stones on ground, can hardly walk but yuh do, keep puttin' one foot in front of other and it hurts on souls of feet, but yuh keep going. Then yuh get to smooth part of track, when yuh don't think of feet cause it doesn't hurt. Soft sand she's cool and lulls yuh to thinkin' this track alright, but round next bend more stones. If yuh try gettin' off that track then bushes closes in, yuh have to pick way through and him slow and scratchy, so yuh gets back on track. Track she can get badder and badder but yuh godda get back on, else yuh won't know where yuh going.' It was the longest conversation Ningan had had with anyone since Connie left and it felt good to let his mouth run on.

'So John Rhodes, you godda get back on track, keep walkin'. Me fell off, gone round in circles, head full of sadness, teamin' round like ants with a stick in their nest. Then him birds with yellow heads flies across sky, makes me think, him nature spirit do good things, maybe I bedda get back to livin'.'

'Yuh know Mr Rhodes, my life she been bitch, as whitefella says.' Ningan smiled, he liked the word "bitch", it sounded good when he spat it out.

'Yeah, I changed day father killed, day I met you. That day I ran back to mother, I scratched, eyes red from cryin' and was tremblin' like kangaroo without fur.

For a moment Ningan stopped talking, the anger and sorrow of that time made his chest feel tight. He had never spoken about it, it was locked up inside him and never been released until now.

'Mother, she ran to me, I couldn't talk. Elders came to look, they knew when no father, no men, no food. Mother she went in bush and wacked herself with tree branch. Elders went, no one come near, like I had bad sickness no one want. I very sad felt like it my fault everyone die, wished you hadn't saved me.' For a moment Ningan sat with a far off look in his eyes before carrying on.

'Women brought mother back to camp when sun gone, she covered in blood where she'd had go at herself and she not speak. She not want me, talk like I not there. Rest of tribe not speak me either. I had to grow up to be man pretty damn quick. Initiation time came and I never sit at mother's fire again. I was very lonely, then Guda, she comes along.'

A slight smile turned up his lips at the thought of her, followed by a frown when the memories closed in. 'She pretty like a flower, dark eyes mouth always smiling. She older than me, she follow me when I go off on my own. I never sat with tribe, I closer to animals. She sat with me, I tell her about black snake and hornet or things that flew over. I not afraid of creatures only humans. I was bit wild, like creatures I watch. She lovely, soft voice got me thinkin' things be alright, but things went bad.'

He couldn't speak for a moment as he swallowed a lump that made his throat tight. 'She had piccaninni in her belly and tribe they think it mine. I never do that to her, she too good and clean, but I got blame. We both got beaten and baby came, into the sand, blood and mess and in middle a tiny baby. She cried and I spat on her, she not good and clean.' There was still a note of disbelief in his tone. 'Tribe still think it me, I left camp that day and never go back.'

Ningan sighed at the unfairness of life but had come to terms with the way the spirits worked. 'I bin walkabout all time since, that

'bout fifteen seasons behind. Then I met Connie, 'nother bad
mistake.'

He shook his head. It was hard to believe the two women in
his life that made him feel alive and sent his heart racing, he had lost.
Sometimes his body yearned for a female but the spirits must have
someone special ready for him. One day he would be loved and it
would last.

The body that was leaning against him began to stir, the eyes
fluttered, the lips parted and the tongue sheepishly licked the dry
lips. The whitefella mumbled croakily and let out a sigh as though it
was all too much effort.

'Now, Mr Rhodes, don't move, I gunna get food for yuh.'

Moving the whitefella's head from his lap Ningan gently
placed it on the ground. He dragged some dried leaves from the
surrounding area and made a pillow, scooping it under the
whitefella's head. He knew they liked to sleep with a pillow and
wanted to make him as comfortable as possible. Rising, Ningan
looked down at him and thought what a shrunken man he looked, but
he would soon make him better. Give him some good tucker, take
him down to the water to get the dust off him and he would be as
good as new, in body, he wasn't sure about his head though.

Ningan spent a few hours hunting for food to help the
whitefella's recovery. Berries were good for making him wee, lizard
heart make his heart beat better, the flesh of a bush turkey good for
his strength and the oil of the tea tree would kill any badness that
was left. It was all stuffed into his food pouch and taken back to
camp. The whitefella hadn't moved while he was away and Ningan
made a fire. He cooked the meats slow wrapped in leaves in the
ashes. Leaves from the tea tree he mixed with water and ground with
a stone to form a smooth paste, which he would later put in a drink.

The cooking aromas caused the whitefella to stir and
mumble. His eyes flickered but this time opened slightly and then
quickly closed as the harsh brightness of the day hurt them.

'You wake Mr Rhodes?' A grunt came from the prone figure.
'You like him smell? Umm…him good tucker.'

Ningan tried to encourage the whitefella but the only
response was when he rolled onto his side in the opposite direction
to the fire. Ningan sat still for a moment, contemplating how best to
deal with this man who carried on like a piccanini. He turned the

meat to let the juices run into the fire and send more good smells in the whitefella's direction.

'Yuh know things could be badder for you,' Ningan said it with a resigned sadness in his voice and continued, 'you could be abo.'

He turned back to his cooking, the food did smell good but he had lost his appetite. A few moments later he heard a rustling behind him.

Ningan turned and smiled at Mr Rhodes who had rolled back in his direction. 'Now, you eat?'

The whitefella leaned up on one elbow and nodded. Ningan beamed down at him, he felt so relieved that he wanted to live after all. He rushed over, helped him to a sitting position. He was still very weak but Ningan knew that if he had the will to live he would be alright.

They rested under the shade of that tree for a few days, its long slender limbs sheltering them from the harshness of the sun's rays. Ningan knew every crack and crevice of its trunk and what lived on it, since there wasn't much else to look at while John Rhodes got better. He had worked on the whitefella in both body and soul, feeding him up on all the goodness that nature could give. He talked to him all the time, which was hard because aborigines are known to be a quiet, thoughtful race, not like the whitefella who gabble on all the time. Eventually Ningan stopped chattering like a demented galah as John Rhodes started to respond and very slowly he began to talk.

The first words he said were, 'Call me John.'

Ningan beamed.

At first John didn't say much, there were long silences between them and Ningan talked about the weather or the way the ants were behaving but didn't ask any questions. Finally John began making excuses as to why he was in such a state and the reasons behind his desire for death. Now the roles were reversed as Ningan listened and John talked. His words were like the water trickling down a creek, slow and meandering until the flood comes and it gushes forth taking all the debris in its wake until finally the water recedes leaving the riverbed more eroded but clean and smooth. John's words flooded out with all the debris of remorse and heartbreak, washed from him leaving him scarred but relieved.

What would happen now, Ningan wondered? Would the whitefella just get up and walk into the bush to be alone again. Nah, they were friends, they knew each other inside out.

John

The droning voice seeped into John's brain. It was comforting and went on in the same monotonous tone, but that was good. It was soothing. It was a warm buzzing in his ears, it was another person, he was not on his own. He was reminded of when he was a child and nanny used to tell him stories and he would close his eyes to let his imagination weave round the characters. Occasionally the voice got excited or dropped to a quiet sadness that made his subconscious jump into action and his ears listened, then the voice would lull him off again.

It was always nanny who told him stories, never his mother. He would never have snuggled up to her, she was thin and hard and only ever went mad at him. This voice was deep and mellow. He caught snatches of information about a death, a child on his own and lost love. John laughed inwardly at the comparison to his own life, death, children on their own and lost love. Was that what everyone's lives consisted of?

The voice he could hear sounded young, it was a man's voice but it lacked that tone of years of experience. That sort of weariness that age brings. The words were simple, straight to the point with no educated nuances to make it false. He liked that voice, he wondered who owned it, but didn't want to open his eyes and look.

He felt the warmth of the day and a harsh light glaring through his eyelids. Later the leaves on the tree rustled and a chill wafted over him. He knew it was evening then, a darkness on the other side of his eyelids meant it was night and still he couldn't be bothered to move. His head was resting on something warm, something living and he could feel a pulse throbbing, keeping someone else alive. It was like the heartbeat of a mother, an unconscious bodily function that told of life and warmth. In his lucid moments he felt things being put in his mouth and he swallowed as though he was a baby being fed. John dozed, his body was so tired he just wanted to sleep. Sleep away the terror, the sadness and rid himself of the tightness in his chest when he was awake.

The ground under his back felt hard and unyielding but that was like a punishment, not letting him get lulled into a comfortable position. Bits of twig stuck into his skin and he could feel ants crawling in his legs, but he had no impulse to brush them off. He wondered what he would do if he felt a snake slithering over him, would he jump up or would he continue to lay here and not care whether he was bitten? He didn't think the person who was watching over him would let that happen. Was it God? Was he in heaven, had he died and gone to a better place? No, he didn't think clouds would be so hard and lumpy, but maybe they were, who knows? Perhaps he was in a coma. He had heard of this where people lay for days, months or even years and can hear things but can't move. It was all very strange and he was too tired to think about it.

Once again he woke and the yellow light on his eyelids told him it was daytime. His brain felt refreshed, he tried to open his eyes but the glare forced them shut again. He groaned involuntarily and a voice answered his stirrings.

'You wake?' The voice sounded further away. 'You like him smell?' John didn't think this person was speaking to him. 'Umm, him good tucker,' the voice went on.

The words made John's nostrils flare and his sense of smell was suddenly awakened. A savoury smell drifted up his nose and he felt his stomach rumble in response. It was a pleasure that he had no right to enjoy, he didn't deserve it, he was a killer and must be punished. If the law wasn't going to do it he would have to do it himself. He rolled away from the voice and smells, into a foetal position and tried to close his mind to temptation.

The next words made John's morbid thoughts of self retribution die.

'Yuh know things could be badder for you. You could be abo.'

It was a very strange thing to say but the depth of feeling in those few words made John turn back to the living.

His squinting eyes took in the campsite, the cooking food and the aborigine who was crouched in front of the fire poking meat with a stick. There was no one else. Was this blackman the voice that pulled him back from the brink? The incongruity of the situation struck John as funny, he wanted to smile but his cracked lips made it more of a leer. He felt emotional but wanted to thank this blackman, but the words wouldn't come.

As the lump in John's throat threatened to turn him into a jibbering jelly he tried to make light of things. 'Call me John.'

The blackman looked pleased. John didn't know what to say, he felt a bit of an idiot but the blackman began chattering so John didn't have to say anything. Food was placed on a rock beside him, he ate as he listened and tried not to let his thoughts seep inwards, back to the darkness within.

It was so companionable and this fellow was such a character John felt like smiling at times. Some of the words spoken to him while he was in and out of consciousness came back to him and with a shock he realized this was the chap who had been talking about lost love and lonely children. It hardly seemed conceivable to look at him now, his mouth full of big white teeth, his smiling eyes and his gangly arms and legs. Then there was that comment about being an abo and John became aware that this blackman was just as vulnerable as he.

Little by little John began to talk, he tried to make excuses for his actions at first. His voice was croaky but he took sips of water and mouthfuls of food and his energy and confidence began to slowly return. His excuses sounded pathetic even to his own ears and he began to tell this total stranger what led him to this doleful situation.

The sun was high in the sky when John finally stopped talking and he looked around him as though he had been unaware of anything else. The blackness inside had escaped like the putrid smell of rotting flesh when released to the air and a wave of relief washed through. For the first time in ages he noticed the beauty of the day, heard the bees buzzing and the breeze rustling the leaves of the tree. It was as though he was reborn and the heaviness of that other life, had been lifted.

The blackman, who he gathered was called Ningan, sat stoically nearby, his lanky languid body looked comfortable in his crossed legged position but there was a slight dint of worry on his brow. John liked Ningan, he liked him a lot and wanted to remain close to him. There was something between them, something invisible yet powerful, something that meant they would always remain friends.

John felt the infected skin on his lip split as he smiled but hardly felt the pain his action caused. Like a newborn foal he got to his feet and put his hand against the tree to steady himself. Ningan ran to his side and supported. John had to stop himself from throwing his arms around this man and hugging him. Men didn't hug each other.

Another day was spent with John making little forays into the bush getting his strength back. Fortunately Ningan had picked up all his belonging that had been scattered along the way so John did have shoes and a hat. The medicinal qualities of the tea tree came into play and were rubbed on John's sun burnt face and arms and also helped his scabby feet. They were so sore he couldn't get his shoes on and began walking bare footed like Ningan although the blackman had years of hard skin coating the soul of his feet.

The following day they struck out from the campsite. Both looked back at the spot where their bond of friendship had been struck and tried to remember the surrounding area so they could come back one day. It was a place neither of them would forget. Their pace was very slow to start and John limped badly but they were in no rush, they had nowhere they had to be and no one to bother about them.

Ningan immediately took the lead and began to show John his land. They were heading to a remote part of New South Wales the northwest corner, which Ningan knew like the palm of his hand, he informed John. The land was flat with hillocks popping up intermittently as though they had been built on purpose to deflect from the lands monotony. Long green grass brushed their legs and spring flowers made a carpet of yellow that rippled in the breeze. The contrast between the land and the bright blue sky was startling with the horizon like a straight line drawn with a ruler by a giant hand.

John took a deep exhilarating breath, the air smelt clean and pure. For the first time in years it felt good to be alive and the feeling made John's raw emotions come to the surface. This is stupid, he thought. The slightest thing and I feel like I'm going to turn into a blubbering wreck. He watched the loping movement of Ningan in front of him, he was beginning to know all his idiosyncrasies, the way he scratched his head when he was thinking as though it would help the process, the way he walked with his hands on his hips to cool his armpits and the way he held his head when he was listening for something that John couldn't even hear.

They had many stops during the first few days while John was regaining his strength and some of the things Ningan gave him to eat were best just popped into the mouth without too much thought.

During their rest periods they inevitably began to talk and John was astounded when he realized Ningan thought he knew him from years ago. At first he kept going on about how he had saved his life when he was a boy and now they were even. This incident in Ningan's childhood John had no memory of. There was a time when John was in the army when he did go to the outback to quell a black insurgence. That turned out to be a dozen blackmen camped on a sheep station which the owner took umbrage to. They were trying to win back their ancestral lands but of course they were overpowered and moved on. He remembered vividly after that event coming across an aborigine camp where everyone had been killed. Their bodies lay scattered on the ground with bullet wounds and bitten and torn flesh where wild animals had had a go at them. They had buried those bodies for decency sake and moved on.

After that gruesome discovery, the plight of the blackman always saddened him but once he got back to civilization and the hubbub of normal life, he more or less forgot about those forlorn bodies. That type of sick incident happened a lot to the blacks back then and it was inconceivable that those dead people could have been Ningan's kith and kin. But John didn't want to disillusion Ningan so he went along with his account of events and let him believe it was he that saved him. He may not be so keen to stay with him if Ningan knew he wasn't his saviour from years ago.

Judging by the sun they were heading east and after a week of walking they hit their destination. John had got used to plodding along. At first it was daunting, the idea of walking all day, but there were so many things to see. Ningan pointed out the life teaming in this bare, flat, land. He learnt so much in that week he felt like a child again whose brain was soaking up information like water soaks into sand. His eyes began to seek out wildlife and try to see them before Ningan but he never managed it.

They were moving towards an area that still had water, Ningan told him. Before the heat of summer dried up the water holes they would cleanse their bodies and drink their fill. Red river gums lined the banks and the long grasses gave way to rocky outcrops and red soil. The river looked enticing to their dust covered bodies and John sat for a while with his feet dabbling in the shallows. The coolness was almost erotic as the current streamed between his toes and cooled his feet. His blisters had healed with Ningan's ministrations and after a week of walking he felt stronger both physically and mentally.

He longed to let his body feel the cool current of water and wash away the dirt and dust of the outback. John lowered himself into the inviting water, clothes and all. He dug his toes into the riverbed and moved his arms about trying to stay on his feet but the pull of the current tore at his clothes and he over balanced. With his head underwater he panicked.

It was happening again, he tried to reach out for them but his fingers kept missing them. They were too wet and slippery, the face of Beattie swum in front of him and he could hear Anna giggling. They were going further and further away and he couldn't do anything about it. The swirling green water sent him tumbling over and over and he was fighting for breath. He was powerless to save them, but this time he would go too. He wouldn't be left on his own he would join them in their watery graves. John let himself be pulled by the water, a feeling of calm came over him and he let all the air out of his lungs. He was bumped against stones and scratched by tree roots but he was oblivious to it. His body jolted when his free fall down the river stopped. Some one grabbed him and pulled his head above the water.

'John, what you doin'?'

'Leave me alone.' John tried to struggle from Ningan's grasp. 'Let the river take me.'

'No, no, you silly devil,' Ningan cursed him.

Ningan's words penetrated the fog in John's brain and he wrenched himself back to the living. He shook his head, trying to clear it of the memories the water had evoked. He couldn't believe what he had just done. It had all came back to him, once the water had covered his head, that feeling of helplessness.

Ningan got him to the bank and John couldn't stop saying, 'Sorry, sorry, I'm sorry.' He wasn't sure who he was apologizing to, his wife and daughter or Ningan.

Once he was on the bank again John felt foolish, but Ningan didn't let him linger there too long.

'Come on John time we were off again.'

John nodded. He thought he was getting over his grief and sadness but this little fiasco had shown him he was a long way from recovery. But even though the experience bought back painful memories, the blackness in his soul had not returned. At least he was free of that.

PART THREE

1914

CHAPTER 15

Maggie

Maggie was told not to stray too far from the house, but at twelve years of age she felt she was old enough to go down to the docks and see the Christmas decorations. She was dying to show them to Dawn. It was slow going with a toddler although Dawn was pretty steady on her feet. They strolled along at a snail's pace and looked into the houses as they walked. Where they lived people didn't have much money to spend on decorations, but some people had made an effort and she could see paper streamers dangling across windows. It was the big clean up before Christmas, and women were out scrubbing and polishing as though their lives depended upon it. It was a good excuse to turn the house out and even Maggie's house hadn't escaped the ritual. In fact that was why she was out with Dawn, her mother said to take her out of the way for an hour so she could get on with the cleaning.

Thoughts meandered round in Maggie's head as she walked. It was very hard for her mum, she worked at that big shop called Greetbys during the week and only had the weekends to do all the housework. Of course she helped her as much as she could. Her main job was to take care of Dawn when she got home from school and cook the tea. Her mother was quite fair with her and didn't expect her to do a lot of housework since she did the majority of the cooking. She kept the room she shared with Dawn tidy and didn't mind helping round the house.

Billy worked long hours down at the docks, leaving early in the morning and coming back very late sometimes. She always kept his dinner warming over a pan for when he came in. Sometimes he would bring back a little treat when something fell off a wagon and the contents spilled.

After a slow dawdling walk they finally reached the harbour and Dawn clapped her hands with excitement when she saw the water. A chubby brown finger pointed at the sparkling expanse of water. Her little face creased into a grin, her eyes reflected the dazzling waves.

This picturesque harbour never failed to enthral Maggie. 'Isn't it pretty,' she commented.

It was the week after they arrived in the city when they first saw the harbour. They had been walking down a street, not sure where they were going when they rounded a building and there it was. With the sun glistening off the water, Maggie thought it was the most beautiful place she had ever seen. The lapping sound the water made against the harbour wall and the cool breeze that wafted across that great expanse of Port Jackson Bay was wonderful.

She still got a thrill now as she leaned against the metal railings watching all the activity that bustled in front of them.

She held Dawn on her hip so she could see. 'Look Dawn, that ship is going away.'

Dawn's attention became focused on what Maggie was pointing at.

'Bye bye,' the toddler's voice piped as she flapped her hand at the huge vessel pulling away from the dock. Maggie smiled and joined Dawn in frantically waving even though the passengers probably couldn't see them.

Dawn buried her face in her sister's shoulder as the deep blasts from the ship's horn reverberated round the quay area and heralded the beginning of its journey.

'It's alright.' Maggie patted her on the back and Dawn peeped out when the noise had stopped. 'Down you go.'

The little face looked up at her as she was lowered to the ground. Maggie was full of love for her little sister. She was so cute. Her brown skin was the colour of a sailor's forearms that had been exposed to the sun for weeks. It was a healthy, sun kissed look not the pasty colour of her skin. And her deep brown eyes were so dark you could see your own reflection in them. Dawn's springy dark hair was something Maggie envied since hers was straight, blonde and boring.

They walked further round the quayside and watched as people got off the ferryboat that arrived from Parramatta. Maggie longed to go for a boat ride but of course she didn't have any money. One day, her mother said, they would all go for a ride.

Billy kept promising to take her but somehow he never got the time. He was all grown up now or so he liked to think. Maggie had to admit he was very tall, a lot taller than her or even her mother. At fifteen he was skinny with big feet and hands and he was too strong to play fight anymore. His muscles were hard from all the lifting he did at work. He swung Dawn about and made her giggle but he didn't seem to have any time for Maggie anymore. He was very serious and reminded them at every opportunity that he was the man of the house. It got a bit tiresome at times, Maggie had to admit, but he was good the way he tipped his wages up to mother every week.

Sometimes Maggie longed for their old life at the homestead, with mother home all the time and a house full of fun and laughter. That was before her father and the twins died. Things seemed to go down hill from then on, but it was no use complaining, there was no one to listen if she did.

They walked up the hill to Government House. By the time they got there Dawn was tired and whingey. She knelt next to her and pointed at the huge Christmas tree that stood in front of the stone building. There were coloured lanterns hanging on the branches that bobbed in the humid breeze and a star on the top that looked down upon them all. Dawn just stood and stared, her tiredness forgotten. It was the first Christmas tree she had seen. Maggie pointed and said 'star' until Dawn repeated her word.

Other families were milling about, mothers and fathers with their children and Maggie wished she was part of a proper family.

A child holding its mother's hand pointed at Dawn. 'Look mummy,' she said. That baby has dirty skin.'

The mother hurriedly shushed her and they moved away. Maggie immediately put her arms round her little sister to defend her from hurtful words, picked her up and began walking home. Their trip had been spoiled for Maggie by those innocent words.

The following day was a school day and Maggie had a long walk after she had dropped Dawn off at Mrs Tulley's house. Her mother left much earlier than her and Billy was away before any of them were up. So it was down to Maggie to take Dawn to the neighbour, who only lived a few doors away, and pick her up on the way home. Her mother paid to have the baby looked after and since Mrs Tulley had four children of her own the money helped put food on their table.

On the way to school Maggie began to worry about the arithmetic test she had that afternoon. Her stomach churned at the thought of it. She knew she would fail again. The humiliation of having to stand up in front of the class when her result was read out made her shudder. Once again she would look like a real dummy.

It was a year since Maggie started school, and she hated it. In the beginning she was treated as though she was backward because she had never attended school before and they tried to teach her simple stuff like the alphabet. Of course she already knew all that, her mother had taught her quite a lot. She was the butt of their jokes and they called her Maggie magpie.

She was already tall for her age, her mother said it was her outback upbringing, the sun constantly shining on her head that made her grow. But of course it was because her father had been tall. She had found it hard to settle into school life, all the back biting and jeering that went on and a lot of it aimed at her. But they stopped their sniggering when it was sports day. She smiled at the recollection. She had won practically every event she was in, the potato race, the running and the jumping. Although it wasn't really lady like to do that sort of thing she had a talent for it and could even beat some of the boys. It had been one of the happiest days at school when her name was read out for doing something good. But then everyone knew her name, even the teachers and it was Margaret Lang do this or Margaret Lang do that. She hated being called Margaret.

Monday mornings at school she didn't mind too much. They had assembly when the headmaster talked about something really boring, like what was in the newspaper that day. Quite often he spoke about their "young bodies" being kept clean or well fed or whatever, she always thought it sounded strange. There was something about him she didn't like, and the thought of sitting outside his office when she failed her arithmetic test made her shiver. They usually had spelling on Monday morning, which Maggie was good at. Her mother used to teach her to spell when they lived at the homestead.

By lunchtime her stomach was doing somersaults and she couldn't eat her lunch.

'Are you alright, Margaret?' Mrs Moore her teacher asked. 'You look a bit pale.'

Maggie saw an opportunity. 'No, Mrs Moore.' She tried to look ill and pathetic. 'I feel sick.'

She knew that would throw the teacher into a whirl because if there was one thing they hated it was when children were sick everywhere. Especially Mrs Moore, sometimes it made her sick as well.

'Oh dear.' She stepped back from Maggie as though she had something catching and said, 'I think perhaps you had better go home, Margaret.'

'Yes, Mrs Moore.' Maggie answered in a sort of croaky voice.

'Will you be able to get home alright on your own?' Mrs Moore kept her distance as she spoke. 'Or do you want someone to go with you?'

'I'll be alright.'

Maggie heard the teacher's sigh of relief.

Once outside the school gates Maggie's stomach stopped churning. When she got round the corner she walked with a spring in her step. She hummed all the way home and decided it was such a glorious day, now she had no arithmetic test, she would pick Dawn up early and they could go to the park. Of course Mrs Tulley would ask why she was not as school so she would have to feign sickness again.

She put her school bag down when she got to the front door of Mrs Tulley's house and was just about to knock when she heard sobbing. It was that sort of hiccupping sobbing that little ones do when they have cried for a long time. Who could it be, probably one of Mrs Tulley's children? The sound was so upsetting Maggie was worried she was interrupting some family quarrel. She crossed to the open window and as the breeze made the closed curtains billow out, she saw Dawn sitting on the floor without a stitch on, sobbing like her heart would break.

At that moment Maggie froze as Mrs Tulley walked into the room.

'You little black brat,' the woman spat. 'You've weed on my floor.' She grabbed Dawn and forced her face into the puddle and the child screamed.

For a moment Maggie was so stunned she couldn't move. Dawn's shrieks went through her head and all the while Mrs Tulley was saying, 'you little black bastard.'

Those words made a flicker of anger ignite in Maggie and without even thinking she yelled, 'Stop it, stop it.'

There was the sound of heavy footsteps running down the corridor as Mrs Tulley ran to the front door and threw it open. 'What're you doing here?'

Maggie tried to push past her but the older woman's fat stocky shape prevented her. The flicker of anger burst into a raging fire and Maggie gritted her teeth and shoved Mrs Tulley against the wall. 'Get out of my way.'

Running into the front room, she scooped her hysterical sister up in her arms and stormed back down the hall.

'You'll pay for this.' Maggie spat at Mrs Tulley with such hatred her voice was shaking.

There was a brief hint of fear in Mrs Tulley's eyes before they hardened. 'Get out of my house you cheeky brat and take that black bastard with you.'

Maggie was pushed from the house holding her screaming naked sister as though it was she who had done something wrong. Some of the neighbours who were outside turned and walked indoors, not wanting to get involved as Maggie stormed down the street to her house and slammed the door.

Once she got the baby home, she cuddled Dawn in a rug and tried to calm her. The baby's chubby cheeks were wet with tears and her little body shook with sobs. Maggie's heart was thumping in her chest at the injustice of her sister's treatment. Was this just a rare occasion or had this sort of thing been going on for months without any of them knowing? She had wondered why Dawn began crying every morning on their way to Mrs Tulley's and clung to Maggie when she tried to leave. Things began to slot into place, like how Dawn scoffed her food down in the evening as though she hadn't eaten all day, which was probably the case. How she had nightmares during the week but had none at the weekend. And the bruises on her arms and legs, she thought had been caused by the toddler falling over. The horror of Dawn's treatment made Maggie seethe with anger. She hugged and rocked the child to calm her down. Finally the baby fell asleep in Maggie's arms. As she sat nursing her sister Maggie vowed that she would never leave her with anyone else again. She would give up school and look after her herself.

Of course she couldn't tell her mother what she had planned. She thought if her mother couldn't get some one else to look after Dawn she would have to give up her job and then they would have no money and nothing to eat. Maggie couldn't face that again after what they had been through when they first came to the city and none of them had a job and they were sleeping on the floor. So it was better if her mother didn't find out what was going on. The money her mother gave her to give to Mrs Tulley for minding Dawn she would keep for herself, and if they ever ran out of anything she would be able to buy it. Or she could just save it under her mattress and eventually give it back to her mother. Dawn would thrive, she could teach her things and there would be no one calling the poor little mite names or treating her like an animal.

With the Christmas holidays coming up she had time to plan how she would deceive her mother. Since Billy and mama went out before her in the morning and were home after her at night, she needn't worry about being found out. They were both so tired when they got home, they didn't ask many questions.

Christmas had been and gone and this year they all received presents. Billy had even brought home a little tree that stood on the windowsill. It had been a devil of a job to keep Dawn off it, but they'd decorated it with bright buttons and coloured paper and attached homemade biscuits to some of the branches. Her mother began buying ingredients for a Christmas pudding, made and stored weeks before Christmas.

Maggie kept being reminded of that Christmas they had with Ningan two years ago, when they had sat under the trees and eaten until they were so full they couldn't move. This time they were crushed into the front room with blow flies zipping round them trying to land on the food. It seemed hotter than the outback with no cooling breeze and it was so stifling it was hard to enjoy yourself.

She missed those times at the homestead. They didn't have any animals now, Jess and Bob were left up country with Mr Sullivan from the shop and Blue Boy had been sold. She missed the freedom they had, when she and Billy used to roam all over and do as they pleased. She didn't have to lie to mama then about going to school, they were taught at home.

A few weeks after Maggie had left school the postman brought an official looking letter in a buff coloured envelope. It was addressed to her mother and since she never got any letters, Maggie had a feeling she should open it and see what it was. Inside was a letter from the headmaster asking whether Margaret was still ill, or if there was any other reason why she had not been at school for the past few weeks. At first Maggie panicked then decided to answer the letter herself, on her mother's behalf of course.

She tried to write like her mother. In the letter she explained that Margaret was now going to a different school and that they would be moving to a new area in the next few weeks. Maggie thought that excuse would stop them writing again. She forged her mother's signature, destroyed the letter from school in the fire and posted the reply back even though it cost the price of a stamp. She couldn't take the risk of someone from school asking questions. Once she had dealt with that little problem she felt happier.

Since she had taken over the care of Dawn the baby had thrived and was now a much happier child. Maggie loved her new role and fantasized about when she was married and had her own house. Sometimes she cooked the tea imagining she was doing it for her own husband and children. She would hum as she worked and talk to herself. Sometimes she would pretend her imaginary husband walked in the door and she would swing round from the range and say, 'Hello my darling, have you had a good day?'

Dawn, who was usually playing on the floor, would squeal with laughter, and Maggie's dream would dissolve. She wanted a husband like Billy, hard working and caring.

The warm weather meant that Dawn had a nap in the afternoon, and when she did Maggie would lie next to her and sometimes nod off herself. One day of oppressive heat they were laying down upstairs, waiting for the southerly buster to hit, when Maggie heard someone downstairs. She froze where she lay, panic and fear making her sweat. What should she do? Confront the thief or keep quiet and hope Dawn didn't wake. There was the slamming of drawers and banging of cupboard doors and Maggie suddenly decided she couldn't sit by and let someone ransack their house. Armed with a poker from the upstairs fire she crept to the top of the stairs. Fear made her hands sweat and the poker slipped in her grasp. Her heart pounded as though she'd been running and her mouth was as dry as the desert sands.

'Whose there?' a male voice boomed at her.

The voice made her spring into action before the thief decided to come upstairs and hurt Dawn. Maggie ran down the stairs. She raised the poker ready to attack and yelled, 'Get out of this house, you......' The words died on her lips as she nearly ran into Billy.

'What are you doing here?' she asked annoyed that he had got her so worked up.

'I could ask you the same thing?' Billy looked at the clock on the wall and then at Maggie.

She tried to think of an excuse. 'Oh erm, the teacher let us out early.'

'Don't give me that.' Billy stood with his hands on his hips.

One of his fingers was heavily bandaged and Maggie tried to change the subject.

'What have you done to your hand?'

'I crushed it at work, so they sent me home.'

'Oh you poor thing.' Maggie was overly dramatic in her sympathy. 'Is it sore?'

'Never mind about me finger, what're you doin' here and where's Dawn?'

'Shh, she's upstairs.'

Maggie realized she had been found out and that Billy would not accept any pathetic explanation as to why she was at home. She sighed, she was going to have to tell him, and hoped she could convince him not to tell mother.

CHAPTER 16

Constance

As Constance washed the clothes in the tub her mind began to wander as it usually did when she was doing boring chores. She felt sure something was going on between the children. Billy and Maggie seemed secretive and she had seen them giving each other meaningful looks. Whatever it was it couldn't be that important. Everything seemed to be running smoothly, Dawn was looking healthy and less grizzly. She'd become such a sweetie. Maggie adored her and sometimes it was as though she was the mother.

Constance rubbed the clothes up and down the washboard, stopping now and then to let her thoughts have full rein. She still felt guilty that she'd told the neighbours that Dawn was an orphan from the outback. She knew what the consequences would be if she said she was her half-caste child. The very idea that a white woman would want to sleep with a black man was unimaginable to some.

Since they had moved to Sydney the relationship between her and Billy had improved. He had taken on the mantle of head of the house with a great deal of maturity and responsibility. She'd been surprised when he got a job and started giving her his pay packet. With the two wages coming in they could afford this small house, put food on the table and still afford to pay someone to mind Dawn while she was at work. The area they lived in had recently been renovated and all the very old houses that were once full of vermin and harboured the plague ten years ago had been demolished. The ones that were left standing were the more substantial limestone terraces, one of which Constance managed to rent.

As she slopped the clothes into another bowl for rinsing she shuddered at those awful days when they had first arrived in the city. They had nowhere to go and Constance had a baby that was only a few months old. She had this misconception that Flo Maguire's boarding house would be just how it was. She couldn't visualize their old friend anywhere else, which was a bit naive. So that was where she went initially, only to be disappointed. The boarding house was no longer there. A new house was built in its place. She had been in a pickle that day. She didn't have much money left and was beginning to think they would have to go up country again and live as squatter.

After scanning the pages of the Sydney Morning Herald she had found a room near the city. It had a mattress on the floor and a rickety table with two chairs but it was a roof over their heads.

She found work fairly quickly and Billy soon had a job too, which was a relief. They moved out of their little room a month later and were very lucky to get this house.

As Constance wrung out the washing she thought back to that interview she had with Mr Rhodes at Greetby's. It was a year ago now but she still remembered how strange it was. She had seen his picture in the paper the day before and Constance had read the story of the death of his wife and daughter. It had brought tears to her eyes, since her own grief for her husband and twins was still quite raw. She remembered muttering under her breath, 'poor man' and she found it hard to believe there was any foul play as the newspaper tried to make out. And then to have him sitting in front of her when she went for the job was unbelievable. As she had spoken to him she remembered noticing lines round his eyes and the deep hurt and sadness reflected through them. She felt as though he was self conscious, hardly surprising with his face splashed across the newspaper. Constance stopped her wringing for a moment and gazed out of the window. In that short time she had spent with him she felt an unfamiliar closeness, which was ridiculous, she thought, as she continued squeezing the water from the clothes. But he was very handsome in a melodramatic sort of way.

Soon after she had started at Greetby's she had heard that Mr Rhodes had gone away and no one seemed to know where to or for how long. Since then Mr Simms had been the boss, he was all very efficient but not half as nice as Mr Rhodes.

Constance shook her head at her musings and berated herself inwardly for not getting on with the job. She had so much to do and standing around daydreaming would not get it done. When she thought about work her other little problem came to mind.

Dan Turner kept popping in to see her. Mrs Potter got very upset when he loitered about the department in his working clothes obviously not looking for gloves. At every opportunity he came in and asked her to go out with him. Constance wondered if she should accept one day just to stop him coming round, but there was something about him that she found unsettling. She wasn't sure what, probably his persistence. He seemed a nice enough man, bit young for her. He could probably have any girl he wanted with his looks.

Constance felt tired, not surprising after being on her feet all day at the shop and having to come home and start more work. At least she had got the washing out of the way and Maggie could hang it out for her in the morning. She flopped down in the battered old armchair and put her feet up. She stretched, yawned and snuggled into the chair.

An unfamiliar noise woke her in the night but she was too tired to register what it was. Half asleep she stumbled up to her bed and slept fitfully. A little while later she heard Billy come in and after that nothing until the birds woke her at dawn.

As Constance came out of the house the following morning on her way to work she noticed a commotion at Mrs Tulley's. There was a policeman at the front door. When Constance waved she didn't return her wave but seemed to ignore her. Fortunately it was Saturday and Dawn wouldn't need minding today. Constance wondered what was going on, but it was none of her business and she was in a hurry to get to work.

When she got to the store there was lots of tittering going on with girls whispering together. Constance tried not to get involved in their gossiping. Mid morning Mr Simms made an appearance and took Mrs Potter to one side. Constance was tidying one of the drawers of gloves and overheard their conversation.

'Have you heard the news, Mrs Potter?' Mr Simms said.

'If it's what they're all chattering about, yes Mr Simms. I have.' Mrs Potter puffed her chest out and folded her arms. 'Am I right in saying that Mr Rhodes is coming back.'

'That's correct.' Mr Simms hesitated before adding, 'we're not sure when yet, probably in a few weeks. So Mrs Potter could you make sure your department is ship shape and try to sell as many gloves as you can in the mean time.'

'Of course, Mr Simms, we will do our best.'

'Thank you, Mrs Potter.'

Constance felt pleased, it would be good to see Mr Rhodes again he was such a nice man. She hoped he'd come to terms with his grief. She knew how hard it could be.

After work Dan was waiting for her. She managed to put him off walking home with her. She knew he was following her and had done many times before. It annoyed her, but she didn't want to antagonize him so she ignored him. He was harmless enough.

Once in the house she shut the door and went upstairs to get changed out of her uniform. She laid the black skirt and white blouse over the chair and glanced out the window. Dan was standing on the corner looking at her house. A shiver ran down her spine.

The next moment the silence was shattered as Maggie and Dawn arrived home calling her name.

'Mother you'll never guess what?'

Constance rushed down stairs all thoughts of Dan put to the back of her mind.

'What, what's happened?'

'Mrs Tulley had all her windows at the back smashed in last night.' The glee in Maggie's voice was obvious.

'Oh poor woman.' Constance put her hand over her mouth, then added, 'ah, that'll probably be why there was a policeman at her door this morning.' She frowned at Maggie. 'But that's nothing for you to be so happy about. Oh dear, I hope it doesn't complicate things with her having Dawn on Monday.'

Hastily Maggie added, 'I shouldn't think so.'

Constance continued as though the child hadn't spoken. 'Perhaps I'd better go around and see if there will be a problem. I wonder who broke her windows?'

'It's alright mother, I'll go round and see her.' Maggie swept out the door before Constance could argue.

Dawn was standing in front of Constance with her hands raised saying, 'Mama, mama.'

'Come here my little precious.' Constance scooped her up and nuzzled her neck making the baby laugh. It was as though Dawn had been born to make the losing of the twins more bearable. She was a bonny child, always laughing and lately saying a few words, although Maggie seemed to be the only one who could decipher what they were. Sometimes she reminded Constance of Ningan, the deep brown eyes that looked steadily at her and the mischievous look she had.

Before she had finished fussing with Dawn, Maggie was back.

'Yes everything is fine for Monday, Mrs Tulley says,' Maggie blurted out.

'Oh good.' Something about the way Maggie was behaving made Constance suspicious. She decided she must go and see Mrs Tulley herself sometime, she hadn't spoken to the woman for months which seemed daft when she was minding her child everyday.

When Billy arrived home later in the day there was much whispering going on between him and Maggie. Constance wondered what their secret was.

Sunday dawned warm and sunny and Constance decided she would get her jobs done early and then they could take a picnic to Observatory Hill. It wasn't very far and she knew Dawn and Maggie would be thrilled. By late morning with help from Maggie and Billy all the chores were more or less done and she packed bread, pickle, half a meat pie that was left from the previous day and some scones Maggie had made earlier. Of course Billy wouldn't come with them so she set off with the girls. They put a rug down under the branches of a huge gum tree near the top of the hill and looked out over the harbour. It was a beautiful spot and not many people were about.

They ate their food but Maggie seemed unusually quiet when Constance asked her about school. She didn't have very much to say

and changed the subject. As soon as they were finished eating
Maggie took Dawn for a little wander around the park and stood
with her near the railings showing her the harbour. Constance settled
back against the tree and closed her eyes.

She could feel someone stroking her arm and assumed it was
the children. Sleepily she asked, 'What's the matter?' She felt
someone very close and the next minute she was being kissed,
passionately. Her eyes flew open as the man ground his mouth
against hers trying to make her part her lips. She struggled and tried
to push the attacker away. Suddenly she realized it was Dan. He
broke off his kiss and she jumped to her feet.

'What do you think you are doing?' Constance was very
angry.

'What you want me to.'

'Don't be ridiculous. Whatever gave you that idea?'

'You did.'

'No,' Constance was shaking her head, 'I never did any such
thing and you know it.'

He grabbed her ankle. 'Sit down,' he ordered. 'You'll
frighten the kids.' He looked across to where the girls were standing
and added, 'We wouldn't want that, would we?'

The tone was threatening. Constance sat down and tried to
stay calm for the children's sake.

'That's better,' Dan said. 'Now we can have a proper
conversation.'

Constance pretended she wasn't bothered by his behaviour.
She was pretty sure she could fight him off if she had to. Years of
working at the homestead had made her nearly as strong as a lot of
men but she felt wary of him.

'What's your first name,' he asked. 'Flora, Lizzie or perhaps
Mary?'

Constance didn't really want to tell him, but since he already
knew where she lived and her surname she said, 'Constance.'

'Constance eh? He smiled. 'It sounds a bit English to me,
but you are aren't you?'

She nodded and felt like a bird being watched by a cat and
decided to turn the conversation away from herself. 'Tell me about
you.' She tried to sound as though she meant it.

'You don't really want to know about me, do you?'

'Of course I do, we've known each other as acquaintances for a few months now but I don't know anything about the real you.' She didn't really want to know, he could tell her any old flannel.

He started telling her about his job and the blokes at work. He looked down and picked at the grass in front of him as he talked. Maggie and Dawn had started walking back to their mother but stopped when they saw the stranger. Constance inclined her head to indicate they must leave. Maggie immediately realized something was amiss and quietly walked Dawn out of the park.

When they had gone Constance was less worried but still needed to find a way of escape. After he'd been yammering on a while he looked up and noticed the children were gone.

'Where've the kids gone?' He looked round for them.

'Oh they wondered off home.'

'So who's is the black one?' He was very blunt and practically spat out the word 'black'.

The lie immediately sprang to Constance' lips. 'She is an orphan from the bush.'

'What did you want to lumber yourself with her for?'

Constance couldn't let the distaste she was feeling for this man show in her voice. 'There was no one else, she was left on our step.'

'And you were so good hearted you just had to take her in.' He shook his head. 'I knew you were a really nice person the first time I saw you.' He gazed into her eyes and added, 'And my opinion of you hasn't changed a bit. In fact...' he looked at the ground, 'I think I'm falling in love with you.'

Constance gulped. He looked up at her with deep admiration in his eyes. She was lost for words. 'Dan... I'm....really....', before she could finish he interrupted her.

'I know... you feel the same way.'

She knew there was nothing she could say that would alter his delusion. He was convinced of her love for him. She needed to get away before he turned nasty.

'Dan I really have to go now.' She spoke quietly, trying not to antagonize him.

'I understand you're too emotional to talk any more.'

She nodded her head, anything to escape. She stood up slowly and gathered the picnic things.

'I enjoyed our little talk.' He smiled which made him look young and vulnerable.

Constance nodded agreement with a false smile fixed to her lips.

As she was about to walk off, Dan said, 'Now we've told each other how we really feel, what's the next step?'

'I don't really know Dan.' She walked away without looking back.

By the time she got back in the house she was trembling. She leaned on the closed door, barring the outside from coming in. She could do without all this drama with Dan.

'You alright mama?' Maggie asked. Constance nodded. 'Who was that man?'

'Just someone from work.' Constance sighed deeply and sat at the table. 'Put the kettle on for me, love.'

She was so distracted when Billy got home he kept asking what was wrong with her. Eventually, after the girls had gone to bed, she told him what had happened. She made light of it, didn't want him to think she was worried or upset by Dan.

'He's harmless really,' she said when she had finished her account of events.

'Is he?' Billy had a look on his face that worried his mother. His eyes were hard and his mouth was grim. 'Everything will be alright mother, don't you worry.'

Constance sighed with relief, she felt as though she was making a big issue out of nothing. What harm had Dan done? It was a schoolboy crush, but Dan was a bit too old for one of them. Somehow she was going to have to get rid of him, but how?

Billy

After Billy left his mother he went to his room. He was very angry with her for getting herself into such a dicey situation with some bloke from work. She tried to sound as though she wasn't upset by the incident but he could tell she was. What made that fella come onto his mother? Was his mother making eyes at him? The thought made him feel sick. She was too old for that sort of thing. He'd have to get the bludger sorted out like he had Mrs Tulley.

He lay on his bed and stretched. His feet rested on the wooden bed end and his long body sank into the sagging flock mattress. Sighing he thought, now he had another problem to sort out. As head of the family he felt a great sense of protectiveness to his mother and sisters, his girls he called them. If anyone did anything to upset them he felt as though it was a slight to his ability to take care of them, which was probably a bit extreme but Billy took his role very seriously.

Since he had started working at the docks he had toughened up physically. At fifteen he was tall for his age and the last twelve months lifting and carrying had built up muscles in his arms, chest and legs. He enjoyed his job and had made friends with some good blokes. Some of them were rough as blazes but they always looked out for him, probably because he was the youngest worker there. He tried his best and was proud when he was told he'd done well.

It was all so different from the solitary existence of the outback and Billy loved it. All the male company, the joking and laughs they had, although some things went right over his head, but he pretended he knew what they were talking about. It was usually stuff about girls that he got lost on. He thought he'd heard it all on the sheep station but these blokes knocked spots off the exploits of an outback sheep shearer. He couldn't let on that he was green as grass when it came to the opposite sex. He would like to have a girlfriend, some time but just at present it took all his energy to work long, dockers hours and take care of the women at home. And he really didn't need his mother getting herself into a tricky situation with a bloke who had a head full of sentimental shit.

He shook his head as he thought of the long way they had come since they lived up country. That was one decision his mother had got right, the move to the big smoke had been a good one. Memories came back to him as to why they had come. Once again it was his mother getting herself mixed up with a fella only that time it was a black fella.

He had forgiven his mother for that little fiasco, he had to, but the hurt and disgust had gone on a long time. As for Ningan, he'd needed a woman. The needs of a man can be pretty hard to satisfy, bit like an itch that won't go away.

It all seemed like a long time ago now. In that couple of years
he had grown physically and mentally. He remembered thinking
after he got his mother and the baby through the whole childbirth
thing that they needed him. At that point he decided he would
always be there for them and take care of them.

Billy rolled onto his side and tried to banish the thoughts of
the past. The future was looking good and now he had some mates
that helped him out now and then, he didn't feel quite so exposed to
the injustices of the world. His eyes were heavy with the onset of
sleep even though his brain was whirling, but the weariness of his
day's toil soon overrode his thoughts.

He slept fitfully. Dreams flashed through his brain. The twins
were calling him, pleading with him not to let them die. He was
digging a grave and they were watching and crying. It was pouring
with rain and everything was wet and slippery. Dulcie lost her
footing and slipped. She was sliding into the grave and she grabbed
for Ben. He began slipping in too. Billy ran to them and began
pulling at their clothes. He couldn't get hold of them, it was too wet
the material of their clothing was slipping through his fingers, the
weight of their bodies dragging on his arms. He heard the tear of
fabric as Dulcie's thin frock began to rip. Desperately he tried to get
a firmer grip of her but he couldn't because he had Ben in his other
hand. His feet were slipping on the graveside, his arms were burning
with the effort and he couldn't hold them much longer. He had to
decide whether he let them go, or fall into the darkness with them.
Dulcie was pleading with him not to leave them and Ben was just
looking up at him. His innocent blue eyes put all his trust in Billy.
As Billy's body lurched closer to the hole he let them go. Dulcie's
screams made him put his hands over his ears, as they fell in the
hole. He looked into the blackness but couldn't see them, it was too
dark but the screaming continued.

A scream woke Billy from his dream-filled stupor. For a
moment he didn't realize where he was but the nightmare was so
vivid in his mind he knew the screams were his. He was covered in
sweat and his hair was sticking to his head. He took some deep
breaths, sat up and reached for a smoke out of his top drawer. With
shaking hands he lit it before opening the window wide so his
mother wouldn't smell it in the morning. The first light of dawn
touched the rooftops and he filled his lungs with the freshness of a

new day before popping the smoke back in his mouth. There was no point going back to sleep now, he may as well get up for work.

The walk to work made the remnants of his dream slip away as he strode along the city streets. It was surprising how many people were out and about so early. There were street sweepers and barrow boys taking their wares to the market in the Queen Victoria Building. It was still cool in the deep shadows made by the tall buildings, the sun hadn't yet touched this man made gully. Billy wallowed in the coolness knowing it would soon be roasting on the quaysides where he was heading. He nodded or shouted 'gudday' to some of the workers he passed every day and felt his spirits rise as he mixed in the world of the employed.

The eight miles of wharves that nestled in Darling Harbour, Woolloomoolloo and Pyrmont were like a bustling metropolis of lumbering ships with nippy pilot boats manouvering these monsters to shore. Once at the quayside the dock workers and stevedores swarmed over the vessels like the people of Lillyput in "Gulliver's Travels". Steam cranes stood like sentinels waiting to spring into action when the unloading began. The backdrop to this hive of activities was the warehouses. Great sheds that ran the length of the wharves, big cavernous structures where the wind whistled through and they always felt draughty, where huge quantities of foodstuff, building materials and human provision were stacked in towering piles, dwarfing the workers underneath.

Billy loved it all. He loved the masculine domain, the camaraderie with his fellow workers and the dominance of the big ships. He marvelled at how such heavy monsters could stay afloat on the ocean waves. He still had his secret dream of going to sea one day. Just at the moment he couldn't leave his girls, but one day he would. A smile came to his lips as he reached the gates of dock number ten and some of the other workers ruffled his hair as they passed him.

'Bugger off,' he yelled good-naturedly, trying to tidy his hair with his fingers.

A lot of the blokes he worked with were Irish and he could listen to them talk all day in their lilting accent. At first he couldn't always understand what they were saying but now he got the gist of what they were on about.

His mate Mick O'Leary was leaning against the fence waiting for him.

'Gudday Mick how yuh goin?'

'I'm fine, Billy boy and yourself?'

'Ah, I'm alright mate.'

'You'll not be sounding so sure of that, is there something the matter?' Mick suggested.

'I'll tell yuh about it later.' Billy said.

'Is it woman troubles you'll be having?'

'Yeah could say that, Mick.'

The Irish lad who was only two years older than Billy put his arm around his shoulder and hugged him roughly.

They laughed and stumbled into the warehouse pretending to box each other. When they emerged on the dockside they were serious and ready for work. They went their separate ways and began the muscle wrenching, sweaty day in the life of a dockworker. They were lucky they had permanent work and were not part of the gang that were hired daily.

It was quite a fluke Billy thought how he got this job. That day he had walked his legs off looking for work all over the city and was so fed up he had gone to the docks to sit and rest. He had settled himself on a wharf post his legs dangling over the water. He remembered the soothing sound as it lapped against the wood and the cooling breeze. He could see baby fish swimming below him and watched mesmerized as they darted about.

He was dreading having to go back and tell his mother that he still didn't have a job. He was desperate to move out from that awful room.

A voice behind him nearly made him jump out of his skin.

'Penny for 'em.'

When he turned round a burly man in waistcoat and bowler hat was walking past. Billy hadn't even noticed him. The man stopped and spoke to him.

'What's a strong lad like you sitting here feeling sorry for himself for?'

'How do you know I'm feeling sorry for myself?'

'Well aren't you?' The strange man smiled almost daring Billy to deny his words. 'It seems to me you need something to occupy your time.'

'Yeah, well if I had a job I wouldn't be sitting here like a great jessie.'

'Well if it's a job you want I can sort you out in that department.'

For a moment Billy sat wondering if this bloke was fair dinkum.

'Come on lad, you look as though you could be good at fetching and carrying.'

That was the day he started work for Mr Webb and he'd worked for him ever since. He still couldn't believe his luck.

Billy's thoughts turned back to the present. This man pestering his mother needed sorting out.

The morning on the docks passed fairly quickly and it was soon lunchtime. A hooter sounded to signal it was time to knock off for lunch. The dock workers all sat round on bits of cargo and ate their food. Billy and Mick sat together and began eating as though their lives depended upon it. They took big mannish bites consuming their food in minutes. Not a word was spoken between them until they had finished when they both lit up a smoke and settled back to rest.

For a few moments they didn't speak until Billy broke the silence. 'Thank your brothers for me will yuh?'

Mick looked at him and before exhaling said, 'what do you mean?'

'Well I presume it was them that came and sorted out Mrs Tulley for me.'

'Oh that, that was just a wee warning.'

Billy gave a slight chuckle. 'Well thanks anyway.'

'Don't be thanking me Billy boy, but if there's anything else you want sorting just give the O'Learys a shout.' The silence made Mick look at Billy. 'Is there something else?'

'Well, yeah.' Billy was having pangs of guilt, he should be able to solve his own problems.

'Spit it out son.' The older boy was speaking to Billy as though he was a lad who didn't know how to tie his shoelaces.

'Give it a rest, Mick. I'm not yuh son.'

'Sorry mate.' Mick looked sheepish. 'Come on let's be having yuh, tell us what's the problem.'

Billy told his mate all about the incident with his mother the previous afternoon.

'What's this bloke's name?' Mick had a mischievous glint in his eye.

'Dan Turner, me mother knows him from work.'

'I'll look into it Billy boy and get back to you.'

'Thanks.' Billy got up ready to go back to work but was stopped in his tracks by his mate's next words.

'The first one was a freebee but this one will cost yuh, alright?'

Billy felt a cold fear seeping into his body as he answered hesitantly, 'Alright.' What was he going to do now? He couldn't take it all back, say forget it and look like a real drongo. And he certainly didn't have enough money to pay them anything. Filled with dread Billy wondered what sort of repayment they would want. Perhaps they wouldn't be able to find this Dan Turner bloke and then they could forget about it, but somehow Billy knew that wouldn't happen.

A few days passed and Billy heard nothing. He began to think perhaps it would all blow over until Mick came up to him one day and said, 'We got the low down on this friend of your mother's.'

Billy felt like sinking through the floor, but instead answered, 'Yeah?'

'Yeah and you'll never guess what?' Before Billy could answer Mick went on, 'he works down here.' Mick was nodding his head with a silly grin on his face.

'Really?'

'Yeah, he's a wagon driver for one of them haulage companies. Evidently he's down the docks most days picking up loads.'

Billy couldn't believe it. 'Well I'll be damned,' he muttered under his breath.

'So, he shouldn't be too hard to sort out.' Mick slapped his hand to his forehead as a new idea came to him. 'I've just thought.'

'What's that then?'

'You could be in on it, since it'll probably be done round here somewhere.' Mick looked about him for a likely spot. 'Yeah, I'll tell the brothers you'll be giving us a hand.' For a moment

Mick's enthusiasm waned as he peered at Billy through squinting eyes. 'That is if you're up to it?'

'Course, yeah, count me in.' Billy tried to sound cocky and confident but his insides were doing somersaults.

Everything went quiet on the topic for over a week and Billy wished they would get it over and done with. He wondered if his part in the payback would be services rendered and no money need pass hands.

As they arrived for work the following day Mick sidled up to Billy and whispered, 'After work, warehouse number eight, be there.'

If it wasn't so serious Billy would have laughed at the subterfuge Mick used as though they were spies or something, doing stuff that was illegal. All day Billy felt ill, his hands trembled as the hours ticked by and the end of the day drew near. Mick had told him bits during the midday break. Evidently Turner was collecting a big load from a ship that was docking in the morning. The boys were going to take their time and Turner's load would be left until last. So it would be late by the time they got to his and while this bloke was waiting around for his cargo to be loaded the O'Leary's would do him over. Of course no one would dob them in since they were all a bit afraid of the O'Leary's and everyone would pretend they hadn't seen or heard a thing.

Billy just wanted to escape, wanted to run away back to his mother and give her a good thrashing for putting him in this spot with her flirting and eyeing up the fellas. Anger was building in him, anger at the situation he now found himself in. He shouldn't have to look after the womenfolk in the family he should have a father to do that. But there was just him against the world, no one to back him up. He thought the O'Learys were a nice big family, helping people out but now he knew the truth. They were a load of thugs, maybe even criminals and he was involved with them. He still liked Mick as a mate and they had some good talks but now they had their claws in him he knew he would have to do whatever they said or leave his job. He'd just have to go along with it.

The sun began slipping towards the western horizon and the amount of haulage wagons being loaded grew less. By the time the sun had gone down behind the warehouse roof of dock number eight there was only one wagon left. At first it was cool in the late afternoon shade but as the breeze blew across the waters of the harbour it became chilly. Billy shivered and rolled down the sleeves of this shirt.

Dan Turner had gone off somewhere, fed up with waiting for his load but as Billy stood leaning in the doorway Mick hissed in his ear, 'He's back.'

A few men appeared as if by magic from around the corner of the warehouse as the wagon driver wandered towards his wagon. Billy was propelled towards him by Mick, who was holding him under his elbow. The other men all moved in the same direction. The wagon driver seemed oblivious to their presence until Mick thrust Billy ahead of him and into the gaze of the stranger.

For a moment Billy stood like a spare part, alone. A trembling went through his body as though he was freezing but he wasn't. He could hardly form any words, his teeth were chattering together but he did manage to get out, 'Are you Dan Turner?'

Cockily the driver answered, 'yeah, what's it to you?'

The way he looked down his nose at Billy and the tone of his voice were like a signal to the boy. Anger began to override fear, who did this bastard think he was? Messing with his mother, upsetting her, thinking he could just come into their lives and spoil things.

Billy began walking towards him with determined tread, his anger mounting with each step. As he got within spitting distance of him he sneered, 'You bastard.' He lunged for the wagon driver before he had a chance to defend himself, shoving him in the shoulder sending him flying across the cobbled yard.

'What the bloody hell are you doing?' Turner tried to scramble to his feet but Billy ran over and kneed him in the face. The wagon driver got a grip on Billy's clothes and pulled him to the ground. The youngster was only a lightweight, easily thrown off as Turner began to retaliate. He rained punches into Billy's body before the O'Leary brothers intervened. Billy struggled to his feet and watched as the brothers laid into Turner. The sound of boots hitting flesh and the occasional crack as a bone was broken was sickening. Suddenly Billy realized they would kill him if he didn't stop them.

'Stop, stop it.' He pulled at the men, shouting, 'Get off him,' and eventually they did. Dan Turner lay absolutely still.

'Want to have the last kick, Billy boy,' one of the brothers asked. 'Go on, one or two more and he'll be on the meat wagon.'

'No I bloody don't.' Billy began to walk away. 'Just leave him, I think you've done enough damage.'

'Only helping you out mate.' It was Mick who spoke. The brothers moved away from the beaten man, one or two mumbled something Billy didn't hear and the eldest said, 'Sort him out Mick, and we'll see yuh at the pub.'

'Sure thing,' Mick replied as he walked towards Billy shaking his head. Was he next in line, was Mick going to hit him? He backed away from him.

'What are yuh doing, Billy boy?' There was disbelief in his tone. 'You're not afraid of you're old mate Mick, are yuh?'

Billy stood still and Mick put his arm round his shoulder and squeezed him. Billy stood rigid. 'You don't want to be frightened of me mate,' Mick said. 'Come on, let's go to the pub and I'll tell yuh the rules of the game on the way.'

'What about him?' He nodded towards Dan Turner who had begun moaning.

'Don't worry about him, the street cleaner'll be along in the morning. With a bit of luck they'll put him in with their rubbish where he belongs.'

Billy felt dirty, his guilt at being responsible for the bloodied mess of humanity that lay on the cobbles made his revenge sour. 'He might die before morning.' Billy tried to move towards the brutalized body but Mick held him in his grasp.

'No he won't. He'll be right.'

Billy let himself be led away from the scene of his introduction to the brutality and control of the O'Leary brothers. From now on he wouldn't tell Mick about any problems he had.

CHAPTER 17

Emily

At any time the image of Daniel Turner on top of her thrusting into her could intrude on Emily's mind. She clenched her fists trying to make the memory disappear, but the jarring of the carriage on the road only simulated his actions. She pushed her body into the seat and sat rigidly, trying to minimize the movement. Clenching her legs together she hoped never again to feel that rush of air on her thighs as her most private parts were exposed. She looked out from the carriage and tried to concentrate on anything but the horrific experience of that day but the memories engulfed her.

The moment she had regained consciousness she felt violated. Blood dripped from a gash on the back of her head and her body trembled. Unsteadily she got to her feet, still frightened that he may leap from behind a rock and attack her again. She managed to stumble to a grove of trees where she would be out of sight from the road. She couldn't face anyone, not in this state, her clothes were ripped and dirty and she longed to have a bath and wash the smell of him off her. She sat trembling and whimpering in her hiding place until it was dark. Eventually she staggered to her feet and stumbled back to Brunswick House.

As soon as she walked in the kitchen Mrs Lovelock made a fuss and asked what had happened. She felt too ashamed to tell anyone of her plight, people might say it was her fault, that she must have seduced Daniel for him to do such a thing. She didn't want gossip to spread round the neighbourhood and she especially didn't want her mother to find out. She told cook that she was out walking and fallen down a ravine. She had piled on the tears which were authentic and cook had shushed her and made her have a bath and go to bed. Fortunately she didn't see the old aunt and it seemed as if cook believed her.

Like a coward Daniel Turner didn't return to Brunswick House. Mr Simms told them he had gone to help his brother, a lie made up to explain his swift departure. Mrs Lovelock had made a remark about how strange it was that Emily's accident and Daniel going missing happened on the same day. She asked her if he had hurt her and Emily emphatically denied it.

It was two months after the incident that Emily realized she was pregnant. The first missed period she put down to the upset of it all but when she missed a second time she knew. She felt desperate, trapped in a situation not of her making, a situation that would get her sacked and shunned. She would have to get rid of it, but how? There was no way she could afford to go to a back street abortionist. Her mother had told her the story of a friend who died during this procedure.

She scoured the books in Mr Rhodes' library for information on the subject and eventually found a book called "The Physiology of the Human Body". There was a chapter on the reproductive systems with information about the first three months of a woman's gestation period. It said that a woman was prone to miscarriage in the first ten weeks of the period and must rest during this time to avoid damaging the foetus. It emphasized under no circumstances do any horse riding.

Emily only had a few weeks to get rid of it and it seemed there was only one solution, she would have to learn to ride, something she had never had any inclination to do. She was frightened of horses. She would have to master her fear or bring a bastard into the world. Riding a horse couldn't be that hard, lots of women seemed to do it.

Yet again she went to the library, for more information. She seemed to find an answer for everything in a book. In her bedroom she avidly studied the pictures about horse riding and the equipment used. She began visiting the stable to try to conquer her fear of horses. The new stable lad thought she was an accomplished horsewoman when she started talking about the various pieces of harness.

Eventually the day came when she had to put all her reading into action. With shaking hands and dread in her step she approached the stable. She asked the new man to harness a horse for her. He obliged without question although he did look a bit puzzled when she said she didn't want a side saddle. She managed to mount the horse via the mounting block without too much trouble. As she wriggled into the saddle trying to grip the bridle, the horse took off with her on its back. In that moment her fear of being crushed under its galloping feet out weighed her fear of pregnancy and she clung to the horse's neck in terror. She was bounced up and down on the horses back like a rag doll in the hands of a frenzied child, before the horse unseated her.

The crash when she hit the ground knocked the wind from her lungs, the pain in her right arm seared through her shoulder and into her head. The stable boy came running and carried her groaning to the house. Emily couldn't remember an awful lot after that. The doctor came, she was told she had broken her collarbone. One thing she did remember was the warm wet feeling between her legs the day after her fall. She should have been happy that she had miscarried but a depression descended on her, she had killed her unborn child. As she lay in bed being cared for mainly by Mrs Lovelock, who made comments about how accident prone she was these days, she vowed that she would have vengeance on Daniel Turner. The only light moments in those dark days were when Thomas came to visit her.

When Emily thought back to that time she couldn't believe she had actually done such a thing. She could have killed herself, where had she got the courage? It was like a drama from one of those romantic novels she read, not something that an ordinary person like Emily Smith would do. In one respect she felt quite proud of herself for getting herself out of that situation without anyone knowing that she had conceived but at other times a sour mood came over her, the whole episode leaving a nasty after taste, a feeling of being tainted and soiled. She was no more the young innocent.

She pushed the memories into the dark caverns of her mind, no one need ever know what had happened to her. A chilling thought seeped involuntarily into her musings, there was one person who would know she had been with another man, her husband, whoever he may be. She'd cross that bridge when she came to it, at the moment she was off men, except of course Mr Rhodes.

The wagonette stopped, bringing Emily out of her melancholy reverie.

'Come along, Tom.' She clasped his hand. 'Let's go and buy you some new clothes. I'll have to put a book on your head to stop you growing.' She smiled at him, what would she do without him?

John

Twelve months in the outback had taught John Rhodes a lot. He had learnt how to skin a wallaby, light a fire with next to nothing and how to survive. He had learnt the aboriginal way of doing things. Ningan had been a good teacher and John had been a slow student to start, but more important than all the ways of finding water and different berries to eat, John had learnt to like himself.

The wide open spaces filled with nature's beauty had made him and his problems seem insignificant. The magnificence of the sky at sunset, that glowing redness that looked like the earth and sky were on fire, could not be matched with anything manmade. The chorus of cicadas on summer evenings, chirruping incessantly, drowning out anything else until they stopped abruptly as though a signal had been given, leaving the ears ringing and an eerie silence. The days that could be so hot that everything was still, the only sound the rustle of leaves from the warm breeze that made the temperature soar. A heat haze shimmered in the distance with an enticing mirage of water. He had been nervous the first time he heard the distant thumping noise that grew louder and louder as a large family of kangaroos bounded past. The bird life was a constant source of pleasure, the colours of the various species from the pink and grey galahs, to the bright colours of the parrot family. The night sky so clear he felt as though you could almost reach up to pluck a star from the heavens and the friendly moon that shone peacefully down on the absolute blackness of the outback.

Beside John as he witnessed all these things was Ningan, giving his interpretation of nature's strange and mysterious ways. They had long talks over the campfire some nights and at other times they were quiet, filling themselves with the peace of the place. John found out all about Ningan's upbringing and the disappointments that seemed to plague him but the blackman never complained about his past. It was the way the spirits worked, they played games with people and never let you feel complacent about anything. He had an unerring belief that one day, in the future everything would turn out for the best. Not just for him but for John too. With such optimism how could John dare to think otherwise?

At first John had only looked inward and dwelt on the bad hand fate had dealt him, to have to roam around the outback to get away from the guilt, the gossip and the grief. His thoughts of suicide began to fade when he admitted to himself that he probably wouldn't have the guts to do it anyway. But as the weeks turned into months his state of mind began to improve and the pleasure of the little things made him smile. Like the cuteness of a joey peeping from its mother's pouch or the antics of a kookaburra that swooped down and tried to eat some left over cooked meat only to find it was too hot to handle. John found he was smiling more and more, a sort of inane grin that appeared at the strangest of times. Sometimes he would look at Ningan and they would grin together for no reason.

After a few months his mind began to wander to his past, and his son. He thought about what he might be doing and who was looking after him. He began to think about him every day and wondered if Thomas remembered his father. What did he think of a father that up and left him when he was needed most? John dwelled on all the people in his life and how they had treated him. His mother, who he always thought tried to avoid him as much as possible by putting him in the hands of nannies. There had been plenty of those over the years but he never got that attached to any, as he knew they wouldn't stay long. His father was always off, involved in some new venture and hardly had time for his son.

His marriage to Beattie had been a mistake. He was looking for an escape from his parents and she came along at the right moment. At first things had been fine, they seemed to the outside world like the perfect couple but in the bedroom things were a little different. Beattie didn't like the coarseness of making love, it was a chore to her and it was amazing that they actually had two children. John loved her in some ways, her dark beauty and certain mannerisms, the way she smiled that made two dimples appear on her cheeks. She was as dark as John was fair, two complete opposites in many respects.

The great love of his life was his children, Anna who looked just like her mother and Thomas who was the spit of him, so people said. His son was all he had left and he didn't know if he could take rejection from Thomas. He may hate his father.

For months John fought with his emotions and couldn't put himself in the position of being hated and detested again. In the outback these things were irrelevant. Ningan and he had become very close and John didn't think he could walk away from him. He was truly indebted to his friend.

The other person he began to think about was Constance Lang which was ridiculous. He had only met her briefly. But in that short time she had a profound effect on him, probably because she was the only one who showed a bit of sympathy and understanding in his time of torment. He knew nothing about her, but wanted to know everything. He wondered if she still worked in the glove department. John smiled at the preposterous idea that she may be unattached, still working at Greetby's and be interested in him.

The unchanging sequence of seasons gave very little clue to the time of year. Autumn and spring seemed to have disappeared. The winter months turned quite chilly at night then gradually grew warmer until summer, when the nights became nearly as hot as the days. John had no idea which month or even day of the week it was, one day just rolled into the next. They hunted when they were hungry, rested when they were tired and walked the rest of the time.

On a couple of occasions they came upon civilization in the form of line gangs. These men maintained the telegraph lines, miles of drooping wires attached to tall wooden poles that punctured the land in long monotonous lines. The telegraph line was the link to the outside world for the country folk and a very important piece of equipment that had to be kept pulsing through wind, rain and anything else nature threw at it. The telegraph gangs were usually a good bunch and were singing Christmas carols when John and Ningan happened upon them. John had no idea it was Christmas and his thoughts immediately went to his son.

They spent the day with the gang and all talked about what they would be eating back home, except Ningan who happily tucked into kangaroo steaks without any thoughts of Christmas pudding with brandy sauce. They cooked on an open fire, filling the bush with the smell of sizzling meat. Their rendition of Christmas carols was heard only by the bush animals. The following day they all went their separate ways. None of the blokes asked why John was roaming around the outback with a blackman.

January merged into February and the year seemed as though it would be just like any other, stretching on into more days of the same. John began to get restless and bored with the bush. The Christmas experience had unsettled him more than he cared to admit. He became moody with Ningan and battled to raise a smile. He lost his appetite and became quiet.

Eventually Ningan broached the subject. 'Now, mate, what's a madda?' he asked casually.

'What do you mean?'

'Well you look as though ants got in yuh bed.'

'What?'

'Or yuh best friend's gone off with yuh dillie bag.'

'What are you talking about, Ningan?'

'That's what I'm talking about.' Ningan nodded his head, 'Something's tipped your wagon up.'

'Yeah, well, maybe.' John sighed.

'Time you went back.'

John looked sharply at Ningan. 'Oh so you want rid of me do you?'

'No mate, walkabout not for city bloke anymore.'

They were sitting round the fire and John poked at the flames dispiritedly. 'There's a lot at stake though...' John went on to explain to Ningan all the worries and fears he felt.

'You'll do it.'

John nodded his head. 'Yep, but what about you?'

'What's a madda with me?' Ningan looked down at himself.

'Nothing you fool.' John smiled. He felt anxious asking him the next question. 'Would you consider coming back to Sydney with me?'

Ningan was quiet for a moment and scratched his head. He nodded as though he had reached a decision and said, 'Try an' stop me.' He was grinning all over his face and John felt like hugging him.

It took them a few weeks to get themselves sorted. They had to find a town where they could get clothes for Ningan, a shirt at least, he insisted his pants were fine and said he wouldn't know what to do with two pairs of pants. The ones he had were a few years old and had probably been washed only a handful of times.

John looked like a tramp. He had a ginger beard which clashed horribly with his blonde hair, that was shoulder length and scruffy. His hands were calloused but he did have a healthy colour to his skin. They had to get spruced up and spent a day by a water hole washing everything they had. They laughed and ducked each other in the water. John felt boyish and excited, splashing and bombing Ningan. His friend retaliated with vigour. It was probably the last bit of uninhibited silliness they would have together before they returned to the staidness of civilization.

John did manage to telegraph Samuel Simms and inform him that he would be arriving in due course, but from where they were situated in the back of woop woop it could take them weeks to get back.

Ningan

During the journey back to Sydney, Ningan stared out of the window of the train. He couldn't understand how whitefellas could live on top of each other like that. And there were no trees or decent birds only little dull brown and grey ones.

More and more people squashed onto the train and bumped against each other and said, 'Excuse me'. They left a gap around Ningan as though he had fleas. It was worse than when sheep were penned ready for shearing, Ningan thought. He stared openly at people and watched them look away under his gaze. He had no idea people really lived like this. He wondered if it was a special roundup they were going to and asked John if this was so.

'No,' John said, 'they're just going to work.'

Ningan thought it must be a big sheep station they all worked on.

When they got off the train the people streamed down the platform just like sheep do at round up, but once through the gate they all swarmed in different directions. Ningan was puzzled, were they all supposed to go their own way? Shouldn't some one be there to herd them all together?

John dug him in the ribs as he stood speechless watching the Sydney crowds and said, 'come on mate, you're holding everyone up.'

Ningan turned to see more people coming up behind him and walking round him. He jumped out of the way shaking his head. Once the herd of humans had gone, leaving just a few stragglers coming up the rear, Ningan relaxed a bit until they got out onto the streets.

As far as the eye could see was stone and brick. Buildings reared up in front of him and the skyline was a strip of blue seen through the gap between roofs. It was like being in a rocky gorge with a herd of cattle rushing past. Ningan went to step off the pavement but was wrenched back by a pull on his arm as a huge carthorse and dray trundled within inches of his bare feet.

He darted between wagons and strange carts, following John, honking noises blared in his ears. By the time they got to the other side of the road he was sweating like he'd run for miles. They walked along the street and everyone going in the opposite direction looked at them. Were they staring at both of us or just me, Ningan thought? They did look a bit out of place with all these whitefellas in their smart clothes. John looked messy with his beard and long hair and swag hitched over his shoulder. Ningan decided he looked even worse with his new pants riding above his ankles and a secondhand shirt that was too short for his long lanky frame. His hair was a mess of curls hanging to his collar and flopping over his face. It was the first time in his life Ningan had thought about his appearance.

As they walked, he could tell John was feeling nervous but he wasn't sure why. It could be from having to get through this dangerous place or facing the people he had left behind. Perhaps they should have stayed up country but then Ningan would never get to see his daughter. That was the main reason he had come. His daughter may be the only child he would ever have.

He remembered how he felt when Connie took her. It felt like a rock was sitting on his chest and the blackness of night travelled everywhere with him. He had gone into the bush, cut a long branch from a mulga tree and stripped all the leaves off it. He flayed himself with the branch to rid himself of the sadness in his heart. It was an aborigine custom he had seen women do when they had lost a child at birth or when a man had lost a wife. It was a way of releasing the grief, if your body was hurting you couldn't feel your mind hurting so much. He had done it to himself for days and eventually walked from his isolation bleeding and scratched but feeling less wretched. So now was his chance to see her. As he looked around the Sydney streets with hundreds of people rushing everywhere he decided it would be like finding a lazy ant in an ant hill.

Walking through this city was not like the bush where they got a good pace going and kept it up all day. Here they dodged round people and Ningan was getting more and more frustrated and his feet were beginning to hurt on the hard manmade ground.

John

To John's surprise he found the crowds of the city oppressive. They walked from the station and John tried to remember if it was this busy last time he was here. He realized in those days he usually travelled in his carriage driven by Dan and didn't actually fight against the minions rushing through the streets. When they reached Greetby's they ran up the stairs like boys who weren't supposed to be there. It all seemed unreal after the time together in the bush.

Samuel Simms was waiting for them in John's office. It was good to see him, they hugged and patted each other on the back, something John had never done before in his life.

'How yuh goin' mate?' John asked.

Sam laughed at his outback slang and said, 'you look well, boss.'

Ningan was introduced and Sam shook his hand. Good job he was an open minded bloke, John thought.

Clean clothes and a barber transformed John from a native to a businessman, on the outside at least. Once cleaned up, he thought about Constance. He'd love to see her but it would only cause tittle tattle.

The ride back to the house was filled with Sam telling him about the business, and the improvements he had made. The department store was going from strength to strength and they were making profits in all departments. John was eager to get back on with things and take charge again. It sounded as though Sam had worked wonders with the business but the competitive streak that had lain dormant in John for all these months now began to surface. The wrangling, negotiations and the lure of staying one step ahead of his competitors were enticing him to plunge back into the merchandising fray. With Ningan by his side he felt he could do anything.

They should do something to celebrate his homecoming, involve as many people as possible, show his thanks to everyone who had carried on his business and home without him. Yes, a big thank you to everyone, a works picnic, where all they had to do was come along, he would pay for everything. The exhilaration of his homecoming and the feeling his depression had gone spurred John on. But he still had to face his son.

The overwhelming welcome he received when he got to the house made all his worries, except one, disappear. The introductions were slightly strained when Ningan shook hands with the great aunt. John caught the look of distaste in her eyes as Ningan must have, but he winked at his friend who stood grinning from ear to silly ear. When John got to Emily in the line of servants he could see tears in her eyes.

'It's so lovely to see you, Mr Rhodes,' she said and he knew she meant it sincerely.

'It's nice to be home, Emily.' John said it with a confidence that was lacking when he left. 'Now, where is my son?'

'He's upstairs in the school room.' Emily looked apprehensive.

John caught her look and ran for the stairs calling as he went, 'Thomas, Thomas I'm home.' He could feel his heart pounding even before he got anywhere near the top of the staircase. He ran to the schoolroom and flung open the door.

Thomas was sitting at the table drawing. John walked up behind him the sound of his shoes echoing on the wooden floor in the silent room. The boy didn't acknowledge him. John's worst fears were being realized, his son had chosen to shut him out of his life. As he stood next to him he glanced down at the drawing. Bright colours danced across the piece of drawing paper, childish images in red, yellow, green and blue.

The hand holding the crayon stopped. 'I finished it.' The young face turned and looked at John. 'It's for you.'

John gulped before saying, 'well, it's very good, I think you have your dad's talent for drawing.' He made the inane remark as his heart hammered in his chest.

At that moment Thomas stood and turned suddenly. He clamped his arms around his father's waist and held him tightly. 'Never go away again, papa.' The emotion in the child's voice made tears prick at the back of John's eyes.

'I won't son, I will never leave you again.' John spoke the words with a vehement passion. He lifted his son in his arms and they hugged each other tightly. The boy's body shook as he cried with relief and emotion.

CHAPTER 18

Maggie

The ferry boat steamed down the Parramatta River and Maggie leaned over the railing and let the breeze tangle her hair and blow into her face. It was the most wonderful feeling she had ever experienced. The spray gently cooled her as the bow of the boat crashed into each wave sending a fine spray over the nearest passengers. The shoreline was mostly bush with clusters of sandstone boulders scattered along the water's edge. Other boats plied up and down the river and Maggie filled her senses with every new sight and sound. She had waited a long time for this boat ride and she was enjoying every minute of it.

Her mother sat on an inside seat out of the wind and Dawn ran back and forth between the two of them. Every now and then she would shriek with excitement and Maggie would shush her so as not to draw attention to her. Maggie didn't want anything to spoil her day, especially not snooty people who judged you only by the colour of your skin.

Maggie thought back to a few weeks ago when mama first told her about this picnic. In fact it came at just the right time for she was feeling guilty and anxious about the school thing. She still hadn't got round to telling her mother. She had been on the brink of confessing all when her mother told her about the works picnic.

Maggie decided not to mention it, just in case her punishment would mean she wouldn't be able to go to the picnic. She vowed that as soon as it was over she would tell her mother exactly what had been going on, and with Billy's help she may convince her that she really didn't need to go to school any more. Such thoughts Maggie put firmly to the back of her mind, it wasn't the day to dwell on anything to do with school.

Mama looked lovely in a new frock she had bought. It was a summer, florally dress that was nipped in at the waist and showed her trim figure. She'd let her hair down and curled it with rags so the ends were soft and springy. Maggie had to admit that coming to the city had done mama good. She was taking more pride in her appearance and had to dress smartly for work. It was a lot different from the way she looked when they lived up country. Then she was always a bit untidy with dirt under her nails and greasy hair when there wasn't enough water to wash it. Now she looked completely changed, for the better and Maggie was very proud of her.

Mama had made her and Dawn new dresses too. Hers was in pretty material and her mother had made it like one she had seen in the shop where she worked. She looked down at her gathered skirt. It had been starched so it crinkled when she sat down and she could feel the petticoat that had been made to go under it, tickling her legs.

As the boat slowed ready to dock Maggie felt so excited she couldn't sit still. Coronation Park extended down to the water's edge and it all looked so clean and tidy. The slight rocking of the gangway as she walked down made Maggie cling tightly to the rope rail and peer anxiously at the dark gap of water between boat and wharf. It didn't look very safe to her, one slip and she'd be in that cold greasy murk, drowned or squashed by the rocking boat. She breathed a sigh of relief when she stepped on dry land, her mother followed, carrying Dawn and placed her on the ground when they were safely away from the quayside.

Colourful flowers bloomed in the borders, the grass was mowed really short and trees stood tall and proud, everything was so tidy. There were people everywhere, strolling, smiling and laughing. It was almost unreal, thought Maggie. It was as though this was a happy place, where nobody thought bad thoughts or did bad things. She smiled and wondered if this is what heaven was like.

Emily

As the carriage approached Coronation Park Emily recollected how she had travelled this route once before, only then she was sitting up front with Daniel and Mr and Mrs Rhodes and the children were in the back sniping at each other. She had been very happy then, before the tragedy of that day.

Things were a lot different now. She was with Mr Rhodes and Tom, as though she was the lady of the house, as though they were married. Emily looked across at John, as she called him in her mind, and smiled. He was chatting to Tom but returned her smile over the boy's head. People looked up at the carriage as it passed and Emily wondered if they looked like a happy family. Would her clothing give away the fact that she was only the governess? She looked down at the summer dress she wore which cost a month's wage. Not as expensive looking as something Mrs Rhodes would have worn, but from a distance no one could tell the material was cheap. Emily sighed contentedly to herself.

People were staring at them. The smile slid from Emily's lips as she realized they weren't looking at her but at the black man who was driving them. Emily couldn't understand John bringing a black man to live under their roof. Everyone knew they were heathens, not to be trusted. They killed white women and babies and went walkabout whenever they fancied a change, so her mother said. When he first arrived Emily locked her door, fearful that she would get stabbed in the night, but as the weeks passed she became braver.

His devotion to John was a bit excessive and the black man's face lit up whenever John entered the room. Emily wondered why. Was he just trying to get in his boss's good books? She guessed there was more to it than that? It was only in the last few days when they were all full of excitement at the prospect of the picnic that Ningan had actually spoken to her and that was to ask her what pattern she was going to paint her face for the big corroboree.

At first she was confused by the question and took a while to realize what he was talking about. She had seen pictures of aborigines with their faces painted and decided to go along with the game.

'The pattern of the dingo,' she answered, just to see him scratch his head and that puzzled expression come to his face.

Before the carriage had fully stopped Tom pulled her arm. 'Come on Emily. Let's go on the merry-go-round.'

She was dragged towards the shrill laughter of the children's ride. John had gone in the other direction.

Maggie

They could hear music coming from the bandstand. It was the first time Maggie had heard a brass band. She and mama strolled with Dawn in the middle holding both their hands. Every now and then they would swing her and she would giggle. When the toddler began to tire they sat on the grass under a tree and delved into the basket that held their lunch. It was a feast that Maggie had been dying to get her teeth into, her mouth watered when they unpacked a savoury pie, a fresh crusty cob and home made scones with a bottle of cold tea to wash it down.

They sat quietly, chewing their food and watching the passing parade of people. There was so much to see. Dawn had to be helped to eat as she was so excited she wouldn't sit down for longer than two seconds before she was on her feet again, trying to run off.

As they ate a stranger came over and began talking to mama. He was very handsome and well dressed and Maggie couldn't help staring at him. Mama seemed pleased to see him and was smiling fit to burst. It was as though he was an old friend of hers that she hadn't seen for a long time.

After a little while she said, 'Maggie, this is Mr Rhodes.'

For a moment Maggie gaped, this was her mother's boss. She suddenly felt very tongue tied and shy. 'Hello,' she managed to mutter.

'I'm just about to announce the running races, are you going to be in it Maggie?' He had a lovely soft deep voice.

'Yes please,' she answered quietly.

'But I'm afraid we don't have a race for little one's like you.' He gently ruffled Dawn's hair and she looked up into his face and smiled.

Maggie watched her mother relax, Dawn's dark skin hadn't put him off, which was amazing for someone as posh as him.

They moved across to the running track and Mr Rhodes and mama talked as though they had known each other for years. Maggie walked behind holding Dawn's hand. It was good to hear mama sounding happy and this Mr Rhodes seemed a nice boss.

The sight of the running track set the butterflies in Maggie's stomach to flapping about until she felt physically sick. Probably eating too much pie didn't help. She lined up waiting for her turn, took off her shoes so she could run in bare feet and tucked her skirt in the leg of her knickers, not very lady like but she didn't care. She just wanted to win.

As she stood chewing on her bottom lip, waiting for her race a voice behind her said, 'Hello, how is your new school?'

Maggie turned abruptly and came face to face with a Lizzie Stead from her class. 'Um… hello.' She plastered a fake smile on her face. 'It's very nice thank you.'

'It was very strange the way you left, with no by your leave, just gone.' Lizzie always had a sickly way of talking as though she was eating sticky toffee at the same time, a sort of slow chewy drawl that irritated Maggie.

'It just worked out that way.' Maggie had no intention of elaborating and getting herself in a tangle of lies.

Fortunately they had to move up for the next race. At least the shock of seeing Lizzie stopped Maggie from being nervous.

'On you marks, get set, go.'

Maggie flew along the track as though demons were chasing her but in fact it was only Lizzie Stead. With the wind in her hair and her legs pounding Maggie felt exhilarated. She didn't seem to run very much these days, it wasn't something people did in the city. She breasted the tape that was held along the finish line first, long before Lizzie who didn't win anything because she was as slow as a cart horse. Maggie loved to win and felt so pleased. Her old classmate was forgotten as Mr Rhodes presented her with a silver medal and shook her hand. She couldn't contain her smile and sat down on the grass next to Dawn and let her play with her prize.

The ladies race was announced and Maggie pleaded with her mother to go in it. 'Go on mama, you'll beat them easy.'

'No, I'm not a fast runner.'

'Yes you are I've seen you chasing around the homestead after chickens fast enough.'

'Shh, that was a different time,' her mother lowered her voice.

Maggie was quiet then, wondering at her mother's words but Mr Rhodes took up the persuading. 'Are you having a go Mrs Lang?'

'No Mr Rhodes I don't think so.'

'Oh, be a sport.' He smiled that winning smile at her and added, 'it'll be fun.'

'Alright then, if you insist.'

Maggie yelled at the top of her voice, willing her mother to win as the ladies bounded down the track, breasts and bottoms bouncing. Her mother streaked to the finish line only slightly ahead of a little woman that scurried along like a mouse being chased by a cat. It was the funniest thing Maggie had seen in a long time and she was doubled over with laughter when her mother breathlessly made her way over to her.

'I'll never listen to you again Maggie Lang,' she gasped. 'That was awful.'

'You were brilliant, mama.'

Her mother looked all flushed, her hair had come out of its pins and stray buts fell over her face.

'That's as may be, but I'm all sweaty now, and I dare say I smell.' She shook her head and muttered to herself, 'What will Mr Rhodes think of me.' She began trying to tidy herself and Maggie felt proud of her mother, for even though she looked a bit dishevelled she was still very pretty.

'Come on mama, you have to go and get your prize.' Maggie practically pulled her to the prize table to be greeted by Mr Rhodes.

'Congratulations Mrs Lang.' He reached out to shake her hand.

'Her name's Connie,' Maggie said.

'Connie it is then, congratulations Connie,' Mr Rhodes said.

As he shook her hand he leaned across and kissed her lightly on the cheek. The flush that ran up her mother's face made Maggie clap her hand over her mouth to stifle a giggle.

By now Dawn was getting fidgety and Maggie asked her mother if she could take her for an ice cream. Mr Rhodes seemed to be glued to mama and suggested they walk round the park while the children went off and enjoyed themselves. He even gave Maggie the money for ice creams.

Constance

Constance felt as though her face was still burning. She was too old and had seen too much of life to be getting all silly over an innocent peck on the cheek. As she calmed herself and tried to tuck stray pieces of hair in their pins she noticed a woman and boy near Mr Rhodes.

He introduced her to Thomas his son and Emily his son's governess. Constance could sense the governess's defensiveness, almost like a lioness protecting her young. She shielded Thomas as though she needed to protect him. Thomas was the spit of his father

When Mr Rhodes asked her to take Thomas on the swings she enquired if he was joining them.

'I'll be along shortly,' Mr Rhodes said.

Emily seemed annoyed at his response and stormed off clutching tightly to Thomas' hand.

Once they were on their own he asked, 'would you like to have a little walk?'

Constance wondered why he was paying her so much attention when there were plenty of other eligible ladies about but couldn't stop herself from saying, 'that would be lovely Mr Rhodes.'

'Oh, and call me John if I'm to call you Connie.'

They walked in silence for a while. John looked handsome and debonair in a pale suit with light blue tie that was almost the same colour as his eyes. The tan he acquired while he was away complimented his looks and the sun had bleached his eyebrows and lashes. There were white lines at the corners of his eyes from squinting into the sun. Constance was trying to catch all these features by glancing sideways at him as they walked.

He began to tell her about Thomas in a proud fatherly way but whatever direction his conversation took it lead inevitably to the recent tragedy in his life. He invited her to sit on a bench and for a moment he stared at the river, in a world of his own as if she wasn't there. His whole demeanour had sagged and his eyes looked pained as he stared across the water.

Constance sat still, feeling the turmoil he was suffering. She touched him on the arm. 'Are you alright, John?'

He looked round at her, startled for a second and then nodded. 'Yes, I'm fine.' Again his eyes scanned the water. 'That's where they died, this is the first time I've been back to this place.'

She noticed his eyes had that glazed look of unshed tears when he turned to her. His sadness brought back memories of her loss. Her twins dead before they had time to enjoy any of life's pleasures and Jack, a strong, hard man weakened from illness until he died.

'I know how you're feeling,' Constance said and John looked at her trying to read the expression on her face. He smiled briefly.

Standing he held out his hand to her. 'Let's walk some more.'

They changed the subject and talked about Greetbys. They laughed about some of the stranger employees and John gave her a history lesson of the company's beginnings. They discussed their children's attributes and personalities, Sydney in general, the latest scandal and their favourite shops.

They walked some of the more secluded paths not wanting the wagging of dozens of tongues making up a romantic liaison before it had even begun. Constance felt so comfortable in John's company, not like the wariness she had felt with Daniel Turner or the strict standards of the men she met at work. This was like putting on a pair of comfy old shoes, she just wanted to sigh with pleasure all the time.

Maggie

Maggie dragged Dawn towards the ice cream vendor and sat on a bench while they ate. Dawn's ice cream began to melt down her arm and Maggie frantically mopped at it with her only hankie. She managed to wash her little sister at a drinking fountain before they moved on to watch other children on the slippery dip and swings. Maggie was dying to have a go but it was awkward, Dawn was too small to go on any rides. They walked away and went to watch the band playing. There were people dancing in a pavilion, elegantly gliding round the dance floor perfectly in time to the music. Other people were being served tea and cakes, sipping the hot liquid with their little fingers poking up in a silly way.

Dawn was beginning to get tired, and Maggie hitched her onto her hip and carried her around. Her little head lolled on her big sister's shoulder but she was too heavy so Maggie had to sit down with her.

She saw her mother walking with Mr Rhodes and wondered what it would be like if her mother were to marry him. She imagined life with Mr Rhodes and all his servants. Perhaps she would be drinking her tea with her little finger poking up if they lived in his house. He would be her stepfather, not her real father.

Maggie had a sudden vision of her real father, so strong, like a warrior, going into battle riding off into the country. His craggy face always smiled at her and some of the things he used to say made her laugh, like when food at the camp was so bad it would "choke a brown dog." Maggie wondered why it had to be a brown dog and not a black one. If her father was ever making something and she asked what it was, he used to say, "it's a wigwam for a goose's bridle". She remembered how he used to cooee when he came back from being away when he got within earshot of the homestead. They used to run out and greet him. He never hugged them or anything like that he wasn't a huggy, kissy person.

Maggie was annoyed with herself for letting thoughts of her father make her feel sad on this wonderful day. She glanced down at Dawn who was now sleeping on the bench with her head on Maggie's lap. She looked once more at the children on the swings and longed to have a go. Gently she lowered Dawn's head onto the bench and slipped out from beneath her. The toddler wriggled and made herself more comfortable, moving her chubby little arm up to use as a pillow. Maggie decided she would easily be able to watch her from the swings. She ran to get on the only empty swing and clung to the metal chains. It was hers and she wouldn't get off until she was well and truly ready.

The boy on the next swing said, 'bet you can't swing higher than me?' He looked small and puny. No competition, thought Maggie.

'You're on,' she said as she dug her feet into the ground, jerked the swing backwards and then lifted her feet and swung them back and forth to get into her rhythm.

His voice beside her taunted her. 'You're garbage,' he said, as she propelled her legs back and forth faster.

'Oh yeah?' She was gritting her teeth with exertion as the swing glided through the air, but each time she passed the ground her dress trailed in the dust. She tried to hitch it up but he was getting higher and laughing at her. She tightened her grip on the chains, fearful of falling.

'Beat yuh,' the boy called. 'Scaredy cat.'

'I'm not, I just have to get back to my sister,' Maggie said.

As she spoke she looked across at Dawn. For a moment she thought she was looking at the wrong bench, but it was the right one. Dawn wasn't on it. Panic gripped her, desperately she tried to slow the swing, sticking her legs out straight trying to halt the momentum. When it had nearly stopped she jumped off and heard a ripping sound as her new dress snagged on the wooden seat. She was too worried about Dawn to think of her dress and rushed through a screen of trees that sheltered the children's play area. She stopped and searched the lawns, as she tried to imagine where she would head. There was no sign of her. Maggie began running, not sure which way to go but the urgency of the situation compelled her to hurry. She immediately thought of the river and headed in that direction. She scanned the shoreline, but she couldn't let herself dwell on the thought that she may have already fallen in. No, someone would have seen her, tried to stop her going near the edge, she couldn't just plop in the water without anyone noticing, could she?

She turned back the way she had come, it was a big park, Dawn could be anywhere. Maggie wondered whether to enlist her mother's help but decided she would try to stay calm, she would be sitting somewhere waiting for her. She raced back across the park, stopping now and then to look more methodically. At least there weren't as many people about as there were before. Her heart was pounding with apprehension and her hands were trembling when she spotted her mother.

CHAPTER 19

Daniel

Daniel Turner had heard all about the great Greetby gathering, the picnic that the all-important John Rhodes had decreed should be held for his workers. It was all the news round the streets of the city and even the newspapers had mentioned it. The return of Rhodes to the land of the living had also made the papers, stories about a new man coming back from the bush, full of bright ideas to improve the lot of his workers. A load of bullshit as far as Dan was concerned.

He had made quite a sacrifice coming to this bloody place today but he needed to know how Connie felt about him. He had been too scared to see her at work or follow her home in case that son of hers was about. Dan had discovered who had been behind his beating, her son, one Billy Lang and the O'Leary brothers. Well he would get them back big time, but he needed a plan, which he hadn't worked out yet.

After his beating he had managed to crawl back to his room and stay there, practically unable to move for a week. His landlady kept knocking on his door asking if he was all right and eventually came in and began taking care of him. She fed him, gave him drinks and kept telling him he should see a doctor. She even went to his boss and explained that he was ill and would be back as soon as he could manage it.

That was three months ago and even though Dan tried to get back to work, he lost his job, which was probably a good thing because he was nervous about going back to the dock area. If those O'Leary's knew he was alive when he should have been dead they would kill him. He'd had to revert to a bit of petty thieving once he lost his job but now worked at the brewery. His injuries had been bad, he had a couple of cracked ribs that were finally beginning to heal and the bruising on his body had gone. But there was definitely something wrong with his left leg, it was still very painful when he walked and seemed to throb all the time, but it was too late to go to any doctor now. He would just have to put up with it until it eventually healed.

Dan hovered at the side of a bottle brush bush, the drab colour of his clothing in complete contrast to the bright red flowers. Everywhere he looked people were enjoying themselves, laughing and giggling, fathers playing with their kids and mothers laying out rugs. Small groups littered the grass, spreading out their picnic fare around them.

He spotted the beer tent and pulling his hat down over his eyes, limped painfully across to it. He looked in before entering, bought his beer and returned to his vantage point with a beer in each hand. He settled himself on the grass half screened by the bush and watched the goings on near him. His eyes wondered to her.

Connie sat on the grass with her daughter and that black baby. The children were pointing and Connie looked as if she was explaining things to them. She looked wonderful in a white dress that showed off her long neck and top of her chest. It was low cut for summer but not slutty, she would never be like those women that like to tease men with bulging cleavages. The sleeves of her dress ended just below her elbow and Dan could see the slimness of her forearms and wrists. She had taken off her shoes while she sat on the rug and her bare feet were slim. Her dress had ridden up slightly and he could see her ankles and part of her calf. Dan smiled to himself and thought she really was a beautiful woman.

The saliva glands in Dan's mouth began to water and his stomach rumbled as he watched them eating. After drinking his beers, he went off to the refreshment tent for a mutton pie. By the time he had queued for his food, been to the beer tent for a couple more and returned to his spot, someone had joined Connie. At first Dan couldn't believe what he was seeing. It was John Rhodes back from the dead and chatting up his woman.

'What a cheek,' Dan muttered to himself.

As he watched resentment began to grow in him and he gulped at his beers as though the amber nectar would sooth his gnawing jealousy. Rhodes reached down and pulled Connie to her feet. She laughed at some private joke between them as he picked up their basket and walked away with her.

'Bugger it,' Dan swore to himself.

It looked as though Rhodes was leading them towards the field. Dan moved from his hiding place and watched where they were going. He downed his drinks and followed them at a safe distance. At the field there was a running track set out with people gathered on both sides ready for the races to begin.

Dan found a spot at the back of the crowd and watched the races, which began with youngsters. The first race was mostly boys and when Dan looked at the finish line he saw Rhodes shouting for his son to win. Ah yes, Dan had forgotten about his son Thomas. It looked as though the little brat had done all right while his father was away. Rhodes caught his son in his arms at the finish line and swung him around. He saw Connie's daughter running and doing very well.

Dan watched all the races, getting more and more bored with each one. Until it came to the women's race. Connie moved forward to line up. He smiled, she was game for anything that one. The race was off and Dan's heart was filled with joy as he watched Connie running barefooted. She streaked along, her breasts bouncing and her bare legs exposed up to her knees as she ran. Her hair came loose from its pins and flowed out behind her. She was a picture of athletic excellence as far as Dan was concerned. His heart filled with pride, and he felt so emotional he just wanted to hug her to him. He made his way to the finish line and knew she must have won. But before he could approach her she had gone to the table for her prize. Rhodes was handing her a little silver cup and as he shook her hand he leaned over and kissed her on the cheek. The crowd cheered and Connie went bright red.

The anger Dan felt made his stomach lurch and his hands tremble. Why was she doing this to him, why was she teasing him? He slunk to the back of the crowd and headed once more to the beer tent. He needed something to give him a bit of Dutch courage. He was heedless of who saw him, he didn't care, his confidence and good intentions had been flushed down the pan and he was getting more and more annoyed. After downing his drink in one go he had another and then staggered from the tent.

By the time Dan got back to the field the races had ended. Connie was nowhere to be seen but her daughter and the black brat were sitting on their own. He knew Connie wouldn't be far away. He looked around and spotted her with Rhodes walking down by the river. He stumbled across the grass and looked down upon them from a bank of trees. They were strolling as though they hadn't a care in the world, then they would stop and look at each other. Rhodes pointed something out to her in the river and she patted his arm.

'Yes yuh silly bitch, that's where he drowned his wife,' Dan wanted to scream out to warn her. His head was lolling and he couldn't stand without the support of the tree.

'I'm gunna get that bastard Rhodes....he's got everything and he still wants my woman.' Dan couldn't feel the tears that were streaming down his face. 'Don't you know Connie, you're the only woman I've ever really loved?'

He spoke the words but no one could hear him. He sank to his knees and put his hands together and prayed. 'Please God, let Connie be mine, I need her.' He slumped down on the ground. 'No, you bastard, you wouldn't let me have a bit of happiness would you?'

As Dan spoke he heard a twig crack close by. He stopped his ranting for a moment and turned his head to where the sound came from. Another creak made him ask, 'Who's there?' Bloody kids, probably, you can't get away from them.

Emily

It was good to see Tom enjoying himself, she hadn't seen him laugh so much in a long time. She waved to him as he went round and round, a grin of pleasure fixed to her face. After a few turns Tom complained of feeling sick and he did look very pale. She took his hand and wandered around the stalls fascinated by all the strange yet interesting things. He was intrigued by the coconut shy, the strongman competition, the lucky dip and lots of other activities that were going on.

Once his stomach had settled he began to feel hungry. They went in search of the refreshment tent, where Emily had a well earned cuppa and Tom scoffed down a meat pie.

The races were next and Tom tried to persuade her to run. She knew she looked ridiculous when she ran and didn't want to look foolish and besides, it was not something the mistress of Brunswick House would do. She clapped like mad when Tom raced, even though he didn't win. His father lifted him at the finish line and hugged him.

She was surprised when the ladies were running, John was shouting for one of them to win. Probably one of the shop girls, she thought, but a hint of jealousy niggled her. When the race was over and the lady in question won, John cheered like a workman at the dog races.

Emily moved nearer to John curious to see who had his attention. At the trophy table he handed the shop girl a silver cup and planted a kiss on her cheek. Emily went cold. He had never kissed her, even after everything she'd done for him, like educating his son and keeping his secret. She still had that letter telling the world that he was going off to kill himself. Well, that little shop floozy was no match for her. She was a governess, with intelligence and not some trumped up flirt showing her legs in a stupid race.

She felt in fighting spirit when John turned to her and said, 'Emily, I'd like you to meet someone.'

She came face to face with a woman much older than herself. 'This is Constance Lang,' he said with a softness to his voice.

Emily fixed a smile to her face, and subconsciously pulled Thomas to her, as Constance said, 'pleased to meet you.'

Emily could only trust herself to nod.

'Come along Connie, now the races are finished we can have a walk.' John still hadn't stopped grinning. 'I believe Thomas wants to go on the swings,' he said to Emily, dismissing her.

She grabbed Tom's hand. 'Come along if you want to go on the swings.'

The anger that was brewing in Emily made her grit her teeth and drag Tom so he was running to keep up with her. She couldn't let that woman have her man, she had to go back and see how this little friendship developed.

Tom protested when his ride was cut short. 'I've not been on long.'

'Yes, but there are other children waiting.' She was not going to give in to Tom's demands today.

She wondered how she could follow John without Tom thinking it odd. She'd have to make it into a game. They darted from tree to tree keeping very quiet as befitted a hunter and his prey and shadowed John and his shop girl.

Emily observed their body language as they sat on a bench. They talked and laughed and John leaned towards her. It was as though there was a thread that joined them getting tighter and tighter.

As Emily watched she realized John had never been like that with her. She was always the servant, he was friendly towards her but that was all. He would always regard her as one of the staff. Her dream of becoming his wife was melting like ice on a hot day, she felt humiliated and hurt. She stood absolutely still, she didn't know what to do, her world had been destroyed.

'Are you alright Emily?' Tom whispered beside her.

She could hardly speak. 'Yes.'

She wanted to be alone. She didn't want Tom to see her upset. The dreams of her future had shrivelled and died and something inside her had died with them. Hope.

'I think it's about time we went to see Aunt Hilda,' Emily suggested. Tom pulled a face. 'She might take you for tea and cakes.'

Once Emily was on her own, she sat on a bench, shielded by trees where no one could see her away from the happy families and couples holding hands. She didn't seem to be very good at relationships especially with men. She could let her disappointment and sadness have full reign, but her reverie of recrimination was interrupted by rustling in the bushes nearby.

A man's voice said, 'Yes yuh silly bitch that's where he drowned his wife.' The words were slurred but full of vengeance and hatred. Emily thought he was speaking to her.

There was something familiar about that voice. She peered through the trees and could just make out the shape of a man half hidden in the bushes. She didn't know whether to run for help but curiosity made her move closer. She put her hand over her mouth as she recognized the person speaking. It was Daniel Turner. Emily froze afraid that he may see her but he appeared to be completely absorbed in watching some one else. She followed the direction of his gaze and realized it was John and Constance he was spying on.

Although Emily swore vengeance on this man she was still afraid of him. Again he shouted but this time what he said made Emily gasp involuntarily.

'I'm gunna get that bastard Rhodes….he's got everything and he still wants my woman.'

Emily couldn't believe what she was hearing. Thoughts scurried round her mind, one chasing the other, emotions surfaced, revenge, jealousy and anger. What would he do to her if he saw her? She stood motionless behind a sturdy old eucalyptus tree, wondering and waiting. He shouldn't be able to get away with what he did, it would live with her forever. He was scum, the world didn't need his type, he shouldn't be allowed to live.

Emily clenched her fists, she wanted revenge so badly. She looked at the ground, a large stone lay in front of her. Could she smash it over his head before he turned round to stop her? Was she strong enough to kill him?

Daniel

Movement in the bushes made Dan Turner look up from his vulnerable position on the ground. Fear gripped him when he saw who was standing over him, but he tried to sound unafraid.

'Oh, it's you.' The rock being held above his head came down on his skull as he yelled, 'No, no…' His words stopped midstream as unconsciousness blacked out his senses.

CHAPTER 20

BILLY

Billy was heartily sick of hearing about the work's picnic after weeks of people going on about it. It was all Maggie seemed to talk about.

When he mentioned it to Mick at work he said, 'Well Billy boy, why don't we go?'

'Because we're not invited, that's why,' Billy retorted.

'That doesn't need to stop us, after all it's in a public park, anyone can go into the park.'

'S'pose you're right, but it'll just be a load of giggling women from Greetby's.' Billy was not very interested in the idea.

'Exactly, my boy, women, lots and lots of women.'

Billy smiled and shook his head. Mick always fancied himself with the women and with his dark good looks he seemed to attract them like moths to a lamp.

'We might even find one for you Billy.'

Billy raised his eyebrows and said sarcastically, 'Oh yeah, they're going to be all dribbling down their chins when Billy Lang walks in the place.'

'Don't under estimate yourself, my boy.' Mick cocked his head and studied Billy. 'Some female might be attracted to tatty blonde hair and peach fuzz.'

'Ha ha, and you can stop calling me "your boy".'

Somehow Billy got talked into it which he didn't really mind until he found out some of Mick's brothers were going too. By then it was too late to get out of it. But looking on the bright side it was a big park and he could go off on his own if he wanted to.

It was typical spring weather, a slight nip in the air when they started off in the morning, which developed into a beautiful sunny day. Billy decided he would try to enjoy himself, but he would steer clear of Maggie and Dawn. He didn't want Maggie saying anything that the boys could later rib him about or have to explain the presence of a black child in their family.

Mick was right about one thing, the place was heaving with women, all dressed in summery frocks with lace and ribbons bobbing all over them. They definitely were a pleasure to the eye, but as yet Billy wasn't all that interested in women. It all seemed a bit advanced for him, he didn't mind admiring them from afar but that was about it. To actually talk to one was not something Billy really wanted to do, he didn't know how, for one thing and he didn't want to make a complete fool of himself for another. And they did giggle a lot and Billy wasn't sure whether they were laughing at him or not. No, it was all too much of an ordeal. Mick had given him a few pointers on what to do, but Billy couldn't envisage himself ever doing any of it. He had noticed that the girls did look at him more since he'd grown a bit. He must be close to five foot ten. He couldn't imagine what it would be like to have a girlfriend.

Thoughts meandered round Billy's brain as they strolled around the park. The next thing, they were in the beer tent and Mick had bought him a drink. Billy had never had a drink until he met Mick. Since them he seemed to drink quite a bit. He downed the beer in two swigs, it was a hot day and he felt thirsty.

The effect was amazing, his confidence grew almost immediately. The second drink he sipped more slowly. He began chatting to Mick about anything and everything and hardly waited for his friend's reply before nattering on about the next thing that had been fermenting in his brain, which the alcohol had released.

Mick steered him out of the tent and Billy looked around at the bevy of beauties that littered the grass. One young lady, sitting under a nearby tree with her friend, smiled at him as his eyes met hers.

'You're in there, Billy boy.' Mick nudged him towards her. 'She's panting for yuh.'

Billy began to laugh. 'Is she hell.' Mick did exaggerate.

'Ah well, if you don't take this opportunity you might not get another one.'

She was displayed on a picnic rug like fruit on a market stall, plump, fresh and rosy. She had light brown hair, which was loose to her shoulders with a ribbon tied round it to keep it off her face. Her face was pale and delicate, her cheeks slightly pink and her eyes dark. She had on a dress that showed a hint of her collarbone and the sleeves stopped just below the elbow. She was looking steadfastly at Billy with unconcealed pleasure. He smiled at her and she returned his smile. Her friend brazenly looked at the two mates.

'See what I mean?' Mick voice was quiet in Billy's ear almost like his own sub conscious telling him what to do. 'Go and say hello, son, it can't hurt.' Billy felt a pressure on his back and he stumbled in the direction of the two girls. Mick caught him under the elbow and propelled him closer. They stood in front of the two young ladies. The girls had to look up to them. Billy felt gawky and uncouth, his big hands fidgeting in front of him.

'Hello there,' Mick said in a tone that sounded more posh than Billy had ever heard him speak before. 'Would you mind very much if we joined you?' Mick began to sit on the grass before the girls had answered and Billy gingerly perched beside him.

Before the ladies could protest Mick introduced himself. 'I'm Mick O'Leary and this is Billy Lang.' He nudged Billy's arm as he introduced him but Billy couldn't think of anything to say.

'Please to meet you.' The one who had smiled earlier said. 'My name is Alice and this is Aileen.'

'Alice and Aileen is it?' Mick said with a half smile as though he found it amusing.

'Do you have a problem with that?' Alice sounded annoyed.

'Not at all, I think they are the two loveliest names I've ever heard.'

Billy thought that was a bit over the top on Mick's part, he was really laying on the blarney. He was quite content to watch the interaction between these two and not get involved but Alice commented, 'your friend's not very talkative is he?'

'Ah,' Mick went on. 'Our Billy doesn't run off at the mouth, he's a mite shy.'

Billy could feel the blush rush from his neck to the roots of his hair and his hands began to sweat.

'Bit like Aileen here.' Alice spoke about her friend as though she was a deaf mute, at which Aileen raised her eyebrows to Billy in a look of disbelief. Billy couldn't help smiling at her expression.

'Do you girls fancy a walk?' Mick asked.

'Only if you get us some refreshment first,' Alice cheekily suggested.

'Righto, wait right there and we'll be back in a minute.'

The two lads jumped to their feet and strode across to the beer tent again.

Mick thrust another glass of beer into Billy hand and demanded, 'Drink up son before we get back to the women.'

Billy did as he was told, he downed it in minutes and then burped loudly. Moments later they strolled back to the ladies with two warm glasses of orange cordial and sat down beside them again. The conversation between Mick and Alice resumed with the Irish man gabbling on about their jobs, his family and anything else that came to mind. Billy had to admit he was a bit of a card, he had the ladies in stitches at some of his stories, he wished he could be like that.

'We'd better get on if we're going for a walk,' Aileen reminded them.

Mick pulled Alice to her feet, but Billy wasn't game enough to do the same to Aileen so she struggled in an ungainly fashion with her long skirt hampering her ascent. She brushed the grass from her skirt and looked annoyed.

The third beer began to work on Billy and he felt as though he was walking in thick mud. His head felt floaty and his limbs heavy. He would have loved to have a lay down but of course he couldn't.

Mick took Alice's hand and they walked in front, with Billy and Aileen trailing behind. 'Are you alright?' Aileen asked.

Billy nodded, and slurred, 'Jus fine.'

After a few hundred yards, Mick and Alice stopped and sat on a park bench. Billy was in a quandary, they couldn't all fit on the bench and he didn't want to cramp Mick's style. He headed for the next bench, and by the time they passed them, Mick and Alice were getting to know each other very closely. Their lips were clamped together and they were oblivious to the rest of the world. The sight of them together sent a tingle down Billy's spine, and he could feel a bulge beginning in his trousers. This response sent another wave of redness up his face and Billy just wanted the ground to swallow him up but Aileen pulled him down on the next bench.

He sat with a gap between them at first until she looked at him with an expression that melted Billy's fears like butter on a fire, his untapped emotions sizzling under the surface. His eyes became riveted to her breasts that fluttered under her cotton top each time she took a breath. She was speaking to him, but he couldn't take in what she was saying, her words seemed to be coming from a distance away. His heart was pounding his blood drumming in his ears, and he could feel his erection bulging in his trousers as though it had a mind of its own. He looked at her face, her eyes looked puzzled and a little wary. Her lips were pouting, soft and slack and he leaned over. He kissed her hard, one hand around her back pulling her to him, the other had nowhere to go but on her breast. As soon as it landed on its mark, she squealed, reeled back from him and slapped him with a resounding blow across the face.

Billy was suddenly sober and very embarrassed. Aileen pushed him away and got to her feet. 'You cheeky thing,' she spat at him. 'What do you think I am, some whore or something?'

'No, no, I'm so sorry,… I don't know what got into me.'

'The drink, that's what got into you,' and with those words she stormed off.

Billy put his head in his hands. 'Oh God, what was I thinking?'

The feeling of being a complete and utter fool overwhelmed him, he stumbled to his feet and tried to get as far away from the situation as he could. He would never hear the end of it from Mick. His head was aching, his mood was treacherous and he felt like striking out at someone. He wanted to hide, and made for a clump of trees and bush that was screened from prying eyes. Like a wounded animal he needed to lick his wounds and hide himself away or in Billy's case soundly scold himself for being such an idiot.

Maggie

'Mama, mama.' Breathlessly she tried to tell her what had happened. 'Dawn is missing.

'How could Dawn be missing when you were looking after her?' Her mother changed from relaxed and smiling to stern and angry.

Mr Rhodes was still with her. 'Where did you leave her?'

'At the swings, she was asleep, I thought I could just have a swing before she woke up, but when I looked again she was gone.' Maggie said it all in one breath, she felt so bad. She had put the urge to have a babyish ride before the responsibility of looking after her sister.

'Right, Maggie.' Mr Rhodes didn't sound panicky or annoyed. 'You head towards the entrance and your mother and I will go back to the swings and see if she has returned.'

Maggie had begun running before he had finished his sentence. She stopped for a moment and looked round. Her heart was pounding from all her rushing about and the fear that something terrible had happened to Dawn.

There were horses and carts beginning to move out the gates as people began to leave. Fear gripped Maggie, Dawn was fascinated by horses. She walked towards an area where horses and carts were parked, trying to calm herself and get her breath back. She didn't want to frighten her little sister if she was near any horses.

As Maggie scanned the area she saw a man holding something. He had his back to her, was it a child or just a sack of feed. As she got nearer she could see a child's leg. Could that be Dawn?

She felt nervous as she approached him, but as he half turned she could see he was holding her baby sister. What was he doing with her? Dawn didn't seem to be crying or protesting in any way. Had he picked her up from the swings and was he trying to smuggle her out of the park. She had heard of such things happening especially with black children. Who did this bloke think he was, trying to take their Dawn away. She got to within a few feet of him, he still had his back to her. At the last moment she gulped at the lump of fear and anger that welled in her throat.

'Hey mister, you've got my sister.'

Constance

Time passed quickly and John retrieved his fob watch from his breast pocket and exclaimed, 'Good heaven, look at the time.'

'Yes,' Constance said. 'I had better find my girls, Dawn will be exhausted.'

As if the thought of her girls conjured up their image Maggie ran towards them.

'Mama, mama.' She was very agitated. 'Dawn's missing.'

Constance couldn't help replying sharply. 'How could Dawn be missing when you were looking after her?'

Maggie gabbled on about leaving her asleep at the swings and then her disappearing. The vision of a small toddler roaming aimlessly around this enormous park, sent a shiver down Constance' spine, but John seemed to take control. He told Maggie where to look. As she ran off Constance wanted to run too but John calmed her.

'Don't worry she'll be alright.'

She looked into his eyes and the reassurance she saw made the fingers of terror at losing another child recede slightly.

They walked towards the swings looking in every direction, trying to study the children that were jumping, squealing and laughing, waiting for that spark of recognition at seeing the face they sought. But she wasn't there. Constance was glad John was with her, she didn't want to be on her own.

Turning from the children's play area they headed for the main gates, her mind grappling with a thought. Perhaps she had walked out onto the road. As they rushed in that direction they say Maggie in the distance. She was standing talking to a man. The fear in Constance' heart made her catch her breath. As they got nearer she saw the man had a small child. It had to be Dawn.

'Thank God...' Constance said as she watched the scene in front of her.

Each step that took them nearer brought the scene more into focus. Maggie was talking to the black man and seemed animated. As Constance watched, she threw her arms round the stranger. Although Maggie may feel indebted to this man she would never hug a total stranger. What on earth was going on over there, Constance was baffled by the turn of events? She could see the man put Dawn down on the ground and continue talking to Maggie. As she got closer there was something about him she recognised, the way he stood and held his head. The image brought back memories of days in the outback and finally she knew who it was. Before she could say or do anything John said the name she was thinking.

'Ningan.'

Constance stopped as though she had been struck. She looked at John. He was beaming all over his face and waving.

He repeated the word. 'Ningan,' and then added with a sigh of relief, 'Ningan me old mate.'

She was still walking towards Maggie and could see that she had Dawn in her arms. She looked across and waved at her mother, a grin plastered from ear to ear. Constance was too stunned to wave back.

She walked on as though she was heading into a situation she had no control over, one that could rip apart the new friendship with John Rhodes. But how could he know Ningan and what was the black man doing here?

She stopped when she was a few feet away from him, the man who had saved her and her children from starvation, the man she had grown so fond of, the man that had given her a black child. The bond with this bushman was stronger than she felt for John Rhodes. She walked up to Ningan and threw her arms around him.

'It's good to see you, Ningan.' She buried her face in his neck and smelt the black mustiness of him, she had missed him more than she realised.

Now it was John Rhodes who was speechless.

CHAPTER 21

Ningan

He climbed to the top of the ancient rock and squinted into the sun. His land stretched to the horizon in every direction as flat as his outstretched hand. It was where he belonged. Where the soil was red and the trees were like old friends, their pale bark and dusty leaves so familiar to him.

A movement caught his eye, a big red kangaroo, as tall as a man, bounded across the scrub land, followed by a smaller female with joey in her pouch. They were a family, they would stay together for as long as the spirit world let them live on this earth. They glided through their natural terrain with no fear of attack, their only predators being man and starvation.

A flock of galahs were feeding off the ground, picking among the fallen leaves and dried grasses. The thumping of the kangaroos sent them flying into the air, with flashes of pink under their wings. They circled above the trees as if someone was telling them where to go. None of them flew away from the flock, they were with their own kind and stayed together. If one of those galahs were brown instead of grey and pink, what would happen to it? But there were no brown galahs, not that he'd ever seen.

As his vision changed direction a kookaburra flew from a eucalyptus tree and swooped down on a snake. It was so quick Ningan nearly missed it but as it flew back to its perch the snake dangled from its beak. The bird bashed the snake's body against the bark until it was limp. The kookaburra told the world of its triumph with a raucous laugh that echoed off the rocks. The bird had killed the snake for a meal. The law of animals meant they only killed for food or to protect themselves. Not like the law of men, sometimes they killed for pleasure or revenge or just because they didn't like the way you looked.

His thoughts went to his daughter and he knew she was cared for and loved. But she would still be a black person in a white man's world. She would grow into a fine looking lubra. He would come back and visit her and one day take her walkabout and show her his country.

Maggie was a kind big sister, with her mother's golden hair and eyes of the sky. It surprised him that she was so pleased to see him. He reminded her of a past life when she was happy before death destroyed everything. She was learning about the injustice of men and trying to protect Dawn from it.

And Connie, she looked different. All tidy and held together, no flowing hair or bare skin. He liked the old Connie better when she didn't bother how she looked or care what people thought of her. He still felt a rush of happiness when he saw her.

It was strange the way the spirits worked. They had woven a web of friendship and love that had bound him to John and Connie. He heard they were getting married. It was how it should be, two white people together. Their pathways had connected, thanbarran as Ningan's people would say. It could only be the work of a very cunning spirit. If he told that story round a campfire to his people they would think he was a good storyteller.

Billy was a man now, built tall and thin like a tree. He had some friends who would get him in trouble. Billy told him he needed to get away, so he was going to work on a boat, he used to talk about that when they were in the bush. Now that Connie didn't need him, he could go and see other places.

Ningan had heard that someone had been killed at the picnic, but no one seemed too sad at this death. He had heard Billy and the teacher Emily talking about it as though it was some sort of secret. Emily was also going away, taking her jealousy of Connie with her.

Ningan had repaid his debt to the whiteman who had saved his life when he was a boy. He knew that man from those years ago was not John Rhodes, he wanted to believe it was but in his heart he knew it wasn't.

The breeze that pulled his hair was cool as dusk began to fall. Birds gathered in the protection of the mulga bushes and twittered their final song of the day. The sun dipped to the horizon and the sky turned orange. Ningan sat as still as the stone he rested on and watched the sun go down on this day.

Tomorrow he would start a long walk, back to his tribe, back to his people, back to his family. He would be a black man in a black man's world, he would blend in with their coloured skin and his beliefs would be shared. It was time to go back.

Printed in Great Britain
by Amazon